'I could not tear myself away from this beautifully written Italian saga about women keeping families together against all odds during Mussolini's despotic rule. Will bring tears to your eyes... I recommend this epic book highly.'

- Angela Petch, bestselling author of The Tuscan Girl

'*Under the Light of the Italian Moon* is a moving and eloquent tale of choosing love in times of war, fortitude in times of hardship and hope in times of heartbreaking loss. Anton's masterful and touching tribute to the women of her family is not only an important addition to the literature of the lived experiences of the wars, but also to that of strong, brave women triumphant in great adversity.'

- Indie McDowell, Founder and Director, Atsede Clinic, Secretary, Global Alliance of Independent Midwives

'Anton has brought to life the history and importance of the role of the rural Italian midwife and shows the world how these women brought children to the light in the middle of 1920s and '30s Italy despite intense difficulties and pressures.'

- Gaetano Manfreda, Head of Didactic Service, Department of Women's and Child Health, University of Padua

'A rich tapestry of Italian life through a turbulent time in history, exploring love, loss and sacrifice through the lives of a remarkable family of women.'

- Debbie Rix, bestselling author of The Italian Girls

'A moving, charming, poetic story, intelligent and well-written. And romantic, too. I was absorbed.'

- Nicholas Coleridge, bestselling author of A Much Married Man

UNDER THE LIGHT
of the
ITALIAN MOON

Inspired by a true story of love
and women's resilience during the rise of
fascism and WWII

Jennifer Anton

Published by Amsterdam Publishers, The Netherlands

ISBN 9789493231016 (ebook)

ISBN 9789493231009 (paperback)

ISBN 9789493231023 (hardcover)

Though based on real events and characters, this is a work of fiction and the author's imagination.

This book is written and edited to British English spelling and standards.

Cover design by www.cabinlondon.co.uk

Poem An Hour of Passion/On Ora de Passion with permission ©2014 olremle/Francesco Bof

For Nancy and Vivien

PREFACE

This book was given to me by the Italian women in my family. Despite many of them having been gone several decades, they reached me. They seeded questions about their lives in my head, starting in 2006, when I was pregnant with my daughter. That same year, after my post pregnancy didn't go well and my grandmother died, getting the answers became an obsession.

I collected stories sitting at kitchen tables in Plainfield, Illinois, over cups of coffee and powdered *pizzelle*. My daughter joined me on trip after trip to Italy, where I shared *aperitivi* of prosciutto and prosecco while listening to translated memories of cousins well over ninety years old. We toured privately through dusty back room "museums" in the University of Padua and sat with the priest in the low-lit rectory of Fonzaso, reviewing records and parish bulletins from the 1930s. We stood in cemeteries, looking at names on marble gravestones, black and white pictures of my ancestors peering out from mausoleum walls.

The lives of these women were remarkable, but the door had been closed on them. Whispers from the past forced me awake at six a.m. each morning. *Tell our stories, Jennifer. Write the book.* Their lives were indelibly attached to the time they lived in. Fascist Italy. World War Italy. Catholic Italy. These topics too became a learning obsession. How did fascist Italy impact the lives of a woman with a husband abroad, a midwife, their families? Beyond memories of aunts and cousins, priests and literature, research by professors such as Victoria de Grazia and Richard Bosworth helped me understand.

Stories collected. Research soaked into comprehension. Taken then with a thread of imagination and woven together into the book you hold in your hands. The imprint of two World Wars on a town in northern Italy. The bold resilience of women. The love of husband and wife. A way to live on forever in text.

It all begins with women.
In them, Heaven and Earth transfer. Creation comes to life, and all of humanity springs forth.
In the mother's powerful womb, the transition from Godly to worldly takes place.
It was Mary who gave birth to eternity and redemption.

The strength of the world is in its women.
The power of the world is within its women.
Yet it is the women we erase.
Some women are unwilling to be forgotten or to forget.
Particularly if they are Italian.

PART I

CHAPTER 1

November 1914 Nina Argenta stared at the altar, trying to concentrate on the Mass since there was no chance of escape. The warm fragrance of incense surrounded her, and the priest's recitations combined with the candlelit sanctuary made it hard to keep herself awake. It was Sunday, and like every Sunday of her ten years on Earth, she sat dutifully, bored by the teachings of the ancient text that is the Roman Catholic Holy Bible.

Under the vaulted ceiling of the *Chiesa della Natività di Maria*, the Madonna statue at the side of the church watched her. Candlelight illuminated the blue veil and gentle expression of the Blessed Virgin casting a shine, like polish, on one side of her face and leaving the other in shadow. Nina shivered, tugging her sweater around her shoulders. The yarn, thick under her fingertips, made her feel secure. It had been a gift from her mother on Nina's birthday two weeks before – the birthday they shared.

"We are born on the cusp of two moons, passionate and loyal. A gift for my gift," her mother had said when she gave Nina the present, blue to match her light eyes. It covered the once-white dress she wore that had belonged to her older sister. She leaned against the solid wood of the pew and studied the colours in the paintings of Frigimelica and Forabosco hanging on the grand church walls. Garments of rich burgundies like dried blood, sparkling golds, skin on a flat canvas painted to project luminescence and curve. It was easy to distract yourself from Mass when surrounded by such intricacy.

The women of her family sat to her right: seven of them in the row behind the nuns, a place of honour. The Argenta women occupied the same pew every Sunday. Onorina, four years her senior, perfect and pious, kept her eyes closed and prayed with a sparkling rosary threaded through her clasped hands, oblivious to the three youngest sisters who fretted next to their mother. Her father and younger brother, Vante, sat in front with the other men. Men in front, women in back, separated by the nuns. Nina's older brother, Antonio, had not joined them today. At breakfast, tension had hung between him and their mother, which she assumed was why he missed Mass. The priest would surely notice. Mamma would be disappointed. Nina knew how it felt to let her down.

The chapel veil sitting atop her head slipped as she looked up at the imposing crucifix that stabbed down above the altar. Adjusting the lace, she missed a prayer response, causing her mother to look over with a lifted eyebrow. Adelasia Dalla Santa Argenta was not a woman to make angry, especially not during Mass. Her wooden spoon would be waiting at home to beat your *culo* if you weren't good. She had a reputation for sternness not only with her family but with the entire town. As the only trained midwife in Fonzaso and the villages surrounding, she had delivered every child Nina knew and had earned the nickname, *La Capitana,* The Captain. It was said even the priest feared her.

Nina could see her father, Corrado Argenta, through the heads and habits as he shifted from side to side. His eyelids drooped in boredom, but he glanced back from time to time to check on his wife and mother, both of whom he feared as much as the children did. Nonna Argenta, small and severe in her black dress and head covering, was the only one besides Onorina entirely consumed by the Mass. *Nonna looks just like a strega,* thought Nina, *missing only a broom to fly away on.*

Nina let out a relieved sigh when it was time for Communion. *At last!* Mass would be over soon, and she couldn't wait to be by the fireplace, reading her book after helping Mamma and Nonna prepare the polenta for supper. She walked up the marble aisle, inching forward behind the nuns, then knelt at the altar and held out her tongue, awaiting the body of Christ. Receiving the wafer, she gave the sign of the cross and stood to head back to her seat. The taste of creamy paper stuck to the roof of her mouth and she contemplated why God would want children to have sore knees and numb bottoms to get into Heaven.

Passing rows of men knelt to pray after Communion; she saw the large Pante family filling two benches in the front of the church. Pietro, one of her sister's classmates, leaned unceremoniously in the pew, trying to help his tiny brother fix his shoelaces, tied together so he would trip. A messy redhead crouched in the seat behind them was the likely culprit of the prank. The Pante boy finished helping his brother, then sat back on the pew, catching Nina's eye and giving her a quiet smile. She hesitated before returning it. The Madonna was still watching her. *I should be praying after receiving the body of Christ.* She returned to her seat, then knelt again, bruised knees on cold wood, to await the end of the Mass.

"*Fratelli e sorelle,*" Don Segala proclaimed after he had completed the liturgy. "I would like to ask for a special prayer today. Another group is leaving tomorrow for America. They will travel to Genoa and take a long ship ride. *Signori,* please join me here on the altar." The pews squeaked, echoing in the church as a group of five men and three boys walked to the front. To Nina's surprise, the Pante boy was one of them. *Was it possible such a young boy was going on that voyage?* There was an earnestness in the way he stood next to the other men who were a head taller than he was; his face was sombre. He stuck out a proud, lifted chin: smooth, unlike the others. A patched brown jacket, cut too wide, hung on his slender physique. *I wonder how many brothers have worn that jacket before him.*

The priest called out each of the men's names. "Lord, please bless these men and give them a safe journey to America. Allow them to prosper there and, if it is your will, bring them safely home to their families here in Fonzaso." The parishioners united in an "Amen". As Pietro returned to his seat, he peered back towards the Argenta pew, gave a wry smile and nodded. Nina tried to see if he was looking at her or her sister, but Onorina was quick to bow her head again. The Madonna was watching her, too.

Nina knew many men were leaving Fonzaso to find work abroad. She had overheard her father mentioning it to her mother – the *emigranti* – but she never imagined such young people going. It unsettled her, and her heart raced as questions filled her head. Pietro Pante, who lived with his family a few streets down, who went to school with her sister, was leaving for America.

America!

The furthest she had travelled was to Padua with her mother, and Bergamo once. *How exciting! What will happen to him? What would it be like to sail on a ship, miles away, to a new country? To start life over far away from Fonzaso?* The Mass ended and the parishioners rose in song. Nina lent her voice with fervour and when she looked again at the Blessed Virgin, it seemed the Madonna was smiling at her.

After Don Segala and the altar boys completed the processional, the congregation advanced out of the church like a tiny parade. Organ music erupted from the doors, transforming into clustered conversations, and the piazza buzzed in dialect. As Nina skipped down the church steps into the autumn air, Mount Avena soared in front of her, rising majestically into the sky, its grey limestone cliffs slashed with zigzags of greenery. The November sun warmed her shoulders as she squinted at the peaks of the snow-capped *Dolomiti,* the pre-Alps, that hugged Fonzaso and split Italy from Austria.

Nina looked higher, past the church bell tolling over and over in the campanile, and saw the little castle in the mountain, the *Eremo di San Michele.* On one of their walks foraging for mushrooms, her father had taught her that centuries before, the people built a chapel in the mountainside dedicated to Saint Michele, protector from evil. He told her they used to make houses of wood, and fires were frequent, so they installed a guardian to live next to the chapel in a caretaker's house that looked like a miniature castle. The citizens paid him a self-imposed tax of one large bag of cornmeal each, and he ensured the bell alerted them to fires that could devastate the town. Nowadays, they built more buildings with stucco and stone, but the guardian remained in this place. *Is he lonely?* Nina wondered. *Does he have his own Mass on the mountainside? Can he see me down here in the piazza?* In school, the nuns said that the *Eremo di San Michele,* or San Micel as they often called it, was the only thing travellers going from the Trento or Vicenza provinces heading to

Belluno could recall as they journeyed over the road called Paolina that the Romans had built. It comforted Nina to know that the man in the castle watched over them.

"So, you made it through Mass, Ninetta?" Papà came up behind her, speaking loudly above the rest of the chatter. The strength of his voice startled her, as usual, yet she couldn't help but smile at him. Each word was a booming announcement when he was near other men and Mamma wasn't around.

"Papà, you're not going to America, are you?" Nina asked, squinting up at his big ears.

"America? No! I'm happy here in Fonzaso getting to see my Ninetta every day. Why, do you want me to go?" He poked her shoulder and tickled her neck.

Focused on getting her answer, she looked at him seriously. "Now they are sending children, aren't they? The Pante boy, Pietro, he can't be old enough to go off without his family. You wouldn't send Antonio or Onorina, would you?"

A smile spread across his face and he teased, "Oh, it's not me you want to go – you are dreaming of America!" Heads in the piazza turned at his pronouncement.

Before she could ask more, Teodosio Pante came to say hello. Corrado nodded a greeting. "Teo! I was just telling Ninetta about your boy heading to America." He slapped the other man on the shoulder. "Why don't you come by the house tonight for a drink? I've invited some of the others too. We'll toast them before they leave! I'll give them a bit of my grappa to take with them."

"*Perfetto,*" Teodosio said. Patriarch of the massive Pante brood, father of fourteen, he had already sent one son to America. "Any excuse for your grappa is welcome. By the way," he lowered his voice, "have you broken the news to Adelasia yet?"

Corrado bristled, glancing at Nina, then back to Teodosio. "It's fine," he murmured, unusually quiet. "Come over tonight. In time, she'll get used to the idea."

"Used to what idea, Papà?" Nina asked, pausing from kicking a stone while she waited for them to finish. *What does Mamma not know? It's never good for her not to know something.*

"Don't worry, Ninetta," Corrado tried to calm her. "Everything will be fine."

Nina turned to see Mamma exiting the church last, along with the priest and nuns. She appeared as solid as her reputation in a grey dress that covered her completely from her broad neck to her strong ankles; she was twice the size of Papà. Her mother, Don Segala and the nuns stood talking on the steps of the church; they had important matters to discuss, always.

Nina and Corrado made their way around to greet the Corsos and Ceccons. The men smiled and patted Corrado's back, asking him about his work in the sawmill, challenging him to games of *bocce,* and inviting him to the taverna for beer. Nina greeted her school friends, and the children chased each other around the piazza, relieved to be released from the confines of the church. Soon the sun dipped, the chill deepened and the families of Fonzaso made their way through the winding streets to terracotta-topped houses with fires burning inside. Nina looked up at San Micel once more and felt the guardian watching as the people dispersed into tiny streets and alleyways. Joined by Adelasia, the Argenta family made their way to the Via Calzen.

The cobbles fanned out like a carpet of shells beneath their footsteps as they walked home from church. Smoke from burning leaves and chimneys wafted into the mountain air as they passed the houses of the Corsos and Bofs, neighbours since before the *Risorgimento*. Although Nina was aware of Vante's excited chatter next to her, she found herself distracted by thoughts of America, ships on the ocean. *What do they eat in America? It's so far away, it's another world.* Soon the family approached their two-storey stucco house, the balcony pushing from the front casting a shadow in the midday sun. *Do their houses look the same? Will Pietro's new house look like this?* As the family reached their home, Alberto Giocomin came into view, shivering outside without his coat. Nina realised she hadn't seen him at church either.

"Adelasia, thank God!" He tossed up his arms, hurrying to Nina's mother. "I ran here. Lucia is ready to have the babies. Can you come?" His round face was creased with anxiety as he spoke to her mother.

"*Sì*," she assured him. "It's early, but with twins, this happens."

Lucia Giocomin had grown an enormous belly with two babies inside her, but the rest of her body was stick thin, which made her appear wobbly. Nina felt sorry for the woman every time she saw her at the fountain fetching water. Adelasia turned to her husband and children. "I'll be back after supper." She nodded at Corrado. "No need to wait for me." Without pausing for his response, she rushed into the house to grab her *ostetrica* bag and within moments her sturdy frame passed Nina at a half-run with Alberto at her side. Nina watched them as a little of her fantasy for the Sunday afternoon fell away, knowing that her mother would not be there. She listened to the pair's footsteps clapping on the stones down the Via Calzen until Nonna Argenta shook her from her thoughts. "Always putting other families first," the old woman muttered in her crackly voice. "It's no wonder..."

Her cackling trailed off and Nina broke in, imitating her mother's certain tone and straightening her shoulders as Adelasia had when she spoke to Corrado.

"The polenta is already made," Nina said, stretching herself taller in what she considered an adult way. "And I can make the sauce myself. Mamma taught me, for times when she has to be away."

They ate polenta with sauce made from tomatoes grown on their terraced patch of land along with delicious hot-baked cheese from the milk of a goat they kept across the yard. The creamy flavours warmed them as much as the heat from the stone oven.

Although she was proud of the Captain's status in town and appreciated it afforded them many niceties other families could not afford, Nina couldn't help but look over at the empty seat where her mother belonged. When her younger sisters began fighting at the table, she scolded them like an adult. They'd almost finished eating when Antonio plodded down from the attic where he and Vante slept next to dried corncobs and husks stored for the fire. He brought a stack of them down with him and threw some into the flames before he sat. Then he ate his supper, staring into the dancing heat, and returned to the attic straight afterwards, without saying a word. Nina frowned, thinking of his absence from Mass, his absence from their family today. He was never this quiet.

After they finished their afternoon meal, Nonna Argenta sat on the bed she kept in the sitting room behind the stove. The autumn sun descended early and the house was dark except for the glow of the fire. Shadows flickered around Nonna while she knitted, happy to rest while Nina, Onorina and

Vante cleaned up. The little ones had retreated to the girls' bedroom upstairs to play. Corrado had gone up to speak with Antonio.

All work finally done, Nina found her book, still in the place she had left it that morning, and slipped into the sitting room, plonking down in the cushioned rocking chair. As she arranged herself, she was careful not to get too close to the fire whose embers snapped and sent specks of gold into the air. Warmth flooded the room, and the lingering scents of their recent meal infused the space with comfort.

Nina opened the book to the page where she'd inserted a prayer card of the Blessed Virgin to mark where she left off. After the first sentence, her older sister glided into the room, interrupting her reading. Nina couldn't help but peek over her book to study Onorina, who sat across from her on the sofa, sewing. Everyone acknowledged Onorina's beauty. Her black hair escaped its tie in curls around her face, framing her dark eyes. Unlike Nina, whose body was one long line, Onorina, now fourteen, had grown elegant curves. Even her stitches were graceful. Nina studied her own awkward hands at the end of skinny wrists. Graceful she was not. Of course, Nonna had tried to teach her to sew, but she was never good at it. Even a simple bag she made as practice had turned out so misshapen, they had cut it into rags for the outhouse. She sighed. *At least I can make sauce.*

Her mind drifted back to the announcement at church. The latest *emigranti. What if Onorina left for America like Pietro Pante?* Don Segala said the men would work in coal mines; if Onorina went, she couldn't do that. *What could she do? What else is there?* Nina put her book down and walked past her sister, through the kitchen and out the door, stepping outside to stand in the patches of grass the frost had not yet claimed. The contrast from the warmth of the house to the chill outside shocked her, and she was acutely aware of her surroundings. Her breath shone in the cold air. Through the nearly bare tree limbs, she could see San Micel and the little castle. She stepped one foot at a time, turning around slowly. Mount Avena, long and continuing, then Mount Vallorca. The mountains encircled her and felt like walls closing her in from a world she didn't know.

The afternoon passed peacefully into evening, except for quarrels between the littlest girls. If Nina or Onorina didn't intervene, Aurora and Evira, six and three, would fight as Evira loved to take Aurora's doll and hide it. The older girls stirred, aware that they should get ready for bed before Nonna came to urge them into their room. A noise came from outside – *Mamma!* Nina thought. The children straightened up at the sound of her coming through the gate. As the church bell rang for nine o'clock, Adelasia opened the door and stepped into the foyer where the girls ran to her.

"Mamma! I made the sauce like you taught me!" Nina exclaimed, proud to give her mother the news.

"How are the twins?" Onorina asked.

Adelasia's face flinched slightly before she got her expression back under control.

"The babies are doing well. A boy and a girl – healthy and a good size. They already have names! Carmine and Renata." She smoothed Nina's hair and ambled to the sitting room. "Lucia is happy but tired."

"Mamma, what's wrong?" Nina asked, sensing her mother was holding something back. "If everyone is well, why do you seem sad?" Adelasia sat, folding her dress underneath her with one hand and holding her lower back with the other.

How far did Mamma have to climb with her heavy bag to get to the Giocomins' house? Nina considered how difficult the walk up the mountainside was.

"It's nothing. I'm home now. I have things to do here. Now, did your father leave me any polenta or is it gone?" Nina rushed with Onorina to the kitchen to prepare a plate for her.

CHAPTER 2

As Mamma finished eating in silence, Nina held her book in one hand, reading, while her other hand twirled around in the murky water of the pot, scraping dried polenta off the sides after it had soaked. Corrado lit a cigarette across from Adelasia at the table. The smoke streamed towards her mother as she wiped her mouth and handed Nina her plate. Adelasia crossed her arms, leaning back in her chair, eyeing her husband as he smoked. "I saw Signor Pante with some of the others as I passed the taverna. They mentioned they're on their way over for a drink."

"Don't worry; we'll meet outside. I know you're tired," he said. He stood up, rested his hand on her shoulder, and she reached up to press it.

"Where's Antonio?" she asked.

"Upstairs. He ate and went right back up," Corrado said.

Men's voices got louder outside and came towards the house.

"Here they are!" He reached for his coat, then headed for the *cantina,* eager to share his homemade grappa.

"Nina, will you bring the glasses to us?" Corrado always

asked Nina to carry out tasks like this. She knew he was proud of her and thought her pretty with her brown hair and blue eyes.

"*Sì*, Papà," she answered. Her mother rose and headed upstairs.

Nina peered through the window before opening the hutch to pull out the glasses and put them on a tray. *How many men are there? Papà, Signor Pante, his son and two others.* She studied Pietro Pante's smooth cheeks in contrast to the stubbly faces of the others. *He's too young for grappa. Papà doesn't let Onorina have it,* she thought, piling four glasses on the tray and proceeding out the door.

"If you like my grappa, you can sell it for me in America!" Corrado patted Pietro on the back, then clapped his hands, his voice rising to a near shout. "I should charge you for it now that you'll make your fortunes abroad!"

As Nina distributed the glasses, he settled down. "Ah, time for a drink. Ninetta, look, here's Pietro. You were asking about him this afternoon. Heading to America!"

Nina shrunk, embarrassed to have Pietro know she'd mentioned him. He glanced at her, his face grave, lost in thought. She preferred him smiling.

"Nina, we need another glass!" Corrado chided fondly, already starting to pour.

"Sorry, Papà!" She ran into the house, grabbed the glass and returned in seconds.

"If he's old enough to work in America, Pietro can have a little grappa," said Corrado, speaking to the other men at the table. Nina handed Pietro a glass. As she did, a cold gust of wind kicked up, causing the table to quiver and Pietro's hair to fly wildly into his eyes. He pushed the locks off his forehead, then smiled at her and said, "*Grazie.*" She liked the way he met her eyes while the other men ignored her before she took her tray inside. Back in the house, she couldn't resist another peek at them. The small group were already enlivened by the anticipated grappa, their voices interrupting each other and hands rising and falling to emphasise each point.

The men around the table joked, their hot breaths making steam in the night air. Pietro relaxed on the bench as Corrado filled the glasses to the brim with his homemade concoction and passed them around. "*Salute!*"

"*Salute!*" The glasses clinked before they knocked back the potent liquor.

Pietro choked as the liquid burned his throat, but he stifled his cough.

"Another?" Corrado poured before Pietro put his glass down.

"*Basta!*" Pietro exclaimed, his voice hoarse, "that's enough for me."

Corrado laughed. "*Un altro bicchiere?*" He held the bottle out to offer them another glass and the others happily obliged. "*Uomini del mio cuore!*" he exclaimed and poured everyone another.

"So, you've decided there is nothing in Italy, and all of you are leaving!" Corrado proclaimed, his face beginning to flush as he pounded on the table with his fist.

"There's nothing to do but farm. How can we ever make real money? America's the only way," said Luigi Ceccon. "Besides, I'd be surprised if Italy didn't get pulled into the war soon. We aren't going to pick a fight, but we'll have to choose a side and stay there. At some point, we'll be in it."

"Let's hope Salandra keeps us out," Pietro's father said with feeling. "It was the right thing to do, refusing to help Germany and Austria."

"And what if they come after us?" Luigi demanded. "We'll be fighting in our backyard!"

"Let's change the subject!" Corrado interrupted. "Talk of war is disheartening. What's the name of the ship you're on?"

"Ah! She's the SS *Verona*. A good Italian name!" Ludovico Vieceli exclaimed. "We're trusting her to get us there safely. The *Titanic* is still in the back of my mind. I'll be nervous about icebergs until we get to America." He shuddered, making the sign of the cross and kissing his knuckle.

"*Mio Dio,* that was awful. Sunk like a brick. Two years of my own troubles since, and I still think of it. I don't think I'll ever forget..." Luigi lamented and took another drink.

"All of those people," Pietro said, his voice pensive compared to his companions, "heading towards their dreams... only to have them end in the ocean."

"It's true, young Pietro," nodded Corrado. "You said it best." There was a respectful pause before he shook the boy's shoulder and took another drink. "Tell me, how do you feel about going to America? What are you going to do there besides find your fortune and marry a beautiful blonde American girl?"

"He'll be with his brother," Signor Pante cut in. "Angelo found work for him in a mine in Pennsylvania – he paid for his ticket. Pietro will help the family, as he should. After he repays Angelo, he'll send money back to Italy, and when the time comes, he'll settle back here and help us build up this country."

"Actually," Pietro said, emboldened by the alcohol and the company of men, "I think I'll like America." He avoided looking at his father and twirled the empty glass between his fingers. "I might end up settling there."

"Nonsense, boy!" his father scowled. "Your entire family is here. America is a temporary way for you to help us make ends meet with sixteen mouths to feed. You'll change your mind when you get there. We didn't reunify this country so everyone could leave it!"

Pietro's cheeks flushed. "I know the family needs me, Papà! I know it well enough since you tell me every day!"

The table hushed as Pietro spoke up to his father in front of them.

"A toast!" Corrado urged into the sudden awkward silence.

"Yes! A toast! To America, and to Italy too!" Ludovico lifted his glass to them.

After another drink and a round of back slapping, each man left with well wishes and a jug. Teodosio hung back with Pietro to speak to Corrado. The two men stood up to smoke, leaving Pietro at the table. He overheard bits of their conversation.

"She knows?" He heard his father ask.

"She knows," Corrado confirmed.

"I'm sure she's upset, but I'm telling you, it's the right thing. Antonio needs to get out of here."

Nina made excuses to Nonna Argenta that Papà needed her so she didn't have to go to bed. She wanted to hear what was going on. Something was off. Her mother had climbed two flights of stairs to the attic to speak with Antonio. She never usually went up there. Coming out to collect the glasses, Nina found Pietro sitting alone at the table.

She strained her ears to pick up her father and Signor Pante's conversation.

Pietro started to fill the tray. "Let me help," he offered.

"I can do it," she insisted. She knew she sounded more impatient than she felt, but now that he was helping her, it was even harder to hear the men's murmured conversation over the clinking glasses. Giving up, she headed towards the door. After a few steps, she turned to face Pietro. "He's going too, isn't he?" she asked, her eyes questioning as she met his. "My brother, he's going to America?"

"I think so," he said quietly.

"Why? Why would he leave? The family? Everyone?" She set the glasses down and crossed her arms into the comfort of her cardigan.

Pietro drummed his fingers on the table and lifted his eyebrows. "It's hard to explain."

"I'm ten. I'll understand."

"*Allora,*" he sighed. "Well, for me, I've got thirteen brothers and sisters. We work all year long to feed everyone, even so, it's not enough. Life is hard here." He leaned towards her and lowered his voice. "And... it's also... I want to try something new, to be my own man. Make my own money."

Her blue eyes studied him, only partly comprehending his words. "So, it's money then? They don't have lire in America, do they?"

"No." His voice was strong again, his face eager for the next day's adventure. "Dollars and cents. Pennies and such."

"Okay." She brightened, an idea coming into her mind. "If you come back here, bring me one."

"A penny?"

"*Sì!* A penny. I want to see this American money!" She smiled at the prospect.

"I will." His eyes crinkled in the light from the door before his face became serious again. "If I come back."

She nodded. "Just in case, I'll ask my brother, too."

"Makes sense." He laughed. "Hedge your bets."

"What?"

"Nothing. I'd better be going." Turning once more, he headed slowly back towards Corrado and his father, still talking in the alley.

"*In bocca al lupo!*" Nina called, wishing him good luck.

"*Crepi!*" He spun in a circle on this heel, flashing her a smile before he closed the gate and strode purposefully past the two men.

Entering the house, Nina found her mother sitting at the kitchen table with her head in her hands. Were those tears drying on her mother's face? Mamma was never undone.

"Mamma, don't cry." Nina set the tray down and went to her.

"It's my fault," she said, more to herself than to Nina. "He's leaving because of me."

"No, no, Mamma. It's not your fault. He wants to go to America and be his own man," she said, repeating Pietro's words without understanding what they meant.

"I've been away too much. Now I'm paying for it. I even picked the perfect *ragazza* for him, but he still wants to go." She leaned her face into her open palm.

Nina looked around the kitchen, frantic to come up with a way to comfort her normally unshakeable mother. Adelasia was the sun they revolved around, depended upon. Nina's mind couldn't fathom uncertainty in Mamma. She cursed her brother for hurting her this way.

Her mother reached to pull Nina tight to her, holding the girl to her heaving chest, smelling of soap and olive oil. "Promise me you'll never leave me. My Ninetta, my gift." She smoothed Nina's hair with her strong fingers.

"Why would I leave you? I won't ever."

Nina felt the solid arms that clasped her relax a little, but the heart pressed against her ear was still thumping. As she searched for more words of comfort, the door opened, Corrado stepped in and hung up his coat. Releasing Nina, Adelasia dried her eyes and straightened her back, letting out a deep breath.

"Ninetta, the others are in bed. It's already much later than you should be up," she said, back to her directive manner. She spoke to Nina but meant it to chastise Papà.

"Goodnight," Nina kissed her mother's damp cheek and ran to her father for the briefest hug before starting up the stairs. As she climbed, she heard their voices behind her.

"You drink and smoke and talk of war while I bring babies into the world and try to keep our family together."

"I could tell you knew when you came back. Who told you? I figured we'd discuss it tonight." His tone was apologetic, the sound of a man wanting to avoid a fight with his wife. "I shouldn't have asked them over. Not tonight."

"You should have told me first. But what's done is done. I spoke to Antonio. Give him money for a ticket. He's leaving next month. I can't hold him back."

Later, when the children were in bed, Adelasia made her way to the bedroom. She washed her hands and thick forearms in the basin; strong arms that had pulled countless babies into the world, then put on her nightgown. She glimpsed herself in the small mirror on the wall and the words of her mother "*Che brutta!*" flashed in her mind as always. "How ugly!" her mother had always said of her. But it didn't matter. She'd grown into an adult, a thirty-eight-year-old woman with children of her own, and she didn't care if she was ugly; she was capable. She had done things that most women never would. She brushed her long black hair which only came out of its chignon at night, took her wooden rosary from the box on her dresser, and went out onto the balcony to pray.

"Hail Mary, full of grace, the Lord is with thee. Blessed art thou among women and blessed is the fruit of thy womb..." She paused. She had become an expert on fruits of the womb. Women and birth. Now, she worried. Her firstborn, her son, was leaving. Was it her fault for going away to Padua to study when he was young? Did he feel she had abandoned him despite her letters and gifts? Was it a mistake to have left him so long in the care of her mother-in-law who had few kind words about her? Did she not provide everything he needed?

A son leaving his mother like this proved she had done something wrong. Every day of her life she fought against being useless and homely, as she believed she was as a child, her mother always favouring her brother, Vittorio. Always pointing out where she fell short. But midwifing had come naturally to her. It was something she was good at, and her size and stature, the exact things that her mother called out as *brutta,* reassured the women she helped. The joy of bringing a new life into the world, seeing the look on a mother's face as she held her newborn child, gave her such a sense of satisfaction and accomplishment she could push away the belief that she would always fall short in life, never earn her mother's love.

God had called her to help women; to help them with the act impossible for any man to complete, the enormous burden and joy only women were capable of, the ability to be the source from which life itself sprung. After her fourth child was born, the priest offered her name to a programme within the University of Padua to train rural midwives. She could read, she was a staunch Catholic and the perfect candidate to service the women of Fonzaso and the surrounding villages so the doctor could attend to other needs. To the dismay of her mother-in-law and befuddled husband, she had explained to them she would be away for the winter, kissed her babies, packed her bags and left. She trained under Doctor Truzzi, who was renowned for completing the first successful caesarean section in Italy. Every week she wrote to her family. When she returned, she was more confident than ever about how she could improve the birth experience for mothers and their babies. Nina and Vante had run to her, happy for their mamma to be back and to be out from the reign of terror of Nonna Argenta. But Antonio had refused to hug her, and it took weeks before the stubborn child would forgive her for leaving them.

When she had climbed up into the attic bedroom and sat on the corner of his bed on the quilt she had made him when he was a boy, he'd said to her, "Mamma, I won't find a woman like you to marry. I'll have to be the provider. I can't do that here." She couldn't argue with him. Perhaps if she were an ordinary mother, Antonio would have stayed.

As she kneeled praying, it was clear what she had done; she had driven her eldest away to the unknowns of America by putting her vocation ahead of her family. She finished her prayer, "Holy Mary Mother of God, pray for us sinners. Now and at the hour of our death. Amen."

1919

"Vittoria nostra, non sarai mutilata."
Our victory will not be mutilated.

– Gabriele D'Annunzio

CHAPTER 3

September 1919 Nina stood in front of the wood-framed mirror propped up in the corner of the room she shared with her sisters. She rarely found herself alone in the compact space and almost never spent time in front of the mirror. The war had shaped her. When the men of Italy battled the Austrians in the Alps above Fonzaso, she'd been a child with dreams of the world outside her beloved town. Four terrible years had passed. The young men who hadn't emigrated fought with the *Alpini,* a brave group of men trained to fight in snow and ice. Many had not returned. Those who had were changed forever, inside and out.

Nina had continued to attend school, but as the war started, the curriculum changed, and instead of learning of Galileo or the Egyptians, topics that fascinated her, the focus became national pride, Italian heroism and headlines. One headline irked her. The teacher brought in an article with the title *Italian Migrants Return to Participate in the War.* Antonio had sent word that he had settled in Salt Lake City. He'd enclosed a picture of himself in cowboy clothing taken in a photo studio. It confused her. While she was glad he wasn't there to fight in the mountains, to come back with nightmares and lost limbs or die in powdery crevices, she knew he wasn't really a cowboy.

She watched the Austrians invade their town, rip houses apart to burn for firewood, leaving neighbours out in the cold. Even now, skeletons of houses remained. During these past four years, Mamma rose to become a near saint in Fonzaso, delivering the babies of the heroes of the war. Adelasia was always away – sometimes in Fonzaso, sometimes in the surrounding villages and other times, the worst times, in the mountains. She travelled as far as was needed to help pregnant women, often at her own risk. One night, at the height of the war, the doctor came knocking at midnight to take her with him to a woman deep in the mountains. Nina overheard him ask her, "Do you have your gun?" in a serious whisper. Adelasia replied with her usual certainty, "I don't need a gun. I have my cross."

The Argenta family contributed to the war in this way, with the shield of Adelasia's Catholic faith and the sword of her ability to heal and bring life. Nina thanked God that Vante was too young and Corrado too old to be called up.

At fifteen, Nina had experienced the responsibilities of a much older woman. She was the one who supported Mamma's work. *I am her gift,* she thought. *She depends on me to lighten her burden.* Throughout the war, as the destinations north and south of them and the sound of far-off explosions echoed in the air, Nina stayed up each night, reading by candlelight and listening until Mamma returned. It was Nina who warmed whatever food they had and watched her eat, spoonful by spoonful, knowing from her damp skirts and bloodied knees that she had slipped climbing in the snow; seeing in the blank sadness of her eyes she had witnessed unimaginable things. It was Nina who scrubbed the blood out of Adelasia's clothes, checked the supplies of her *ostetrica* case, and took the heavy satchel from her mother's frozen hands after the woman had nothing left to give at the day's end. She watched Mamma's exhausted face, and as the men killed each other in the mountains, Adelasia patched them up, delivered their children and prayed for their salvation.

One night, two years into the war, when Nina was only twelve, her mother had come home more sombre than usual. Adelasia had sat down, staring ahead, while Nina put her dinner in front of her.

Mamma turned away from the food, and when she spoke, a disgusted curl of a frown appeared on her lips. "Bodies. All I saw in the mountains today were bodies, limbs, pieces of people. I saw a man's leg in a tree."

"Mamma, please don't tell me this. You're scaring me." Nina reminded her mother she was a child, she didn't want to know any of this.

But Adelasia continued, numb from the day and seeming to want to make sense of it by saying it aloud to someone, even if it meant confiding in a young girl. "It's a circle. Women create, men destroy. We feed the beasts." She let out a disgusted laugh, shaking her head and continued, "Creation in the wombs of women must overcome destruction at the hands of men," she said, her eyes bloodshot, the candlelight flickering on her round face. "I bring life into the world; men take it, I try to save it. But God didn't give me the ability to resurrect, and I'd rather bring new life than have to fight to hold it."

One night, when Adelasia was away in the mountains, Nonna Argenta died. The old woman complained until her last breath that her daughter-in-law was never there for her own family, and when her last spiteful statement pierced the air, her eyes froze open as if in fear of her own judgement. In the end, Adelasia was the one who organised her funeral and carried out her wishes of having white lilies around her head.

When the war ended, Fonzaso found itself with more struggling families, and fewer able-bodied men to work the fields and feed their children. Her brother's friends had fought alongside Britain and France in the Alps and returned without the promised gained territory in Austria. So much blood and nothing gained. There was a bitter taste in the Italian mouth. Then came the epidemic, the Spanish flu that killed many of her childhood friends and their family members. By a miracle, the Argentas suffered no deaths. Nina formed the sign of the cross, thinking of what she'd survived. *Praise be to you, God, and to the Holy Virgin for helping us through.* The war had finally ended, and the King awarded Fonzaso for the bravery its residents had shown. Despite the small population of only a few thousand, the King deemed it a city. Pride filled the hearts of the people. On that autumn day in 1919, the scent of fresh-cut vines and flowers filled the air with possibility and Nina managed to squeeze a few minutes in the house alone while the entire town prepared for the festival.

As she studied herself in the long mirror, she was delighted by her new body. At fifteen, gone was the straight-line figure she had known as a child. The changes began as a nuisance, even hand-me-downs were a luxury as they made do through the war. Eventually, she realised her body and Onorina's were no longer distinctively different, and she marvelled at the outcome. Under her cotton dress, her breasts were pert and filled the bodice. She ran her palms down the sides of them, grinned and wiggled for herself in the mirror, laughing.

"*Che bella,*" she said aloud, smoothing the fabric inward to her waist and down over her hips. These too had changed. The roundness of her bottom below her torso was distinct.

"What are you doing in here?" Aurora swung around the doorframe and into the room, surprising her.

"*Mio Dio!* You scared me!" Nina laughed and wriggled her chest to her little sister. "I'm marvelling at these."

"Ooh. I'm waiting for mine! Maybe they'll be like Mamma's!"

"That would be something!" Nina said. Their mother's robust size meant her bosom was the largest in the town. They giggled. Throughout the war, while Nina was Adelasia's support, Aurora had become hers. The girls kept each other sane by joking in a way they couldn't around others. Aurora was good-natured and funny, four years younger than Nina and so different from Evira, the second-to-youngest sister who seemed to have taken Nonna Argenta's place as the complainer in the family. She had a spiteful tongue and disposition that made them feel Nonna hadn't left them at all. When Aurora was alone with Nina, they were friends, but sometimes, as the older sister, Nina had to chastise her when she and Evira were at each other's throats.

"There's a group of young men playing *bocce* with Papà. I don't think I've ever seen them before," said Aurora, flopping on the bed.

"*Sì.* I saw them in the piazza. Probably booth merchants for the *feste*. Papà will try to win money off them and then have them over for grappa," Nina said.

"*Allora*, I heard they are *emigranti* coming back to visit. One of them is a Pante, back from America." Nina paused at the mention of the last name, Pante. She liked how it sounded like Dante, the writer of *The Divine Comedy* she had recently read, and she had a vague memory of liking the name for other reasons. Aurora kept talking, "Wouldn't it be nice if Antonio came home to visit? I hear some of the boys are back from Britain, too."

"Antonio won't visit. He's happy playing cowboy in America. He's let Mamma down. It's disgraceful how little he's written – like he gave up on the family entirely. Other men send money back; he sends nothing but silly photos. I think the war was his excuse to cut ties." Nina opened the window to let in some fresh air. "I remember that Pante boy. He's Onorina's age, I'm pretty sure. Where is she, anyway?"

"I don't know, she likes to be with her friends. They're talking about marriage and babies and who's been flirting with whom at the *filó* while they shell peas together."

Nina laughed as she smoothed her chignon and poked her sister.

"Pff. I don't care about any of that, but I can't wait to dance to the *Alpini* band! It's been too long since we had a proper celebration." She hummed, skipped and shook around the room dancing into Aurora who pushed her away and laughed. "You're crazy!"

"And that's why you love me!" Nina said, giving the girl a squeeze.

The families and neighbours of the Argentas slowly emerged from mourning their lost and welcomed home their broken men. Nina's favourite author, D'Annunzio, had turned into a war hero and was bravely arm wrestling for Fiume, a territory on the north-east corner of Italy which was in the crux of an international argument to hand it over to the Slavs.

Corrado regularly came home from the taverna complaining. The world seemed unwilling to recognise the Italian contribution to the war and the promises of the London Treaty. But with the pleasant weather, even Corrado, who bantered all day about politics, succumbed to the sentiment in the Belluno province. The *Fonzasini* were ready to embrace joy. In the countryside, the summer heat dwindled, crops were coming in, and people preserved produce and prepared for winter while the *feste* were on everyone's minds. They held the first in Frassenè, and the last, Nina's favourite, was the *Festa dell'Uva*, celebrating the harvest of the grapes and winemaking. Fonzaso always hosted it. Everyone took part in the preparations. Corrado, who loved to sing, had been rehearsing the choir at the church hall for the celebrations. Legend had it that years ago he had used his voice to woo Adelasia, singing like Casanova to her until, embarrassed by the attention, she agreed to marry him.

Later in the day, Mamma called that supper was ready and, as usual, Corrado had lost track of time, so Nina grabbed Aurora to run and fetch him from the church.

The girls bounded down the Via Calzen and turned onto the Via Mezzaterra, dashing through the wafting scent of baking bread from the *panificio* and sounds from open windows of clanging utensils and shouting mothers as their neighbours sat down for their midday meals. Reaching the piazza, the *chiesa* stood out, a distinct peach at the foot of the dark cliffs like cream into coffee. Breathless and laughing, they approached the church steps and rested there for a moment before standing to head inside. The great wooden door opened, squeaking on its hinges, and out walked a young man in a light-grey suit that hung loosely over his broad shoulders. He had hair that was cut short on the sides but was otherwise mildly chaotic, curling near his forehead, and smiling eyes with dark slashes of brows like accent marks. *I know him somehow,* Nina thought. Her heart, still beating from the running, refused to slow. Aurora ran ahead, leaving Nina on the steps, transfixed. The man loomed tall above her, lit a cigarette and brought it to his lips, then sauntered down the stairs with his long legs kicking out gracefully. When he reached the step above her, he paused. His brown eyes observed her with an air of incomplete recognition, then he smiled, his jaw square. A scent surrounded him, a cologne of wood, tobacco and spice. No one she knew wore cologne except on holidays. His eyes were familiar to her, smiling overturned crescents.

Eternity passed in a moment as they stood, peering at each other on the steps. Her heart was wild in her chest. *Un colpo di fulmine.* A lightning bolt of love. She had read that somewhere. She pushed the silly thought out of her head.

"*Ciao,*" he finally said, taking a puff of his cigarette and looking intently at her. Still smiling he cocked his head, emitting an air of confidence the young men she knew did not possess.

"*Ciao,*" she replied, trying to catch her breath.

"If you're part of the choir, it seems you're late. They're finished."

"I don't sing. I've come to get my father, he's leading them."

He nodded his head as though she had confirmed something for him.

"I knew you looked familiar. You're the Argenta girl, Corrado's daughter. I remember you when you were little. I was at your house years ago, the night before I left." He spoke with a unique accent, less fluid, in dialect.

She regained her senses and replied, "Yes, that's right. I'm Nina. Nina Argenta." She pointed to the church. "I have to get my father."

"I was just talking to him. I came back two days ago, and we've been playing *bocce.*" He paused and studied her. "He won some money off my *amico* and I volunteered to bring it over to him. I didn't recognise you at first. I'm Pietro. Do you remember me?"

A wind kicked up and pieces of her hair escaped its chignon, flying wildly around her eyes. As she reached up to tuck them back into place, she noticed the way he looked at her. *I must look a mess.* But the look on his face was not one of disgust. It was something else she was unfamiliar with.

Instead of answering his question, she asked him, "So, did you end up in America?"

"Yes. I go back in three weeks."

"Where did you go?" Her curiosity compelled her to stay on the steps though she climbed two more stairs towards the door while they spoke.

"Pennsylvania. Lots of Italians in the mines there."

"You missed a war," she said, noticing black lines deep in the knuckles that held the cigarette, at odds with his elegant appearance.

He took a puff, and paused before responding to her, "It must have been awful." He shook his head, meeting her eyes.

"This piazza was full of Austrians in every corner. They even took over San Micel. But, we survived," she had run out of things to say. "I should go."

"I'll see you at the *festa, sì?*" he asked, his voice rising with interest.

"Oh, yes, I'll be there. *Ciao.*" Nina padded up the steps into the church, trying to remember what she had come there for and was thankful for Aurora who ran over with their father to accompany them home.

The next day, after breakfast, the girls cleaned up. Corrado announced he was going to the *bocce* court, as he did almost every day, his work at the mill more sporadic with the younger men back.

"Ninetta, can you be a love and bring me lunch?" he asked. It wasn't often he requested her to bring him lunch as he usually ate at the taverna or came home.

"*Sì*, Papà," she said. "Mamma brought fresh salami home last night. The family in Giaroni who had the baby owns a *macelleria*."

Adelasia had returned home before dawn and was fast asleep snoring upstairs.

Ninetta collected eggs, swept the house and ensured her siblings did their chores. Once Onorina finished canning dozens of tomatoes and carrying them to the *cantina,* she washed her slender hands in the basin, draped her scarf around her shoulders, and left, presumably to meet with friends to prepare for the *festa,* reminding Nina to take Corrado his lunch. Onorina looked striking with her burgundy scarf and coal-black hair. Born on Saint Valentine's day, her sister seemed to emanate love. It was obvious why so many young men in town admired her.

Nina was eager for the day ahead. If she was lucky, Pietro might be at the *bocce* court. She packed a lunch of salami and bread into a basket and headed down the street. The sun was warm on her neck and the basket swung in the crook of her arm. The trees on Mount Avena were still lush orange and green, bursting with leaves, and the church at San Micel gleamed silvery white against the rock.

She reached the *bocce* court just as Onorina, burgundy scarf flying behind her, left with three friends. They exchanged waves goodbye with the men playing. One of them was Pietro. Nina held back. Onorina and her friends were of marrying age; it was their time. It shouldn't surprise her to find them here flirting.

After a fresh coin toss, Nina spied Pietro coming for his turn. He grabbed the *pallino* and wound up dramatically, like the American baseball players she had seen in the newsreels when Papà had taken them to the cinema in Feltre last month. He leaned forward and released the ball in a gentle but firm underhand throw. The other men chuckled and shouted, "*Americano!*" and, "*Dugador de beisbol.*" He laughed with them, and she found herself laughing too. As she approached the side of the pit, he spotted her and grinned. He threw his other ball with the same overdramatic movement; it landed within inches of the *pallino,* causing the other men to groan at his luck. After patting their backs good naturedly, he jogged over towards her.

The sun was in his half-moon eyes as he squinted and smiled.

"You're giving them a run for their money," she said, shifting her basket from arm to arm and returning his brilliant smile. She was flirting, she realised, and it was new for her. She wondered if he noticed how she'd changed. The way his eyes lingered lightly on her told her he might have.

"I miss these *bocce* games. Your father's good," he said. He stepped closer to her and angled to take in the game, his shoulder almost touching hers.

"He should be. He plays every chance he gets. I came to bring him his lunch. He won't even come home for that. You'll find him in the taverna later. His other home."

"Corrado." Pietro chuckled fondly watching the man take his turn. "I'll never forget the grappa he gave me. My throat will never forget either. I used it to clean my room in America."

"He's so proud of his recipe. He thinks it's what stopped our family from dying of the Spanish flu," she said. Pietro studied her as she spoke and she felt she must be depressing him with her tales of survival. *He has his own worries in America, certainly,* she thought.

"Your sister was here a few minutes ago. Your father reintroduced us. She just left," he said.

"Oh." She stopped, distracted. "Yes. I'm sure she's headed to help finish plans for the *festa*."

Her heart sank. *Of course he would be interested in Onorina.* She was enchanting in a way Nina could only dream to be. He crossed one leg in front of the other and cocked his head sideways, as though trying to read her expression.

"Do you dance?" he asked, interrupting her thoughts.

"*Si*, I dance. I haven't in a while, but I do," she said.

Before he could say anything else, Corrado finished his toss and came over.

"Ninetta! I see you've been talking to Pietro. He's been entertaining us since he's been back. Showing us how to play baseball like the Americans." He patted Pietro on the back. "And he's been telling the men how to gather coal using the mules. He's smart, this one. We'll miss him when he goes again."

"I'm sure you've been having a lot of fun with your visitor, Papà. I hope you haven't won too much money off him. Here's your lunch," Nina said and handed him the basket as one of the men yelled for Pietro to take his turn.

"*Ciao*, Nina!" Pietro called as he backed up looking at her then turned to jog back to the game.

"*Ciao*," she shouted back, too eagerly. She surprised herself. Something was different when he smiled at her. She sighed. *He's practically American,* she thought. *And it wouldn't be me he'd be interested in anyway.* At least he came back to Fonzaso to visit, unlike her brother. And he was easy on the eyes. She smiled. The boys she'd been around in Fonzaso were nothing like this near stranger. He was infinitely more interesting, and she tried to push the distinct thought out of her head that maybe he was meant to be hers.

CHAPTER 4

The day of the first festival arrived, and the Argenta house buzzed with excitement. Corrado planned to drive the family across the Cismon in the donkey-pulled cart. Vante, Aurora and Evira were preparing to compete in the three-legged race and egg walks. The song, 'Quel Mazzolin di Fiori' had been running through Nina's head all morning and she secretly dreamed she would get to dance with Pietro. Onorina pinned her black hair in a style she had seen on a cinema poster to create elegant waves from her forehead to her ear. She could have passed for a film star herself. Adelasia wore her Sunday best and closed the house as the others scurried to the cart.

When they were about to leave, sounds of hooves clattered on the road towards them, and another cart pulled up the Via Calzen. The driver, an older man, shouted to Adelasia. "Are you the midwife? Can you come? Something's wrong with my daughter! She's with child, and there... there's blood," he said, his eyes wide and voice strained, uncomfortable to be talking about the subject.

"Where is she?" Adelasia called over to him, already lowering herself down from the family cart.

"At our farm. Up in Faller."

It would take more than an hour to get there. Nina saw her mother considering. In a moment, she spoke, "I may need help. Is there another woman in your house?"

"No, *signora,* just me and her husband. He's with her."

"Ninetta, come with me," she directed Nina with a brush of her hand.

"But, Mamma!" cried Nina. It had been so long since she'd danced to a band. All her friends would be there celebrating – and Pietro.

"*Basta!* I need your help. Come, *dai, dai,*" her mother called without looking back for confirmation as she headed into the house to change and grab her bag.

Nina frowned, jumping down from the cart. It would be of no use to ask why Onorina couldn't do it. It was her time, and festival season meant that by next spring she'd have found someone to marry. Nina lamented as she climbed into the stranger's cart and her dreams of dancing with the handsome Pietro Pante faded.

The air in the room in Faller sickened her. She was used to helping Mamma, but today she longed for fresh mountain air and music, not the cloying smell of a moaning body about to give birth. The woman wasn't in a critical way; the men had overreacted. A trail of blood mixed with fluid, pink like the juices from strawberries, soaked a spot under her, but the baby wasn't coming soon. "She's not ready," said Adelasia knowingly after examining her. "Help me move her off this." They changed the soiled bedcover, replacing it with papers and fresh linens. Nina boiled water and prepared her mother's equipment while Adelasia checked the baby's heart rate with her Pinard horn.

"Good, Ninetta. Knowing your way around a birth room is a useful skill," her mother complimented her as she set the tool on the nightstand. *I'd rather not have the skill and be at the festa!* Nina thought. This wasn't the first time her mother had mentioned her midwifing. It scared her, as if she was being apprenticed against her will to someone else's dream.

It was five o'clock in the evening before the woman's contractions got closer and, at eight-thirty, Adelasia used forceps to help pull out the child. At last, the baby appeared. The rattling cry of the newborn cut through the stifling room, and Adelasia held up a little girl, tiny legs kicking into the air with folds of skin on the thighs and an oversized head for her mother's slight body.

"The first girl and she's already giving you trouble. This head of hers proves she'll be twice as smart as the men in this house," Adelasia laughed. The new mother held Adelasia's hand and thanked her as the child sucked away on her breast. Nina smiled at the scene and pride filled her heart seeing Mamma this way, but the thought of what she had missed tugged at her mind. By the time they'd cleaned up and begun their journey home, it was already midnight. Adelasia and Nina sat tight together in the cart as the man sat up front driving them home. The closeness to her mother made Nina feel like a child again, safe and small. Adelasia was quiet for a long time watching the countryside; something was on her mind, something Nina couldn't guess.

When she spoke, she told Nina in a low voice, "I'm glad she had a little girl. Now she has someone to keep her company in a house full of men. She won't have to watch her die in their wars or leave to build lives away from her." Nina could see her brother was on Adelasia's mind. There were days where she had walked in on Mamma, looking at the studio-cowboy picture. It was as though he had died. Nina sighed and looked at the moon, radiating gold into the sapphire sky like the halo around the Virgin Mary's head. She could see carts in the distance making their way back from Frassenè and the first festival of the season had passed by without her.

The next day, Nina slept in after the long night in Faller. Onorina came back from an early morning of washing clothes at the river, singing and talkative, and Nina pulled her pillow over her head so she didn't have to hear. When her sister's friend, Giovanna, came over for coffee, she overheard them laughing and talking about what an excellent dancer Pietro Pante was and how Toni Bianchi had lost his balance and fallen into the band while showing them where shrapnel had entered his leg, making everyone laugh. They spoke of the drama of a fist fight that had broken out over politics when they were leaving and it sounded thrilling compared to Nina's night. She groaned, punching her pillow. She would not miss the *Festa dell'Uva,* only a few weeks away. After dressing, Nina came downstairs for coffee at the same time as Mamma.

"Can I pour you a cup?" her mother offered.

"*Sì,*" her tone expressed her foul mood.

Adelasia filled the cup halfway with coffee and the rest with milk; she mixed in two sugar lumps then tore off a piece of bread from yesterday's loaf and plopped it in.

"*Pane e caffè,* there you go," she said, pushing it across the table to Nina. She made herself one and pulled up a chair.

"Thank you for yesterday. You must be disappointed to have missed the *festa*."

"I don't care."

"Of course you care. But your time will come soon enough." Adelasia patted her hand then added, "Don't worry about your chores today. I'll get Vante to help; he doesn't mind. He's a good brother. It's a beautiful day. Go for a walk."

"*Grazie,* Mamma." She dipped the bread into the coffee, eating it with a spoon. Comforted by her mother's affection, she cheered up. The next festival wasn't far away.

Time sped by as the yields from the maize came in and the whole Argenta family worked to husk it and take it to the mill to be ground into cornmeal. They picked berries and beans, preserving them for hours every day. Having experienced the shortages during the war, the family were experts in using every vegetable that was good enough to eat. Once, when Nina was in the garden collecting courgettes, Pietro had been in a nearby field walking with the other men, gesturing with his hands. She imagined he was telling them about working in the mines. He'd looked her way but hadn't waved. Had he seen her? Later that week, she was at the shop with Onorina and he'd walked in. As she opened her mouth to greet him, Pampo, the bothersome red-headed boy from the village nearby, came to ask her opinion about what cheese his mother would need for her recipe. Pietro spoke to the elderly shopkeeper, bought tobacco and exchanged words and smiles with Onorina before the shop bell rang and he left again. He had glanced over at her with raised eyebrows, but she was trying to help Pampo with his question, and she left frustrated at a missed chance to speak to Pietro and another credit for her sister.

On the day of the *Festa dell'Uva* the weather was blustery and the tents of the merchants whipped and shook. No one wanted to cancel, but the conditions were less than ideal. It seemed it would rain any moment. Nina looked out the window, cursing her luck. The door to the house opened, and Corrado entered along with a gust of wind.

"Bundle up! The *festa* is still on. Even if we have to huddle under blankets, we won't be cancelling!" he announced. Everyone let out a cheer and grabbed their scarves and coats. Nina tied her chignon tight to avoid the wind making a mess of her hair. Vante, Aurora, Evira and little Luigia tied blankets over their shoulders like capes as they marched to the piazza where the festivities would begin.

In the *Piazza Primo Novembre*, the *Fonzasini* huddled next to each other on either side, leaving space for the parade. Nina scanned the crowd for her friends and Pietro. To her surprise, Onorina grabbed her arm and shouted at her, "Come with me!"

Nina allowed herself to be pulled across the piazza towards a section of the crowd where Onorina's friends stood, anticipating the celebration, next to a row of young men in linen pants and wool caps. To Nina's nervous pleasure, Pietro was with them.

"Squeeze in!" yelled Toni Bianchi, a wilful and brawny young man who had spent time abroad in Canada, come back to fight in the Great War and returned to find his father had died of the Spanish flu. He pulled the two girls next to him with Onorina on his side, forcing Nina between her sister and Pietro. "Hello there," Pietro said, jostling as the crowd pushed and pulled to get the best view of the parade. The wind tossed his curls. "You weren't at the *festa* in Frassenè!" he nearly shouted and she didn't have time to respond to him as the crowd cheered. Each cart rolling by celebrated winemaking and depicted a different step in the process. The first cart came through the crowd, adorned with twisted grapevines covering every surface, and one of Onorina's old classmates, Bettina Napoli, waved from the carriage with a wreath of vines on her head. She was supposed to wear a Roman goddess costume, but with the cold and wind, whatever she wore was hidden beneath a coat. The girl held tight to her crown to keep it from blowing away. The crowd shoved forward and tightened, pushing Nina against Pietro on the right and her sister on her left. To her secret delight, the pressure of the crowd on Onorina's side was rising, and she had the distinct impression Toni was instigating it, pushing closer to her sister and forcing her into Pietro. She could feel Pietro's warm body under many layers and they laughed, cheering as each cart went past. Pietro's hand brushed against hers, sending an electric current through her belly. As the carriage drove by with old men and small children stomping on grapes in a vat, the skies opened and a light rain fell, flying about in the wind. Someone lifted a large blanket behind and above the group and Nina found herself squeezed underneath it, protected from the rain with Pietro. It was oddly intimate despite the entire population of Fonzaso and surrounding villages gathered around them. They laughed and shook their heads, unable to hear anything through the shouting crowd, accordion music and roaring wind. They cheered along, laughing at the absurdity of the entire situation and the thrill of being close until someone released a corner of the blanket and the wind ripped it away. The group screamed in surprise as the rain drenched them.

Pietro's hair was soaked, his damp curls stuck to his forehead as chaos started around them, everyone running for cover from the storm. Nina imagined her hair must look wild, most of her chignon loose. The organisers announced the *Alpini* band would play in the Corsos' barn. "Are you coming?" Pietro shouted to Onorina and Nina over the madness in the piazza and the intensifying rain. "We'll see you there!" Onorina called in response, pulling Nina again with her.

"What was that about?" asked Nina, when they found cover under an umbrella someone handed them.

"What was what about? It's a *festa!* Have fun, *sorellina!* Your life is too serious!" Her sister was in an exceptionally good mood, even though her waves were damp and would soon frizz. They were the first into the Corso barn as the *Alpini* band started and the accordions hummed.

The exhilaration of the cold and the extraordinary situation of the festival took away any inhibition Nina had of being first to dance, and she and Onorina bounced to the music as soon as they entered. Onorina was an excellent dancer and they both swung their hips, dipping and spinning with the music. Nina finally felt free. She twirled under the timber roof, giving in to an abandon she hadn't felt since childhood, since before the awful days of the war took it away.

A flood of people soon joined, swaying and waltzing around them. Nina's cheeks hurt from smiling and she danced with everyone. The temperature rose in the barn, making the air muggy with the earthy smell of rain and hay. Where was Pietro? The men passed bottles of wine and raised them to allow the liquid down their throats, swigging and handing it on. Her father appeared and lifted her around, then swung her sister. Vante and her little sisters stamped past, clapping their hands and twirling as the music played. It reminded her of the weddings she'd attended when she was small before the war. Everyone wanted to dance with her then, and she never wanted to leave the floor. Women swished their skirts, men slapped their thighs and when the *Alpini* band played 'Quel Mazzolin di Fiori', a cheer went up for the favourite song. Nina spotted Pietro through the boisterous crowd, but as he was about to break through, a young man with red hair swung her away. "Hey, Pampo!" someone shouted at him and gave him a wink as he swung Nina on the dance floor. She wanted to get away, annoyed at his awful dancing and even worse timing. She watched as Pietro found Onorina and gave her a twirl, both of them swaying to the music. Nina tried to move away from the redhead but the barn was too packed with bodies and he swung her again. This time, she lost her balance and, with two steps, trying to catch her footing, fell into the crowd.

"Whoa there," a low voice hummed in her ear as strong arms wrapped around her, catching her from her fall.

"I remember you telling me you could dance," Pietro said, smirking at her in a kidding manner while he pulled her into his arms.

"Don't blame me. A girl has to have the right partner," she quipped back, surprised by her own words and immediately taking in the heady scent of his cologne, wood and spice mellowed by dried rain.

'La Monella' played, and Pietro put his hand on Nina's lower back, guiding her in an easy waltz to the quick tune. No one had ever held her in such a way; his palm was firm on her lower back, possessive, as though sending a message to everyone in the room. He was smooth on his feet, confident. They spun around in the packed space until the other dancers parted enough to allow them to travel. As the pace of the song picked up, Pietro became animated; he raised his eyebrows, dipping her and teasing with his movements. Nina liked how he moved. He was smooth but didn't take himself seriously, and it was exhilarating to be twirled around in his arms. His hair had dried into a wild flop covering his left eye. She resisted the urge to push it back for him.

"Did you learn to dance like this in America?" she asked, as he spun her and then pulled her back close to him.

"I've learnt a lot of things in America." He leaned towards her and changed the subject. "Do you ever go to the movies?" he asked. When he spoke to her, he had to get close to her ear so she could hear him over the band. She felt the heat from his breath on her neck.

"*Sì*. In Feltre and we're meant to get a small picture house behind the church soon. I especially love American films!"

Pietro grinned at her, searching her face as if memorising her features. "Why weren't you at the last *festa*? I saw everyone else in your family but not you. Onorina was the star of the night."

"I'm sure she was," Nina frowned, a chill going through her at the mention of her sister. "I had to help my mother. Babies don't plan around events," she said, breathless and annoyed the conversation had headed again in Onorina's direction. How many times had men tried to get information about her sister through her? Was Pietro the same?

"You want to be a midwife too?" It was a serious question to ask in the middle of a dance floor but his brown eyes made her want to share her thoughts with him.

"I want to matter to the world," she admitted. "My mother has figured out how to do that." He spun her again, then looked at her seriously.

"You do and you will," he said. *Un colpo di fulmine.* The lightning bolt returned as his words sunk into her like she had been waiting to hear them all her life.

The song changed again and, this time, Corrado appeared, took Nina in his arms, and spun her around the barn. Losing sight of Pietro, she was tossed away again as Corrado seized her mother for a rare dance. She kept moving to the music as Pampo came up once more; this time she shook her head at him, unwilling to let him have her hand. He stayed nearby anyway, gesticulating towards her. For a moment, she thought she saw Pietro frowning on the other side of the barn as the annoying *ragazzo* danced at her. Nina smiled awkwardly, feeling uncomfortable, not wanting to be rude but miserable about the change in circumstances. Pampo grabbed her wrist and twisted her roughly again. This time, she stepped with intention away from him and inched into a corner of the barn where observers sat on stacks of hay. She searched the space until a flash of burgundy drew her attention. On the other side of the barn, there was Onorina, again in the arms of Pietro. He had her sister's scarf tied around his neck and was making the same animated faces at Onorina he had made at her. Nina felt the blood drain from her face and her urge to dance died, replaced by the desire to escape. Her siren of a sister could enchant any man; and why shouldn't he fall in love with her? Hours before, it seemed like Onorina was steering Pietro her way, but, as she batted her eyes and grasped onto the ends of her scarf around his neck, it was clear she was interested, too. Nina wove her way through the crowd to the exit, pushing away tears with the palms of her hands, and ran up the moonlit stones of the Via Calzen and home to her bed.

CHAPTER 5

The festival had been one of the best nights of her life, but it was cruel that she was still too young to enjoy it as her sister did. She had always prided herself in not caring about boys, but she could not get Pietro out of her mind. She spent the day alone in the woods, collecting chestnuts among the trees of Mount Avena and feeling sorry for herself. When she came back to the house and opened the door, she encountered a familiar scent combined with coffee. Pietro Pante sat on the bench stirring the espresso her mother had made him, wearing a brown flannel work shirt and looking at ease.

"Sit down," Adelasia said, gesturing towards a pulled-out chair. "Pietro was telling me about his life in America."

Nina hesitated, unsure what she had walked in on – the anger at seeing the burgundy scarf around his neck still burned into her memory.

"I've only come back to drop off the chestnuts. Where's Onorina? I'm sure she'd love to hear."

"Please, join us. I've been boring your mother about life in the mines. Probably not very interesting for you," Pietro said.

He cleared his throat, then fiddled with his cup. When he met Nina's eyes, the corner of his mouth turned up, and a dimple appeared as he made a slight wink at her.

She blushed and excused herself. "I'm sorry, I'd love to stay but I've promised a friend of mine I'd meet her for a walk to San Micel and I'm already late."

"Well, I expect Signor Pante will be disappointed," said Adelasia, as she searched for something in the cupboard.

Nina paused for a moment, unsure how to react and embarrassed her sister wasn't there.

"It's been lovely to see you." Forcing a smile, she rushed out the door. She walked at a fast pace up the Via Calzen and paused after turning the corner, considering which friend's house she should head to and shaking her head at the uncomfortable situation in the kitchen. What had he been doing there?

"Running late, aren't you?" Pietro's voice surprised her as he appeared around the corner. He closed the space between them and her heart thumped at their proximity.

"I didn't want to leave before giving you something," he said.

"When are you leaving?" she asked, trying to sound composed.

"Tonight. But I'll come back. Here." He pulled something from his pocket and reached for her hand. The feeling of his skin on hers again sent a current through her. He pressed a small, warm object into her palm; when she looked down, she saw it was a shiny circle of copper. An American penny.

"You remembered." Her face broke into a smile.

"You weren't an easy kid to forget."

She hesitated, feeling the warm penny in her hand. "Are you sure you want to give me this? I might want more next time," she joked, surprised at her comfort in teasing him.

He paused at her comment, as though he was breathing it in. "Next time, I hope to give you more."

They held each other's gaze for a moment before she swallowed and glanced at her shoes.

"I should go," she said, wondering why her mind was empty of any more meaningful conversation to keep him near her.

"I'll see you, Nina." His eyes looked sad as he flashed her the wry smile she remembered him having as a boy.

"I'll see you," she said, and they went their separate ways.

She headed to San Micel, squeezing the precious American penny tight in her fist.

Standing outside the church at San Micel, the entire city of Fonzaso sprawled out below her. From the main piazza, a series of winding roads connected to streets of homes and paths curving into the mountains. Houses staggered on inclines into the base of the Dolomites, stone and stucco homes with burnt-orange tiled roofs. The blue-green Cismon River ran over rocks past the town, splitting it from neighbouring Frassenè. Nina sat for a long time, overlooking the town, contemplating the past week's events. *Pietro*. His closeness during the parade, his smile at the *bocce* court, his words before he left. She could swear something was there, but she questioned herself, given the way he was with Onorina. She had no experience with men. Regardless, she would have to wait for her time. He was heading back to America. When would he be back? Would he ever return?

When she arrived home for dinner, the house was a flurry of activity; utensils clanged as Luigia and Aurora set the table with their best dishes while Evira pretended to rearrange pillows in the sitting room. Vante brought in firewood and stoked the fire.

"What's going on?" asked Nina.

"Where have you been?" Vante asked. "Have you heard the news?"

"What news?" asked Nina.

Aurora interrupted with glee, "Onorina! She's engaged!"

"What? When?"

"Today! He came over and asked Mamma and Papà and they said yes and now Onorina is getting married!" Aurora hummed a wedding song and feigned walking down the aisle with her hands holding an invisible bouquet.

Nina's heart pounded and her body went numb. The room spun in a frenzy around her. It all made sense. *That's why he'd been here!* Pietro had been sitting with her mother having asked for Onorina's hand. As she considered it, his words rang through her ears differently. "A kid you couldn't forget," he had said. To him, she was a silly young girl who'd asked for a penny. The younger sister of the most beautiful woman in town. How stupid she was, imagining he'd been flirting with her! How embarrassed she was for the way she'd flirted with him! He would be her brother-in-law! It was too much, too humiliating. She wanted to run away. She had made a complete fool of herself.

Before she could turn to go back outside for air, she heard her sister upstairs shrieking with delight. Onorina bounded down the steps, radiant and looking too lovely for their plain house. Her eyes sparkled with excitement, and she grabbed Nina in a hug.

52

"I've been waiting for you! I couldn't wait to let you know." Onorina squeezed her.

"You'll be my bridesmaid. The wedding will be in the spring. Toni's taking me to Canada! Mamma made him promise we'll come back after he makes some money of his own."

"Toni?" Nina said. "Canada?"

"Yes! Toni Bianchi proposed this afternoon. We're getting married! He and his mother are coming over for dinner to discuss the details and celebrate!"

Nina released the air tightening in her chest and collapsed onto the divan, suddenly light-headed. Her sister was marrying Toni Bianchi and moving to Canada. Pietro Pante was on a train to Genoa then leaving for America. Would she see him again? Would she see her sister again? She didn't know, but, despite it all, a great relief came over her.

"Yes, a dictator can be loved.
Provided the masses fear him at the same time.
The crowd loves strong men.
The crowd is like a woman."

– Benito Mussolini

CHAPTER 6

As Italy tried to come to terms with the fallout of their mutilated victory in the Great War, the country suffocated under the cost. Adelasia could buy less with her lire as prices inflated. Fights had broken out all over the city, angry farmers fought the political suffocation of the elite *signorotti*. Violent rebellions broke out, with Don Segala supporting the poor *contadini* to his own detriment. He was taken away at the request of the bishop and the *chiesa* was closed.

Anger at the socialist government's failure to do better for Italians laid the ground for a new leader to rise. Benito Mussolini, a soldier and journalist, pushed on the wounds and offered himself and his idea of fascism as a solution. He pulled no punches; he was resounding and clear and wanted to return Italy to greatness. His voice boomed on the radios and his fuming image appeared on the front page of every paper.

Nina turned eighteen on 24 October, 1922, the same day a stone-faced Mussolini declared to his cheering followers, "Our programme is simple: we want to rule Italy!" And he did, with truncheons and fear and bravado. But it stopped the chaos of everything else, the struggle for power and control that even in Fonzaso had led to madness. What *il Duce* brought seemed orderly to Corrado and others who were sick of the surrounding turmoil, so the Blackshirts marched on Rome on 27 October and on 28 October King Vittorio Emanuele III handed over the government to Mussolini. Italy came under the rule of a puff-chested, sour-faced little brute of a man, and Corrado and almost everyone else approved.

A few months later, Nina held Chiara Sebben's sweaty hand as she pushed. "It won't be long and you'll meet your baby," she said.

"One more push, Signora Sebben, you can do it," Adelasia urged as she extracted the baby from its mother, the cord, as purple as an aubergine, twisting between them.

"It's a boy!" Adelasia announced as the baby cried out for the first time, testing his little lungs.

Signora Sebben's exhausted face turned to elation at the sight and sound of the new person she'd added to the world. Adelasia wrapped a towel around him and handed him to his mother while she attended to the afterbirth. The woman studied the child's face, her heart reflecting in her eyes, and tightened the towel around him to keep him warm. A snapshot of the scene held in Nina's mind, like a medallion of Madonna and child. The woman held her baby's little finger and kissed it, then he opened his tiny eyes into slits to the blur of his mother, knowing her from the inside out. What a tremendous thing birth was and what a gift Mamma had for helping the process! Nina admired the Captain in action, and the outcome more often than not was this beautiful moment when mother and child met.

Nina took the baby to clean him off, running her finger

over his pebble toes and soft skin. Someday, she would love to be a mother. A husband was required first, and both Corrado and Adelasia had taken to reminding her of this and pointing out potential bachelors since a few months before her eighteenth birthday. The young men in town didn't interest her. She had been around these rural boys all her life, and none of them stirred her, none of them made her feel like she had about Pietro Pante, years ago. He was a world away. She'd rather join her mother as a midwife and limit her duties as a wife, especially if her only options were men from the province. Since she desired to be a mother, she'd have to settle on a man. She handed the baby back to his mother and his tiny mouth found her breast to nurse. The woman touched his cheek as he sucked. Nina was moved. She hoped one day she would know that kind of love.

The SS *Paris* neared Genoa in late February 1923, and the wind was crisp. The ocean tossed up a spray, sending the salty sea into the air around the deck where Pietro stood. He lifted the collar of his grey wool jacket. The jacket was good quality, a newer style, and had cost a decent amount of his pay. He didn't mind spending money on things that would last and was aware it gave him a slight air of distinction. It was nothing compared to the elegant attire of the passengers on the new ship, but if he stood tall, wore his leather gloves, and walked confidently past the gleaming windows and brass art nouveau décor, he did not look out of place.

He had taken his time buying the jacket, finding a shopkeeper who would take his money and be kind to him. Many didn't like doing business with what they considered a dirty *wop*, an Eyetie with permanent coal dust under his fingernails and in the creases of his hands. After he'd returned from his last trip to Italy, he had moved from labourer to miner; the work was daunting, and the conditions dangerous, but it allowed him to send more money to his family in Fonzaso, and to save. In the spring, he had lost a friend to an explosion, and another in the autumn when forty tons of top rock fell on him the week before his wedding. As a single man, Pietro's expenses were low, but he paid attention to the mining families and understood what tough lives they lived. The company housing rent, the food and supplies from the company shop, the costs of keeping tools sharp and clothes cleaned and your family fed didn't leave much, and the risk of injury or death was high. But moving back to Italy was financially impossible and his family depended on his earnings more than ever. Besides, after more than eight years, America was home. The Pante family could not survive on their small landholding and he shivered to think about how destitute his family would be if something happened to him and his money stopped flowing back. Their dependence on him made him question the mission he was on returning to Fonzaso.

He had come back for Nina.

As he considered it, he didn't have much to offer her, but he was compelled to return. He remembered his last trip back. He'd been twenty-one years old and was only visiting, a reprieve for him after many tough years working in the mines with his brother, first as a driver boy then as a labourer. His brother, Angelo, had oversold everything about working in the mines. It was like a death sentence. From sunrise to sunset, you were underground breathing coal dust, and the dangers were great. But when he wasn't in the mines and he could stroll down the main street and watch movies, he felt like he belonged there. Coming back to Italy had been a vacation into his old world, like stepping into a dated postcard with worn edges.

Everything changed the day on the church steps when he encountered Nina Argenta. It was as though Botticelli's Madonna had appeared before him. Her eyes bore into him, twinkling with joy or mischief, likely inherited from her father. He'd known her much of her early life, but nothing had prepared him for the feelings he had at that moment, as if time halted and the Earth revolved around them instead of the sun.

Everything about her captivated him. Her clear blue eyes, her pink lips like an elongated heart. Her nose, long and sculpted, could have been considered more Roman than her northern Italian roots suggested. She was wildly beautiful the night of the festival when her hair escaped from its chignon and he loved how, when she laughed, it was unbridled, taking over her entire body. He watched her dancing to the band before anyone else; she let nothing hold her back, and she emanated joy. But there was more to her. Her humour charmed him and her duty to her mother was something he could relate to as he tried to live up to the expectations of his father. It seemed they could understand each other, if he wasn't mistaken. He could tell the war had been hard on her but she was strong. Pietro knew there would be others interested in her. Although her face held a peaceful serenity, the twinkle in her eyes and the curves of her body would make any man consider her a delight for a wife. He had written to his family, attempting to ask casually about a variety of people from the town but he had no answer about Nina.

On his previous visit, he had mentioned his interest lightly at first in a comment to Corrado over *bocce*. Corrado had looked at him, knowingly, and told him not to get any ideas. It wasn't her time, and Adelasia would be the only one to consider changing that. He needed the courage of entering the mines every day when he went to speak to the Captain. She wasn't surprised, having seen them together, laughing under the blanket during the parade, but she told him the same thing Corrado did.

"It's not her time, and I'm not sure how you would be the right person. Ninetta won't want to move to America," Adelasia said.

"What if she stayed?"

The thought was logical but a stretch. He knew other women whose husbands were abroad but none who married them knowing they were leaving and planning to live apart.

"If you feel the same when she's eighteen, come back. If she wants to marry you, I won't stop her," she told him.

She must have known what a challenge that was and thought the likelihood was low he would return before Nina found interest elsewhere. But Nina's words had spurred him on. "I might expect more next time," she had said to him. She was making a joke about a penny, but he hoped she would accept what he offered her, which was only his love and a promise. All he could do was propose to her, hope there wasn't someone else and pray she'd consider him. He remembered the orange-haired nuisance who was always around. *Damn that Pampo,* he thought, frowning. Thinking of her with him made his jaw tense. He hoped he wasn't too late.

The sun was already beginning to set as he arrived home, tired from the intense journey. "Welcome back!" Pietro's brothers and sisters shouted, hugging and kissing him on each cheek in a flurry as soon as he opened the door. He tried to greet each one and comment on how much they'd grown. "Are you hungry? Come, eat," they called. They fought to take his bags, pull out his chair and guide him to a seat prepared for him at the table. He laughed. It was nice to come back from America and see his family had missed him. Even his father made a fuss over his homecoming, insisting he eat something immediately. As he lifted spoonfuls from a plate of risotto, he glanced out the window. A figure lifted a pitcher away from the water fountain at the end of the road. It was her! Nina stretched and he watched her. His dream was in front of him. He sat, spellbound, pretending to hear his siblings talk but completely focused on Nina. Her dark hair was pulled back, tendrils loose around her face, softly curling around her forehead, a blue scarf tied over the rest of her hair. The cold air made her cheeks flush pink and dark lashes shielded her eyes from the sunset reflecting off the snow. She wore no coat, only a shawl covering her dress. Placing her hands on her hips, she stretched again, an elegant line forming from her waist to her breast and along her neck, her eyes closed. He wanted her. He wanted to kiss the neck, the breasts, the lips, to put his hands in her dark hair, to get lost in her scent.

"Pietro." His mother interrupted his thoughts. "You're not eating your risotto. What's wrong, did you lose your taste for my cooking?"

"No, Mamma. It's excellent!" He took two large spoonfuls to please her and then stood up.

"I'll be right back." He grabbed his jacket and glided out the door.

"Where are you going?" his mother called after him. "You just got here!"

He turned up his collar, straightened his sleeves and ran towards the Argenta girl at the fountain.

Nina was preparing to carry the pitcher the rest of the way when a voice came from behind her and someone hopped over the low brick wall.

"That looks like it's heavy. Let me help."

She turned to face the voice, arming herself to deal with a bothersome admirer. Lately, several young men had been lingering around, trying to get her attention. Annoying her.

"I'm strong enough," she said, not glancing up to see who it was until she had shifted the pitcher onto her hip. She then lifted her eyes in a bored expression.

Her breath caught as she recognised him and their eyes met. Lightning in her heart wielded her speechless. He was here! In front of her in the cold snow! Not in America, not in her dreams. The smiling brown eyes looked back at her and the untamed hair hadn't changed. Nonetheless, he was different, older but stronger too, and even more self-assured.

"Ah! That's right. Why would Nina Argenta need any help from anyone?" he chided her.

"You're back," she said, a thrill rising in her as she said the words. She couldn't feel the cold anymore; her heart pumped blood fast through her system. "Have you come to stay?"

"Not to stay, but for a while. I just arrived. Mamma's been feeding me." He patted his stomach and grinned. "May I carry it for you?" he asked again. She nodded, and he lifted the large pitcher with ease. His shoulders were broader and more rounded. His cologne drifted off his jacket, rich and warm. She could feel herself pulling towards him again; how badly she wanted his scent to encircle her, how much she wanted to feel his hand on her lower back like when they'd danced together.

"You've been gone a long time, no?" she commented as they walked.

"Yes, working as much as I can, in Pennsylvania."

"Are you still in the mines?" she asked.

"I am. But now, I'm officially a miner. Bit of a step up from labourer. Not that it's impressive."

She felt his eyes studying her as he spoke. "Do you like it?"

"Not really, but the money's better than anything I could make here, that's for sure, and besides, I like America."

The radiance drained from her face and jealousy took over, as though America was another woman.

"America must be amazing and exciting. You must dread coming back here!" She could see from his face she'd surprised him with her comment but his voice was tender when he spoke.

"America's nice, but there are beautiful things here I can't find in America." His words were soft, stroking, and he kept his eyes on her. She blushed and looked away.

Too soon, they arrived at her front gate.

"Well, thank you," she said, hesitating before opening the gate and leaning against it to prop it open.

"Wait – tomorrow, may I take you for a walk? You can fill me in on what I've been missing."

She reached to take the pitcher from him and their hands touched, hers cold and his warm, sending tremors up her arm.

"You know, Onorina married Toni Bianchi. They live in Canada." She tried out the information, studying his face for a reaction, adjusting the pitcher on her hip.

"I heard. You can tell me all about it tomorrow." His face revealed nothing.

"Fine then," she said, warning herself to proceed with caution this time, but the flame in her stomach was growing.

"Nine o'clock?" he offered.

"Make it ten; I have chores. I'll meet you at the *bocce* court when I'm finished," she said. She turned to go into the house. "Welcome home, Pietro."

He smiled at her. "Nice to see you, Nina."

She walked inside and left him standing on the other side of the gate.

CHAPTER 7

Pietro was waiting for her the next morning and she studied him as she approached the empty *bocce* court. He stood at the edge, hands in the pockets of his grey jacket, elbows pointed out in a stance that told her there was nothing boyish about him anymore. His skin was still taut, but there were faint lines on his forehead; the mines had put their mark on him. *Is he meant to be mine?* she wondered as she got closer. Upon her arrival, he grinned, and his eyes danced. She bit her lower lip. He was perfection.

"Good morning. I'm glad you came. I was worried I'd have to come to the house to find you. I'm not quite ready to face your mother, and I'm sure your father will ply me with grappa," he said, laughing, running a hand through his hair.

"I told them you might come for *aperitivo*. They're eager to spend time with you. It's not every day someone comes to visit from America."

"I'd love that! Should we head up to San Micel?" he asked.

"*Sì*. It's not too cold today and the sun is out so the view should be clear." She tried to relax as she spoke. He was here, and he had asked her to walk to San Micel, which meant they would have much time to talk. As they walked through town towards the path in the woods, they realised they were being followed. Three children trailed behind them, keeping their distance but giggling. One of them was her cousin. Of course, they could never go unchaperoned! Whether they were following of their own accord or her parents sent them, it wasn't clear. Nina and Pietro ignored them and continued with their plan.

They scaled the path up to the little castle, twigs snapping under their feet with every few steps. Snow sprinkled Fonzaso with white, and dusted the trees, like powdered sugar on warm *crostoli* biscuits.

She told him what she had been doing over the past years and about the recent births and funny stories of husbands and children of the women she helped attend.

"Mamma has been busier than ever," she said as they avoided icy patches and walked in the worn pathway of others' footsteps.

"She's lucky to have you to help her."

He wanted to know about everything. Odd for a man to care about women's business. She liked his interest.

"I help her all the time. Did you know I was born on her birthday? I think she believes it means we share a mind, but she's wrong."

"Don't you think like her?"

"More than my siblings do. But I'm not her. She's much tougher than me." Nina laughed and continued, "I know one thing. I don't want the life of everyone else here. But I'm not sure I'll get a choice."

They climbed more until reaching a break in the trees revealing the vista below. Smoke curled from chimneys, white puffs smouldering into a blue sky. She became breathless as they ascended the steep trail and she could feel him watching her. As they reached the indentation where San Micel stood, the expanse of Fonzaso and beyond lay before them. The town gleamed below in the winter sun.

"May I ask you a question?" he leaned on the balustrade as he spoke.

"*Sì*," she said.

"How do you feel about America?" Pietro asked.

She paused. She used to think a lot about America, before the war, but she wasn't ready to tell him.

"It's a place, I guess, like any other. Am I wrong? My brother went. We never hear from him." She kept her eyes low.

"You're right and you're wrong," answered Pietro. "People live and raise families and work and have neighbours but it's also new and fresh and feels alive."

She studied him as he talked about America and looked over the expanse of Fonzaso, his breath coming out in puffs as it met the air. His face held a determined look.

"You love it there, don't you?" she asked.

"My family here leads a simple and difficult life. They're born; they work to survive by toiling in the fields and depend on the weather. If I live here, I worry my children and my children's children will lead the same life. Sometimes I think rather than earning money and bringing it back to live better here, as my father wants, I should settle there for good."

"What's wrong with leading a simple life?" asked Nina. She was challenging him but, in her heart, she knew what he meant.

Pietro stopped and smiled at her. "Nothing. It's not bad if you don't mind going hungry for half the year. I do find it repetitive and a constant struggle. Maybe less for you and your family because of your mother being a midwife but certainly for someone like me. Remember, I'm one of fourteen. I want something special for my children, and I'd like to raise them in America where there's a chance for them to do something extraordinary instead of working in a field until they die."

Nina smiled at him, remembering how he had mentioned he wanted to be his own man, years ago when he was young and had coughed on grappa. He was the same, a boy grown into a man.

"Is it better for them to work in the mines?" she asked seriously.

"No. That's the problem. Working in a field is better than being underground every day. But it doesn't pay. I won't mine forever, and I don't want my children to have to."

They stood looking over the vista; their observers played below, waiting to determine their next move.

"And what about you, Ninetta? What do you want?" She noticed he added the endearment to her name.

She regarded him cautiously. "I know I want a family of my own."

He turned to look at her.

She wished he would come closer, keep her warm, instead of standing at a distance observing her answers.

"Is that all you want?" he pressed.

"When my brother left for America, it broke my mother's heart. I promised her I wouldn't leave her. I want to keep my promise. I don't want to leave Fonzaso. Not now." She hesitated. "But to be honest, during the war, I dreamed about taking a ship across the ocean. I wondered about America. Perhaps someday an adventure will be in store for me."

He grinned.

She shivered.

"You're cold. Let's go back, I'd like some coffee. Shall we return to your house and call off the guards?" She glanced at their group of small spectators.

"*Andiamo.* Let's go," she said.

Back at the Argenta house, Nina's family welcomed Pietro and offered him grappa, which he turned down, to Corrado's displeasure, but he promised to accept a glass of wine after coffee, which appeased him. Papà was eager to fill Pietro in on Mussolini and the politics of Italy and to hear what they were saying in America. As they sat together having an espresso, Luigia, now ten, prompted by Evira, twelve, flicked water from the staircase to tease them. Pietro, good-natured, pretended to chase them up the stairs to catch them, which left the girls in peals of laughter. Everyone got on with Pietro except Adelasia, who watched him quietly, made her excuses, and went out to check on a mother. Nina didn't let it spoil her happiness. Did her mother not like Pietro? America was far away and this man visiting her home lived there. Was Pietro Pante threatening Mamma's plans to keep her close, to continue the family business of midwifing? Nina didn't want to know and didn't want to worry about the future because, as the fire warmed them, and as she sipped Marsala with her father and Pietro, she was happier than she had ever been in her life, and it seemed everything was just as it should be.

They agreed to walk to the altar of *Sant'Anna* the next afternoon, as they both had many chores in the morning. It had snowed overnight and Fonzaso sparkled. They walked together up the incline, their followers from the day before again a few metres behind.

"My father has never been to *Sant'Anna* but my mother and sisters come here all the time," he told her as they climbed.

"It's a special place for women." She looked towards their destination, remembering some of the touching scenes she had witnessed there. "I've only seen my mother cry a few times, once when my brother was leaving – it was the night you were at my house – and the other times at *Sant 'Anna*. It's as if she saves her gratitude and sadness and leaves it at the feet of the Madonna and Saint Anne; they're mothers and daughters, so, they understand."

He listened and was quiet. As they passed the wooden Stations of the Cross along the path, her soul soared. The weather was frigid. Icy winds slid down from the mountains, but her coat was warm and in Pietro's company, her heart beat much faster. The snow crunched beneath her shoes and twice she slipped, prompting him to catch her lightly. She would have fallen headfirst if she knew he would rescue her in his arms the way he had caught her the night of the festival. *Stop it, Nina*, she told herself. *Don't show him your eagerness.*

In the late afternoon sky, the sun was slipping behind the mountains near neighbouring Frassenè, creating an orange glow over the rooftops, and the moon was angling to take over.

"Ninetta, have you ever been in love?" he asked her, avoiding her eyes as they walked past the eighth and ninth stations.

The question took her off guard, and she focused on the stations in front of her as she thought how to answer.

The eighth station – Jesus meets the holy women of Jerusalem.

The ninth station – Jesus falls for the third time.

Thinking of a response, her throat constricted and her body went numb; she checked to make sure none of their followers were close enough to hear.

"What would I know of love?" she said. *What do I know of*

71

dreaming every night of someone you cannot have? Of being in love with a man you think loved another and not any other, but your sister. What do I know of lying in my bed dreaming of being embraced by a man thousands of miles away?

"I've been stupid about love. A young girl's fantasy, I suppose," she said to him.

They approached the tiny white altar surrounded by vineyards and she changed the subject. "Mamma has convinced the new priest to allow for a little building to be built here someday, around the altar. He's trying to win everyone over since none of the women wanted Don Segala replaced. He's growing on them." She touched the side of the decaying altar. "It will be wonderful when it's finished. Someday when they raise enough money." As she pranced joyfully around the area in the snow, her coat swung open and her chocolate hair whipped around her ears. Pietro dug his cold hands into the pockets of his coat and smiled. She could feel his eyes continuing to follow her.

"I'll be right back, I'm going to pray," she told him and headed back to the grotto near the Madonna statue. Icicles hung around the shallow cavern entry, glistening like diamond teeth. She ducked under them and knelt on a thin wooden platform beneath the statue, taking her rosary out of her pocket and starting a quick decade of prayers. On the third Hail Mary, she heard him behind her, and saw his outline in the corner of her eye, kneeling in the snow, hands clasped in prayer. There was something so sweet in the gesture, it almost made her cry. Her heart softened as calm washed over her. She completed the last prayer, ending in an Our Father.

No sooner had she finished than she heard a thump behind her and a muffled groan. Turning, she saw Pietro, still on his knees, holding his face and wiping his cheek. "*Mio Dio!*

What happened?" she exclaimed. He pointed to a large icicle that lay menacingly in the snow. "It got me," he joked.

"Let me help," she said, rushing to lean over him. He took his hand down. Despite his smile, there was a slight cut on his eyelid, and flakes of melting snow dusted his hair and face. Nina gently wiped the snowflakes off his eyelashes and cheek with her fingers, murmuring words of comfort like a mother with an injured child, before she sensed how close her face was to his. She studied his features; the creases by his eyes, his full lips and the stubble on his jaw sharp beneath her fingers. Finally, he stood, close to her, frozen in the moment. "Come with me," he said when she broke from his gaze. He caught her hand and helped her up a steep part of the hill above the grotto, leaving their onlookers busy in a snowball fight below. "I want to show you something." He led her back behind the cavern where the Madonna stood and into a cluster of pine trees. "Look, come here." He pointed and she could make out a tiny wooden shed covered by foliage and snow.

"What is that?" she asked.

"It was my hideout," he said, pushing away branches and getting closer to the entrance. "Where my brother and I used to go when we were young, before I left for America." A rueful smile flickered across his features. "It feels like it was yesterday."

She stepped around to see it more clearly. "I would have never found it. It's perfectly hidden," she said, ducking under the brush, stepping closer to him.

"We meant it to be like that. Our siblings couldn't pester Angelo and me here. We covered it with wood and vines and hoped it would stay a secret."

"And you're sharing this secret with me?" she teased. "I'm honoured."

There was a brief silence before he spoke. "I have another

73

secret to tell you, Ninetta." His voice softened and he turned her shoulder to face him. She cocked her head, examining him and savouring his touch. What would he say next?

"You have a crazy idea in your head I would have cared about your sister marrying Toni."

She pulled away, embarrassed. "Please, I don't want to talk about this," she interrupted.

"Why do you think I came back?" he asked. "To see my mamma?"

She quieted, scared of what he would say, and realised how alone they were. Her heart cartwheeled.

"Ninetta, remember meeting on the church steps? Or that night at the *festa*? Can you honestly not know? Can you not feel what I feel for you?" he pleaded with her, a tender smile on his lips.

She blinked back tears. Of course she remembered. Those were the moments she replayed in her head. The priceless jewels of memories she kept locked away in her mind and took out to admire when she was alone. How could they pour out of his lips, more special because they were shared?

"I never had a thought of Onorina! It's always been you." His expression was earnest as he told her, "You're in my dreams. I want to talk to you every night. I've been waiting so long for you," he said, his eyes glowing with love.

"You were never interested in Onorina?" she asked. She remembered the longing on Pietro's face. It was not for her sister but for her. *Of course!* She had always hoped but never dared believe it could be true.

"You captivated me from the day I left when we were both children. It grew to wonder and then…" He stopped, looking at her for permission to proceed. "To love," he admitted. "Can I ever hope you feel the same?"

She shook her head, astonished. When she looked at him,

her eyes filled with tears. "I've loved you since before I knew what love was," she whispered, crying and laughing at the insanity of the moment.

He took her hands. "I want to marry you, Ninetta. I can't offer you much. It won't be easy for you if you come with me. I'm a miner, I'll probably never be rich. But I want you to be my wife. I've known it for a long time."

"I'm not sure what my parents will say." Slowly, the reality of what she was considering hit her. He lived thousands of miles away in America.

"I spoke to them. Last time I was here. Your mother told me if I came back and you wanted me, she wouldn't stop you. She probably didn't believe I'd return. I think she hoped you'd find someone else. You haven't, have you?"

Nina looked down at his hands, rough and clean, but still blackened. "She won't stop me, but she won't give her blessing, either," she said, feeling the weight of the choice in front of her. What would it mean to marry Pietro Pante? To her, to Mamma?

"I've come all this way for you and I won't give up if you can't come with me. There has to be a way," he said, searching for solutions. "You... you can stay," he stammered. "She would give us her blessing if you stayed. But do you want me? Tell me you want to be my wife because, if you do, I'll do anything for you. I'll love you until the day I die." He bent towards her and placed the softest kiss on her lips, restraining his passion expertly at first. When she didn't push him away, he allowed his mouth to take hers more urgently. "Will you marry me? Will you be my bride?" he whispered, pulling his mouth from hers.

"Yes," she said, her eyes meeting his.

"Are you sure? We'll have so much to figure out. It won't be easy," he said.

"Together, we will find our way."

They headed back down the path, the mountain wall at their backs and the sun casting its last glow, making shadows of them as the moon took its place in the sky. They went home to tell their families the news.

CHAPTER 8

April 1923 She stood outside the *Chiesa della Natività di Maria* as Aurora fretted with her veil. The candied scent of cherry blossoms mixed with April grass filled the air. It was the perfect day for a wedding.

"Make sure you keep this nice. I'll be wearing it next," Aurora teased. "So far, it's been good luck." Onorina had been married in the same veil, and she was far away in Cape Breton, Canada, with her first baby, Mary. She'd written to congratulate Nina on her engagement to Pietro.

Nina grabbed Aurora's hand in hers. "Am I ready, *sorellina*? Do I look like a bride?" She wore a simple white dress her aunts had sewn for her with embroidered flowers on the collar and a matching sash, blue, like the Madonna's robes. It fit her beautifully and its collar of azure flowers brought out her eyes like topaz jewels.

"I wouldn't be surprised if he weeps at the sight of you. You're beautiful, Ninetta."

"It's almost time. Everyone's in their seats," Luigia announced. "Here's Mamma."

Adelasia huffed to the church, dressed in her best clothes.

She had pulled out a special little hat with netting on it for the occasion, and even wore a little lipstick.

"Mamma, you're so pretty!" Nina said.

"Ninetta," she said. "My baby." She squeezed Nina's hand in hers.

"Mamma, you had many babies after me," she laughed, surprised at her mother's overt affection.

Adelasia cleared her throat and fretted with the hat, not used to such fussy attire. "You are my Ninetta. You were my gift. You'll be a good wife. Pietro may live abroad, but he is an honest man. You get to stay here and he'll send money so you can have a good life." Nina clenched her teeth into a forced smile at her mother's comment. The practicality of it took away from the romance of the day, but her mother's approval, albeit on condition of her staying, meant everything. Especially after watching her first two children move away.

"I'm glad you approve," Nina said.

"Now, go marry him," Adelasia said and squeezed Nina's hand again before slipping through the grand church door.

Corrado's arm felt spindly under her shaking fingertips as he guided her down the aisle. Diamond patterns on the terrazzo floor stretched under her wedding slippers. She squinted, squeezing her fingers into his bicep for assurance. *Papà,* she thought fondly. Sunlight gleamed through the arched windows of the church, casting light on the blues and reds of paintings in elaborate gold frames she could see through the Venetian lace veil. Music vibrated from the organ, matching her pace as she glanced from side to side at smiling guests. Zia Angelina, her uncle Vittorio's wife, was there without him with tears in her eyes, holding their daughter. Evira appeared bored, but Aurora, Vante and Luigia beamed at her along with their mother. Pietro's side was boisterous, paying no attention to her and goofing around in the pews. *My family,* she smiled. Marrying a man who lived abroad in America – that was something. A man she loved and who loved her. It didn't always happen like that. God blessed her; the Virgin Mary must be helping to answer her prayers.

On tall columns, soaring above either side of the altar, stood statues of *San Paolo,* pious with his sword, and *San Pietro* holding the keys to Heaven. The saints watched over them as she walked under their gaze to emerge in front of her own Pietro.

Corrado lifted the lace veil and placed it over the top of her head. He handed her to Pietro and her small hands slipped into his calloused ones. She looked at him, staring first at the buttons on his shirt, then his collar and then into his eyes.

How handsome he was! The skin was smooth on his neck above his jacket, and his smell was familiar. His hair was in perfect place today except for one loose lock that curled over the middle of his head, threatening to fall forward. He smiled at her then and she saw her future.

The vows went by in a whirlwind; the organist played *Ave Maria* and Nina reminded herself to never forget this moment as she looked at her husband with love in his eyes and the paintings of the church behind him.

"I declare your marriage in the name of the church of *Santa Maria della Natività* of Fonzaso," Don Cavalli announced. "Pietro and Nina Pante."

Her heart leapt. Life would never be the same. There would always be the time before this moment and her life after. Nina lifted her face and Pietro leaned down and pressed his lips to hers for the first time as man and wife.

Afterwards, their families held a party on the Via Calzen. Each of the houses strung lanterns over the street to create an archway of light. Her family went to stay at the homes of various relatives to allow Nina and Pietro the house to themselves for two nights. Nina rode in a cart with Pietro to the altar of *Sant'Anna* and the Blessed Virgin. His arm was warm around her waist and he tightened her towards him. She could feel his palm on her side and this intimacy gave her a heady pleasure. When they arrived, he took her hand and helped her out of the wagon and into the darkness, lighting a candle to help her find her way to pray to the Madonna. The soft earth gave way under her wedding slippers as she walked the path to the Virgin Mary statue. She laid a thick cloth on the wooden platform and knelt before her.

"*Santa Maria,* thank you and your son for this beautiful day. Please help me be a good wife to Pietro. Help me love him, support him and bear him children. *Madre di Dio,* please give us the gift of children and help me be a good mother in your example. Please bless my mother, Pietro's mother and all the mothers and children in the world. Keep them safe in your care."

Nina breathed in the fresh sweetness of the four white rose blossoms she'd brought with her and laid them before the Madonna statue. Would God give her four children? Would the Virgin assure it? She stood and turned to walk back to Pietro. After taking three steps, a nervous thought came to her, and she ran back to the Madonna and knelt again.

"Virgin Mary, please also help me and give me the strength to get through tonight," she whispered. Making the sign of the cross, Nina hurried back to the carriage.

"Wait there," Pietro called out as she approached.

She stopped. Her heart raced from the chilled evening air

and her anticipation. She peered back at him. "What is it?" she asked.

"Just stop and let me look at you."

She was self-conscious under his gaze and her lids dropped to cover her eyes.

"I want to remember you like this forever. In the moonlight, with Fonzaso behind you, the night you became my wife. You look like Botticelli's Maria," he reached his hand towards her and helped her into the wagon then whispered in her ear, his breath warm on her neck, "But you are my Ninetta."

She brushed her hair in the room she shared with her sisters, then padded across the hall and twisted the knob of the master bedroom door. Pietro stood by the window, unbuttoning his shirt. He turned as she entered and she looked at the bedpost, too nervous to meet his eyes. He crossed to her and slid his hardened palm up her arm, sending currents through her body. His fingers caressed her throat and moved to where her long hair met her neck, calloused leather on silk.

"Ninetta," he said from deep within his throat, desire coming through. His fingers twirled a piece of her hair and he stroked her chin with his thumb. She curved it towards him and closed her eyes. He brushed his lips against the spot on her throat where his fingers had been, and more waves ran through her body.

"You smell like oranges and powder," he whispered. His mouth made its way to her ear; he took the lobe between his lips as his hands slid upwards over her hips, her waist, and found their way to her breasts. He slid his hand in the opening of her cotton nightdress and cupped her softness. His hands were rough and cool against her warm skin and when he rubbed his thumb against the peak of her breast, she shivered and grabbed his shoulders, gasping at the sensation.

"It's okay." He put both his hands in her hair, fingers massaging her scalp as he brought her face towards his for a kiss. Her tongue met his; she didn't know what to do but her body responded, arching towards him. "You taste of Chianti," he whispered. She was inside his scent, her lips on his neck. It was her turn to breathe him in. She quivered inside, her entire body on fire. Reaching up, she pushed back his hair and wove the locks through her fingers as she had wanted to for so long. Then, with a boldness she did not think she possessed, she pulled up her nightgown. He helped it over her head and stepped back. She watched him take her in.

He finished undressing, his eyes still on her, and she did not have time to be embarrassed at his gaze before he pulled her onto the bed. She could feel his eagerness to possess her, and he laid her down, her hair sprawling across the sheets, breasts parting as his chest crushed hers. They finally belonged to each other.

"Dance with me." He looked at her seriously, pulling her off the bed. It was the middle of the night, but neither of them slept. The moonlight lit a knot in the wood on the warped floorboard she had never noticed before. Everything was new, intensified as though Raphael's brush strokes had repainted the world for her. Nina laughed nervously. He extended his hand. She stood naked with him in the moonlight and pressed her body to his, holding his gaze. He devastated her. Her rules, her private decisions, were in question and shaken. She was dancing naked in her parents' room. "You amaze me," she said, meaning it. He pressed his hand to her back as they swayed back and forth, the wood floors creaking below them. "Shhhh," Pietro whispered.

Nina was content, but she wondered if she should be. Should she not be embarrassed? To want to cover herself? *Not now*, Nina thought. *Now I will give him anything he wants.* Pietro pulled back and spun her around. She laughed aloud again, this time not out of nerves but surprise. "What are you doing, you crazy man?" she asked.

"Don't you know?" he whispered in her ear. "I'm trying to get you to fall in love with me."

"Really?" she questioned. "It's late for that, no?"

"Why would it be too late to fall in love?"

"Because I am already in love with you," she said.

"Well, then, fall again," Pietro said, and dipped her smoothly, cradling her in his arms and then twisting her onto his lap as he sat on the bed. He pushed back her hair and held her face in his hands, kissing her with a mounting passion.

"I'll never stop falling in love with you," she whispered.

CHAPTER 9

The scent of saffron, white wine and onions permeated the kitchen and Nina poured the Arborio rice into the boiling mixture as it crackled over the heat. Her fingertips were gold from the thin filaments of saffron, a gift from one of Adelasia's families. She wiped her hands on her apron.

The first meal for my husband, she thought. Pietro would say he liked her cooking no matter how bad it was.

I married a kind man, she thought. But she wanted to please him. She bit her lip, remembering the night before. *I certainly pleased him last night,* she smiled to herself. She hadn't expected to enjoy the secrets of the marital bedroom, but Pietro was patient and knew exactly what to do. She hoped he hadn't learnt *that* in America. She pushed the thought from her mind. He took pleasure in every part of her and feeling so desired unlocked something in her. The neighbours were close; she hoped they hadn't heard.

The rice bubbled, and she stirred in butter and cheese. She grabbed a few pieces of wood and tossed them into the stove; embers flew out, just missing her apron. How long would Pietro be? He had gone with Corrado to the courthouse to finalise the purchase of a house. To be able to buy a house! One benefit of Italian inflation; Pietro was paid in dollars and old widow Angarani had passed away, leaving a tiny house with steep steps and two small bedrooms available at the top of the road. Pietro liked the idea of something solid to spend his money on. They could always sell it to family. And things were stabilising somewhat in Italy. The new prime minister, Mussolini, was committed to picking Italy up from its post-war poverty. There was nowhere for him to take the country but up. Bounty was in front of them, she was certain.

She took the rice off the heat and let it sit, covered by a towel, while she prepared the table. Two spots. She smiled.

Two spots for a few months, she thought. And then he would have to leave again to start his next contract. She frowned at the thought but was cheered again, seeing Pietro come through the gate. He bounded into the house with a handful of spring flowers.

"It's done!" he said, grabbing her around the waist with one hand and handing her the flowers with the other. "The house is ours! We can move in tomorrow!" He spun her around, burying his face in her hair, kissing her temple.

"I'm going to get used to you and being married and then you'll leave," she pouted at him like a spoiled child.

"Let's not think of that yet."

"No. Let's eat and celebrate!"

He lifted the towel, peering into the pan. *"Risotto allo zafferano.* Almost my favourite," he said.

She frowned.

"But your mother said it was your favourite! I made it because she said..."

He wrapped her in his arms. "It was my favourite, but I had something else in mind for supper." He picked her up, carrying her towards the stairs.

"The food will get cold," she laughed, wrapping her arms around his neck.

"I don't mind," he reasoned. "We can warm it up later. Risotto always tastes even better that way."

They fell into a pattern, working side by side, getting the basics for the house and planting in the tiny landholding Pietro had received from Corrado, who had insisted on providing a dowry as a gift out of his and Adelasia's allotments. It wasn't much, but it was enough for them to make a start. She grew used to catching Pietro watching her in the field, waving and smiling. He was more affectionate than most men she knew. He found any opportunity to touch her as he piled beans and onions in her basket or when they washed their hands in the fountain. As she spent time with his family, she saw that he and his father were alike in this way. When his mother, Margherita, sewed, Teodosio would sit so close to her, he had to lean to the side to avoid the needle every time she pulled a stitch. It was endearing. She knew Pietro didn't always see eye to eye with his father, so she kept her observation of this similarity to herself.

Nina listened as Pietro discussed politics with Corrado and Vante. News of a conflict in Corfu came, making it clear Mussolini was a powerful leader for Italy. He sent troops to occupy without regard for the League of Nations. He didn't back down and everyone agreed it showed Italy was protected in his care. Nina was more worried about family matters, specifically if their marital relations would result in a new life, a family. If she had to wait until he returned, it would be years.

One night, just before he left, she told him about her

worries. "We've been married for only a few months, but we'll be apart for years. It's not fair," she said.

"Every single day since we have been married will give me enough joy to last me a year," he said to her lovingly.

"Don't you dare stay away that long!" She tried to make the conversation lighter but tears pressed on the back of her eyes.

"Are you sure you don't want to come with me? It's a hard life but we would be together." He looked at her tentatively, they both knew her response.

"I can't break my promise, Pietro. It would kill my mother to have another of us move away. We agreed. Please don't make me feel bad about it now." She blamed her promise to Adelasia, but she knew she wasn't ready to leave. Her heart felt torn in two.

He pulled her close. "I've wanted you my whole life," he said. "And now that I have you, I'm going to do everything to make you happy. I'll get home to you as soon as I can."

Nina lay underneath him, with his nose and mouth attending to her throat.

"I'll take the smell of you with me wherever I go," he whispered, burying his face in her hair, cradling her with one arm around her back and the other below her head, holding her close to him as he took in her scent with a deep inward breath. He exhaled and peppered light kisses along her neck. They started as tiny, clipped kisses but as he continued to breathe her in, his lips became greedy and he let his tongue taste her throat. She groaned with pleasure as she lost all sense of reality, the reality that he was leaving, the bulky canvas bag in the corner representing years away from her. A tear trailed down her face, plunging onto her breast. He kissed where it wet her skin.

"Ninetta, I'll never really leave you, I'm always with you," he said. He pulled her across his lap like a child and turned towards the open terrace door. "Do you see the moon? It's beautiful tonight, isn't it?"

She nodded her head. "It's lighting everything."

Pietro smiled. "It's our moon. *La nostra bella luna.* It's the light there every night. You can count on it. Sometimes it may look far away, the clouds may cover it, but it's there. Sometimes it is small and hidden but it's there. Sometimes it will be like this, taking over the sky and filling us with light, but no matter what, it's there. It's like us. You'll look at the moon every night and so will I, on the other side of the ocean. I'll see it when I come up from the mines. It will be you, welcoming me, covering me in your love. You are my moon and I hope I'll be yours."

She turned to him and stroked his cheek. She planted a kiss there and another on his chin and shoulder. He shuddered, and she knew it meant he wanted her again.

"*Sì,*" she said. "We'll be each other's moon until you come back to me."

She stood at the train station in Feltre to say goodbye. He would travel through Montebelluna to Padua then Milan to Genoa, where his ship would leave for New York. He had a long journey ahead, and they had agreed she would stay, but now, how could she let him go?

"You stay here. Be good and help your mother. I'll be back before you know it, and I'll send money every month, as much as I can, so you can buy more animals. Some chickens, maybe a pig. You'll have your hands full."

"I don't care about the money but I will cherish your letters. Write often, money or not."

The train whistled and her throat tensed as if she'd swallowed a pomegranate. She laid her head on his chest and he held her and kissed her forehead. As the train stopped before him, he kissed her mouth deeply and held her close to him.

"*La mia sposa, amore mio,*" he whispered. My bride, my love. He pulled away, keeping her gaze as he got on the train and waving goodbye as it pulled away. She stood on the platform as the others left. After praying a Hail Mary, she made the sign of the cross, then turned to take the bus back to Fonzaso, alone.

CHAPTER 10

Fatigue hung on Nina like a thick carpet. She sat in her mother's kitchen cleaning beans with her sisters. The pile of green curls grew in front of them on the table as they snapped and pulled the strings, then threw the beans into a colander for washing. The juices made Nina's fingers raw and the earthy smell made her mildly nauseous, but she kept going to have company.

The home Pietro had bought was just a few houses down, at the end of the Via Calzen, perpendicular to the street and had a balcony with unhindered views of the *Eremo di San Michele.* His scent lingered in the halls at first, then disappeared and as the weeks passed, she put away the razor he forgot near the basin. The house was empty without him and she was scared to be by herself, like being a child again. She spent as much time as possible at her mother's or visiting Pietro's relatives. While she knew it would please him for her to get to know his family, helping in their kitchens made her sleepy and the mess in their homes overwhelmed her. Every family lived to a different standard, and she was used to the Captain's orderliness. The Pante homes had charmed her when Pietro was there, but now they mildly irritated her. Nonetheless, she continued to visit to be a good daughter-in-law.

Adelasia had received a letter from Onorina, happy in Canada and doing well with their shop. Little Mary was proving to be a very smart child. She was crawling early and learning to talk.

"It's wonderful that Onorina and Toni are doing so well. Mamma says they are very enterprising," said Luigia.

"No doubt supplemented by Toni's bootlegging," goaded Evira. Her nasally voice made everyone cringe. "I'm sure there was a reason she asked for Papà's grappa recipe in so much detail!"

Aurora made a face at her and changed the subject, "*Allora*, Nina, have you had a letter from Pietro recently?"

"Yes. I just received one. He's working hard. He tries not to make the mines sound bad but I worry about him."

"What do you think America is like?" asked Luigia. "Do you think it's nice? Like in the movies?"

"Pietro says it's the most amazing place in the world. He says it opens your mind to a new way of thinking and people can become great and rich there with hard work." Nina slowed her peeling; she rested her head on her hand and her wrist bent at its heaviness.

"Is that what you want, Ninetta? To be a rich American and to leave us behind like Antonio did, like Onorina did?" Evira asked, lounging on the divan as her sisters worked. Evira had always been lazy, but Nina was confused by how cunning and jealous the girl had become.

"No. No, of course not," she answered. As she stood up to take the beans to rinse, a wave of dizziness overcame her. She grabbed a chair to steady herself, faltering as the room spun.

"Nina!" cried her sisters. They rushed her into a chair.

Aurora grabbed her hand and fanned her with a newspaper. "Luigia, get her a glass of water. Oh, *Madonna mia!*"

"Are you all right?" Luigia asked. "Are you sick?"

"I... I don't know. I'm just tired. Let me lie on the divan for a few minutes."

"Evira, get off your *culo* and let her lie down." Aurora swatted at their idle sister with the paper.

Luigia returned with the water and the girls helped their sister to the sofa. Nina lay her head on the small pillow. Her body was thirsting for sleep. She closed her eyes as their voices drifted further and further away.

When Nina awoke, she was still groggy. From behind half-opened eyelashes, she could see it was already getting dark. The moon peeked out from behind the clouds outside the window. Utensils clattered more quietly than normal as everyone prepared for dinner, trying not to wake her. She opened her eyes to see Adelasia carefully laying out plates on the tablecloth. She finished setting the table and, seeing Nina awake, ambled towards the sofa, grinning.

"How long have I been sleeping?" Nina asked.

"Oh, two or three hours." Mamma sat next to her and smoothed back her hair.

"That long! I'm still tired. I must be ill," Nina said.

"Well, you aren't," replied her mother. "What you are is pregnant. When was the last time you bled?"

Nina hadn't considered it. She had been busy setting up her home, unpacking, writing to Pietro and helping her mother. "It's been a couple of months. I forgot about it."

"Well, there will be a baby by spring," Adelasia said.

"Are you sure, Mamma?" she asked.

"I think I know what I'm talking about."

Nina smiled and lay her head on Adelasia's broad lap. "Pietro will be so happy!" she said. Their dreams were coming true. She reached down and stroked her stomach. *My baby,* she thought. *Pietro's baby.*

She lay the next night in her bed, the moon shining bright and lighting San Micel outside her window. In her hands, she clasped a new letter from Pietro.

Cara Ninetta,

La luna è bella stasera, amo questa notte perché sei con me. The moon is beautiful tonight, I love this night because you are with me.

His letter was warm in her hand. She read it four times. This letter would always be with her. She would keep it close to her until they were together again. His words made her love him more, as if he were wooing her from thousands of miles away.

Tu sei tutto quello di cui ho bisogno; sei tutto. Tu sei il lago, la montagna e il cielo. You are all I need; you are everything. You are the lake and the mountain and the sky.

Oh, how she loved him. How she missed him! She wished she didn't have to be apart from him at all. Perhaps if she found work she could help bring them together sooner. But what could she do? There was no work in Fonzaso. She was helpless. She concentrated on the last words of the letter.

Quando sarò a casa, ti bacerò due volte per ogni giorno che sono stato via, e ti ricoprirò di tutti i giorni e gli anni di baci in una volta sola. Sii paziente, aspettami. Ti amo, moglie mia. Baci, Pietro. When I am home, I will kiss you twice for every day I've been away, and I will cover you with the years and days of kisses at once. Be patient, wait for me. I love you, wife of mine. Kisses, Pietro.

She smiled. Yes, she was in love and she was having his child soon.

Caro Pietro,

My love, I'm missing you every day, and I still can't believe we're husband and wife. Pietro, I have happy news. I'm having a baby! Mamma guesses it will come in early spring. I know it will be impossible for you to come home so soon, but maybe there's a way you can plan an earlier visit. I've already been making sleep gowns and tiny socks and preparing the house. My sewing is awful, but young Luigia has proven quite good at it, so I embroider and she sews. Daydreaming about the baby gives me something to think about that is close, knowing you are far away. A lot is changing in Fonzaso. The mayor and the city council have been replaced by a Podestà named by the King. Papà is happy, he says things are finally getting some order in our country and he's being paid better than he used to at the mill. I'm just grateful for our news and hope you are happy and safe in America. I dream of the day we will see each other again and you can hold our child in your arms. Until then, Pietro, I am praying for you. I'm there with you, holding you when you come home from the mines at night. You are with me always, especially now. I am so excited – our life, our family, is beginning. Please, take care and come home to me and your new son or daughter.

Cento baci, ti amo.
Tua Ninetta

Weeks later, as she pulled out the chair to sit at the table, the fire crackled, startling her. Nina held the latest letter between her thumb and forefinger. It was smooth and damp in the corner. He had held this in his hands. Tracing the stamp with the tip of her finger, she closed her eyes and brought it to her nose, hoping for the scent of him, then brushed her lips against the paper. It was the closest thing she could do to feel him. She slit open the envelope, taking care to keep it intact. The paper inside was thin and folded in half. She fingered the crease. His thumbs had pushed on the paper and made the fold. He would have sat for a long time, bending over his table with his pen tight in his hand to write three pages. She tried to slow her rapid breathing and her stomach tensed awaiting the first words. The luxury of a long letter. His handwriting was tight and precise. Her tears came with the salutation. *I love you my wife, my moon – Ti amo moglie mia, luna mia.*

Cara Ninetta,

I wish you could have seen the joy your letter brought me. A baby! Of course, our love would bring it about with God's help. I envision a beautiful little girl with blue eyes like yours or a son, a lanky little boy. This news keeps me smiling even on my rough days, as my love for you brought me through until now. This baby will have the best of both worlds – the style and passion of being Italian and the fresh, optimistic outlook of an American child. I'll work hard, Ninetta, I promise, to save to come home as soon as I can to you and the baby. It's difficult with these mining contracts, but I'll do what I can. You are so beautiful to me. I would love to see you pregnant with our child. Thank God you are in the excellent care of your mother. There are no more capable hands in the world than the

Captain's. It gives me peace to know you are with your family and sisters.

He went on to tell her about his life and enquire about his family in Fonzaso.

Lives of the families in the mining town are rough; I won't lie to you. Ninetta, I promise, I am saving to make a life for us. Angelo assures me our savings are growing. Find some money in the envelope and please give a little to my mother. As God has blessed us with each other and now, this child, we will be together soon.

Amore mio, mia moglie,
Baci, Pietro

An evergreen filled the corner of the room opposite the fireplace and fresh pine mingled with the sweet scent of baking in the kitchen. The nativity scene Mamma bought years ago in Padua stood under the tree and the Virgin Mary looked down adoringly at baby Jesus in the manger, his hands outstretched to welcome the world.

It was Christmas and her mother's house was full, but Nina felt alone. Her Zio Vittorio's wife, Angelina, and her two little cousins were celebrating with them. Little Rina was three years old and excited about *Babbo Natale* and *La Befana,* the old witch who visited in January during the Epiphany and would put oranges or onions in her shoes depending if she was good or bad. Zia Angelina stared intently at the fire and held her baby, Maria. Zio Vittorio was spending Christmas in

Paris. No one explained why; the tension could be read in Angelina's face.

Aurora told stories of the year Evira received a piece of coal, worse than an onion, in her shoe. Evira pulled her hair and whined to Adelasia to make Aurora stop embarrassing her. Vante bantered in the kitchen with her father, speaking in an animated fashion about Mussolini's bold efforts in Greece. It was incredible how excited her father and brother could get about things that had no real impact on their lives. Nina's mind was with Pietro. Wishing that his arms could be around her for Christmas. She longed to nestle her face against his neck and feel his soft tuft of messy hair against her forehead. How she missed him! Her belly was taut under her hand and had grown large; she was getting slower with just over two months until the baby was due. It rolled in her womb and she marvelled at the feeling of life inside her.

"A gift for you." Adelasia handed her a small package.

It was wrapped in delicate, metallic tapestry paper surrounded by a thin, gold string. Turning it in her hands, she caressed the paper. It was exquisite even unopened.

"Mamma, where did this come from?"

Adelasia was already busy wishing Vante and Angelina a *Buon Natale* and preparing to roast chestnuts. Pulling open the paper revealed a soft black velvet box. Curious, Nina eased off the wrapping, careful not to rip it. It was special to her, a gift in itself, and she set it to the side and held the square velvet box in her hand. She popped it open. In it lay a delicate gold medallion of the Virgin Mary, no bigger than a thumbprint. She'd always admired the larger one her mother wore, but this one was perfect for her neck. There was a square of folded paper tucked into the box. She pulled it out and opened the letter, recognising his handwriting.

Cara Ninetta,

I wish I was with you this Christmas, but since I cannot be, I wanted you to have a special gift. You've always admired your mother and her medallion of the Madonna. Here is one of your own. I wrote to the Captain and she helped me get it for you. I imagine you, expecting our child, and you are even more beautiful to me. It's the only thing I need for Christmas – to know you are safe and that our baby will be here soon. You will be an incredible mother. I miss you.

Buon Natale, Ti amo moglie mia,
Pietro

On the bottom of the letter, he'd drawn a little crescent moon. She smiled. There was a man partway around the world who loved her and whose baby she was carrying. He had conspired with her mother to give her this present and note. There was something wonderful about that.

Life is good, she thought.

The new year would hold great things for them. Nothing could stop her happiness.

CHAPTER 11

February 1924 When Adelasia placed Nina's son, with his black downy hair, on her chest she wanted to bottle his sweet, creamy smell and send it to Pietro. Sunlight shone through the lace curtains of the birth room and filled her heart as it soared to San Micel and above to the skies. In her whole life, she had never been so happy.

Teodosio proved to be a content baby, yet her entire world shifted to revolve around the newborn. They agreed through their letters to name him after Pietro's father and nicknamed him Teo. Adelasia came to Nina's new house, or Nina would bring the baby to hers and Corrado would tickle and make noises at him. Nina always believed Corrado was a wonderful father, never scolding or violent like the fathers of her friends, but he was an even better *nonno*. As she took care of their house, fed, bathed and cuddled Teo, there almost wasn't time to long for Pietro. From his letters, she knew the work in Pennsylvania was hard. She read between the lines that it was also dangerous. When she held the money he sent in her hands, before thinking of the things she could do with it, she considered his sacrifice and prayed he would be safe. She thought about her bereft Zia Angelina, how her Zio Vittorio was away in Paris and never wrote, never sent money back. How easy it was for men to move away and forget their families, like her brother, like Zio Vittorio. Her husband was different, she was certain her Pietro would never abandon them.

At the end of June, Corrado shared news from the taverna: the word from Rome was the socialist leader, Matteotti, had been kidnapped and was presumed dead; people said Mussolini was behind it, but there was no proof, Corrado adamantly argued. Nina listened to his political babbling, but in Fonzaso the sun shone and Rome was far away. None of the madness of men worried Nina that summer. She was in her own happy world, with her son. Her only thought when she heard the news was, *His poor mother.*

Summer meant the town was colourful with crimson-red geraniums and roses flowing from grey terraces and entryways, but it was hot. Nina shooed the *zanzare* away from Teo as they tried to bite his chubby thighs. At church, at the markets, he gave her cheeks gooey open-mouthed kisses and pulled her hair out of its bun. Everyone commented on his cheeks. "He looks like a cherub!" they said and pinched him. It was irresistible; they were so plump. He gawked at everyone and reached out to them, ever curious. She snuggled him to her and was happy to retire early each night, sing lullabies and lay him in his cradle then fall fast asleep, exhausted but happy. He was her little man of the house.

Nina always anticipated the autumn festival season, her favourite time of year when the weather cooled. Her curious boy would enjoy it with her this year. She imagined walking him from stall to stall showing him the trinkets for sale, spices, clothing and bric-a-brac of all colours. They would dance off to the side of the crowd and she'd watch him clap his little hands and make funny noises with his mouth open as though he was singing with the band. She dreamed of his life even beyond festival season, imagining the day Pietro would meet him and teach him his *bocce* skills.

One afternoon, at Adelasia's, Papà played with Teo, shaking a toy in front of the boy. Teo giggled in delight and squeezed his *nonno's* finger. "Ninetta, this is the most handsome *bambino* ever born in Italy. Why have you not had his picture taken yet?"

"Oh, Papà," she said. "He's not even five months old. He won't sit still for a picture. But you're right. I should send one to Pietro before he's grown too much."

Corrado frowned below his moustache. "I'll pay for it. We'll get his picture taken in Feltre this week." He picked Teo up, and the baby squealed in delight and pulled on Corrado's whiskers. "And I will keep the picture in my pocket so I can take him everywhere with me!"

A few days later, Corrado proudly drove them to Feltre. Nina could not believe the difficulty of getting two people dressed for a photograph. She tried to keep her hair in place, her necklace out of the baby's grasp, his gown straight, and made sure he was fed and happy. When they arrived, they waited in the hall until it was their turn. Nina did what she could to stop Teo from putting items from the waiting room in his mouth as he grabbed for everything new around him.

When it came to their turn, Teo sat on her lap with his tiny toes sticking out of a pinstriped dressing gown and Nina held him close to her with his pudgy hand squeezing her finger. He wore little socks, but kept pulling them off and sucking on them, so Nina let him go barefoot. On his head was a cap his Nonna Margherita, Pietro's mother, had knitted him: white, with flowers on each temple sticking out like stuffed bear ears. Corrado made faces behind the photographer to get the baby's attention and the boy let out a loud cry.

"It will be a beautiful picture," said the photographer, a rotund man from Padua, with a raspy voice and a cough that kept interrupting his directions. The photographer shook a rattle to stop Teo's cries, but it was in vain. When the man handed the toy to him, Teo calmed down and popped it in his mouth. Nina pulled it out in an instant and looked up at the same time Teo did. The camera snapped with a pop of flash.

"Isn't he the most handsome child you have ever captured?" Corrado half asked, half told the assistant the next week when they picked up the developed photograph. "That's my grandson. His father's in America. Someday he'll be a wealthy American businessman or perhaps an actor, the next Rudolph Valentino. This *bambino* is meant for great things!" The photograph turned out near perfect. Teo was adorable and angelic, the chubby cherub he was. His lips were a tiny heart puckering in between apple cheeks and Nina couldn't wait to send it to Pietro. She appeared more serious than she'd hoped but didn't care. No one who saw the picture knew how difficult it was to get the perfect shot.

The house felt like a home, a compact but attractive white stucco with a dark timber balcony and roof. A square patch of grass in front ended at the side of the neighbour's house. Nina would lay a blanket down and let Teo roll over while she cooed at him and pointed out the *Eremo di San Michele* in the mountain. The property had a sizable shed on the left side of the house where she stored tools, wood for winter, kept their goat and chickens. Another shed housed a pig, all bought with Pietro's money. Maintaining the animals and the hillside allotment where she grew vegetables was a lot of work. Vante was helpful and Nina didn't know what she would do without him. Caring for a baby was more effort than she ever imagined but she was content.

One afternoon, Mamma came to visit and Nina prepared coffee in her silver *Napoletana,* heating the *caffettiera* on her stove. The rich smell of coffee brewing filled the room. Teo napped while they drank and discussed recent births Adelasia had attended. The Marcons had a son and he was a huge child, but Stella Marcon had so many children, even such a large baby slid out in an hour. They giggled like girls until their sides hurt at this and Nina thought, *How wonderful to laugh with Mamma now,* as she wiped a tear of amusement from her eye. Adelasia calmed her laughing and commented, "Can you hear that?" A smooth *coo coo coo* came from outside the house. "You've got an owl on your roof. Did you see it? Don't listen to the old *nonnas* who say they're bad luck. God doesn't leave room for superstition."

"I hadn't noticed," Nina said, pouring more coffee despite the warm day. No matter how hot the day was, coffee was essential.

"I heard from your sister. She's ready for another one. And they're taking boarders to make more money." She took a sip then added, "I'm grateful for her letters. A daughter doesn't forget her mother, she always writes, but a son..." She trailed off.

"Not mine! Teo will be a true *mammone,* he'll live with me until I die and I'll raise his children too," Nina said, her blue eyes sparkling with motherly joy.

"Where is my little grandson? Sleeping so long – I want to snuggle him. Wake him up," Adelasia said as she gathered their dishes and pushed them Nina's way.

Nina picked up their cups. "He has been sleeping a while; he's teething, so he's not resting well. Let me check on him." Adelasia finished cleaning up while Nina walked into the living area where Teo was sleeping soundly in his cradle.

"Mamma, come here. I think Teo has a fever. Probably the teething, but he's very warm," Nina said. Adelasia walked over and touched his cheek.

"*Madonna mia,* he's too hot!" Adelasia exclaimed, looking seriously at Nina. "We need to get his fever down."

Nina hurried to soak a rag with cool water but what she had in the house was tepid from the heat of the day. She lay it on Teo's head. He barely opened his brown eyes to look at her. They were glassy and Nina's heart sank.

"Give him some cod liver oil and I'll grab more cool water." Adelasia was in her directing mode as she always was in urgent times. She ran outside, down to the fountain to fill a jug with cooler water.

On her way back in, Adelasia noticed the owl, now sitting on the balcony. *Stupid superstition,* she thought.

"Shoo!" she yelled at it. "Go away!" The owl glared at her with saucer eyes, remaining in its place.

When she entered the house, Nina held Teo in her arms; his head swayed.

"Mamma, he was fine this morning. What could have happened?"

"It's just a fever; we'll get through it," Adelasia spoke calmly, leaving Nina to hold Teo while she went through and pulled out anything they could use to treat the temperature.

Hours passed. The baby was still hot, too hot. They made more coffee. Soon it was evening and Corrado would stop by to find Adelasia if she didn't come home. Teo, exhausted, slowed his tossing and fell asleep. Nina massaged his little fingers and kept the cool rag on his head, praying the fever would break soon.

Adelasia left to tell Corrado she would stay with Ninetta and Teo. She didn't want to worry him but asked him to fetch the doctor. It would take time to get him because he was at his lodge high in the mountains to escape the summer heat. When she returned to Nina's, she stroked the baby.

"His fever is lowering, give it time," she said.

They agreed to take turns sleeping and watching him through the night. Adelasia insisted Nina rest first and when she could no longer keep her eyes open, she woke Nina, who had never completely fallen asleep. The owl cooing outside kept her from resting. As Adelasia dozed, Nina prayed. She watched Teo's tiny chest rise and fall, his cheeks flush, his fluffy hair matted to his forehead with sweat. The rhythm of his chest lulled her and before long they were all three asleep.

Hours passed before a deafening cry from Teo broke the silence in the house. Nina was on her feet in seconds, she ran to him and pulled him from the cradle. His legs were pulled tight into his chest and his neck was stiff even as he twisted his body from side to side.

"Mamma!" she screamed.

Adelasia hurried over, snapping to alertness, and felt the boy. "His fever is raging."

"My *bambino,* my *bambino,*" Nina cried.

Teo screamed, convulsing back and forth. They rolled the

cool rag over his head, his chest and his back. Nina cursed that the water wasn't cool enough to make a difference. For an hour they went on fighting the fever until poor Teo was spent. His glazed eyes looked past her; she wrapped him in a light blanket and rocked him.

"*Ninna nanna bambino.*" She sang a lullaby to him, her voice shaky and exhausted. She traced her finger over his cherub cheek and it was too warm. His body was bent and his muscles would not relax. She rocked and rocked. Adelasia changed the rags. Nina fell asleep.

She awoke to Adelasia squeezing her arm. "Come. Put Teo down. Have something to eat. You need to stay strong for him." Nina kissed the baby's forehead, which was still hot but much less than before. She lay him down with great care and met her mother in the kitchen.

"What is it, Mamma?" Nina asked.

Adelasia's eyes were red. "Eat, Ninetta. You need your energy. Let's hope the doctor comes soon and can help. I've not seen a fever like this," Adelasia said. Nina shook her head, agreeing. She took a bite of a hard-boiled egg; it lodged in her throat and she washed it down with cold coffee left in the cup on the table. Having no appetite, she went again to check Teo. From a few feet away, she could already see what she prayed she would not. There was no movement in the cradle. There were no more feverish cheeks. Teo was gone.

CHAPTER 12

The black cotton of her mourning dress stuck to her in the summer heat, but she could no longer feel and she no longer cared. If the heat suffocated her, so what? She was dead anyway. Buried with her child. Deep in a cave, like her husband, the miner, darkness smothering her. Both the Argenta and Pante families shared in her misery, but she couldn't believe anyone else could be in the place with her. He had grown inside her. He had entered the world through her. She had fed him with her own body. She had held him until he was cold.

Aurora washed her and pulled back her hair every day. Nina leaned into her mother and sister like a child. With a husband abroad and a dead son, she could not be alone in her own home and instead spent the month after Teo's funeral staring out the window from her mother's house. She could not come to write the letter to Pietro about Teo. It was pointless for him to come rushing back; he would have never made the funeral. It would have only added to her guilt. She was sure it was her fault. Adelasia wrote to Pietro for her daughter:

Pietro,

I am writing this letter with a broken heart to let you know your son, Teo, died of meningitis. He went quickly. Ninetta and I did everything we could, but he passed within hours. Nothing could stop his fever or cure what came over him. We could not have saved him. The doctor said there have been cases in Padua, too.
Ninetta is devastated, as you can imagine. She adored your son and was so proud of him. I am doing what I can to help her and she will stay with us as long as she needs to get through this. Pietro, I know this news will break your heart as it has broken all of our hearts but please be strong and understand Teo is with the angels and there will be other babies for you and Ninetta.
I am enclosing a photograph of Teo that Nina had taken before we lost him. I'm sorry this is the first time you will see him. We are heartbroken. Please be strong for Ninetta's sake.

God Bless you,
Adelasia

The letter got to Pietro two weeks after Adelasia mailed it. It sat in the post office while he worked underground at a camp on a new mine installation. When he picked up the envelope, he questioned the handwriting before opening it. Miners dealt with the worst tragedies. Pietro had witnessed his peers buried under piles of rock and blown to bits in explosions. He knew of miners who suffocated in shafts and others who fell and went missing in deep caves, but he never cried about any of those things. Thousands of miles from Fonzaso, in a post office in America, a miner broke down in public and cried loud enough for the entire street to hear.

In mid-August, over a month after the funeral, the clouds rolled into Fonzaso and the temperature dropped. Nina sat at the table at her mother's house watching the downpour. The family had gone to church for *Ferragosto* Mass, celebrating the assumption of Mary into Heaven, but she refused. God had taken her baby. She could not come to terms with it and she hadn't been in the church since the day they laid him to rest. The power of the rain and the lightning called to her. She wanted to feel it on her skin and she calmly rose from her seat and walked outside, carefully closing the door behind her. The rain pelted down, and she lifted her face to it as it beat on her cheeks and blurred her vision. She put her hands out and turned them to the sky, feeling the concentrated force of the drops exploding on her palms. She squeezed her hands together in two fists. They were good and real, these tears from the sky. Anger at the loss of her son welled up within her. Swinging open the gate, she ran. Her shoes splashed through puddles and the rain mixed with her tears as she let go. Her heart contracted and burst at once. None of it was fair! She sprinted forward, her feet wet in her shoes, beating hard against the cobbles of the Via Calzen. She passed her own house, knowing exactly where she was heading. "Mary!" she thought. "The Madonna will give me peace." Her legs found the path up the hillside. Her mourning dress stuck to her thighs; the wet, black sleeves clung to her forearms. She envisioned Teo's sweet face, Pietro and her on their wedding day, her mother at the funeral and she cried, her heart pouring out with the rain. *Ave Maria* played in her head, the song getting louder as she scaled the hill. The song they played in the church for him. The apple cheeks. Fragments of memories circled in her mind. The tiny wooden coffin. A painting of the Virgin rising into Heaven surrounded by cherubs. The mourners staring at her, pitying her. Why? Why did God punish her this way? When she reached *Sant'Anna,* she stood, staring at the altar, her chest heaving from the exertion, certain her heart would explode. She fell to the ground, not feeling the chill of the rain, wanting to hurt. If she hurt physically, maybe the tearing of her heart for her baby boy would ease. She clawed into the gravel, grabbing handfuls, squeezing it and letting the sharp rocks stab her palms and rip under her nails. Then, with everything she had, she screamed. A horrible drowning wail joined the thunder. Like a maniac, she dug at the rocks and threw them until she was spent and her fingers were bleeding and raw.

With slumped shoulders, Nina walked to the statue of the Virgin Mary where she had prayed for babies the night of her wedding and collapsed, wet and cold and dirty at the Madonna's feet. She wept there for her son to the only one she thought could understand.

Soaking and bloodied, she made her way back to the Via Calzen and the house she hadn't been in since that awful day. She opened the door, scanning the room for traces of Teo.

Silence.

There were the muslin rags they used to cool him and the rattle they had used to distract him. She tightened her arms around herself, feeling the ribcage that had appeared as she had eaten little these past days. She leaned on the wall to steady herself. Her knees were unsure. Grabbing one of the cloths, she put it to her nose. There he was – the sweet, biscuity scent of her baby. Her breasts ached as a warm wash of milk flowed into her already soaking blouse, her body still yearning to feed him. Tension in her throat released into an ugly moan; crying and groaning, she covered her mouth as her sobs shook her body. She would never see her baby again, never feed him from her breast and feel his little fist on her skin. It was cruel. More than anyone could bear.

In the fury of caring for Teo that day, she must have knocked her cup over onto the floor and a pool of liquid had eaten away at the wood. Still sobbing, Nina knelt to pick it up from the ground, but found she couldn't lift herself. She hugged the leg of the table and pressed her cheek to the solidness of the wood, like a child holding on to their father's leg.

"Why, God?" she asked into the silence. "Why Teo? What did I do wrong? Why did you take him from me?"

The door creaked open and Adelasia crept in. Nina was only vaguely aware of her, peering around, then, hurrying towards her, crouching to pull Nina up.

"Mamma!" Nina cried and buried her head into her mother's shoulder.

"My child. You're soaked. What have you done to yourself? Why didn't you tell me you were coming here? I would have cleared this up."

"Nothing matters anymore. Teo was Pietro's and mine and only I was able to know him. Everything is ruined. Teo is gone. My life is nothing."

Her mother closed her eyes. "Your life is not nothing," Adelasia stated firmly. "What has happened is awful. We all mourn Teo with you, but you need to get your strength and continue with your life. You're only nineteen years old. There's more beauty and heartache to come. I know it's hard to believe."

"Mamma, you can't understand. I *can-not* breathe without him. I can't breathe!" Nina's eyes implored her to see the pain.

"I understand more than you know." Adelasia pushed her lips together and closed her eyes before continuing, "Ninetta, you can't stay in this house alone surrounded by your memories. You should leave Fonzaso for a while. I want you to help me. The clinic in Padua where I did my midwife training has a place for you. I've already spoken to Don Cavalli. You can leave in September and stay with our cousins there. A change of scenery will be good for you, keep your mind occupied."

"But how can I leave? What if Pietro comes back? What about the house and the animals?"

"It's decided, Ninetta. I'll write to Pietro myself and let him know where you will be if needed. I'll take care of your house; Aurora and Vante can help with the animals."

Nina had no words to argue. She was empty. "Fine." She left it in the hands of her mother. There was no fixing the situation; it was easier to follow directions as she had no path of her own.

Adelasia stood up, slapping her thighs in finality. "It's done."

CHAPTER 13

Voices hummed around Nina while she wallowed in her thoughts. She sat with her family but was separated in her despair. She overheard Corrado telling her mother the body of Matteotti, the socialist leader, had been found stabbed several times with a carpenter's file. Mussolini denied being involved. To Nina, it was background noise. Nonetheless, she prayed for his soul when she heard the violent way he died.

Despite her intense sorrow over Teo, Nina followed Adelasia's orders and left Fonzaso for the training in Padua. She had no baby to care for, no husband in the country and she couldn't bear to stay in the house with the memories. Her life had been blessed, but now, as she thought of Teo, she couldn't see a future in front of her. All she could see was her baby. She could still feel his chubby arms. Had it not been yesterday she was kissing his toes and biting his cheeks?

Oh God! she thought, *how could you take him from me?* she kept asking. God had abandoned her. She had taken her life before for granted. When she married Pietro and became pregnant, she'd been content. She scorned her contentment. She wanted to punish herself for the two or three times in

Teo's short time on Earth she let him cry too long to teach him to go back to sleep. If he had a lifetime to live, those choices would have made him into a happier child or a better man, but since his life ended after only five months, it made her feel cruel. If only she could relive those moments. She would go to him and hold him all night. She would snuggle his warm, little body for as long as she could if she knew one morning he would be gone. These thoughts consumed her every moment and while she accepted the fact that she would live with this pain forever, she didn't have the energy to disagree with her mother about going to Padua. She would learn about delivering babies when hers had died. Didn't Mamma recognise the harshness in that?

Corrado took her to the train station in Feltre. She kissed him goodbye, trying to ignore the sad eyes that watched her walk away. No one at the station knew her; it comforted her to be alone. She could carry her pain anonymously, a girl in a black dress and kerchief. A young woman going on a trip. She stared at the platform, waiting for the train. *What would it take? One, two, three steps? Just before the train comes?* The pain would stop in a second, with a flash of metal and the blare of a horn.

She couldn't do it.

As a Catholic, she believed eternal life was impossible if you took your own on Earth. She would close off any opportunity to see Teo again forever. And there was something else, something outside of her faith, giving her pause. She waited for the train to pull up and stop in front of her and then she stepped on to take her seat.

The room in Padua was more than sufficient: with a wide bed, a chest of drawers for her things and a window overlooking the city. She marvelled at its expanse, a vast difference from Fonzaso.

"Do you want some coffee?" Her cousin, Tinetta, an elegant middle-aged woman, peeked around the door. Nina untied the scarf from the nape of her neck and laid it over a chair.

"*Sì. Grazie,*" she said. "And thank you for letting me stay with you."

Tinetta smiled. "You're welcome here as long as you like. How do you like the room? Is there anything else you need?"

"No, *grazie*. It's perfect and what a lovely view of the city."

"I'm glad you like it. Come down whenever you're ready."

"*Grazie mille,*" Nina said.

Tinetta waved her hand to say, *It's nothing* and left Nina in the room. She walked to the window, staring out at Padua. From the corner of her window, she could make out the magnificent cupolas and campanile of the *Basilica di Sant'Antonio*. On the surrounding buildings, rich carvings of Roman goddesses ornamented the balustrades. Rooftops featured statues of philosophers, soldiers, nudes and saints. Each building told a story of the ancient city of Padua where Galileo, Dante and the greatest minds of Italy and the world had come to study, teach and write.

I can't believe I'm here, she thought. It was bittersweet. A short while ago, she was a young mother with no plans to leave Fonzaso unless it was to meet her husband in America. There she now stood in a city, about to train at a midwife clinic. *How quickly life can change,* she thought, dragging her fingertips down the cool windowpane. She closed her eyes and thought of Teo and Pietro. "Be with me," she whispered, then walked out of the room to join her cousin downstairs.

Cousin Tinetta was related on Corrado's side. Her mother and his mother were sisters. Tinetta had married a Jewish man named Federico who was a shopkeeper in Padua. They owned a red brick building and shop in the main piazza near the university. Federico's *macelleria* fared well, selling meats along with pecorino cheese and glossy olives in jars within a charming shopfront popular with locals and tourists. The couple lived above the shop. A second space above theirs provided additional income but, knowing from Adelasia that Nina would come to train at the clinic, they had held off new renters to allow Nina to stay. The apartment was large, more than Nina needed for the short bursts of time she spent there. They had furnished it with comfortable wicker chairs and couches with an abundance of orange and yellow patterned pillows. The walls were covered with postcards from Venice, watercolours from Como and shelves of extra knick-knacks Tinetta had no room for in her finely decorated flat downstairs. There were too many clocks on the walls, multiple pictures of Madonna and child, the Pope and saints Tinetta would never dare throw away but were odd to display in her apartment given she was married to a Jewish man. Saints and crucifixes surrounded Nina, Catholic symbols comforting her in her sadness. By far, the most outstanding feature of the apartment was the view; even from the second floor, the basilica's top gleamed. Each night, Nina would come home from the clinic, wash, sit in her nightgown and look over the city. When the moon rose above the buildings, it cast a glow over the rooftop statues, creating a museum in the sky, and she thought about Pietro. What it would be like if he were here, sharing these moments, sleeping beside her.

The city, so much larger than Fonzaso, gave her much to

explore. Nina walked in the footsteps of great minds among the old buildings of the University of Padua, the first school to bring theory and practice together. Once, she visited the *Palazzo Bo* and snuck into the empty anatomical theatre. All alone, she looked up and down from the third balcony where surgeries were observed and science surged forward, at one point with Italy in the lead. Walking through the ivory-slated galleries made her feel remarkable, smarter and stronger. She imagined her mother as a young wife, just a little older than she was, walking the same halls and she understood. Nina was feeling as though she could take care of herself without her family and she wondered if her mother had the midwife school in mind for Nina before she married Pietro.

The days at the clinic were fascinating. Doctor Alessandro Bertino led the courses and Nina was one of several rural women training. The clinic was loosely associated with the university. Its mission was to ensure women outside the cities had formal knowledge of delivering babies rather than leaving it to rituals passed down to each other, as it had always been. The first day, Nina was surprised to walk into a musty room filled with carved models of wombs and female genitalia on display. The models showed opened bellies, allowing an illustrative view of the baby inside. They had a form depicting every condition: breech babies, babies with cords twisted around necks, babies stuck in the birth canal and abrupted placentas. Nina found it mesmerising to view the body depicted this way, as though a curtain had been pulled back on births she had helped her mother with for all these years.

They began with the basics of anatomy: the role of the pelvic bones and the changes in the body at the various stages of pregnancy. She marvelled at this new information. Even her mother kept much of this a mystery. As a married woman, she was now privy to the secrets. Most of the women training were older than her, and well past childbearing age. These women stayed in housing provided by the clinic. They regarded her curiously and she didn't bother speaking much to them because she had no desire to explain her story. She focused on her reason for being there and left class each day alone.

Nina walked the ancient city by herself, angling past flocks of nuns and priests around each corner, admiring the gold and orange timber-framed buildings rich with frescoes and taller than anything but the church campanile in Fonzaso. Sometimes, she would pray in the peaceful courtyard of the university hospital. She loved the feeling, as she emerged from under the bleached porticoes, of the tall white statue of the Blessed Virgin appearing before her in the centre of the space, her hands opening outwards, willing to take on the suffering and fears of all. Nina stood in front of her for long periods of time and strolled around the courtyard studying the names of the benefactors back into the 1400s and earlier.

She spent hours in the grand *Basilica di Sant'Antonio*, getting to know each corner, and lit candles every day for Teo in one chapel or another. Her favourite chapel in the basilica was the Chapel of the Blessed Luca Belludi with frescoed walls full of colourful images of saints stretching up the parapets to the archways. Surrounded by saints and artwork created with great care by artisans years ago, she did not feel alone.

Nina appreciated her studies, but she still wasn't passionate about midwifery in the way her mother was. Nonetheless, her professor commented on her skills and memory, telling her, "I much prefer to teach rural women like you. They are knowledgeable, yet do not speak up to question me. The city women are always quick to call out if they disagree, but rural women are more amenable to teaching and better listeners. You are a *brava donna*. Excellent work."

Something about the dismissive nature of the intended compliment felt like he had spit on her rather than praised her ,and she clenched her teeth to keep her focus.

She visited the shops under the pointed archways throughout the city, admiring the furniture, furs, lace and wine bottles, but purchased almost nothing. The only place where she spent her lire was one of the small religious shops which sold rosaries from simple to sparkling. She bought one for her mother, one for each of her sisters and one for Pietro. She sent it to him with a letter:

Caro Pietro,

I'm sorry it's been so long since I last wrote to you. It has been a very hard time with Teo passing. At first, it felt like I was buried in the little coffin beside him. I wanted to be. I didn't want to exist in a world without him. I dream about him almost every night. He's in my arms and I'm content, dreamy and full of comfort. I look down, he's gone. I panic and wake up and remember it is true. It's as though the cruellest trick has been played on me. God gave me perfection without a warning that my time with it was not unlimited. Padua has been good for me. I can focus my life, for now, on helping others and the work with my mother. Our family will happen again in time. Until the day I die, I will remember our little boy. Our sweet Teo. Padua is a place to reflect and consider history. I pray every day in the basilica here and light candles for our boy. Being here makes me feel like we are part of something bigger, a greater story to be revealed. I long for the day I can hold you again. Be safe. I can't lose another part of my heart.

Ti amo, cento baci.
Tua Ninetta

Her lessons near completion, Nina was to return to Fonzaso the following week and was savouring her last moments alone in the city. *Il Duce* looked out at her from every newsstand and called from every radio. The fascist party had taken full control of Italy and the papers depicted Mussolini jovially as a powerful leader who would bring Italy greatness. He was initiating new programmes for everything: education, sports, health. The Italian people needed the support and flocked to his offerings. *Good for him,* Nina thought. *And good for Italy.* Who dare say anything against this man when his influence was so positive for the country!

Passersby smiled at her and she smiled back, confident in the city. Months before, when she arrived, she would have been nervous to speak to anyone and use her voice here. Now, she excused herself in a firm but polite manner to cross the crowded piazza and duck into the *macelleria*.

"*Salve,* Federico," she called in a singsong manner. She had shared dinners at his table every night with Tinetta and grown fond of him.

"Nina!" he welcomed her. The man had shown her nothing but warmth since she arrived. She knew he pitied her and that it pleased him to see life had come back to her over these past months.

"What can I do for you this fine day?"

She studied the cheeses and meats.

"I'd like a little bread and *formaggio casata* please," Nina said, rubbing her hands together to warm them.

"Of course, *signora.* Anything for you," he said.

"And you can't stop me from paying today, Federico. It's only right."

"Nonsense, you're family. When Tinetta and I visit Fonzaso, you can return the favour," he said.

"Maybe so. If I had an apartment to give you and owned a shop and the rest, but I'd rather pay you," she said.

"All the same, I won't take your money," he said. "Now, how are your lessons going?"

"They're interesting, but so straightforward compared to what happens at those bedsides," Nina said.

"And we will know soon," Federico said as he scooped the creamy cheese from a chilled container behind glass.

"Excuse me?" Nina asked, pausing and not knowing what he meant.

Federico smiled. "Tinetta is pregnant."

Nina gasped with surprise. Tinetta was older, Nina thought, beyond her time having babies.

"We tried for years and it never happened for us and now – poof!" He gestured with his hands. "And me, I'm so old, people will think I'm the baby's grandfather!"

"Oh Federico, I'm happy for you! Where's Tinetta?" Nina asked.

"She's upstairs, knitting socks. She's so astounded she wants to keep herself busy."

A few weeks later, Nina kissed her cousin and Federico goodbye. She was leaving Padua with a fresh outlook on life and a new sense of Italy. She would write to Pietro as soon as she got back to Fonzaso and tell him her midwifing would help her take care of his family so he could save more money. Two things were certain: Mussolini was *il Duce*, in charge of the country and, though she would never regain what she had lost, Nina was in charge of herself.

CHAPTER 14

A delasia sat at her table reading a letter from the Belluno province *Opera Nazionale Maternità e Infanzia,* ONMI chapter. *Il Duce* had launched the organisation to help with the welfare of women and children. The state was offering a range of services and wanted to alert her, as the registered local midwife. "It's about time," she said aloud. Never one to be impressed by what the government offered, Adelasia couldn't help but give Mussolini credit. His new fascist government was helping the people more than the previous administration ever had. The entire family was benefitting from the demand to grow local grain. Posters on the *municipio* walls reminded them, "Liberate Italy from the slavery of foreign bread!" It was all very promising. Nonetheless, the cynic in her wondered what they would have to trade for these benefits.

There was a loud bang on the door and Adelasia opened it. Her sister-in-law stood in front of her, eyes wide and body shaking. Adelasia coaxed her to come in. "What in the world is going on?" she asked.

Angelina held a letter in her hand. She had tears in the corners of her eyes but otherwise resembled a feral cat. "Everything he said was a lie!" she yelled.

"Calm down, *per favore*. Please sit and tell me," said Adelasia. She helped her onto the divan as her sister-in-law gasped for air.

"I had everything ready, the passports, the documents. It took me months," she cried.

"Yes, I know," said Adelasia. She received regular updates about the challenges in dealing with the *municipio* as Angelina planned to join Vittorio in Paris.

"We were so happy, the girls and me. I even taught them a little French. I wrote to him to explain everything was in order and I received this back." She handed a piece of paper to Adelasia. The letterhead was from Fouquet's in Paris.

Angelina,

Very sorry, but it's not the right time for you to join me in France. I'm not ready for you and can't say when I will be. You are best staying in Fonzaso with the family there. I'll visit if I can.

Vittorio

Adelasia shook her head. It was typical of her brother. When he left for Paris to find work, she sensed he would not return. Vittorio had read about the city when they were children. Stories of the Moulin Rouge, the green fairy and countless debaucheries of Paris intrigued him. But Adelasia prayed he had let go of those wicked thoughts when he married Angelina and had the girls. Angelina was a widow and had lost a child when he agreed to marry her to appease his family since he was already thirty. He knew everyone would regard him as a hero for marrying a woman in such a dire situation, but he had no plans to commit to marital life. He left, almost never sending letters or support home.

In the meantime, Angelina took to doing washing and mending for the wealthier people in town. She struggled to care for her little girls without help from the family. Both girls were adorable, with dark hair cut below their ears and short fringes. Tiny Maria had ears that stuck out of her round head and her sweet face was full of hope and curiosity. Rina, however, was already an old soul. At four years old, she mirrored her mother's unhappy face and shared the feeling of being unwanted by Vittorio.

"Angelina, I am sorry. This is my brother. I'm embarrassed for how he acts. Do you want me to write to him?" Adelasia asked. The woman's head dropped. Her bottom lip trembled, and she was silent for several minutes as her tears dried. When she met Adelasia's eyes, a look of determination blazed on her face.

"No," she said. "It's clear what his choice is. He didn't even send any money back to help us. Nothing. Even with your power, Captain, you can't change a man's heart." She let out a disgusted chortle as she stood from her seat. "I've lost two husbands. One to war and one to Paris."

"It's not your fault," Adelasia called out as her sister-in-law walked away from the house. Vittorio's letter fell to the ground and Adelasia knew better than to chase her with it. She picked up the note, opened it again and sighed. *Men*, she thought. *If they aren't controlled, they destroy everything.* She watched as her devastated sister-in-law walked up the road.

Later the next week, Adelasia had just returned from a birth and was planning to take an afternoon nap. Small fists knocking on her door interrupted her and little Rina came bounding in with her sister in tow.

"Zia Adelasia, we're hungry."

"Have you not had lunch?" Adelasia asked.

No, they shook their tiny heads, brown eyes wide and imploring.

"And no breakfast?"

"No," Maria moved her tiny body side to side emphatically.

"Mamma's been in bed all day," said Rina.

"All day," repeated Maria, folding her hands under her head mimicking sleep.

"Let's see what this is about. Have a pear in the meantime." She pointed to the fruit on the counter. Adelasia wrapped her shawl around herself and headed up the street and into their house. The bedroom was dark. She pulled back the curtains to let a streak of light in. On the bed lay Angelina, immobile, with her eyes open, facing the wall. Adelasia touched her neck. There was no pulse. She held her reaction as not to upset the girls, but sadness pierced her insides. With two gentle fingers, Adelasia closed the woman's eyelids and asked God for her forgiveness. The children stood in the doorway, staring at their mother's bed.

"Come," said Adelasia, trying to cover the cracking in her voice. "Kiss your mother goodnight. She's gone to sleep for a long time."

The girls did as they were told.

"Pack a few clothes and bring your dolls. You'll stay at my house tonight."

As they walked out of the house, tiny Maria looked up to

Adelasia and said, "*Je veux de l'eau s'il tu plait.*" I want water, please.

"What a smart girl, Maria," Adelasia said, knowing the innocent child would never move to Paris.

Maria and Rina were left alone. Adelasia wrote the letter to her brother.

Dear Vittorio,

It's been a long time since you've been home, but you must return to Fonzaso. Angelina has died and without you, the girls are orphaned. How soon can you come back?

Your sister, Adelasia

She included details of the circumstances in which she found his wife, sent the letter to the last address she had on hand for him, and waited. Two months passed before she received a response. When a letter came from France, Maria and Rina eagerly anticipated a reunion with their father. Adelasia read the letter to herself before addressing the girls.

Adelasia,

It's unfortunate Angelina has passed under those circumstances. I'm sure she intended to punish me and force me back to Fonzaso. Nonetheless, it was pointless. I've made a life here for myself and it's not possible to have children here while I work. You can imagine there is no one here to care for them whereas in Fonzaso they have their family. Please make provisions as necessary for the girls. You've always been good at taking care of everything.

Vittorio

Three ten-franc notes he had stuck in the envelope fluttered to the ground, but the girls did not chase them, instead, their eager faces waited for Adelasia's reaction. She straightened up, walking over to them. She put her arms around both the girls who cried, knowing they had lost both parents.

"What did the letter say?" asked Rina through childish sniffles and tears. Adelasia held them both to her robust bosom, then looked down on them with a reassuring smile.

"It says, you get to stay with us forever."

Nina swallowed hard as the train neared Fonzaso, bracing herself. The countryside appeared different to her, but she couldn't explain why. Was it only because she had been in Padua, surrounded by an environment different from her own? Would she return and wither back into the girl she had been in her mother's presence? No, she was ready for whatever would come next. She stepped off the train and into Feltre station, already smelling the crisp air of the mountains. She slipped her hands into a pair of soft brown leather gloves, the one extravagance she had allowed herself and, grasping her suitcase, walked out to meet her father. Corrado greeted her with a tipped cap and easy wave. When, minutes later, the cart approached Fonzaso, the mountains seemed to surround her in an embrace and, to her surprise, it felt good to be back.

Corrado deposited her first at his house, likely on direction from Adelasia. As soon as Nina stepped through the door, the roasted smell of coffee greeted her. It took the edge off her strange sense of nerves and joy to see Mamma, who looked up with anticipation from the table. "Welcome home!" Adelasia said, observing her in a way she didn't recognise. The eagerness of Mamma's desire to ask questions was palpable and Nina could tell it took everything for her to not interrogate Nina on the training. Corrado took her suitcase and started upstairs but Nina stopped him.

"It's okay, Papà. Leave it here. I'll stay at my house tonight," she nodded to him gently and pointed for him to set it in the corner. It bothered her that she thought she saw her mother give a knowing smile, satisfied, her mission accomplished by sending Nina to Padua. But it was true. She was ready to go home.

"Sit. Sit. Have some coffee. Tell me everything. Corrado, hang her coat." Adelasia said, then got up to pour the coffee and laid out a plate of almond biscotti. Nina took one and dipped it into the coffee. The wet biscuit was sweet. It instantly comforted her, like a kiss from Mamma.

The Captain sat down, crossed her arms and launched in.

"How was it? What did you think?" Nina studied her mother before responding. What did she want to know? Did she want to parallel their experiences? See if the training emblazoned Nina with a passion to midwife like Mamma? Did she want to hear her heart had healed? That she was eager to have Pietro come home so they could have another child?

"I'm glad to be home. But I liked Padua and the programme was incredible. It made sense of everything I've seen with you over the years." She was more deliberate in her communication at first, taking her time with how and what she shared with her mother about her time there. They discussed their shared experiences of Padua, there was no laughter, just facts, and updates. Nina brightened when she told Adelasia about Tinetta and Federico expecting a baby. It was hard not to be happy thinking about them becoming parents at such an advanced age.

"I have a favour to ask of you, Ninetta," her mother began, when they had covered everything about Nina's time in Padua.

"A favour? What is it?" Of course the Captain would have orders for her as soon as she returned. Her freedom had ended on the train.

Mamma had mentioned in a letter about Zia Angelina and Zio Vittorio, but now she shared everything, explaining in detail what happened: how her brother abandoned his children and how his wife had died.

"With Angelina gone, Maria and Rina need mothering. Rina is damaged by what's happened, but Maria is still little. If she stayed with you, you could take care of her like you took care of Teo. It would be good for both of you," said Adelasia.

"What? Mamma, she's not my child!" Nina exclaimed, shocked her mother was making such huge assumptions.

"She's our family, Ninetta, and she's only a baby. Barely three years old." She stood and opened a drawer, pulled out a photo and brought it back to the table. She set it in front of Nina. On the left stood Maria, her hair cut short with a bow flat on her round head, so babylike it was hard to imagine she could already walk. To her right was Rina, arms tight to her sides, frowning as though unwilling to give in to the pretence of the photo. "Look at them," Adelasia pleaded. "All I'm asking is that she lives with you and has a room at your house. We'll help raise them both, but she can keep you company."

Nina looked at her mother, confounded. Everything was simple for her. No complicated emotions, just taking care of the problems in front of her. No questions asked. She sighed, keeping her eyes on the photograph, knowing there wasn't a way to say no.

"Only until they're old enough to do something on their own. Let's give them a childhood." Adelasia gently pushed to conclude her plan.

"Okay, Mamma. Bring Maria to my house. I'll write to Pietro and tell him. You're right. She deserves a childhood. They're both precious and they're family."

"*Esatto!* Family!" Adelasia said.

CHAPTER 15

May 1928 As the years passed, Maria became the perfect distraction for Nina. The girl was easy to love, no trouble whatsoever. When she was old enough, she spent her days at school or with Nina's sisters at Adelasia and Corrado's house. Each night she slept in a small bed at Nina's surrounded by a colourful sea of pillows. Nina would tuck her in, pray with her, then return to her empty bed and sleep alone, a photograph of Pietro as a young man aboard the SS *Paris* in a frame on her nightstand. Nina taught Maria to read and to make sauce like Adelasia had taught her. The child looked at both of them as though they held the moon. Her lighthearted happiness seemed to have no bounds. But sometimes, when her sister was around with her sad eyes, Nina could tell Maria knew the truth. It reminded her that her mother was gone, so the charade fell to pieces.

The demographic campaign, *The Battle for Births* had begun to bear its fruit. *Il Duce's* latest focus on Ascension Day, 1927, was on Italian women producing more children, with five being the target. Nina couldn't imagine how some families would feed that many children, even with the new government benefits. Good Italian women, *le brave donne Italiane*, were to answer the call whether or not they liked it. While Maria played with Nina's sisters, Adelasia and Ninetta delivered the *bambini* of the Belluno province.

Caro Pietro,

Will you be coming home to visit soon? It's been so long; I fear I have forgotten what you look like. Have you changed much? Are you keeping safe? I hope so. Come home to me. When you do, we'll both forget this time apart. Thank you for the lovely dress you sent for Maria's sixth birthday. I read her your letters. She finds it so entertaining to get mail. She is a sweet child: funny and curious. She keeps asking where babies come from. We tell her Zia Adelasia brings them. She wants to know where Mamma gets them. We have so much fun laughing at this. I had an extraordinary experience the other day. Signora De Lazzer was to have her baby, and Mamma was in Giaroni helping another woman. I went to her on my own and it was terrible. I won't share the details except to tell you after several hours of trying to help her, hoping my mother would come, I had to deliver the baby with forceps. It was the first time I've had to do that on my own. The baby was blue, the cord was wrapped around his neck. I thought he was gone but by a miracle, using everything my mother ever taught me and everything I learnt in Padua, I saved him. The fear I had when I thought he would die made the joy I felt when he lived that much stronger. His mother was so grateful. She has an older son called Abramo, who Mamma delivered three years ago. He was excited to have a little brother. Signora De Lazzer kept saying how I saved her baby. She asked me to be the godmother to little Domenico, which I agreed to, of course. We call him Nico, and he's very sweet, cherub cheeked. Reminds me of our little Teo, whom I pray for every day. I hope you come home soon.

I miss you. We heard from Onorina and Toni in Nova Scotia. Their confectionery shop is faring well, and they are having another baby. She promises they will come back here. We'll see what promises are kept.

Cento baci, ti amo.
Tua Ninetta

Nina spent the entire day with her mother, checking on the pregnant women in the villages surrounding Fonzaso. It was a long day as they covered a lot of the area, carrying their heavy *ostetrica* bags, and she longed for her bed. She left Maria with Aurora at Adelasia's house where they often watched her overnight. Opening the door of her own house, Nina expected quiet emptiness. But stepping over the threshold, something was different. On the floor lay a large canvas bag, the same one Pietro had left with over five years before.

"Pietro?" she called, not expecting an answer.

Footsteps hurried down the stairs. He appeared as if by magic, an apparition before her.

Oh my God, he's here, she thought, running to him.

The man who stood before her, her husband, had changed again. She held him to her with her hands on his shoulders; she could feel how five years in the mines had made him leaner. Pulling back to run her hand through his hair, she looked at him. Fresh greys had peppered his waves, too early, and permanent grit pulled his eyes down, making his face ashen. The stubble from days without shaving added to the shadow. But he was her Pietro. Their lips met with urgency, trying to become familiar, and she burrowed herself into his chest, feeling the solidness of him against her cheek.

"How are you here?" she whispered, looking up at him, clasping his shoulders to be sure he was real.

"It's been too long. I wish I could have come home sooner," he said. He wrapped his arms around her. His body was familiar but different, more refined, more assured.

She wept in his arms, making their kisses salty as his coarse chin scratched her. Pent-up emotion welled inside her. She was so different as a person but yet, as Pietro kissed her, none of it mattered. She wanted only one thing: she wanted him.

His hands reached into her chignon, her hair loosening in his grip. He pulled back to look into her eyes, his blurring with emotion. "Ninetta. I'm sorry I wasn't here. I hate that you had to go through everything without me."

"You're here now," Nina said and kissed him, needing to. The smell of him and the feel of his lean, new muscles made her giddy. This was her husband. The husband she had married, whose baby had died while he was away in America. The man she'd written to, longed for, and whose features she had almost forgotten. She grabbed his hand, pulling it to her lips. She loved him, he was here, and she needed him. After years learning to depend on herself, she was happy to admit she still needed him. She took his hand and led him upstairs.

Their evening was full of passion. A passion existing only between people who loved each other and had missed one another so much nothing else mattered. They held each other so tightly, bruises sprouted on their bodies.

Afterward, they lay facing each other, naked, unembarrassed in the moonlight. Nina's dark hair cascaded across the pillow, her breasts exposed in the gleam through the open terrace doors.

"Tell me about Teo," he said.

She smiled, thankful for this man who wanted to talk

about his son. She needed to talk about him, too. "He was the happiest, easiest baby. I'd been nervous about becoming a mother, but he made it simple. All I had to do was love him and hold him and he was happy." Her eyes were wet with sorrow. "He would have been a great man. You would have been close. He was like you, so much your son. He made it harder to miss you because you were there in him every day."

Pietro's face fell at her words. "I loved him. I want you to know that. When I got the letter from your mother I was broken, and it's broken my heart every day. I'm sorry I wasn't here. I'm sorry I never got to meet him."

They held each other, her soft, wet cheek against his coarseness.

"He's with God," she said. "We will see him again someday."

She lay back on the pillow, facing him. "I love you, Pietro," she said.

He kissed her. "Thank you," he whispered. "Thank you for loving me."

Nina watched her husband reacclimate to Fonzaso after being home for a little over a month. Breathing fresh mountain air instead of Pennsylvania mine grit, having shaved, eaten the food she and his mother cooked, making love to her every night, he looked reborn despite the few grey hairs. Even his tired eyes morphed back to smiling crescents. He told her she and Italy were just what he needed.

One Sunday, after church, Pietro came home from talking to friends at the taverna, excited.

"Wanna go for a ride?" he asked. He said it first in English, then in Italian, wrapping himself behind her and mimicking a steering wheel with his fists. She giggled in delight at his boyishness.

"Where to?"

"How about *San Martino di Castrozza?* The scenery on the way is beautiful. My friend Stefano said I could borrow his Fiat."

Nina admired her husband; she wondered if she looked restored as well. "Fine," she said, excited for the adventure. It had been a long time since she'd been on a drive, and she had never done so with her husband. There were still more carts and donkeys in Fonzaso than cars. Going for a drive was a luxury.

"Do you drive a lot in America?" she asked. She didn't even know if her husband had access to a car in the States.

"No, not often. But I did once drive to Philadelphia to pick up tools for a site. It snaps with energy. One day, I imagine one of our sons running that town," he said.

She laughed. "You make big plans," she said. She thought about Teo. He could have been such a man. She stopped herself.

"I'll go get the car; can you be ready in twenty minutes?" he asked.

"Okay," she agreed, rushing upstairs to change into one of the gifts he'd brought her from America, selecting a floaty red dress that seemed to fit the occasion and brought out her blue eyes. She applied the tiniest amount of lipstick, then brushed her hair back, pinning it and covering it with a scarf in case they rolled the windows down. It was a perfect day, warm for March in the Dolomites, she only needed a shawl in case it was late by the time they came home.

"You're gorgeous, *signora,*" he said when she came out to see him in the driver's seat. "Care to take a ride with a stranger?" Remarkably, her husband was a familiar stranger.

They needed to get to know each other again. She had much to find out. *What did he do with his time? Who did he spend time with?* Did he still want her to live with him someday or was that just words in letters so he could come back and enjoy her and his family as well as his life in the States? *Oh, I don't care,* she thought as she feasted on the sight of him happy and confident in the driver's seat of the Fiat, his long fingers curled around the steering wheel. His hair fluttered above his forehead and she reached out as he drove to stroke his ear, admiring him. He breathed in and sighed. "God, I love you," he said in an exhale. Pleased she had found something he liked, she settled into her seat with her wrist lying on his shoulder. She stroked his ear from time to time as they went north, passing signs towards Lamon, heading deeper into the mountains.

"Did you know my grandfather was from Lamon?" he asked her. "His name was Gaetano. He was a big chap. Never turned away a bowl of pasta. Ate everything he could find. He taught me to eat dandelions. You should hear what the guys in the mines say when I bring that for lunch."

She laughed, content until they drove a few kilometres north. In minutes, high cliffs surrounded them where the road thinned out, with barely enough space for two lanes. "*Mio Dio!*" she said. They had far to fall if Pietro didn't drive carefully. She kept herself from looking down by taking in the view. Evergreen trees grew up the sides of the bluffs and the sparkling Cismon River flowed between the cliffs on either side. The mountains folded into each other: peaches, pinks and blues slashing each other's horizons, the water reflecting the colours back into the sky. It was like driving through the centre of a masterpiece while it was being painted: the colours mixed and laid but the paint still viscous, fluid and not yet formed, when everything was most vibrant.

"I've never been able to find anything like this in America," he said as another magnificent mountain edge loomed beside them. "I've heard Colorado has landscapes like these, but nothing could be this spectacular."

They spent the day on the foothills, taking in fresh mountain air and watching chamois prance across the rocks. They picnicked surrounded by bluebells and the magnificent view of the grand *Dolomiti*. When they returned under a pink sunset, Nina felt more alive than ever. In the evening, they went to Adelasia and Corrado's house to bring Maria back with them. The house was full, as always.

"Papà," little Maria cried. After three years of letters and gifts, she had long ago adopted the term for Pietro as a novelty and was thrilled to have him in person.

"Zio Vante said you would teach us to count in English," she announced.

"Did he? Very well. Let me teach you, come here." She climbed on his lap to study him seriously as he explained.

"*Uno* is one, *due* is two, *tre* is three," he said. "Say it with me: one, two, three."

"Wona, tooa, tree," she said, her head bobbing with each syllable.

"*Quattro* is four, *cinque* is five, *sei* is six. Four, five, six."

"Fora, fiva, seeks."

"Well done! Keep practising," he encouraged, his eyes glowing with pride at her cleverness.

She went running around the house, repeating, "Wona, tooa, tree, fora, fiva, seeks," again and again.

Corrado poured grappa for Vante and Pietro. He happily partook, telling them how drinking was illegal in America. Corrado found this ridiculous. They filled him in on the improvements *il Duce* had been making in Italy – the *Autostrade* and his programmes for families and even for orphans. Maria and Rina were going to attend free camps near the seaside, to explore the beauty of Italy, thanks to *il Duce.* They showed him their *fascisti* cards. Aurora and Evira picked at each other for stealing each other's clothing, while Luigia offered to sew Pietro a new shirt. Nina soaked it in, enjoying the madness and the noise of their family, with Pietro, her handsome husband, at the centre.

They walked home, stopping by his mother's house to see the medal she had just been sent. Having fourteen children had earned Margherita Pante *il Duce's* motherhood medal, though they joked it was nowhere near the woman he had recently celebrated, with twenty children.

"Twenty children. Can you imagine?" Pietro laughed. "I can barely remember the names of the fourteen of us!"

"I'll take another one," she said, holding her hand on her belly. "I'm not sure, but I think I may be pregnant again."

Nina let herself relax, giving into the happy exhaustion of the first months of pregnancy. Pietro beamed with pride, but they knew the likelihood he would be there for the birth was low. His contract started in December and the mining companies had no flexibility. Even riskier was that if he stayed longer, he'd have to register at the *questura* which meant they could call him for *leva obbligatoria*, mandatory military duty. It overjoyed them to experience Nina's pregnancy together. When they weren't working, they rode bicycles to Seren del Grappa to visit her cousins. Nina secretly observed Pietro as they toured through the *Museo Civico* in Feltre, admiring the paintings and Roman artefacts. They spent the evenings walking up to San Micel to watch the sunset, hand in hand. *How perfect if it were always like this! At least I get this,* she thought. Other women had husbands who never left and were as needy as children. Many of them had awful tempers, beat them and told them what to do. These women didn't have the focused distraction of midwifing, they didn't have husbands working abroad sending money back to them. Every night they slept next to their spouse, always knowing how the day would end. *I don't have a husband sleeping next to me every night, but that means I'm my own woman much of the time. And when my husband comes back...!* She smiled. They were like strangers and lovers and spouses mixed into one. There was a romance in what she had that was different to typical provincial marriages.

One warm summer evening, they climbed to San Micel for a picnic. The stars over Fonzaso sparkled like white diamonds in cobalt between the mountains. Reaching the top of the cliff, they unfolded a blanket and lay in the grass in front of the caretaker's castle with nothing but air between them and the stars. The night smelled of heat from the day that settled on the earth while the trees breathed towards them. The enormous moon, a radiant balloon casting light on San Micel, was so close; it seemed to appear just for them. They lay for a long time, gazing at the sky, her hand enveloped by his. Nina radiated in the moonlight, her belly growing with child. Free from its chignon, her hair fell softly around her onto the blanket, like a sea nymph. She caught him looking at her. *He may not be there when his child is born, but he's here now.* She prayed this child would grow up to know him.

"Ninetta, things seem better here, no? The country is improving. If I save for a few more years, I could come back. We could buy more land... grow wheat for Italy. What do you think?" He propped himself up on his elbow and looked down at her.

Really"? You think it's possible? Wouldn't you miss America?" she asked, enjoying his hopeful energy.

"It could be. Our life would be simple, but we'd be together. I could take care of you. I'd love to get out of the mines, breathe this air and wake up to you and the mountains every day."

"Maybe it's time," she said.

"Maybe it's time," he repeated.

Nina and Adelasia's birthday came in October; Pietro gave Nina a book of poems and prayers and a pair of gold drop earrings set with tiny opals. They went to the festivals together, holding hands, often with little Maria in tow. Nina's body changed with the coming baby and Maria asked her daily, "Why does your dress go up in the front?" But it was obvious the baby wouldn't come before Pietro needed to return to America. It didn't stop them from dancing together to the *Alpini* songs as best Nina could with her protruding belly, and they joked maybe the baby would greet them early if they danced enough.

Before long, the time had come for Pietro to leave.

"Look, look, *topolino* came! This *soldi* was under my pillow!" Maria cheered, running down from her room, a considerable gap between her side teeth and coins in her hand.

"In America, the tooth fairy comes instead of *topolino,*" Pietro told her, hugging her goodbye.

"Not a mouse?"

"Not a mouse, a fairy."

"That doesn't make any sense," she reasoned, unsure of

how fairies got around but clearer on mice. "Can I go show Zia Aurora?"

"*Sì, bella.* Make sure you keep practising your numbers while I'm away." He squeezed her then let her run to Adelasia's house with her big news.

Nina made Pietro a *caffè corretto* to help boost his courage to take on the day, to leave her again. She wanted to make one for herself but her taste for coffee had disappeared with the pregnancy. She was complete when he was there. How could she let him leave again? She would have to go back to being whole without him. He padded down the steps with his rucksack over his shoulder. Her heart fell at the sight of him preparing to leave. Her handsome husband. Her man abroad. Her lover. Nina wrapped her hands around her swollen belly, feeling the baby already up and kicking. *If only I had become pregnant earlier in the visit. He might have met this child before he left.* There was no use in wishing. He would meet the baby someday soon, God willing. She squeezed behind the table onto the bench next to him.

"Promise me, Pietro," she said, her face close to his, her chin on his shoulder.

"Anything," he said, taking a sip of his coffee as his eyes met hers.

"What my uncle did to his family, saying he wanted them to come to Paris then backing out. Promise me you won't do that to us. No matter what changes... or how much time passes... or who you meet. I don't want that to happen to us," she told him. "Promise me."

She hated to say the words, but she had to, for her peace of mind. "Don't replace me. Don't have others, please."

Her insecurity embarrassed her, but she couldn't help it.

He tipped her chin up so her eyes met his. "There could never be anyone but you. Know that."

His brown eyes held a firm resolve that made her believe him and she smiled as he continued.

"You are my life. We'll be together one day. I promise. I promise with everything I am. Soon I'll have enough to come back and take care of you and the baby." He shifted, pushing away his cup, turning to meet her eyes. "You're an incredible woman. More beautiful because of what you've gone through. I can only love you more."

She squeezed closer to him on the bench, laying her head on his shoulder, having to push out the table to account for her expanding tummy.

"Look at what you're doing. It's amazing," he said, putting his hand on her belly. The baby kicked at his palm and he laughed, delighted. "Aha," he said. "I love her, too."

"How are you sure it's a girl? Don't you want another son?" Nina asked, her voice unsteady, Teo always on her mind. "I'm happy with a son, or I'm happy with a daughter. I can't wait to meet the baby someday soon." His voice held sadness. He pulled her to him, his hand remaining on her round abdomen; she stayed folded into him for a long time until he had to leave.

He got up and grabbed his bag. "I love you, Ninetta."

He pulled her into his arms. "It's too hard to say goodbye to you."

"*Ti amo, marito mio,*" she said.

"*Ti amo,* my Ninetta." He stroked her hair, placing a soft kiss on her lips as she tried to savour their last moments together. "*Buon viaggio,*" she whispered as she walked him out the door and down the street where their families stood in the piazza waiting for them, surrounding the car that would take him to Genoa. His family pelted him with kisses, his father embraced him. Pietro held Nina once more before getting into the car. As he drove away, she blew him a kiss; he blew one back, and she watched the Fiat disappear up the road. Handkerchiefs flew in the hands of their relatives like doves flapping their wings around her.

She was on her own again.

CHAPTER 16

December 1929 On a dreary Monday in December, Nina went into labour. Dull, intense pressure squeezed her back. Christmas was in two days, and she had struggled to help prepare the *panettone* with her sisters.

"Go rest," Aurora told her. "I'll come later and prepare a nice bath for you. Luigia will help me. We'll spoil you before the baby arrives."

"*Grazie,*" Nina said.

She napped restlessly on her side through the afternoon. At five o'clock, Aurora came over as promised with Luigia to draw the bath. They brought the large wooden washtub from the *cantina* to the kitchen, boiled pot after pot of water, and closed the curtains. Aurora helped Nina out of bed and down the steep stairs. They assisted her to undress and step into the tub.

"Don't look at me," Nina said. Her belly protruded with the full bulk of the child inside her, her full breasts sprouted with blue veins, like lightning bolts beneath translucent, creamy skin.

"I know what pregnant women look like," said Aurora as

she rolled a towel to put behind Nina's neck. "I can't imagine doing that to my body, though. *Dai, dai,* come on. Let's get you into the water," she directed.

Nina sank in. She moaned as her lower back relaxed, the water relieving the weight of the baby off her spine. The pain had been present in her back since Pietro left, and the heaviness of the baby on her slight frame was taking its toll. Warm water lessened the agony, and she soaked for a long time. The baby rolled; the shape of its heels and buttocks twisted, protruding under her skin.

"Incredible," said Luigia, watching the foreigner within her sister. She helped Nina wash her hair as she relaxed.

Her sisters helped her out of the bath and into her nightgown. The ache in her lower back returned, more intense out of the water. By the time she got into bed, she was wincing in pain.

"Tell me how I can help you," Aurora said. "There has to be something to comfort you. Warm milk? A cold compress for your back?"

Nina winced again. "I'll try anything. It didn't feel like this the last time," she told her sister, unwilling to say Teo's name. Not wanting to remember.

Aurora left to fetch a water bottle and fill it with snow. Nina tried to relax, to think about Christmas and Pietro. She wondered how he would celebrate his thirty-second birthday, if their baby might be born on Christmas Eve, like him. He was born as a gift too.

"Here, try this," said Aurora as she put the compress behind Nina. Nina laid back, propped up on pillows, allowing the cool bottle to deaden the pain while Aurora crossed the room to close the shades. As she exhaled, an excruciating pain tore through her abdomen like a knife ripping her open. She screamed in agony and Aurora jumped in surprise.

"What happened?" Aurora cried.

"It's starting!" Nina gasped aloud seconds before another contraction ran through her middle. She spun with dizziness from the pain. Powerful contractions came with barely a moment to relax in between.

"Run. Tell Mamma the baby is coming, have Luigia boil water, I would do it but... *awwwww!*" She bent sideways with another contraction.

"I can't leave you like this!" Aurora cried.

"*Mio Dio! Vai subito per favore!* Go now, please," Nina shouted at her, wide-eyed. Aurora ran down the stairs and yelled something at Luigia. Nina tried her best to relax and breathe, as she told her mothers to do. A contraction took over again, shooting through like a blade tearing at her middle. She pinched her eyes closed, leaned over the basin and vomited as Aurora returned to the room.

"I need Mamma," she said through gritted teeth.

If Teo's arrival was smooth, Nina's second baby's birth was the opposite. It took hours and hours of angry contractions and coaxing for the baby to arrive. After the quick initial progression, things slowed for a long stretch. Adelasia had to break Ninetta's waters. When Nina thought she could go on no more, Adelasia had her push, and with Aurora by her side, a baby girl entered the world. The little one cried in quick spurts until they wrapped her in a blanket and handed her to Nina.

"I'm so tired," Nina said, barely looking at the baby. "Mamma, I'm naming her after you. Little Lasia. Lasietta."

Adelasia puffed with pride. "You rest. Where's the cradle for Lasietta?" she asked, looking around the bedroom.

"There isn't one."

"What is she meant to sleep in?"

"I burned the old one."

"Fine." Adelasia pulled out the bottom drawer of the chest next to Nina's bed, emptying the contents onto the chair and lining it with blankets as Aurora held the baby. Nina turned her back to them, facing away to sleep.

"She can sleep in the drawer for now. We'll sort out a cradle after Christmas. You need to feed her before you rest," said Adelasia.

"There's goat's milk in the *cantina* and the kitchen. There are glass bottles on the top shelf. You'll need a chair. I can't right now."

Nina fell asleep as her mother and sisters cared for the newborn.

The next day was Christmas Eve. Pietro would have to wait to learn about the gift that arrived so close to his birthday.

From the moment Pietro disembarked from the SS *Conte Biancamano* on 6 December 1929, he was ill. Something told him it was more than seasickness, but he made it through the immigration check. By the time he boarded the train back to Pennsylvania, he was sweating with the flu. Days later, he lay in his bed in the room he shared with his brother, having passed out without even removing his dirty clothes.

Now, Pietro was hallucinating. Ninetta's face appeared before him one minute and the next he was curling over in pain, nausea and abstractness. Everything floated around in his mind – blurry, distorted. He wished she was there. He dreamt of Teo, rocked him to sleep. Pietro retched, he couldn't breathe, he slept. Each day continued like this, and he was aware of his brother coming and going, leaving a piece of bread or glass of water on the bedside table. Finally, Pietro awoke from his abyss, arms wrapped around himself. The bones of his ribs were distinct beneath his fingertips. His lips were cracked, his tongue large and foreign inside his mouth, but he could breathe again. Trying to sit up, the room swerved, twirling, and he lay back. Angelo came into view, sitting in the corner reading a newspaper, with a stack of old papers next to him. Dirty dishes and overflowing ashtrays peppered the room.

"You look horrible. I thought maybe you would die," Angelo's voice sounded strange as it broke the silence with a clear tone now that Pietro's stupor had passed.

Pietro paused, gathering his thoughts. He ignored the comment, then asked him, "What day is it?"

Angelo picked something out of his teeth with his little finger and replied, "December twenty-fourth, Christmas Eve, happy birthday."

Pietro gaped at him; he'd been sick for over two weeks. "Take some of my money – buy a Christmas meal for us. A chicken, something decent to eat."

His brother continued to pick his teeth, stared at Pietro, and then shrugged.

"You have no money. There's nothing left," he stated plainly, then stood to look out the window, turning his back to Pietro.

"What are you talking about?"

"I know you've been in Fonzaso getting fed by Mamma and enjoying your wife, but don't you read the papers?" Angelo sneered and picked up a newspaper from the nightstand, tossing it at his brother. Pietro looked on, still dazed.

WALL ST. IN PANIC AS STOCKS CRASH – ATTEMPT MADE TO KILL ITALY'S CROWN PRINCE

"What's this have to do with my money?" Pietro asked.

"Remember, I told you, I had it with a guy, in the market. It was growing real quick there for a while. Well, the market crashed. There's nothing." Pietro stared at him, his lower jaw dropping, aghast as if a heavyweight boxer had delivered a striking blow. "Don't look daft. You're not the only one who's out. I had a lot more than you and it's gone. I'm starting again."

Pietro tried to push himself up in the bed. He wanted to hit Angelo in the face for his dismissiveness. "*Stronzo!* You asshole! I trusted you! You knew that money was to bring my family together. You knew what it meant to me!"

Angelo dropped the sneer and reasoned as his voice rose to a shout, "I was trying to help you make it happen faster! You don't appreciate nothin' I do! Never have. Listen, don't blame me." Angelo looked at himself in the mirror; finding a hair out of place, he spit into his palm and slicked it back with the rest. "There's more bad news. The company isn't happy about you gettin' sick right when you were supposed to start. I've tried holding your spot, but they've got other guys desperate for work. With the Crash and all... bad times are coming."

Pietro's temples tightened. His head felt squeezed in a vice. His stomach groaned. The world was unravelling.

Angelo strode to the coat stand to grab his jacket. "I'm going out. I'll try to find something for us." The door closed behind him with a thud.

Pietro sat alone in the room – empty except for the tearing of his heart. The money he had saved was gone. He would start over from nothing. Over ten years of savings, ten years breathing soot for money, gone. He thought of the hopeful conversation Ninetta and he had at San Micel. Nausea overtook him and he leaned over to vomit but only heaved, as he had nothing left to expel.

Caro Pietro,

We have a little girl. You were right. We named her after my mother and call her Lasia or Lasietta, as we agreed. She's small and delicate, but she'll grow. She eats well, though it upsets my mother that I feed her from a bottle. She does fine with it and it allows me to do other things. Luigia has made a stack of lovely shirts and dresses for her. I'm embroidering them with her name. You know I've never been great at sewing, but I can embroider a bit. Mamma yells at me for the time I spend stitching instead of holding her or feeding her. Nothing's good enough for the Captain. Sometimes, it's as though everything I do as a mother is wrong. Onorina has written from Canada and said their shop is still doing well but others are struggling because of a crash in the economy of America. Has that hurt you? Is work still there? If not, come home. Come home to me, Lasietta and Maria. We pulled an excellent prank on Maria. Since she wanted to know where babies come from, my sisters laid a suitcase out in the sitting room, filled it with blankets and set Lasia inside. They brought Maria to meet the baby and told her, "The baby arrived!" She was still curious and asked who dropped her off. They told her I drove in a cart towards Venice and met someone halfway who handed me the suitcase with the baby in it. You should have seen her face! She's too smart to believe it. In other news, Vante is engaged and will marry Antonietta Ceccon later this year – just in time to avoid il Duce's tax on unmarried men! Did you hear about that? I hope you are well and keeping safe in the mines.

Ti amo, cento baci.
Tua Ninetta

The rails hummed under the carriage where Pietro slept on and off, allowing himself the luxury of rest. The train ride was long but smooth as they careened past fields of corn and soybeans. The vast plains of the Midwest spread forth outside the window through Ohio and Indiana. In a few hours, he'd hit Chicago then take a bus with other labourers who were being collected.

Rest.

He needed it desperately, like water after a drought. The illness had left him weak, constantly pulling him back into a cottony blur, and his anger coupled with the despair of the years his brother had stolen from him made him weary. It was up to him now. Trust no one. Stay focused on the dream and, by God's will, one day soon Ninetta and Lasia would be with him.

He exited the train and walked with the wave of others towards the station's main hall. Chaos. Joyous chaos. Newsagents, businessmen, secretaries and street urchins surrounded him, bumping into his shoulders, stepping on his feet as they rushed by. The front pages of the papers headlined an Italian named Al Capone and his gangsters. Union Station thrilled, with its grand lobby where lamps of ornate gold ribbons stood on thick columns soaring to the ceiling. Looking up, he ran his hand through his hair. The sun cascaded through the glass ceiling into his eyes, filling them with light. A spark of hope in his heart brought a smile to his face that hadn't been there since he saw his wife. The twinkle in his crescent eyes returned as he murmured to himself, "So, this is Chicago."

Cara Ninetta,

I'm so happy to hear about the birth of little Lasietta! I can't wait to meet her. I'm sure she's beautiful like you. Don't worry about what the Captain says. She's hard on you, but she knows you're a good mother. Take care of yourself. Give Lasia my kisses. The story of Maria and the suitcase made me smile. You can't imagine how those little stories from home cheer me up these days. Something happened. I need to tell you. I'll write soon with a new address. I've left my brother in Pennsylvania and met up with other Fonzasini in Illinois. Angelo took our money – bet it with crooks in the stock market, which crashed while I was in Italy. I can't forgive him. I can't forgive myself for being stupid enough to trust him. We lost over $1500 I was saving for us. I have to start again. Don't worry, Ninetta. I'm glad you are safe in Fonzaso. I wish we were together, but it won't be long. You're better off there for now. Many people here are struggling. I saw such poverty when I took the train from Pennsylvania to Illinois. I got off in Chicago before heading south. The city was magnificent; you would love it. Tall towers into the sky that are pristine white rising over a river and a lake I swear looks like the Atlantic! The buildings are as tall as Mount Avena. I'll show you it someday. All I had was my work boots, the clothes on my back and $30. I wore my grey jacket, which is patched heavily. I did it myself so you can imagine how that came out! You should see how well dressed some people in Chicago are despite the Crash. There are a lot of Italians making news, but not the kind I want to get mixed up with. Alcohol is still illegal, but people make good money from it, anyway. Corrado's grappa would sell! The

Fonzasini here think they can help me find work. Don't worry. I hope I get to meet Lasia before her chubby cheeks grow lean. I'll do whatever it takes to make up what we lost and to bring us together.

Ti amo, moglie mia.
Baci, Pietro

CHAPTER 17

In late autumn 1931, Nina plucked laundry off the line as Adelasia sat nearby watching her, directing her on better ways to fold the bedsheets. The scent of freshly dried clothes wafted between the floating fabric, calming her impatience with the commands of her mother.

"Mamma, okay. I know. This is my house. I know how to fold laundry." She was getting too old to be pushed around by her mother, even if everyone else was used to it.

Adelasia stood and snapped the sheet from Nina's hands, briskly folding it into a perfect rectangle. Then she grabbed pieces one by one with determination, finishing the rest in half the time it took Nina.

"Come inside, it's going to rain and I want to talk to you."

Nina followed the Captain, feeling deflated after her weak attempt to stand up to her. She closed the door behind them and put the basket of clothes on the floor.

"Why do you always have Lasia with your sister or Maria? The girl needs her mother." Adelasia started in immediately.

Nina huffed and leaned against the stove. It was true, she sent Lasia to her sisters often. They were patient with her when Nina found she couldn't be. At night, she embroidered tiny rosettes and vines on Lasia's clothing from her dresses down to her undershirts, allowing her affection to bloom in the fabric she decorated for her child to wear, but she didn't say this to her mother. Recently the girl had developed a terrible cold and Adelasia made her dress in the robes of *San Antonio*. In the recent Argenta family picture, Vante's new daughter, Corinna, sat on his wife's lap and Lasietta on Nina's. The girl appeared eerie as she sat in silence, dressed in her brown tunic, belted with a rope.

"Is this what you wanted to talk to me about, Mamma? How to raise my daughter?" She tried again to stand her ground against the bully that was her mother.

"*Basta,* Nina. *Senti.* Let me tell you about last night. I ended up with two patients at the Turra house instead of one."

"A sick baby? Everything was alright though, *sì?*" Nina wondered why Mamma had not mentioned this earlier in the yard.

"No, a sick husband. Apparently..." Adelasia lowered her voice, her eyes went to the open window. She lifted the heft of her body and stepped across the room to shove it closed. "Signor Turra must have said a few things, disagreeing with *il Duce.* The *squadristi* had visited them the night before and fed him castor oil until he shit himself enough to know to smile and agree with everything Mussolini says. It was awful to deliver a baby with the smell."

"*Il Duce ha sempre ragione. Il Duce* is always right," Nina said, quoting the slogan the Blackshirts repeated. Even Corrado was apt to use it almost daily.

Adelasia put her hands on the table and leaned closer to Nina. "Did you get the most recent letters? From ONMI? They don't want us to tell women how to limit pregnancies. Why should a government dictate what happens in the bedrooms of Italy? The church, okay. But not this man."

"*Sì,* Mamma, I heard the doctors had to take a fascist oath too. I'm sure Doctor Bertino didn't mind signing where his loyalties lie, first to *il Duce* and then to his patients. Have you said anything to Papà about Signor Turra?" Nina got up to brew coffee and saw her mother look out the window as the wind kicked up and tree branches whipped against the glass.

"Please, your father's a happy fascist. He finds reasons to justify it or chooses not to believe it. Evira too, but she's not all there." Adelasia tapped her temple. She sat back and swatted a fly that followed them into the house. "Just be careful, Nina. Alone, you can't beat a tyrant. Better to get on with life, keep the peace. Leave him to his power until he destroys himself. We do our work, but we keep our thoughts and our ways to ourselves. It's our job to take care of the women."

By spring 1933 letters to and from Pietro became less adoring and frequent, more functional. Marriage long distance settled in again while they each focused on daily life. She wrote to him when, in January, the radios announced Adolf Hitler had become the chancellor of Germany. It seemed odd, she told him, a man against a race of people, the Jews, could become the leader of a major European nation, but Mussolini was not concerned by the man so neither was Italy. As she penned the letter, Nina frowned, thinking of Tinetta and Federico in Padua.

She came home each night to make supper for Maria and Lasia. Lasia's early childhood cough had never left despite her clear recuperation, and it became incessant. Everything else about her was healthy, but she would not stop her quiet, dry cough. While Nina loved the girl, the tic maddened her. She knew in her heart Lasia wanted to please her. The child would attempt to stifle her little coughs and go into the room she shared with Maria so as not to bother her mother.

"Lasia, *sara la boca!*" she shouted in dialect, then chastised herself for the way she yelled when she knew the girl was trying. But sometimes, she was at the end of her patience. *What a horrible mother I am,* she thought. *How terrible would Pietro think I was if he heard me?*

If only Pietro would come home soon. It would help her gain patience and perspective. *Am I crazy? What's wrong with me?* she asked herself. Some days, she couldn't smile, she could barely drag herself out of bed. She worried about money. What would happen if bad times came? Pietro was sending less back because of the lack of work in America. She told him to save instead, but it troubled her. What if she needed medicine for Lasia? She was spending as much time as she could delivering babies, which gave her a little money along with useful gifts from the families. The bedsides she stood by, the animals she tended, no matter how tiring, were easier for her than the challenge of watching her own child. She hated herself for what an awful mother she was. How would Pietro react to her behaviour? Would he think she was cold? Teo, that happy, healthy baby who got sick one day and was in Heaven the next – Lasia had none of his vivaciousness. Nina muddled through mothering with guilt and regret.

Caro Pietro,

I sit here in the quiet kitchen thinking of you, the fact you are out in the world, living in America, and I am here as life ticks by. The slow rhythm of life in Fonzaso sometimes paralyses me from seeing the future. It's hard to find energy. I'm grateful for the births that add a hint of variety to the days. You can't predict how and when labour will begin or how it will go. Here in Fonzaso, the young girls look forward to the festivals; the old women are content to watch days go by; I am caught in between. When you aren't here, my life is motionless. The men talk politics and the pride of Italy and Mussolini, but I am not moved. I only want my loved ones to be happy and safe. I have news from Onorina. She's coming in the spring for an entire year! Toni will stay behind, but she'll bring all four of her children. I think Maria will get along with her oldest two, Mary and Adelina. The younger two, Elda and Quinto, can play with Lasia. It's something to look forward to as I wait for you to come back. I hope to see you soon. The years feel long and short.

Ti amo, marito mio.
Cento baci,
Tua Ninetta

In the summer of 1933, Fonzaso welcomed Onorina and her children as though they were movie stars. Onorina emerged gracefully from the back seat of a taxi with her children spilling out onto the Via Mezzaterra, their wide eyes having never seen Italy. Mary, her oldest, guided the other children into their grandparents' house like ducklings who everyone kissed, embraced and commented upon.

"Quinto – you little dear, you look like your papà!"

"Mary – you're so tall! Ten years old? So beautiful. Your mother tells us you are very good at school."

"Adelina, Elda, come give Nonna a hug!"

Onorina and Nina held each other for a long time, tears wetting their eyes.

"Your children are lovely, Onorina," Nina said, holding her sister out to look at her face. She was still beautiful, even more elegant. A swipe of red lipstick made her look modern, out of place in the *cucina* where everything was made of old timber and looked like it had been there forever.

"*Grazie, sorellina.* Where's Lasia?" asked Onorina.

Beneath the table legs, Lasia huddled in a squat, her bony knees wrapped by stick arms, watching the chaos from below.

"*Lasia, lei è tua zia, Onorina, dal Canada,*" Nina explained to the child.

Nina picked her up and sat her next to Quinto so the two children might play together, but Corrado soon shuffled Quinto off, leaving Lasia on her own.

"Come," called Adelasia, bustling around, trying not to run into a child or grandchild. She radiated with happiness to have so many of her offspring in one place. "Let's have some coffee; you must be tired from your journey." She poured and laid out sweets they had made in the weeks leading up to the arrival. A small white hand belonging to Lasia appeared at the corner of the table and grabbed two biscotti, then snuck back to the divan as the rest of the family caught up with the vivacious Onorina.

A few weeks later, Onorina had signed her girls up at the convent school, taken care of paperwork at the *municipio* for Toni, unpacked their things neatly at Adelasia's house, and reconnected with her old friends and her in-laws. Nina marvelled at the whirlwind that was her sister with her beautiful white teeth, her grace at getting everything in order. Nina looked at herself and saw what she hadn't paid attention to before her sister returned, her hips versus the slim hips of Onorina, even after having four children. She observed the light way her sister swept through a room and the town leaving it somehow improved by moving this or that into place, connecting this or that person. Her sister's experience surpassed hers in every area, having lived abroad, learnt another language, run a business. It made Nina feel heavier of heart and body, but she was glad to have the distraction and novelty of Onorina back in town.

Nina didn't love coffee, nor did she love the sun or air or any other wondrous thing people took for granted. Coffee was as necessary as water. To wake up, coffee must be drunk. To socialise, coffee must be drunk. To talk about something serious, you needed coffee. Her mother had rooted it in her upbringing; she could go to Adelasia's in the middle of a hot July day, be offered coffee for refreshment and gladly accept.

Today was one of those occasions as Nina sat with Onorina, watching Aurora fuss about her new kitchen. Their younger sister had married a man named Ippolito Sabbadin and was getting their house in order. Maria was away at the seaside thanks to one of Mussolini's programmes for orphans. She wrote of the wonderful time she was having and the orange-eating contests she took part in with the other children. The heat of the sun dried the rainbow of laundry hanging across the balconies. Lasia sat in the shade of a tree in front of the house on a little chair, resting. She was tired, as usual, with her persistent cough. They gave her a teaspoon of cod liver oil and a half thimble full of grappa so she could rest. Nico De Lazzer came over with his mother to play, happy to visit his godmother and a child his age; but after sitting and pulling at the grass while Lasia rested, he became bored and left. When Onorina's girls came from school, bringing their little brother with them, Lasia stayed in her place as they ran around playing tag.

Nina peered out the window at the children. "How is it God has given me one dead child and one live child who acts as though she is dead?" she asked.

"Ninetta!" cried Aurora. "God has blessed you with another child; she's a beautiful girl. She'll get well someday. *Il Duce* is getting to you. He expects women to be perfect and motherly, seductresses and national heroes. We'll never live up to his expectations. You're being too hard on yourself and Lasia."

Nina looked across the table at Onorina, thinking those things were exactly what her older sister had accomplished. Onorina was the perfect *brava donna italiana.*

"Pff. *Il Duce.*" Nina flung her hand in the air. "Do you know how many women are telling us they were done having babies and because of what he is saying their husbands expect more children? When men have babies, they can decide how many. It's crazy!"

"*Allora,* be careful what you say. You know some people in town will hold any criticism of *il Duce* against you," said Aurora as she laid a plate of pear slices and cheese in front of them.

Nina looked outside again, shaking her head. "She'll never be fully healthy. It's my fault. I was so scared of losing her when I was pregnant, my fears must have gone into my womb. Poor Lasia."

"Don't worry about Lasia," Onorina said. "She will find herself. There's a reason God sent her to this Earth."

Nina put her chin in her hand. She poured herself another cup of coffee and sighed.

The months went quickly with Onorina in town and the liveliness she brought to the family. But each night, Nina lay back in bed and pressed her head to the solid, walnut headboard. It amazed her how fast the days flashed by and the years slipped. Wasn't it yesterday that she was a child herself waiting for Adelasia to come home? Young Maria went to school each day and was happy to play with Lasietta when she wasn't running around town with her friends. But Nina was always tired. She would find time for Lasia later. For now, the girl was getting along. What was Pietro doing? Did he feel like she did? That the years were passing by? Was he lonely? Did he miss her? How would he feel when he met Lasia? Would he be proud of her? Disappointed by her shyness? Or would he love her unconditionally? None of these questions made their way into her letters. Her eyes burned and her body ached. When she couldn't worry about things any longer, she slept.

Christmas of 1933 passed quickly and was more joyful with the children around. Lasia celebrated her fourth birthday with her cousins. In January, Corrado took on the responsibility of playing *La Befana* and filled his grandchildren's shoes with sweets as they slept. The great happiness of having the Argenta women together and the look of joy on Adelasia's face made Nina forget her disappointments in Lasia and her inadequacies compared to Onorina for a time.

By the spring of 1934, Onorina shared with Nina she was contemplating staying another year and having Toni come to visit, but then a great misfortune came upon the one who appeared to be the most fortunate. Onorina's six-year-old daughter, Elda, came down with a cold, a barking cough and wheeze that took her breath away. The girl, who the family had doted on for the good part of a year and who had learnt Italian perfectly, deteriorated before their eyes. Nina watched her sister age years in a month. On a spring day, the family lamented the death of another child as little Elda Bianchi gasped for her last breath then joined her cousin, Teo, in the white marble cemetery of Fonzaso. Ninetta wrote to Pietro:

Caro Pietro,

The joy that came with my sister's visit is over. Her youngest daughter, Elda, died of pneumonia. I feel for my sister, who is distraught and angry. I remember the feeling of losing a child. The injustice. Like being robbed by God. She says they won't stay; she wants to get out of Italy. I think it's probably best. Again, my mother has made arrangements on behalf of the family for Maria and Rina. A wealthy family she knows in Rome through the church needs house help. She has agreed the girls will work for them. She believes it will give them opportunities and knowledge of the world they can't get here. I can't disagree, but I hate to let Maria leave. She's twelve, she wants to go. I think the idea of an adventure appeals to her. Mamma vouches that the family is kind and will treat them more like daughters than help. I have to trust this is the case. They can always return to Fonzaso, so can you. I hope we have you here soon. I miss you.

Ti amo, marito mio.
Cento baci,
Tua Ninetta

CHAPTER 18

Goodbyes to Onorina and the children were like an extension of little Elda's funeral, as if it was part of the mourning. Nina watched her mother close the door quietly on the car full of her loved ones, a woeful look replacing the happiness that was there when they were together, before another grandchild died. A few weeks later, Maria and Rina left for Rome and Fonzaso seemed to go quiet again. Summer lulled on.

August rain poured despite the heat and Nina joined Adelasia to attend to a woman in Arten who was having her first baby. After spending much of the afternoon waiting, it was obvious the birth would take a while longer.

"Perhaps Simona's brother could take you home, Ninetta. I can finish myself."

"Are you sure, Mamma?"

"*Sì*, go get Lasia from my house so she can sleep in her own bed tonight."

Nina straightened the woman's kitchen, taking care to place the copper pots where she thought they were most likely kept. She was accustomed to making herself useful in other people's homes. She enjoyed the sense of authority and purpose her work gave her. The shadow of Simona's brother moved in the other room. As she finished closing the latches on her bag, a tall, flaming-haired man in shirtsleeves thick with muscle ducked through the arched doorway of the kitchen. Ninetta recognised him instantly from his auburn hair.

Pampo.

Since the dancing incident years before, she had seen him doing jobs for various families in the area and once he had childishly whistled at her in the piazza when she walked by. He interrupted her thoughts. "There's no cover on the cart. This umbrella will have to do. At least it's warm outside." She followed him to the door in silence. There was no way she could make an excuse to stay; she had to let him drive her home.

From the corner of her eye, she studied his face. Years and hard work had smoothed his mischievous appearance. He opened the door for her in a gentlemanly way before they ran from the house to the cart in the downpour, him holding the umbrella above her. She tried to pretend his shielding her from the rain in such an intimate way was accidental.

"Thank you for helping my sister," he said as they set off.

"It's no problem; we do it all the time." Her wet blouse clung to the contours of her body and she caught his eyes on her. Embarrassed, she crossed her arms over her chest.

"You're an exceptional woman," he said. The compliment was disconcerting, and she shifted in her seat, wishing she had turned down the ride.

He attempted to cover her, managing the reins in one hand while stretching slightly to share the umbrella or to get near her. The heady scent of his aftershave made her warmly unsteady. She tried to shake thoughts that crept into her head when her eyes drifted over the tanned skin on his neck, the muscles that tensed when he swallowed. She had no interest in him, yet it had been years since she had been this close to a man, and she could sense his attraction to her.

"I'm glad I get to be a *zio* before I leave. I'm heading to Libya the day after tomorrow to work."

"Isn't there plenty for you to do here? Aren't you often in Fonzaso working on someone's roof or someone's land?"

"You can't make money here. It's the same people passing around what they have or paying you in tomatoes. I've got to go. You know how it is," he said, not mentioning her husband. The cart bumped on over the bridge towards Fonzaso, and she jostled against him.

The sapphire night sky surrounded his figure. She worked to avoid meeting his eyes, scared her own would portray the thoughts she was carefully pushing out of her head. She felt more alive in his presence, which meant she had to get away. He would flatter but annoy her tomorrow if he whistled at her in the piazza, but tonight, she allowed him to give her cover beneath his umbrella and tried not to imagine other things. When they got to the Via Mezzaterra, he offered to walk her home under the umbrella, but she declined and thanked him as the mist fell around her. She jumped out of the cart before he came to a stop at Adelasia's house where Lasia was staying.

Peeling the sleepy child off the divan, she carried her home in the warm rain with a racing heart, wondering how it was possible to forget the feeling of being desired.

When Nina awoke the next morning, she found a note stuck under her door. On it, in handwriting she did not recognise, was her name: *Nina*.

Inside, a poem was scratched out in a script that it took her eyes a moment to adjust to. It read:

An Hour of Passion

Among all women
That I have known
It is you that is the most beautiful
Your eyes are the colour of the sky.

When you are around me
The world is more beautiful.
My life passes now and yours starts
If I could reverse time, I wouldn't let you go.

A caress would be enough to put me into Heaven
I'm at my wit's end;
I don't know which Saint to call
Without seeing you, I can't stay
There is chaos inside me.

During the night I dream of you
Give me one hour of passion
The day takes you away; the night is over.

P

Her cheeks heated as she read it. Tucking it into the pocket of her dress, Nina crept upstairs before Lasia awoke so she could read it once more, three times more. The words were like caresses. He was an awful dancer with a shocking hair colour, but the man had a gift with words. Guilt overcame her, and she twirled the weight of her wedding ring on her finger.

It had been so long since she'd been touched. The poem gave her the giddiness of a kiss. Passion seeped from it to her. She should tear it up, burn it – but the years were long. She folded it into a small square and tucked it into the back of her prayer book. She remained faithful to Pietro and always would. This counted for nothing except knowing she was still a woman to be desired.

Pietro toiled every day, trying to make up the money he'd lost in the Crash. He scrimped and saved, with only a few pleasures. He went to see John Wayne movies, losing himself in the films as the cowboys stampeded, guns shooting in the air, and the guy got his girl. He relished watching the spliced international newsreels. Sometimes, they depicted the way of life in *il Duce's* fascist Italy. Even the Americans admired the order and structure, the improvements and the odd charm of the animated Italian dictator.

In autumn, he visited the Chicago World's Fair with a few other miners. He loved his infrequent trips to the city and The Century of Progress Exposition was nothing short of mesmerising. Grand structures depicted a future of great scale and modern lines. Chrysler showcased new automobiles and he revelled at their design, watching the racing Plymouths speed around a track. Twenty cents bought him a ticket on the Sky Ride, a cable car high above the fair where he could see the entire city, suspended on a man-made machine. Industrial progress at its finest.

Guilt caught him when he paid to get into the show to watch Sally Rand. Each one of the men was keen to see the Hoochie Coochie girl herself, known for dancing nude. He sat in the murmuring audience waiting for the performance, feeling embarrassed as the men joked. The house lights darkened as delicate piano notes floated into the auditorium, rising to the bleachers. It didn't seem to him like the kind of music a scantily clad dancer would perform to, it was classical, familiar. Suddenly, a striking blonde pirouetted onto the stage. She began an elegant peekaboo between two screens, twirling large feather fans in the most graceful way. Glimpses of her form between the fans had the crowd holding its breath. As Pietro watched this woman, arching and stretching, the music lulled him, and his mind went to the recent letters between him and Nina; how the tone had changed from the way they used to write. They seemed to have slipped from passion to function, details of daily life, complaints.

He coaxed himself back to the moment and leaned over to ask his friend, Sammy, "What is this song? I've heard it before."

"Shhhh," Sammy hushed him, entranced by the stage, eyes not moving away. "Look at that gorgeous ass."

An older gentleman behind him overheard his question. He tapped Pietro on the shoulder and whispered, "I know the song well. It's Debussy's '*Clair de Lune*'. Moonlight."

Pietro sat back on the bench and pressed his hands onto his knees. On the stage was a woman, the form of her nude body behind a screen. He focused on her shape, the curve of her lower back, the swells of her thighs down to her knees and the smoothness of her calves to her ankles. He wanted a woman to come home to, a woman in his bed, soft skin beneath his fingertips. It was time to visit Fonzaso.

When spring of 1934 came, Lasia trotted off every Saturday morning past the pink rhododendrons to youth gymnastics under the programmes instituted by Mussolini to build a great, fascist Italy. She was part of the *Figli della Lupa,* the children of the she-wolf, under the *Opera Nazionale Balilla,* the fascist youth. The exercise required them to take direction well, move their bodies as they were told and pay the compulsory card fee. This suited the obedient nature of Lasia very well. When she returned, Nonno Corrado would eagerly ask her how it went. It credited him that his granddaughter was such a model participant. He hung a collage with the local fascist faces with pride on the wall – *il Duce* with photographs below of himself and the *Fonzasini* who joined the party first. Underneath were the words: *I swear to execute without discussing the orders of il Duce and to prosecute with all my strength and if necessary with my blood the cause of the fascist revolution.*

Lasia toiled under the guidance of the strict gymnastics coach and sang *Giovinezza* at the top of her lungs when they told her to. Because of this, she often came home with medals which pleased Corrado to no end. He would talk about her commitment and duty to his cronies at the *bocce* court. They also had grandchildren in the programmes, but theirs were nowhere near as accomplished or obedient. Lasia for once was shining and while the purpose of the programmes escaped her, she excelled.

After she returned from her fascist Saturday activities one early afternoon, Lasia sat in her mother's living room looking through a picture book and swinging her legs from the chair. Through the window, she could see a man approach the gate in front of their house. He had fluffy brown hair and wore a plaid shirt; his pants were loose on his hips. Over his shoulder, he carried a bulky canvas sack and his face looked like Christmas morning. Lasia's heart beat between her ears. Dumbstruck, she stared out the window. He opened the door without a knock, and stood in the hall. His eyes focused on the top of the stairs, then a huge smile grew on his face. He was staring at her mother.

In a flash, her mother was down the stairs. He dropped his bag to hold her. For a moment, neither of them noticed Lasia's presence, so she took the chance to sneak out of the house and hide in the garden.

After half an hour, Nina came to find Lasia in the yard.

"There you are! I didn't know where you were. There's someone I'd like you to meet." Pietro peeked out the door. Nina motioned for him to come out. He beamed at Lasia and sat on the garden bench next to her.

"*Piacere*," he said, smiling with his eyes. "Let me look at you."

"Lasia, this is your papà. He's back to visit from America."

The girl studied Pietro. He watched her with an elated look on his face.

"Have you come to take us to America with you?" Lasia asked. Pietro blinked, then frowned. Nina knew he wished that was the case.

"No, but I'm here a while. We can get to know each other," Pietro said. Lasia observed him for a moment, then walked past him into the house, up to her room.

When Nina called her for dinner, Lasia complained her stomach hurt.

Nina and Pietro sat at the table, eating their meal, observing each other.

"She's beautiful, Ninetta. But I think she hates me. I honestly didn't expect that reaction. In my mind, she was a baby, without her own thoughts yet."

"She's still young. Lasia's a quiet girl. She'll eventually open up to you."

"I hope so." He reached for her hand. "I've missed you so much. There's so much to say. So much to tell you." She stood up, walking over to him. She sat on his lap and took his head between her hands, stroking his earlobes between her fingertips.

"All that matters is we're together and we can be a family." He let out a sigh and kissed her hand.

"You are as beautiful as you were when I left. I wish... I wish..." he fumbled with what to say.

"Hush," she stopped him with a kiss. "I know."

That night they made love. They freed themselves of the years between them, the things they had missed, giving in to the longing for each other. Silently, they brought each other to know one another as they were. The mines, the craziness of America, the loneliness, the struggling – they swept it all away. There was only love between them. When they were satisfied, they held each other and slept, as neither had in years.

Lasia tiptoed downstairs the next morning. Her mother's door was still closed, so she assumed she was still asleep. That man, her father, would be in there, too. Arriving in the kitchen, she found Pietro sitting at the table, drinking coffee from her mother's cup. She turned to go back to her room.

"Come," Pietro said. "Sit down."

Lasia approached cautiously and pulled out the chair across from him. Sitting, she stared at the table.

"Do you drink coffee?" he asked.

She shook her head. "No, Mamma says it will turn my skin brown."

The man, her father, looked amused. "Really!" he exclaimed. Pulling an empty cup towards him, he filled it halfway with coffee, half with milk. He dropped three lumps of sugar into it, holding each one up in an animated fashion, then letting it plop into the coffee so Lasia couldn't help but giggle at him. Then, like a magician with a wand, he held the spoon up dramatically in the air, bringing it down in one theatrical movement, stirring with gusto. He slid it across to her.

"*Voila!* Try it," he said. Lasia hesitated. She had never drunk coffee even though she'd always wanted to try it like the grown-ups.

Pietro buttered a piece of bread for her. "Here. Dip this in it."

She reached for the bread, then dipped it in the hot coffee. The butter melted in her mouth and the sweetness of the coffee coated her tongue. She gave Pietro a broad grin, revealing a mouth full of missing baby teeth.

Pietro looked at Lasia, wide-eyed. "I didn't know you were missing so many teeth! You must be rich from the money you collected from *topolino*." She shook her head no.

"No? Well, we'll fix that. Here." He took out his money clip and stripped off the top bill. "In case the little mouse wasn't generous enough."

"*Grazie,*" she finally spoke with an enchanted smile on her face.

By the time Nina woke up, Pietro and Lasia were on their second cup and to Nina's delight, Lasia looked happy as she bounced around the room. *We will be a family again,* she thought. *Even if only for a while.*

The following days were full of joy. They worked side by side in the garden, had dinners at his family's house where Pietro met the new babies and spouses. She stood proudly by him in church, the three of them together in a pew. Pietro drank with her father and Vante as they discussed the fascist system improvements and Mussolini's interests in Africa. Pietro had to be careful as staying too long would mean he had to register at the *questura*, and if they implemented his mandatory conscription, he might have to go to Africa or elsewhere. That would mean no money coming back to the family. But they didn't let this concern them. It hadn't been a problem the other times he'd visited, so they trusted it wouldn't be now. They cheered together as they listened to the radio when Italy won the World Cup. It was almost as though he'd never left.

CHAPTER 19

In the mornings, the sun drenched the room early from their east-facing balcony. Nina let the rays stream through her eyelashes as she observed her husband, lying peacefully on his pillow. She would nestle into him while the fan whirred air across her skin and feel his bare arms around her, fitting like a lock and key. Perfectly conjoined, perfectly bound – while he was there.

One morning, they'd agreed they would have to spend the day apart. Nina needed to help her mother with a birth in Giaroni. Pietro wanted to see about selling their pig to make things easier when he left. The birth was a long one, tedious on the mother as well as Adelasia and Nina. She returned late in the evening, eager to curl into her spot under the covers with her husband. A cloud shifted to cover the moon, and she approached the house in inky darkness.

Nina stepped into quiet stillness in the kitchen. Lasia had slept at her cousin's house. The light over the sink was on and an empty bottle of grappa lay next to an overturned glass on the table. She picked the bottle up to examine it, knowing it was nearly full when she left. One by one, careful not to make the steps creak, she climbed to their room. Pietro was sitting on the bed, still in his work clothes, looking out the window at San Micel, his back to her.

"I can't believe how long the baby took to come. How did things go with the pig? Any luck?" she asked quietly as she unbuttoned her cardigan and hung it in the wardrobe.

He sat immobile. Silent.

"Did my father come over and ply you with alcohol? I noticed the bottle's gone," she laughed nervously, not sure why he didn't reply, wouldn't turn to face her. She sat next to him on the bed. Something was off. Like he didn't speak her language anymore. Their language.

"Did you sleep with him?" he asked, his voice cracking as the words left his mouth. She froze, an icy panic shooting down her spine.

"What are you talking about?"

"Do you think I'm stupid?" He stood, flipping the poem from Pampo onto the bed. "You keep it in your prayer book? It must mean a lot to you."

"No," she whispered. "I promise you, Pietro, it's nothing. I don't know why I kept it."

"Don't lie to me. What happened between you two?"

"Nothing, nothing at all." She was pleading.

"But you wanted something to happen. You imagined what it would be like to be with him." He barely got the words out, curling over as if he had taken a fist to the stomach.

She hated that she had done this to him – hurt him this way. The man she loved brought to this because she had allowed a stupid flirtation.

"Pietro, I'm sorry, I shouldn't have kept that poem. I was stupid... flattered. You have every right to be angry with me but please, I swear nothing happened. It's just a poem."

He grabbed the paper and read the lines aloud. *"When you*

are around me, the world is more beautiful?" He spat the words out. *"Give me one hour of passion? Promise it is not the end? What is this?"* His hand holding the note shook and, to her dismay, tears appeared in his eyes.

"No, please stop, I'm so sorry."

"Do you want him? Do you want me to go away and forget you? I'll never be the same." He swallowed. "Do you know for five years I have been dreaming of you? Of holding you, of being with you, and now..." He pushed his face into his hands; she knew his tears would embarrass him. His body shuddered.

She ached with sadness at the love that put him in this state and for her betrayal.

"Forgive me! Nothing happened. It's you I want. I knew it when we met, I know it now. I'll do anything to make up for this... this silly flirtation. I'll give you anything you want – just forgive me."

She knelt on the floor in front of him and wept too, overcome by the pain and the pure love she had betrayed even in this small way. Despite her attempts to push herself into his chest, he would not put his arms around her; he cried and let her burrow into him. Wrapping her arms around him, she grasped his back tighter – trying to attach herself to him to show they were one as they had always been. Through salty tears, she forced his lips open with hers and her tongue pushed into his mouth, forcing him to let go and forgive her. Cheeks met, she kissed his entire face, his neck, his ears, and reached with both hands to grab his thick hair. She needed to show him she was sorry. To prove to him she was his, only his, always; to give all of herself to him. If she could just pull him close enough, kiss him with all her emotion, she could wash away her mistake, force him to forgive her.

When he kissed her back, she knew his desire for her was stronger than his anger. The fierceness of his love came out in raw lust, as though he wanted to push any stupid flirtation out of her mind and remind her what they had, to claim her heart and her body as his. With her wet cheek against his face and her hands tight in his hair, she felt the surge of his desire to possess her. He pulled down her slip, tearing it as he exposed her breast and took it into his mouth, hurting her as his hands reached around her buttocks, squeezing and lifting her. He continued as he hoisted her again, this time letting his hand grab beneath her and his finger rubbing against her sex. She gasped at the sensation, and he took her open mouth in his as he joined with her, pushing against the wall. Waves of pleasure ran through her and he continued holding her as he released his jealousy and love in one expulsion of himself into her.

In the middle of the night they made love again, slowly but with a new intensity. They clung together as a vision of life without each other flashed in their minds, and the pain of possibility made them recognise their dependence on each other to live.

The awareness that each had the power to hurt the other and to reciprocate such pain wound them tighter together. They fell asleep naked, in a blanket of moonlight.

Forgiveness threw them into a time of passionate motivation to make each day count. It had been so long, forgetting the feel of one another, the smell. With age and waiting they had no qualms and were eager to touch every part, explore skin, hair, marks, limbs. Many days they sent Lasia to play at Zio Vante's house with Corinna, and it wouldn't be long until they made their way back to the bedroom. Pietro interrupted Ninetta while she cooked, when she returned from the market, sometimes right after she made coffee, and pulled her to him, his eyes filled with desire. At night, he took his time, exploring each part of her. His lips tried to memorise the softness of the skin on her neck. His hands glided over the curves of her hips, calves and thighs, over her buttocks and the curve of her back. He lingered on her mouth and explored the sensation of his lips on hers, kissing her with five years of fantasies welling up, possessing her mouth and her body, again and again, to make up for lost time. During the day their lovemaking was urgent and frantic, knowing someone might drop in needing to borrow cornmeal or wanting to chat about America. Over the first two months of Pietro's return, not a day passed when they made love less than once.

When the end of summer came, Nina was pregnant. She was sure from the queasiness in the mornings and the sudden fullness in her breasts. By the time the snow of winter melted and Easter arrived, she and Pietro would have another child. One night, when she was sure, Nina grabbed Pietro's hand and put it on her stomach.

"Pietro," she whispered, "we have another one coming."

He gasped, laughing, and kissed her belly, neck and face.

"Can it be? So soon?"

"It's God's will."

"This time, I'm staying until the baby comes. We'll figure out everything else."

"How, Pietro? Will the work wait for you? What about the *leva obbligatoria*? Won't they make you sign up for military service?"

"I'll take the chance." He held her and buried his face in her hair, his hand on her stomach. "I want to be here when one of my children is born."

It was a happy time at the Pante house. Pietro's return was like a fresh breeze taking over the whole place. Their family was complete: Pietro, Nina and Lasia; a trio. Lasia had someone who was interested in her. Pietro would talk to her for hours. And the house became a place where her cousins wanted to be – especially Corinna. Her mother, Antonietta, was busy taking care of her new little sister, who wasn't eating well and needed a lot of care. The excitement of Zio Pietro coming home from America was a pleasant diversion for her. Lasia and Corinna sat at the dinner table each evening with Pietro and Nina and talked about their days. It was late summer, so conversations consisted of little dramas that happened around the Via Calzen and surrounding streets. Nina brought minestrone over to the table and served it to the girls.

"No *grazie*," Corinna said.

"What's wrong?" asked Pietro. "You don't like minestrone?"

"No, I don't like it," she said, covering her mouth with both hands.

"Corinna! Eat your minestrone!" Nina scolded, pointing at the bowl with her spoon. "Many families wish for a feast like this for dinner." But the girl sat there, looking at her bowl. Pietro bent down close to her face as if to tell her a secret.

"You know, if you put your foot on the floor and push down hard while you eat your minestrone, it goes down much easier."

Corinna peered at him without questioning. She stretched her little foot to the floor, barely reaching, and to Nina's disbelief, finished the soup.

After dinner, they gathered in the sitting room. Pietro sipped wine while Nina mended in her rocking chair. The girls sat at Pietro's feet as he told them about America and regaled them with what he had seen at the World's Fair in Chicago.

"There are tall buildings ten times the size of anything here; they call them skyscrapers because they touch the clouds. Streetcars run on rails between them; you have to look, so you don't get hit by one coming the other direction," Pietro said. The girls couldn't get enough. Corinna said she was eager for the chance to try America out for herself, but the stories made Lasia nervous and she said she hoped never to leave Fonzaso.

Pietro tucked them in every night. For Lasia, it was enough that he was there, but Corinna was scared of the dark and begged him to leave a light on.

"You know, I work in a dark hole in the ground? I travel into pitch black every day. It's my job. But you want to know a secret?" he explained.

"What?" Corinna and Lasia were both curious.

"The secret is, every day I enter the darkness, but I always come out to the light. It will be the same for you. You'll go to sleep tonight – and yes, it will be dark – but you'll wake up to the light tomorrow morning and look forward to a new day."

"Tell me about the mines." Nina lay in the crook of his arm after Corinna and Lasia were asleep. "I heard you telling the girls. I try to forget you go into the earth every day. I pray each morning and night. It must be awful, no?"

"It was strange at first, thrilling. As you know, I was sixteen when I first went down, trying to go along with the group. I hid my fear. When the elevator let us out, the terror set in. No sunlight, only our headlamps, and knowing you are far from everyone living their lives on the surface. You're stuck underground for hours. It can be maddening. But I learnt to focus on the job in front of me... pretend to be a machine until it's time to break or leave." He shifted, reaching over to play with the strap of her nightgown, then ran his lips over her shoulder. "Let me tell you how much you appreciate the sky after you've spent so long in the mines. The sky becomes like an angel, a saviour waiting to greet you, remind you there is beauty and wonder in the world. I learnt I could go under every day, as long as the world was waiting for me above."

"I'll always be here waiting for you," she said and rested her cool hand on his cheek.

"I know you will. You're my moon. *La mia bellissima luna.*" He sighed and wrapped her in his arms.

Pietro spent his time taking care of the things Nina hadn't been able to get done on her own. He reinforced the roof, repaired fences and looked for anything he could do to make her life easier when the inevitable came and he needed to leave again. She told him daily, "If you keep this up, there's no way I can let you go back to America. You're spoiling me too well."

Politics ramped up in conversations between Pietro and Corrado. *Il Duce's* imperialist desires were growing. Abyssinia, which Italy had tried to conquer in the past, was his target. The pressure mounted for Pietro from the local fascists and Corrado told him, if he didn't go back to America soon, it would look bad for the family if he didn't sign up at the *questura*. There was talk at the taverna.

It surprised Nina how quickly Lasia and Pietro became close. He played with her with a patience Nina didn't have, and she caught them several times sitting next to each other with buckets between their knees, de-stringing beans and quietly talking. She was almost jealous of how well they were getting along.

On the first Sunday in April 1935, after Mass, Margherita Pante was born. It was a happy day, and the birth marked the culmination of joy. The household bounced with energy. Pantes, Argentas, cousins and aunts filled each room. Everyone was in the mood for a baby and Pietro and Nina's little girl was a joyous birth. Nina's pregnancy had been the smoothest yet, and when she held her newborn baby with Pietro by her side, she said a prayer of thanks to God for the perfection of her life. They named the child after Pietro's mother. Little Rita was a plump baby, a good eater from the start. Pietro bragged to everyone how sweet she was. He swore she never even cried. Three days after Rita was born, Pietro broke the news to Nina.

"*Amore mio,*" he said, his eyes full of love, "I wish I could stay here forever with you and the girls, but I have to go back to work. If I don't go, I'm only further delaying our being together. If I have to join the military here and get sent to Abyssinia, I'm no good to you or my parents."

"When do you have to leave?" she asked, tears welling in her eyes. It would be harder than ever to say goodbye.

"At most, a week," he said.

Nina held him as tight as she could. She knew this moment was coming, but it didn't make it easier.

"Do what you have to do. We'll enjoy you this week and pray it won't be long until we can be together forever."

Pietro coddled his girls every moment for the next week. He rocked the baby and made silly noises at her. He held her each morning. "My little Rita, my happy little girl, you'll bring a smile to your mamma every day until we can be together again." Rita gave a little toot and Pietro chuckled. "Haha, that is what I expect from you!" He told Lasia stories and went on slow *passeggiate* with Nina, holding her hand, both of them dreading the day they would have to say goodbye. The night before he left, Pietro held Nina. He turned her to face him.

"Ninetta," his eyes met hers, "you've given me everything. You are my life. I'm only living when I'm here with you." She touched his face.

"We're only a complete family with you. Promise me you'll be safe."

"I promise," he said, leaning over to admire Rita, sleeping softly at eight days old. "I'll miss my girls," he whispered, cupping her head and closing his eyes for a silent prayer.

The next morning was painful. Nina awoke early and was feeding the baby in the rocking chair as Pietro slept. If only things were different and he could stay. The past months had been perfect.

How will I get on without him again? His chest rose and fell. His eyes opened, and he looked at her.

"Good morning," he yawned. She watched his mouth, wishing she would have him to wake up to the next day, and every day after.

"I'm not sure it's so good," she said. What she wanted him to say was 'I'll stay'. But she knew it was impossible.

A teardrop rolled down her cheek, and she rocked the baby to calm herself.

"I pray to God it will be soon," she said.

Pietro stood and dressed, buttoning his shirt and pulling on his suspenders; he draped his jacket over his arm, never taking his eyes off Nina.

Eventually, she stood, and he kissed Rita's forehead. The infant yawned with her tiny rosebud mouth and went on sleeping, content.

"Such a good, happy baby," he said.

He packed the last of his things in his canvas sack. Nina lay the baby down in the cradle. "I'll go say goodbye to Lasia," he said. He tiptoed into her room where Lasia lay with her eyes open, knowing she shouldn't get out of bed yet.

"Lasia," he said, placing his hand on her shoulder. "I'm lucky to have been able to spend time with you these past months. You be a good girl. Take care of your mamma and baby sister. Make your mamma coffee sometimes, as I showed you. Soon, maybe you'll come to America with me, see the skyscrapers."

Lasia nodded her head at him. "*Sì,* Papà," she agreed.

Pietro held her, trying to soak in the moment and remember the feel of her little body in his arms.

"Go back to bed, *amore,*" Pietro said. He closed the door and walked downstairs. Nina handed him a sack filled with bread, a flagon of minestrone and a small jug of wine. The tears ran down her face and she reached for him.

"Pietro, I don't know if I can do this," she said. "I don't know if I'm strong enough to do this."

"You are, Ninetta. That's what will bring us back together," he told her. He held her and kissed her goodbye, his warm lips on her mouth.

Pulling back, he turned and, with great effort, walked out the door. He held back tears, ignoring the pain in his chest and the large lump in his throat. He took two definitive steps towards the gate when he heard it, obvious and clear. A baby was wailing; little Rita was crying. Her first cry that he had heard. Overwhelmed, he bounded back into the house, up the stairs to where Nina was trying to calm the infant. Pietro reached for her and, holding Rita, fell into Nina's arms, sobbing like a child himself.

Moments later, he forced himself to leave again and had to run to make the train.

PART II

"War is to man what maternity is to a woman."
Benito Mussolini

CHAPTER 20

S pring 1936 Lasia sat at her mother's dressing table, observing herself in her Communion dress, surprised to be pleased with her reflection. Her alabaster skin was pale and more like a doll's than a girl's, the result of childhood illnesses that had kept her in the shade while the other children helped in the fields and played *calcio* in the piazza. Her nose was regal, but it sat positioned between eyes whose lids sagged to give her a dreamy, uncertain appearance. Her blue eyes were lighter than Nina's, with a translucent quality to them. She had the air of an aristocrat's child, with her well-combed blonde bob, swept across her forehead in the front and pinned down with a barrette. She often clenched her teeth, and she bit her nails to the quick, but Nina made sure she looked polished, and Lasia liked to be clean and neat.

She descended the staircase, taking care at each step so a stumble wouldn't ruin this day. After Mass, they would come back to devour the desserts her mamma and *nonna* had prepared. Lasia's only vice was sweets. She adored boiled candies, tiramisu, biscotti and chocolates. It was the one thing her mother had caught her being sneaky about. Mamma had once made a special tiramisu with fresh raspberries they had picked with Rina and Maria. After the raspberry picking, the older girls had curled Lasia's bob with a hot iron rod. Later, in the middle of the night, her mother came downstairs to find a shadow with a puff of curly hair in the kitchen sneaking thin slices off the edges of the dessert. Lasia was scolded and sent to bed. But, as she came down the stairs today, Lasia could see the pride in her mother's eyes.

Nina admired her daughter as she carefully navigated the steps in her Communion dress. They had purchased it in Padua, and the Venetian lace veil had been passed down in the Dalla Santa family. Even Adelasia had worn it when she was a girl. "Lasietta, what a beauty you are today," she said, adjusting the headpiece, surveying her daughter.

"*Grazie,* Mamma," Lasia replied. Nina went to the cabinet and opened a drawer. "I have something for you." She handed the girl a small sack made of Florentine paper. Lasia opened the ornate pouch and turned it over so its contents spilled into her palm. A sparkling rosary with silver medallions of Jesus and the Virgin Mary slid out of the bag. The light caught the beads. Nina watched as a spectrum of colours danced across Lasia's cheek. "Mamma, *che bello!*" Lasia exclaimed. "*Grazie!*"

Nina kissed her head. "It's from your father. He asked me to choose it and give it to you from him," she said. Lasia pulled away from the embrace first.

Nina watched Lasia lay out the rosary and then fold it evenly around her palm. Her daughter, heading to church as the vision of innocence and the epitome of an Italian Catholic girl.

The Mass was joyous. The little Communionites dressed finely, girls in lace veils passed down from mothers, and boys in the best suits their families could muster. Young Nico De Lazzer, Nina's beloved godson, was also making his Communion. His blond mane, combed elegantly, gave him the appearance of a miniature movie star in his brother's hand-me-down suit. He was the fairest of the boys and waved excitedly at his mother and godmother from the altar. He reminded Nina of Teo. *What would Teo have been like at this age? He would have been a wonderful big brother to Lasia. She would have been more confident in his protection.* She shook the wishful thoughts out of her head and said a prayer Teo was at peace. Each of the children took turns reading, and even Lasia read out a prayer for the faithful, standing on the pulpit. Nina watched her daughter, seeing she was tall enough to need only a small riser to reach the plinth. She bounced baby Rita on her hip. The child was a giggly, gooey joy; she had just learnt to walk, but she loved being held by everyone.

Nina passed her to Onorina who stood next to her, still beautiful but aged. She had returned from Nova Scotia with three children, slivers of grey hair woven throughout her black curls and heavily pregnant. She'd convinced Toni it was time to return to Fonzaso, to the family who loved them and the child she left in the cemetery. Toni gave in to his wife, not least because Roosevelt had repealed Prohibition, ending his side-income. Their savings would go far in Fonzaso. They moved to a house on the Via Mezzaterra, just down from the Via Calzen. It comforted Nina to have her older sister back again. Her beauty, while still obvious, was subdued, the death of her child veiling her with age.

When Mass finished, they exited the church. While the group of Communionites stood for photos, Nina and her sisters noticed a commotion in the piazza. A line of women queued in front of a sign stating GOLD FOR THE FATHERLAND.

"What's going on?" asked Nina.

"Wedding rings. Mussolini's collecting gold for the Fatherland to raise money for the campaign in Abyssinia. Even the queen gave up hers," Onorina said.

"*Allora,* I'm sure the queen has a room full of gold and lots more she could give. Come on," said Aurora, pushing urgently behind them. "They've finished the pictures. Let's go this way. *Andiamo!*" Nina peered over her shoulder as she tried to hurry Lasia away, holding Rita, but her father's voice called to her. "Ninetta!" He ran down the church steps. She waited for him as Onorina and Aurora shuffled on.

"Aren't you going to give your ring? Even Queen Elena gave hers," he said.

"Yes, I heard," Nina murmured as he pulled her towards the queue and took baby Rita out of her arms.

"What will people say if my own daughters don't sacrifice?"

Panic overwhelmed her as she thought of that word – sacrifice. The line shortened; she was nearing the front. Her sisters were nowhere in sight. Nina looked down at her thick band, gold leaves entwined to symbolise the union of two, her and Pietro on an April day like today.

Aurora appeared at her side. "Nina?"

"Where did you come from?" It relieved Nina to have the camaraderie of her sister, but she had no desire to force Aurora into this sacrifice. Aurora looked at her, shrugging her shoulders. "Ippolito's going to Africa. I should give mine." They reached the front of the line, held out their hands, and were helped off with their wedding bands. *Tink tink.* Nina watched as the band Pietro had put on her finger lovingly that day thirteen years ago joined the bowl with many others. She walked home with her hand heavy, wearing a steel band inscribed with *Oro alla Patria,* Gold for the Fatherland, etched cheaply on the outside.

Italy was changing. For some time, Adelasia felt the shift. While Corrado and Vante sat in the evenings eating *aperitivo,* or enjoying glasses of grappa on creaking wicker chairs, they spoke excitedly, championing Mussolini's displays of machismo and efforts for Italy. *Look at the programmes he implemented to improve the schools. Look how everyone is learning proper Italian instead of dialects where we cannot even understand each other,* they said. *Look at how he's allowing poor, sick children to thrive at the seaside and see Italy's beauty! He's giving everyone a thirteenth pay cheque! Good man!* However, Adelasia, listening from the other room as she took inventory of the items in her *ostetrica* bag, adding more cotton wool and simple gauze to aid her bleeding mothers, had a different sense. Over the years he gained power, her job became more controlled, families scrutinised. The King and the government ran the country, but Mussolini should leave families to themselves and the Church! She watched first as he 'became' Catholic, conveniently pleasing the Vatican so they turned their heads at his methods. When he implemented the prize for large families, she scoffed. Was he going to feed and change the nappies of those babies? She believed it to be a grand performance, the typical bravado of a short Italian man given a little power, until the communications came to her detailing the scope of her responsibilities: where they began and where they ended. This was a woman's business! Under the new regulations, guiding women as she had in the past to encourage their husbands *procedure con cautela,* proceed with caution, at certain times of the month, or to have a headache regularly if need be, was against the law. Mussolini wanted Italian babies, so it was the Italian woman's job to make them. A woman's body, it seemed, was a vessel for the state. Adelasia's workload soared. It was a good thing she had Nina to help.

Her annoyance at *il Duce* had escalated over the years, but her complaints about him in the bedroom to Corrado went ignored; his allegiance was undeterred. She always frowned at his logic but didn't push the point. He could never understand. At least he knew to listen to his opinionated wife and tried to appease her for his own good.

That night, as they lay together in the wide oak bed, he told her news from the piazza. Nina and Aurora had given up their wedding bands.

"What are you saying?" she said to him. "This is crazy and stupid!" Adelasia looked at her husband as though he had two heads, neither of them with a brain.

"Give our daughters' rings and husbands to *il Duce!* Give our son to *il Duce* for the country if he asks. You carry that card. You pay homage to Mussolini as if he is Jesus Christ. What aren't you willing to give up? More importantly, what do you seek to gain?" She turned her back to him, but as she did, she thought she saw a hint of doubt enter Corrado's head so she added, "Men's enthusiasm for power will ruin us all!"

Month by month, as Pietro watched the Italian news headlines in American papers, his anxiety grew. Each time he deposited his paltry pay into the bank, he prayed for two things, that the banks wouldn't close again and that his savings would grow faster than the unrest in Europe. Could Mussolini slow down so he could catch up? It was obvious *il Duce* had big ambitions, but Pietro doubted the Italians shared his interest in conquering outside their own country. *He may want an empire, but most Italians were happy enjoying their lives and families. Couldn't he just focus on improving things for those in Italy? Did he have to play Caesar? And what was his relationship with this German Chancellor, Adolf Hitler?* Pietro wondered. He had read about their first meeting in Venice years before and watched as they each enforced their domains: two arrogant men who wrapped their desire for power in the guise of love of their respective country, under the rallying cry of moving their countries back to greatness. Both excellent at using bravado to convince masses of fools and bigots. What good could come of it?

To Pietro's surprise, Ninetta wrote that Toni and Onorina had returned to Fonzaso. Signor Tomassina, who owned the *tabacchi* and *alimentari,* had died and Toni, ever the opportunist while also wanting to please his wife by keeping their promise to return to her mother, bought the shop for a trivial amount. It made him the main proprietor in Fonzaso. A big fish in the smallest of ponds. On one hand, Pietro envied him – never separated from his family and able to provide. On the other hand, he thought Toni was crazy to move his family back to Italy. But Toni had contacts and a gift for negotiation. Maybe it was good for Nina that they were back, but Pietro felt left out and far away.

He focused on what he knew was right for him and Ninetta – a move to America, away from the big egos and insecurities of European leaders. If he were smarter and wealthier, like Toni, he would have already moved them. He would have convinced Nina it was her turn, no matter how much her mother depended on her. Instead, he would have to do what he could, living apart from them until he had the money saved. He needed money for their passages, paperwork completed, a home for them to live in and a job outside the mines. Joliet, Illinois, was a tough city, flat with smoky industry skies, but it was an opportunity for a family life in America. It was a start. The sun beat on his back as he ate a lunch of salami and Coca Cola, a treat he learnt to appreciate and allowed himself every Saturday. The fizzy liquid danced on his tongue. He thought of Lasia's first try of coffee. Someday he would take the three of them to a soda shop and buy them a Coca Cola. He smiled; how American would that be?

Caro Pietro,

I hope you are keeping safe. Have you made friends there? I pray you are well. I can't wait to hold you again someday. Baby Rita is growing quickly. She rolled over early and is starting to walk. She has so much energy! Thankfully, Lasia is a good helper; she gives me a break when it is too much for me. Onorina and Toni settled in. It's strange to have them back in Fonzaso. I'm still surprised when I find my sister behind the register at the shop. They're also talking about opening a bakery soon. Aurora would manage it while Ippolito is away. Having a little new excitement is nice. Onorina's children are sweet and having them all together is making my parents happy. She had a baby girl, and they named her Elda after the one they lost. My mother has not slowed down – as you would expect. Maria and Rina came to visit from Rome. The family they're with is as kind as Mamma said. You should see how chic Maria is! A real beauty. The boys in town were beside themselves when she came to visit. The girls told us there have been violent beatings in the streets of Rome with the fascisti squadrons. I told them if things

don't seem safe, they must come back immediately. They laugh at
my worries! Il Duce has done many good things, but Mamma and I
are getting concerned with the new expectations. What if they bring
us into another great war? How big can this get? The government
has also been collecting wedding rings for the Fatherland. I couldn't
bear to part with mine, and I can't see how my little ring is going to
help Italy. I'm keeping it. I may not always wear it – just so you
know. Sometimes others in town judge you for not doing your part.
Either way, I've been able to get a steel band, so they won't see.
Lasia was beautiful on her Communion day. I'm enclosing a
photograph. Maria and Rina used a curling rod on her hair. I'm not
sure who she looks like. I think your side of the family, no?

I love you so much!
Cento baci,
Tua Ninetta

Nina would have to deal with her lie another day.

Gianna Erenzi's baby wasn't meant to be born until later in the
spring. March, Adelasia said. But her husband had come
banging on their door at midnight: shaking and insistent.

"Adelasia, please, she's having the baby now!"

Adelasia buttoned her dress, slipped on shoes and was out
the door in minutes. She had a duty to this family. Their first
child had been stillborn at only a little over halfway through
Gianna's pregnancy. She had come home quiet and severe, not
speaking to anyone. Later, she told Nina how Gianna held the
baby and rocked her for an hour until the girl was cold in her
arms. Nina had gone with her when they buried the baby and
taken Gianna to the Madonna to pray for her lost child.

Adelasia had observed her second pregnancy closely, advising her to rest, and telling her what foods to eat, ensuring she had fresh goat or lamb to get her the iron she needed. The couple already had a little boy, Carlo, who was shy and who stayed near Gianna rather than running around rambunctiously with other five-year-olds in town. Adelasia cursed aloud when she found out Gianna was pregnant again, blaming *il Duce's* propaganda for influencing otherwise rational minds to make perilous choices for their bodies. She worried Gianna was risking so much when she already had one healthy child. But she thought, *I'm not to judge, I'm here to bring this child into the world.*

Adelasia stayed with Gianna all day and returned home tired but relieved.

"I was able to calm her and stop her labour, but it won't be long. Only God knows if the child will stay with us or go to Him," she told Nina.

For the next five days, Adelasia and Nina took turns nursing Gianna. They massaged her legs but kept her flat in the bed to prevent labour from starting again. They fed her soup and kind, hopeful words. It was a matter of time before the baby came, ready or not. It was still alive. Adelasia could feel it kick and roll in Gianna's belly.

On the following Friday, Gianna screamed out in pain. A new contraction ripped through her, severe and sharp.

"It's starting again," Gianna screamed. Adelasia was ready. She had taken her time to prepare for the tiny new one. It was unlikely the child would live, but she would try. It took only four pushes for the infant to emerge from his mother. His shoulders were the width of a sugar spoon. He was light, Adelasia guessed he weighed just over a kilogram and would fit in a shoebox, but he was alive.

He gave a weak grunt, no louder than a kitten, and Gianna

begged, "He's alive – my God, give him to me!" Adelasia put the minute boy on Gianna's breast. His arms were frail with wrinkled loose skin that hadn't yet filled out – more like the arm of an old man than a newborn. His head was an apple, but out of it sprouted Gianna's husband's black hair. His body, too, had a slight fur on it, common in babies born early.

"We will call him, Matteo, a gift from God," Gianna announced.

Adelasia kept watch over the baby. She tried having Gianna nurse the infant, but it was impossible. His mouth was too small, its sucking reflex not yet developed. Adelasia gave him milk through a thin tube, but he hardly consumed any. She dissolved sugar on his tongue for some nourishment, praying he might live, praying for miracles. They kept him warm on his mother's bosom, calming him with the beat of her heart which he was supposed to hear from within her body. When he remained alive the third day, their hopes rose. They thought God was answering their prayers. But the fourth day, Matteo was feeble and near motionless, the fifth day he didn't open his eyes, his heartbeat was slow. They held him, his father and little brother at Gianna's side. Matteo fell into an endless sleep in the loving arms and lying on the breast of his mother. The last sound he would have heard would be her heart beating and breaking as he left them.

They buried him the next Saturday. It was a dreary day in late January, the clouds were like a blanket below the mountains. Adelasia agreed the best place to bury the small carved box holding Matteo's little body was behind the sanctuary of the Madonna. They did it quietly, and early in the morning. Gianna, face tear-stained and eyes dragging, looked numb and exhausted. She was dealing with the death of a second child but this one, born alive not still, had held her finger, and she had looked into his eyes. With this one, she had hoped he would live and would play one day in the piazza with his brother. She said this to Adelasia as they walked to the sanctuary with Carlo trudging next to them. Overhearing his mother's comment, he reasoned, "Mamma, I think Matteo is playing with our sister in Heaven. They're playing catch with clouds." Gianna's face lightened with tenderness, and she knelt down to Carlo, meeting his eyes. "You're right, *bambino*. What a smart boy you are!" She held him tight.

As Gianna and her family prayed, Nina and Adelasia walked together away from the sanctuary towards the nearby vineyards to give them time alone. They sat on an iron bench facing over Fonzaso, angled close together, arms interlocked. Nina loved holding the pillow of her mother's arm. She felt like a girl again. The vista calmed her as the fog lifted for the sun to pass through, the heavens sparkling on terracotta rooftops below.

"I want to talk to you about something," Adelasia said.

"*Sì*, Mamma?" Nina questioned, her mind shuffling through what family request her mother might make. Serious conversations with Adelasia were always about family.

A sharp breeze slid down from Mount Avena, and they both held their coats closed tight at the collar.

Adelasia started, "You've been very good to me – always been the one to help, ever since you were small. Antonio left, Onorina left, but you stayed with me." She patted Nina's knee. "Even though your husband is far away from you. Even though you've gone through so much alone."

It surprised Nina to hear this admission from Adelasia. "I wasn't alone. You've always been there with me," she told her mother.

"What I want to say is... you should go. When you can, you should go. I'm watching what's going on here..." She paused and shook her head before continuing, squinting as a cloud moved to reveal bright rays. "You don't want to be here if there's another war. Especially without a husband. It's not fair to you or the girls."

"Mamma, you worry too much. There's no chance of another war! Anyway, we have to save more. We've talked about it. He doesn't want us living in mining company housing. We'll have enough saved in a couple years. We can think about it then."

"I have a little saved; I'll give it to you," Adelasia said, her face set with determination.

"Mamma! Pietro would never take your money. Anyway, it might not get as bad as you think. Pietro could come back. Toni and Onorina did."

"I understand. You and your husband have plans, and that's for you to decide. But I want you to know, when you're ready to leave, you have my blessing." Her voice cracked the slightest bit when she said it.

Nina sat on the tiny bench in the vineyard, dumbfounded. She hadn't expected these words from her mother. Whatever was weighing on her mind to cause her to have this discussion had to be important. Nina observed Adelasia. She was the same, sturdy Captain who was never old and never young, but, as if they had only just appeared, she saw that deep lines covered her mother's face. She now observed the wrinkles by her mother's eyes from sixty years of smiling and squinting on Earth, recently deepened by magnificent smiles for her grandchildren. Nina took note of the creases between

JENNIFER ANTON

Adelasia's brows from focusing and worrying over hundreds of mothers and babies, including her own. The ashy softness of her skin. The steel grey streaks of lightning through her crown. Had she always had a slight slump forward in her shoulders or was that new? She was with her mother every day, yet only now did she fully see her. A hint of terror made Nina's stomach drop. *Captains didn't age, they just continued,* she assured herself. Adelasia would continue. She hugged her mother and buried her head on her shoulder as she had when she was small, giving the pillowy arm another squeeze. With the altar of *Sant'Anna* behind them, the two women looked out at the orange glow of the sun reflecting off the houses of Fonzaso, filled with people Adelasia had helped bring into the world.

CHAPTER 21

Summer 1937 Fonzaso welcomed a burst of colour as wisteria and geraniums spilled forth from window boxes like pastel waterfalls over grey stone walls. The countryside was lush with grapevines. On Saturdays, the market brought vendors from around the area to sell their wares: scapulars and prayer books, mushrooms, spices and bottles of olive oil. Neighbours sat on metal chairs, drinking espresso at the café in the piazza and Corrado held court like an impresario. Each evening, people gathered for *filó,* assembling in each other's barns to shell peas or shuck corn together; the young flirted, and everyone shared news. With Toni and Onorina back, life was no longer quiet. The shop was at the heart of town and Onorina became reacquainted with everyone. Since Nina had two-year-old Rita at home, and Onorina had to work in the shop, the Bianchi children were often in the yard at Nina's. They scrubbed out the old pig shed and loved to play house in it with tiny spoons and forks they had purchased at festivals and poked at dead birds as though they were having a feast.

The discussion at the *filó* was kept light, and even though they spoke of the concerns coming from the radio and in the papers, the sun was shining, and the food was plentiful; worrying felt useless. *Was Hitler stripping the rights of Jews? How awful, but aren't my tomatoes extra juicy this year? Mussolini associates with this man? Blackshirts in Rome and Florence have become more violent? Appalling, but have you seen the dress I'm sewing for my daughter's play?* There could be no real foreboding when the sun was warm, the coffee strong and the gardens abundant. Maybe underneath people worried things wouldn't always be as they were now, but what could they do? It was better to bite into the mozzarella, let the juices trickle down your chin, admire the flowers and pretend.

A letter arrived from Tinetta, and Nina was glad to open the elegant envelope but frowned as she read.

Cara Nina,

I hope all is well in Fonzaso with you and the family. How is Adelasia getting on these days? Tell her Padua misses her! We miss you too! Giglio is growing up quickly, and he seems like a man to me! He's twelve and a very talented calcio player. It's his passion, but his father tells him to focus on school because his marks are very strong. I think most boys would rather play ball all day than study maths. He's always had lots of friends, but things are getting difficult for Jews. With his being half Jewish, some boys tease him. He tells me not to worry, and now he is taller than me, pats me on the shoulder like I am his little mamma. It's strange how they go from babies to young people so fast, too fast since he is my only one. The macelleria is still faring well, but we have lost the German tourists who used to spend good money in the shop. They leave, as though disgusted, when they realise a Jewish man owns it. Last week, someone broke the windows, so Giglio and Federico repaired them together. Cleaning slurs off the brick outside is a regular morning activity. We wake up to scrub off what we can to keep the shop presentable. It pains me to see my sweet husband become an old man this way after how hard he has worked his entire life. He shows such dignity despite the disrespect and cruelty of people.

How ridiculous, thought Nina, but now that she considered it, she remembered Corrado mentioning that in Germany, Jews were no longer considered citizens. He was glad Mussolini supported the Jewish people despite Hitler's views. Before, it had seemed odd but far away, disconnected from her own life, a problem that would resolve itself. Maybe even a politically driven rumour. The note from Tinetta made her pause. It was real. What if the hate in Germany continued to bleed down into Italy?

All summer, deliveries filled Adelasia's days, despite Corrado telling her to leave some of the births to Nina and the latest apprentice midwife, Pia. The woman was from Arten, and Adelasia was starting to trust her, but she trusted herself more and tried to be at every birth. She huffed up the mountainside and across bridges, carrying her heavy leather *ostetrica* satchel, and sometimes, Corrado drove her to further deliveries. When she could give Rita and Lasia to Aurora, Nina helped.

Adelasia sensed a dark threat in the air. Memories of the Great War were etched into her mind. As she watched the headlines, saw changes in the government, and looked at her grandchildren, she worried. But what could she do? So she focused on her work and prayed.

Some of the most poignant changes Adelasia saw came from her glimpses into the households of the families in Belluno. She was always discreet about the happenings inside the walls of the homes she served. Through the years, she developed a keen sensitivity to domestic concerns. She could feel the tenseness of a disagreement between husband and wife, notice the lacking of a family that didn't have enough food, sense when a daughter was keeping something from the family, and when a son was willing to move away. She worked around the emotions, softening them when she could for the sake of the mothers and babies, but never got in between. Most recently, she found herself precisely in the middle of a domestic tension, thanks to *il Duce*. Signora Bertoluzzi was pregnant again despite having benefitted from a quiet conversation with Adelasia after her first complicated and dangerous pregnancy. The woman was thin with slender hips and a body not ideal for childbirth. She had nearly haemorrhaged to death the first time, and Adelasia explained to her what she needed to do to ensure she kept her marital duties but did so safely, without future pregnancies. Her husband, however, was a stubborn man who bullied her and, Adelasia believed, took it very far, based on the green bruises on her upper arms and back that she tried to hide. When she heard the woman was pregnant again, she visited the house to monitor the progress. Signor Bertoluzzi opened the door, slurring his words and smelling of alcohol. He frowned as she ascended the steps.

"Why the hell are you here?"

His language took her aback, but she held her resolve. She had dealt with many drunk men. "I came to visit the *signora;* I understand she is with child."

"No thanks to you," he slurred, practically growling, and opened the door, waving her into the cramped kitchen and living area. Dirty boot marks covered the floor, and boards hung loosely from the walls. Had something been thrown hard against them to make them slack? The table was loaded with yellowed papers and grimy tools. Sawdust covered one side. A muddy boot with a missing sole lay sideways next to a child's empty bowl, corn mush dried to its sides.

"She's in there, the lazy bitch. Complaining how hot she is."

Adelasia walked into the bedroom where a stained mattress lay on the floor. On top of it the thin form of Signora Bertoluzzi, with her swollen belly, reached for a child who sat next to her playing with a piece of twine. There was nowhere to sit so Adelasia bent down on one knee at a time to examine her. She hoped she could get up on her own; no one here would help her.

"Signora Bertoluzzi, do you know how far along you are?" she asked.

"Six months," she answered, glancing to see where her husband was just as he slammed the door on his way out.

Adelasia lowered her voice and took the woman's pulse. "I told you how to ensure this didn't happen. It's not safe for you."

"I tried. I did what you told me. My husband, he's the one who decides. I told him not that night. I told him I had a headache." She pushed her hands onto the mattress to sit up. "It made him angry. It made it worse. I'm sorry."

Adelasia looked at the woman's delicate face and body. The *signora* reached to the little girl to play keep-away with the string, smiling at her, and the child crawled over to kiss her head.

"Don't be sorry. You're doing your best. We'll bring this

baby here safely. Take care of yourself. Make sure you get plenty to eat. I need you to gain weight in the next couple of months."

"He won't like it. He likes me slim."

"Then eat all you can when he's out. I'll give my son-in-law a little money for you to visit the *alimentari* and buy something you can eat outside the house. Do your best."

Hoisting herself up by grabbing onto the dusty windowsill, she left the woman, and quietly walked out of the house, taking care to ensure the front door didn't fall off its hinges as she closed it.

"Who do you think you are?"

She jumped at a voice to her left. He stood up from a dilapidated rocking chair. Again, she smelled the liquor as he came close, and her heart throbbed, but she kept herself calm.

"Your wife is in a difficult state, Signor Bertoluzzi. Her body isn't meant for babies."

In two quick steps, he was next to her, breathing in her face, and she was sure he would hit her.

"How dare you interfere in my bed, you cow! I know what you did. I know you told her how she should stop from havin' more babies. I could report you. I'll report you and then when you go to jail, I'll laugh 'cause you think you and your family are so wonderful."

Adelasia tried to remain calm, though no one had ever spoken to her or insulted her this way. She realised this man was dangerous. Straightening her shoulders, she took a deep breath and looked fixedly into his eyes.

"Signor Bertoluzzi, I'm here to keep your wife and baby safe. It's my job, and I intend to do it. Come for me if she has any problems. Good day." She stepped around him, and he didn't stop her. Not until she out of his sight did she slow her stride. Shuddering, she set down her bag along the path back to town, making the sign of the cross and looking up at the sky. For all the climbs into the mountains to deliver babies during the war, for all the gunshots she heard too close to her own head, there was a new danger in the air, and she believed it to be deadlier. Angry and belittled men were capable of great atrocities.

Nina did not feel well and found she had to drag herself through her daily routine. She shivered. Her entire body ached and her throat, which had been prickly for two days, felt like she was swallowing cut glass. She woke, as usual, before the sun was up, watched the sunrise, and said her rosary. It took twenty minutes to complete the Hail Marys and Our Fathers, each bead a prayer, but it helped her start the day. Today it was less comforting, and she wanted to go back to bed. Nina dressed and went outside to feed the goat, feeling each step was an effort. By the time she finished, it would be breakfast. *Maybe Lasia can take care of it today,* she thought. Lasia often helped with Rita, and Nina had to admit, she needed her help because Rita was mischievous and quick. Several times while they were dressing the two-year-old, she had wriggled away and gone running down the stairs naked.

An exasperated Nina would catch her, slap her bottom and shout, "*Basta, basta.*" Enough, enough. Nina was sometimes at the end of her rope. Lasia was a complete angel. Pietro had helped Nina see her in another way. The girl could be stubborn, but there was a genuine kindness about her, and while she was willful, unlike her little sister, Lasia did what she was told and hated to be reprimanded.

By the afternoon, Nina's cold was draining her. Her throat burned in pain. Throughout the day, she didn't have a moment to rest. Thankfully, Vante came over and made her coffee. The warm liquid coated her throat and gave her solace, however short-lived.

"You rest, I'll entertain them a bit," he told her. Vante stayed long enough to play with Lasia and little Rita. Nina was in no state to entertain the energetic toddler the way her brother could.

"By the way," said Vante, after several rounds of hide-and-seek with the girls. "The Bertoluzzi woman is having her baby today. Antonietta told me Mamma was headed over there." Nina, who had drifted off while watching them play, straightened up.

"Vante, no. Loretta Bertoluzzi is sick. Onorina told me she came by the shop coughing, asking for treatments as she held her belly; and I'm sure her husband is still beating her even though she is pregnant. Mamma shouldn't risk herself." Nina thought of the slumping shoulders and the creases in her mother's face. "Can you stay here with the girls? I need to go help her."

"Absolutely not, Nina. You're not going anywhere," said Vante. "Besides, you know Mamma. She's never been sick a day in her life. The woman's made of steel."

Because of her fever, Nina was easily convinced.

"I wish Pia would go instead, but I know Mamma wants to help Signora Bertoluzzi. She doesn't want Pia to have to deal with that monster husband." Nina took a last sip of coffee, thanking her brother. "You should go. I don't want you to get that wife of yours sick. I'm looking forward to a healthy niece or nephew in a couple of months." Vante beamed. He adored his two daughters, but the crib death of his first son had him longing for a child to continue the family name.

"Yes, hopefully a boy, in honour of my Luigi."

In the mountainside, Adelasia sweated in a birth room that doubled as a sick room. She needed the doctor for this delivery but, once again, he was up in his mountain lodge, enjoying the cool air without time for the inconvenience of births. Adelasia tried to save mother and child, but she failed to leave the room with any life. She had lost mothers before, but never a mother and child. Signora Bertoluzzi had little chance with her throat infection and already frail body covered in recent purple bruises. With her long labour and weak state, she died before she could push the baby out. By the time Adelasia delivered the child, he had died as well. Signora Bertoluzzi had no right to deny her husband, instead, she was denied her life, and her daughter deprived of a mother. Adelasia had warned Corrado of the situation. He was to wait outside in the cart with his gun to ward off the drunk Signor Bertoluzzi, who, with a daughter alive and wife and baby dead, blamed Adelasia.

"You stupid woman. You killed them!" he shouted when she stepped onto the porch, having covered the body of Signora Bertoluzzi with the bedsheet and wrapped the stillborn gently in an old towel. She could find nothing else in the house.

"I did everything I could," Adelasia spoke tenderly to the man, despite his abuse. He had just lost his wife and child and his little girl stood barefoot in the dirt wondering when her mother would wake up. "She was sick and not built for children."

He raised his hand to slap her and Adelasia braced for a blow. Cart wheels crunched over gravel, pulling up as Corrado cocked his gun and pointed it at Signor Bertoluzzi. "Hit her and I'll kill you," he said calmly.

Signor Bertoluzzi pulled back his hand, laughing. "No. I won't bother hitting you. I've got *il Duce* on my side. Just wait. You'll never midwife again. I'll see to that."

CHAPTER 22

Adelasia remained in bed the morning after the deaths of Signora Bertoluzzi and her baby. It was several days before Nina could come to see her, only recently recuperating herself. Walking into the room, she found another woman in her mother's bed – a transformation. The slump in her shoulders was pronounced. Ashen skin hung limp on her face, and her rough coughs pulled down the folds under her eyes. Silver had overtaken the black of her hair; she looked as though she had carried a boulder up a mountain and could do no more.

"Look at this." Adelasia handed Nina a folded piece of paper. The official stamp of the *municipio* was on the bottom. It stated a complaint had been filed against Adelasia for negligence. An investigation was to take place. Until then, she could not midwife.

"Now I'm a criminal. Can you imagine? At my age? After all these years! I won't even be allowed to help deliver my own grandchildren." She looked out the window, coughing more. "Maybe it was my fault. That poor woman. That poor baby."

Nina comforted her, then fetched her a glass of Fernet-Branca to help her relax and sleep.

A new routine began. Nina and her siblings nursed their mother while each day she became thinner and slept more. By the time summer was over and leaves fell from the trees, Adelasia, the Captain, lay in her bed, a sick old woman.

A rumbling began from the heart of Mount Avena. At first, it was negligible, light tremors that shook the windows and made unsteady pots crash. The quaking returned almost every day in the afternoon. The *Fonzasini* wondered if a catastrophe was pending. They went about their business, but it gave them fodder for discussion at the *filò*. The more superstitious of them blamed a curse.

Not a day passed when Nina didn't stay with her mother for as long as she needed. No matter the work to be done in the fields or the difficulties of raising a two-year-old, ensuring the goat was milked, or the chickens fed, she came to care for her. She turned Adelasia to make sure she didn't get bedsores. She cleaned her. With her sisters, she carefully held her mother up to change the sheets. When they did this, Nina would hold Adelasia in her arms with Aurora or Onorina supporting the other side, feeling her mother's shrinking body against her. This woman from whom she was born, disappearing beneath her embrace. Her quips were still there, but she said thank you more often and frequently said nothing. Silence from an outspoken woman was a tiptoe towards death.

Adelasia had carried a heavy load and carried it grandly. She had administered over one thousand births, comforted mothers of the stillborn, gone countless nights without sleep.

The passing of her grandchildren had taken its toll on her, as did losing her first son all those years ago, and rarely hearing from him. The Bertoluzzi family controversy was too much. Her cough wouldn't go away, but it was her heart that was weakened beyond repair. The woman who brought life everywhere she went was dying.

On a dark day in late autumn, Mount Avena roared as though lightning was crashing inside it. Copper pots fell off walls, the ground vibrated, and the Argenta sisters held onto doorways at Adelasia's house while everything shook around them. When the rumbling stopped, they checked for damage and called on neighbours. But, besides a few fallen chimneys and a fire that needed putting out, nothing appeared to be damaged.

In November, the daily tremors continued, and the wind blew and kicked up leaves, swirling them in mini tornadoes down the Via Calzen. The first cold fog came, and the carpet of mist was so low it covered San Micel. At the Argenta home, the mood was sombre. Anticipation of coming despair was in the voices and movements of everyone who visited as it became clear Adelasia would not make it through the day. Nina lamented, when you love someone and depend on them for your entire existence, the process of life slipping from them feels gradual then speeds up before they are gone; the way the last bit of sand drains through an hourglass.

Evira, recognising this and being the last of the two youngest to wed, decided to clarify the subject of her dowry. Could she have Adelasia's wedding ring? What about the land? Would Adelasia tell Corrado to give her the larger piece near the spring? Luigia, the youngest, wondering herself, entered the room as Evira was addressing their mother and they bickered over their dowries until Nina ushered them out.

Lasia stood with her cousin, Quinto, in the corner of the room staring curiously at what happened when a person was about to die. At eight years old, she hadn't had a lot of experience with death and observed with curiosity the comings and goings of the adults and the withering away of her once robust *nonna* who she barely recognised but still loved with her whole heart.

"Come here," said Adelasia. The children stepped forward, Quinto looking uncomfortable. Adelasia spoke to him first. "Quinto, take the banana there on the table. Go share it with your sister."

"*Grazie*, Nonna." He grabbed the fruit and scampered out, looking relieved.

When he was gone, Lasia walked to the bed and quietly spoke to her *nonna*.

"I bet he took that banana to the attic to look through your anatomy books. He's always up there looking at those books," Lasia said, looking down at her bitten fingernails.

"Aeh," said Adelasia weakly, shrugging her shoulders the slightest bit. "He can look at them all he likes. He'll never learn anything from those pages. Women will always be a mystery to men." She winked, and young Lasia pulled a stool next to the bed and sat, her knees poking out from her skirt.

"Nonna, will you get better?" she asked as Adelasia smiled at her.

"No, *bambina mia,* it's time for me to go away. We can't all stay forever, or there would be no room for new people."

"I don't want you to go," said Lasia, her sincere childish words warming the room.

"I'm going to Heaven. I'll get it ready so one day, a long, long time from now, it will be just the way my Lasietta wants it."

"With candy and lots of *biscotti?*"

"*Certo!* Of course! All the sweets you can imagine." A rattling cough shook Adelasia's frame.

Lasia noticed the purplish hue on her *nonna's* lips. "What about Nonno?" Tears filled her eyes as she tried to be brave.

"He'll stay with you. Take good care of him, *sì?*" Meeting Lasia's eyes, she told her firmly, "You are my Lasietta. You're strong."

"*Sì,* Nonna," she said.

"You won't forget me, will you?"

"No, Nonna."

"Then I will always be here, *amore*. Always."

At five o'clock, Adelasia asked Nina to bring her children to her. Nina held Rita in her arms, while Lasia stood directly in front of her *nonna* at the foot of the bed. The room was dim other than a streak of light coming through the lace curtains. Around the bed were Adelasia's daughters. Onorina stood behind Corrado, who sat in a chair holding Adelasia's hand as he had for days. Aurora stood next to them, holding her face in her hands, unable to fathom what was happening. Evira leaned on the wall, while Luigia cried.

Vante couldn't be in the room. He sat on a chair outside, staring at his shoes. It couldn't be happening. Adelasia had been so strong. It wasn't time for her to leave yet, was it? At sixty-one, she had filled every year of her life. She had given everything to living and bringing new life into the world.

Adelasia opened her eyes. "I suppose Papà will take my portion of the polenta."

Smiles broke out; giggles gave way to tears. Corrado grinned weakly, leaning closer. He kissed the palm of his hand, pressed it to her cheek. "*La mia sposa, amore mio.*" My bride, my love. After forty years of marriage, she was still his bride, the woman who appeared larger than life and took his heart with her.

Rina and Maria came in to take Rita. They'd made it back from Rome in time to say goodbye. The children cried out – not wanting their *nonna* to go. The girls pulled closer to their mother; they allowed Lasietta to stay in the room while her namesake lay dying. Adelasia's eyes were dark; she had lost so much weight and was a fraction of her previous self, but she was still Adelasia somewhere under it all.

"You have been my life, my children. *Vi voglio bene,*" she said with what was left of her raspy voice. Nina grasped her left hand, Corrado held her right. Aurora, Luigia and Evira each touched the blanket that covered her soft, withered form. With a gentle squeeze of Nina's hand, a great lady left the Earth.

Lasietta looked at Nina who was full of tears.

"Mamma, it's okay," she said. "Nonna is with us. She'll always be right here with us." Nina pulled the girl to her and held Lasia tighter than she ever had before.

Silence hung over the Argenta house. Nina stepped into the room where her mother no longer lay. It had been made-up as though nothing was missing. A delicate crocheted coverlet hugged the bed, peaceful and white. Adelasia's soap and powder scent lingered on the pillows. Nina ran her hand across the dresser. It wasn't expensive but would have been considered elegant even by wealthier standards. She opened the small metal chest on the bureau, remembering the rare times when Adelasia would get dressed up for special occasions while she looked through the chest. Adelasia never minded as she took out each necklace, pair of earrings, bracelets from Venice, coins from Rome and a shell – Nina had no idea where it was from. She'd once asked Adelasia, but her only response was, "It's something I collected over the years." There had been a look on her face telling her daughter perhaps there were stories about her mother she didn't know. There were rosaries, crosses and a scapular under a velvet-lined divider where she found a small stack of old photos wrapped in parchment paper. The picture of Nina with Teo sat on top, then one of Antonio on his Communion day, one of a young woman in a heavy dress (could it be Adelasia?), one of a young man Nina had never seen before, and one of a baby with no name written on the back which might have been any of them or someone else. *Funny how we forget our mothers were girls; they once belonged to themselves and not to their children,* she thought. She studied the picture of the young man. Had there been someone she loved before Corrado? She remembered fragments of things Adelasia had mentioned that she ignored, too busy with her own cares. How Mamma had met Corrado when she attended a birth for one of his family members, how he had followed her around from that point on, determined to marry her, singing outside her window. She regretted not asking for more details about these stories, but it was too late. Had Adelasia loved Corrado when she married him, or did love come later? Nina remembered something from when she was younger about another baby who died before she was born, but Adelasia had never spoken about it. *Was this the baby?* she wondered. She took the pictures, slipping them into her pocket. They were her mother's secrets, her mother's questions to answer, but she was at peace. The life she had lived was complete.

Nina let her tears come. She cried for Adelasia and the tremendous life she lived and for Teo who she knew was now in the arms of his *nonna*. She cried that Pietro never met his son and the belief someday he would in Heaven. She cried for Lasia and Rita growing up longing for their father, for the years passing apart from Pietro and the unknown of when they would hold each other again. There had been good times. There had been incredible pain, but Adelasia had always been there, putting things into perspective, giving Nina purpose. Who would guide her now? She thought of her father's deep admiration for her mother. He had stood in the hallway after Adelasia died repeating to anyone who would listen, "She picked me. She could have had any man. She was so wonderful. But she picked me." He walked around dumbfounded, adrift without his wife, never imagining she would not be there to direct him.

Opening the chest under the window, Nina pulled out one of her mother's sweaters, slipping her arms through the holes then holding the collar to her nose to breathe in whatever she could of the Captain.

"Be strong, Ninetta," her mother had said. "You don't know how strong you are." Adelasia had known so much but she was wrong about this. Nina doubted herself completely. *Who am I without her? My sounding board, my advisor, my confidant, my defender and saviour. She was everything!* Nina thought. Losing this woman was like losing a piece of herself. She couldn't imagine the family ever being the same. Adelasia was the sun they orbited around. She couldn't be gone. This reality made no sense.

After crying alone in her mother's room for a long time, a feeling of calm washed over her. If there was anyone she would want to watch over her family, there was no better guardian angel than Adelasia Dalla Santa Argenta. Everything on Earth, they would have to handle, but Lasietta was right, she would stay with them. Nina looked to the sky, tears drying on her face, holding her arms in her mother's sweater. "I know you're with us, Mamma. *Ti voglio bene.*"

The funeral was a blur, as if Nina was watching herself attend through tears. Her mother lay, peaceful in her casket, in the dress she had worn to Vante's wedding, with her rosary wrapped around her hands. Her peaceful face made her unrecognisable. She was at rest as she'd never been in life. The church filled with people lining up, one after another, to honour the Captain. Adelasia had helped every one of them – adults she'd delivered as babies, women she had taken care of, families she helped create.

"I was breach and she turned me."

"My baby wouldn't feed, so she fed her milk with sugar until she grew. Now, look at her!"

"She saved my life when I was born."

"Without her, I would have died."

"She held my husband's hand in the mountains when he passed."

Nina attempted to speak with each person, but in the dazed state of losing her mother, the best she could do was go through the motions of comforting others as they made their way past her then on to her siblings and father. The children played in the back of the church quietly. They paid their respects but moved on in the way only children can. Nico put a bunch of wild flowers at Adelasia's feet then handed another small bunch to Nina as he hugged her.

"I'm sorry, *santola*," he said.

"Thank you, sweet boy." He made his way to Lasia who sat away from the other children, as usual, mourning her grandmother on her own. He handed her a small bouquet and leaned to give her the slightest hug.

Nina looked over at her brother in his suit shaking hands, standing by his wife. How fast they had grown up. Wasn't it yesterday they were children themselves, saying goodbye to Nonna Argenta? She considered the memories they had together with their mother. She remembered a day they travelled to Bergamo when she was a child. They had cousins there, so her mother insisted they go and visit. Nina had loved the speed of the train rushing past village after village, travelling through the lush Italian countryside. When they arrived in Bergamo, she fell in love with its *piazze*, inclined streets and ornate, eerie churches. Adelasia bought them gelato, which they ate while sitting on the church steps. Afterwards, Nina convinced Vante to race her to the top of the baptistry tower. They pushed past each other on the narrow steps, sprinting until they got to the highest floor, empty of others; a secluded perch high above the city. They had marvelled at the russet dome cap of the *chiesa* and the expanse of Bergamo. Four pillars on top of the dome held a pointed pyramid roof. She had imagined flying over to the space between the columns. There, she could be alone, looking over the city, watching the people living below. She could dance behind the posts, peeking out ghostlike atop the basilica. Her mind had floated as her eyes beheld the city's beauty. The sun had shone over Italy that day, as she and Vante squinted into its rays, content with youth.

After several hours, the crowd left, each of Adelasia's children kissed their mother for the last time and closed the casket. It was hard to watch Corrado say goodbye. His face held a surreal smile, a general air of confusion. They walked behind the casket as Vante, Toni and others carried it to the cemetery behind the church. Don Cavalli said a Hail Mary as they placed Adelasia's casket in the earth, then the family walked home together without their Captain to share a meal celebrating her life. Upon entering the house, they found a letter slipped under the door stamped from the *municipio*. Nina ripped it open and scanned through the words, praying for justice for her mother. She made the sign of the cross. The investigation was complete; Adelasia Dalla Santa Argenta had been exonerated. She would eternally be a midwife. Nina was sure she had just missed it, but after that day, the rumbling in Mount Avena stopped.

Caro Pietro,

We have just finished the funeral of my mother. It feels strange when I wake up, look around and realise she is no longer on this Earth. I can't make sense of it. We've been trying to settle her things. Of course, Evira has been difficult. She wanted to have my mother's ring when she knows it should go to Onorina as the eldest. She's an odd character, so selfish. The other day she made Lasia clean out her oven when I asked if she could spend the day there while I helped with the birth of one of the Corso babies. Papà gave me an envelope Mamma left for us with some money inside. By the time we save, I'll be ready to go. Papà is lost without Mamma, but

Onorina and Toni have him helping at the shop and bakery. Aurora runs the bakery. They can take care of themselves. Vante's leaving for Africa to work. At least he was with us when she died. Her greatest joy was having her children around her. I'll write to Antonio. Let's begin a plan. Is there any news about a job in the factories? What do you need from me? It's time for our life together as a family to begin. I know it. Mamma would have wanted it like this.

Ti amo,
Tua Ninetta

She tucked a prayer card from her mother's funeral into the envelope. Nina walked to the cemetery to brush the first snow of December from Adelasia's gravestone, dropping the letter in the post on her way. She pictured it crossing the Atlantic. Of course, it would travel by cargo ship, but she imagined the letter as a bird, flying over the blue sea with its destination in mind, landing on his doorstep. It was a nice thought, romantic even. She only glanced at the headline in the newspapers at the *tabacchi* shop. On the front page, *il Duce* stood in the *Piazza Venezia* in Rome in front of thousands. Italy would leave the League of Nations, following Germany away from the rest of the world.

CHAPTER 23

On 25 September 1938, Lasia raced home from church as the bells tolled, and the *Fonzasini* bounded out of the *chiesa* to prepare for the afternoon's excitement. Mussolini was coming! *Il Duce* in Fonzaso! She left Mass by herself since her mother went home early after a minor scandal. Her sister had left her underwear at home, and the people sitting behind them had sniggered, pointing it out when her bare *culo* shown through the slat in the pew. Lasia laughed. Rita was always getting into trouble. In the three years since her little sister was born, life was certainly more eventful.

She skipped past Zia Onarina's shop and saw her reflection in the glass. Mamma had tied her hair back with one of Nonna's old ribbons to keep it out of her face. She had found it when cleaning out Nonna's drawers. It was nice to have something of the Captain's giving her confidence. She tucked her crisp white shirt into her black knee-length skirt and stretched her back straight. Despite her bony body, in her uniform and with the words of *il Duce* in her head, she felt strong. *Better to live one day as a lion than one hundred years as a sheep,* he had said. She only ever wore her uniform to school and for fascist Saturday activities, never usually to church. But today was special, everyone was in their regalia ready for *il Duce* to come after his morning speech in Vicenza. The community buzzed. Who could eat with so much excitement? She gulped down her mother's *fagioli* soup then ran to meet her school friends and Nonno in the *Piazza Primo Novembre.*

The band tuned their instruments in preparation, sending notes from songs they had learnt in the *Operazione Nazionale Balilla* into the sky. Today was the culmination of her hard work, her obedience and focus on being a good fascist girl. A perfect *piccola italiana.*

"Nonno!" she called to Corrado who stood outside the taverna looking unrecognisable in his black uniform and tall boots. The party must have outfitted him with the appropriate attire because she was used to him in work shirts and trousers.

"Lasietta!" His voice boomed even louder than usual. "It's a big day! See, you've made *il Duce* proud with all of your awards. I bet that's why he's coming to Fonzaso!" He laughed, squeezing her by the shoulders before she ran off to meet the rest of the girls, who were lining up on the western side of the piazza. As she found her place among her classmates, the piazza filled. Loose lines of boys arranged themselves in front of the girls. They would see Mussolini up close. The sons of the Fatherland. Quinto, her cousin, stood on the church steps with his classmates dressed in their *Balilla* uniforms: black fez hats angled over their right ears, black shirts tucked into grey shorts, grey socks to their knees. *How funny those knees look lined up next to each other,* she thought. A bee flew around the crowd, finding its way up schoolgirls' skirts, looking for a thigh to sting. The girls swatted it, screaming and giggling. Anticipation made everyone over-talkative with nervous energy. *Il Duce!* In Fonzaso! Lasia had never seen such excitement.

Older boys packed in shoulder to shoulder, some punching and roughhousing. Nico's brother, Abramo, stood with a group of other twelve-year-olds who kept timing each other in sprints from their line to the corner of the *municipio,* seeing who could run back before the teachers caught them. Another set of boys dashed by and suddenly, Lasia felt a tug on her ribbon, and her hair fell into her eyes. A boy ran with the strip of fabric like a banner through the pack of people before dropping it among the dust and shoes. She cried out just as a blond head swooped down to pick it up. *Nico!* He squeezed through the crowd to bring it to her.

"Here you go. Sorry about that. Bortolo loves to tease the girls. It's not very nice but..." His voice trailed off as he attempted to help tie the ribbon back in her hair, fumbling their arms and hands. After bumping her nose, he gave up, and she laughed as her classmates giggled around them.

"It's okay. Thank you," she said quietly, flashing him an awkward smile. When he skipped back to his space, the girls around her poked her side and raised their eyebrows, teasing her briefly before someone shouted, "He's coming. He's coming!" The crowd settled as word spread. The fifth-grade teacher slapped one boy running sprints on the head yelling, "Don't you know, *il Duce* is coming any minute!" With a roar, the band started up and *Giovinezza* played as they began to sing.

Visitors from neighbouring towns filled the *Albergo Sant'Antonio* and rushed to the streets for a spot. Women leaned out of second and third floor windows, holding babies on hips, others stood in a line, dressed in traditional costumes with large baskets on their backs holding the tiniest of children in *Balilla* uniforms. Tricolour flags adorned balconies replacing laundry. Green, white, red; the colours were everywhere. At once, the crowd cheered, as a shiny black convertible appeared. *Il Duce* stood in the back, his right arm giving the Roman salute. *"Viva il Duce, Viva il Duce!"* the crowd shouted. Lasia saw Nico raise his hand, she followed his movement. Hundreds of acute angles saluted Mussolini, the only leader of Italy Lasia had known. The man Nonno and her uncles admired, whom her mother and Nonna complained in secret was interfering in the church and women's affairs. His picture hung in her school next to the cross: King Vittorio Emanuele III to the left of the crucifix, *il Duce* to the right. *He is seated at the right hand of the father –* words from the scripture played in her mind. Through the raised arms, she could see the man himself: clean-shaven and square, his face enthusiastically angry, lower lip stuck out in a pout. On his head, he wore a black fez decorated with the *fasce,* a bundle of sticks made into an axe. He looked solid, resolute, inspiring the normally quiet girl to shout with all her might, *"Viva il Duce, Viva il Duce!"* enough to lose her voice praising the leader of Italy.

Six months after Mussolini came through Fonzaso, spring smiled at Nina through the window. The metallic echo of the church bell tolled seven times. Cherry trees lifted their blossoms towards blue skies outside the glass. The cool became temperate. She was reticent. Was it a trick? Would she plan for a sunny day only to see it gradually turn into dismal blackness? *How cynical I've become,* she thought. She knew it was for good reason.

Four years since she had last seen him.

It had been four years today since he'd stood on the threshold, since he'd held her. Every day that passed they were inching towards war. Everyone could feel it. She had seen the papers, heard the stories from the taverna and *alimentari*. The day after Corrado and the children returned from Mussolini's rally, *il Duce* met with Hitler. The idea of formalising a partnership with the man who was swiftly executing his vision for taking control in Europe emboldened him.

But Nina and Pietro had a vision of their own made of hopes and letters. She pulled a letter from the biscotti tin where she kept the most recent ones. The container was full of correspondence about plans, a constant back and forth of possibility. The Depression had made Pietro's work sporadic and low paying. Attempts at strikes to improve workers' conditions added further delays. Each letter had Pietro saving in fits and spurts with little coming into Italy; Nina used what her mother left her to help his parents. It was a tin filled with details of an adventure for which she was finally ready.

She pulled out another letter, not from Pietro. It had come last week from her cousin, Tinetta. Their situation in Padua had deteriorated. They had transferred the shop deed to her father's name since Jews could no longer own businesses after *il Duce* established the Manifesto of Race. It made no sense, but Mussolini passed racial laws to complement his ally in Germany. Some Italians embraced the antisemitism, the others allowed it through indifference. Inaction made them guilty, too. Months before, Nina was appalled to hear on Aurora's radio what had happened in Germany. Angry mobs had attacked Jewish shops with bricks. They ruined thousands of businesses and burned synagogues to the ground. Photos in the paper showed broken glass blanketing the streets. The hatred crept towards them, threatened to surround them, and invaded their relatives. Even Corrado gradually was becoming disenchanted with *il Duce*. Nina noticed not long after he had watched the motorcade he moved the picture of Mussolini and the local fascists to a back room. It was the last time he wore his black shirt. He'd always liked Federico; a man's life being dictated by the state because he had Jewish blood didn't sit well with him. Corrado replaced the picture with a photograph of Adelasia.

Tinetta wrote that her son, Giglio, had been doing well in school, a future as a doctor was a possibility, but they questioned whether he could continue his education. The race laws forbid Jews to study at universities. Even being half Jewish, he was outcast. They were considering if perhaps they should also emigrate to America, asking Nina what she thought based on news from Pietro. She would write to them this afternoon and tell them they should go. Maybe they could meet in Padua and travel together to Genoa. It came down to getting documents in order. Paperwork. How many fates lay on desks in office trays hoping to make it to the top of the pile before the decision-makers went home for dinner. Every minute lost to a toilet break or a long lunch meant another day a family stayed apart. Destinies decided in mundane pauses.

Five thousand miles away from Fonzaso, in America, Pietro was nearly skipping with excitement – he had organised everything to the point he could almost send for his family. He had saved enough to get them passage to America. All he needed were the proper documents. The wife of an Irish miner helped him fill in the forms to make sure everything was just right. Why was it taking so long? He would have to hurry to make the travel plans – with war looming it was getting harder and harder to bring emigrants across. Military in Europe were commandeering passenger boats for supply ships to support the war efforts. Any day he would receive the papers allowing them to join him, he was sure of it.

Once Nina agreed she would come, Pietro hadn't wasted a minute. When he wasn't in the mines, he asked around at the bar about other work. There were steel factories in Joliet; if he was lucky, he could get a job in one of them. Or perhaps a foundry – something above ground, out of the mines. With what he'd saved, the money from Adelasia and a job at a factory, he could (barely) afford to sustain his family here. There was no time to waste. Nina's letters and the newspaper announced *il Duce* was cosying up to Hitler. He'd even put in place anti-Jewish laws, turning Italians against Italians. Pietro couldn't understand why, after the stories of atrocities in Germany, *il Duce* would follow this man. Power. Some men wanted power above any morals.

Unlike most mornings, the pick he carried on his shoulder wasn't heavy.

"You got somethin' eatin' at ya, Pete?" asked Freddy. The Irish immigrant had worked with Pietro for a year but beyond a beer after work, he knew little of Pietro's life.

"No, no," Pietro said, "thinking about the job."

He wished he could get out of today's work so he could figure out the plans for his family. This job paid twice as much because it was twice as dangerous. The site they were mining was drilled deep into a land formation. It was rich in coal, but the risk from the rock overhang and drilling below left them grappling every day with major obstacles. They'd been on the job three months, and the hole was deep. They worked outwards from the base, drilling shafts from the central pit. Six of them descended that morning, their headlamps glowing in the makeshift elevator. Pietro tried to focus as the dank, earthy smell filled his nostrils. He couldn't afford to be preoccupied. Preoccupation meant loss of life. The elevator halted at the level of the indentation they'd dug the week before. They split up, three on each side. Pietro went with Fred and a burly Irishman named Sammy who had forearms the size of telephone poles. They pulled their picks back then slammed them forward, chipping at cavern walls as dust flew around them.

"Hey. Hey, Pietro!" Someone called him from across the other side of the pit. "You got an extra stake over there?"

Pietro grabbed a stake and walked to the pit where the elevator still hung suspended between the caverns. "Throw'er across," the miner shouted from the other side. Pietro grabbed the wooden side rail of the elevator, anchoring himself between the cavern edge and the floorboards. As he tossed the tool across, his foot slipped on the slick ground. In a flash, he lost his grip on the rail, sliding, then free falling into the vastness. Pietro bashed into the edges of the pit, grabbing at the air, panic-stricken. Rock cut him as he scraped to catch hold of anything. He hit another rock. He envisioned Nina. A rib snapped; she reached out for him. He lost consciousness.

His limp body descended the pit until he landed, becoming submerged in muck and still-falling debris.

As Pietro lay unconscious while his fellow miners angled down to rescue him, the post was being delivered to the building where he rented a room. It informed him he had filled out the forms incorrectly. He had printed N-I-N-E-T-T-A as his wife's first name, which did not match her passport. The request was denied.

CHAPTER 24

A utumn 1939

Caro Pietro,

I hope this letter gets through to you. The girls and I are doing as well as expected without you and without word from you. We pray you are safe. Rita is growing and saying the funniest things. The other day at the shop, an old man asked who her mother was. She pointed at me and said, 'She's married.' You should be glad to know your youngest looks out for you. Lasia is still doing gymnastics programmes. My father used to be excited about her awards but he's getting frustrated with il Duce so he just pats Lasia's shoulder without a fuss. I think she misses his old excitement. I don't think he realised his enthusiasm for a party for the good of Italy would bring us to the brink of war again. It seems they may call up the workers in Africa into the army. Vante would have to fight. We've lived through one war and we don't want to see it again. I don't want our daughters to experience what war brings. I still remember the fear those Austrian soldiers instilled in us. I remember being hungry. I remember worse things I try to forget. Papà is lost since Mamma died but is finding great joy in his grandchildren. He takes them foraging for mushrooms in the woods when he isn't at the taverna or bakery. I miss Mamma. It's not the same to midwife without her. I try to be as strong as she was, but I fear that will never happen. I am nowhere near as strong and I have to tell you, Pietro, I am missing you more than ever before. It's been several months since I received a letter. What's wrong? Il Duce has stirred the energy of everyone. Things are odd here. Is there progress in having us come to you? Do you still care? I'm sorry, I know you hate my doubts but I've heard nothing. Soon I'll send a message through one of the other families who have Fonzaso men in Joliet. I hope someone can tell me you are safe. I'm praying. Please write as soon as you can and let me know you are all right.

Tua moglie,
Ninetta

Onorina handed Nina a wrapped *porchetta* as she counted out her lire to pay. Her sister wiped her hands on a towel then came out to straighten the *alimentari* shelves and greet Aurora who was also shopping. She checked around the small space to ensure they were alone.

"Did you hear what they're saying?" Onorina whispered, "Italy will help Germany while that bastard Hitler takes over all these countries. Why would we do that? Italian men dying for them!"

"It's awful," Nina said, "When I think of what we lived through... now siding with the Germans."

"Toni says Hitler has the upper hand. The rest of the world

thinks we're crazy. Has Pietro said anything?" Onorina asked as she straightened the shelves.

"A little," Nina lied, quickly deflecting back to Onorina to avoid answering. "Where did you hear that?" Nina asked.

"Radio London. We get the station, but just barely. I'm glad I learnt English. You'd never hear it on the Italian stations."

Nina nodded, her sister was much more worldly than her, even in her thinking, but she added, "As Mussolini says, '*The press in Italy is the freest in the world*'..." Aurora angled from behind the shelves towards them to complete the sentence, sticking out her chest and lower lip like *il Duce*, "*As long as it supports the regime!*" she said in a low masculine voice. They laughed at her impression.

"Be careful, *sorellina*," Onorina said. "You never know who will walk in. If they hear you mocking *il Duce*, they could denounce you. I pay attention." She motioned with two fingers to her pupils, then pointed around the shop before leaving them to go to the back room for more stock. Aurora rolled her eyes then dropped to a serious expression to address Nina.

"Anything?" she asked. Nina shook her head.

"*Niente*, nothing." She told her sister. No letter, no word from Pietro. Nina had kept her secret from everyone, including the girls, but she recently confided in Aurora she had stopped hearing from Pietro. It had been over nine months since the last letter.

The shop bell rang, interrupting their conversation. Evira entered, her lips pursed and eyes looking accusingly at them. Her face was always a mix of consternation, pain, or annoyance.

"Speaking of someone who would denounce anyone..." Aurora whispered as she turned to study the confectionery treats for her daughter.

"Oh, so you're together but you didn't come to get me did

you?" croaked Evira. "No one came by to see if I needed anything." Her words sounded like a mix of teasing and accusation.

"You're perfectly capable..." Aurora berated her sister, but Nina put her hand on her arm to stop her, addressing Evira patiently, like Adelasia always had.

"*Sorellina,* we happened to end up here at the same time. We didn't leave you or Luigia out of anything. By the way, I made you some fresh pasta. I'm going to have Rita bring it over to you later this afternoon."

Evira scowled as Onorina returned from the back room. "*Salve,* Evira!" she called in a singsong voice, flashing her a beautiful smile, at odds with their sister's sour disposition. Evira picked up a packet of Arborio rice, studying it. "You must make good money, Onorina, with the *alimentari* and the bakery. Nice that you gave Aurora a job there. Nice for Ippolito when he returns. God forbid you'd help my family."

Onorina didn't flinch; they were used to the regular cuts Evira delivered. She complimented her instead.

"I think your husband does very well. You were clever to marry a delivery driver. He can probably pick up a lot of things in the various cities he drives to."

"Oh, I think he picks up lots of things," Aurora quipped below her breath but loud enough for Evira to hear. Nina and Onorina tried not to laugh at the comment but the play on words combined with the stroke of truth were impossible not to find disturbingly funny. It was a poorly kept secret that Evira's husband enjoyed his time on the road. When her daughter was born covered with boils, eyes congealed shut, his escapades were obvious to Evira.

Their sister glared back. "How dare you? What about you, Nina? You don't know what Pietro is doing in America. He could have a whole separate family there. You wouldn't even know it," she taunted, obviously pleased with herself as she made her way casually around the shelves.

Nina drew in a sharp breath. Evira had pushed on a soft spot. She felt tears pressing behind her eyes and forced herself to contain them. Aurora snapped at their younger sister.

"Go home, Evira. You've been *brutta* since you were little and you're *brutta* now."

"Calm down, Aurora." Nina composed herself and tried to cool the rift between Aurora and Evira. Mamma would have wanted her to keep the peace in the family, even if Evira's words cut. "Just go home, Evira. Rita will bring you the pasta," Nina said.

Their sister opened the door, still holding the pack of rice in her hands, and left after emitting a "hmph".

"*Allora,* she drives me crazy. Ignore her, Ninetta. You're too good to her," Aurora tsked, her hands on her hips.

Nina made the sign of the cross. "Give me patience," she prayed aloud, then reached into her coin purse to pay for the rice Evira had taken.

Evira lounged by the window, watching people pass. Her daughter was at Luigia's house since she never felt well enough to care for the girl herself. She didn't tell her sisters she was sick of dealing with a child, sick of her life, tired of them getting everything they wanted. She loved to go to the cinema, imagining her life was like the movies. Greta Garbo in *Grand Hotel* lying on her chaise lounge flirting with a vagabond, or dramatically ill and doted on like in *Camille.* She had a divan placed by the window looking over the street – the perfect spot to lounge, greet passersby and pretend.

Rita hadn't come by yet, but Evira left dishes piled high in the sink thinking she could get the little girl to wash them. As the postman passed, she waved him over and spoke to him coquettishly about the pleasant weather and her aches and pains. He mentioned he was on his way to her sister's house with a letter postmarked from America. "Oh, don't bother walking all the way up the road. She's coming over in a few minutes," Evira lied. "Leave it with me, I'll surprise her with it!" Without a question, the postman handed her the letter; he knew the Argenta sisters and was eager to finish his route.

"I appreciate that," he said. "The incline up the Via Calzen pains my back." He joined her for several minutes in the trading of aches.

"Well, I'm right here. Whenever you have letters for her, you might as well save your back. She's here all the time!"

They spoke for a while, finding common ground in complaining before he left her. After saying goodbye, she studied the envelope, squeezing it to see if it might hold money. Then, after checking the postman was further up the road, Evira buried the letter with its red, white and blue edges under the other rubbish in her bin. Lying back, she let the sun blanket her face while her mind went to reveries of the handsome Clark Gable. He'd been chosen to play the lead in *Gone with the Wind* and was on the cover of every paper leading up to the premiere. She smirked thinking about the delicious fresh pasta her niece would bring over shortly.

Rita Pante stood, arms akimbo, feet spread in a commanding stance, in front of their slatted wooden door. Her brown waves toppled around her ears and gave the impression of a halo turned askew. Beneath her hand-me-down dress, bruises in various shades of blue and green covered her legs, earned jumping over fences and playing kickball in the piazza with the boys. Above her rounded cupid cheeks, her eyes blazed, mismatched to a sweet five-year-old – perhaps belonging to a gypsy or a thief before. They were covered with her mother's thick lashes, which she hid behind to play innocent, or tell a white lie to get out of trouble. Her little hands were never clean, no matter how often her mother bathed her or scrubbed her nails after she flipped buttons in the streets or played leapfrog in the fields. The boys she played with were both amazed by and fearful of her. A rumour circulated among the kids she had boxed someone's ears for calling her a stupid girl.

While she preferred to spend time with her loyal crew of boys, she spent her days at the convent with the nuns who constantly scolded her and the other girls who generally annoyed her. On the way home for lunch one day, she walked with her classmates past the private boys' school, peeking in on their breaktime. Away from the fighting and banter of the others, a boy stood out to her. He looked like he came from one of the families of the *signorotti* and had ink-black hair and eyes to match. She admired how finely he was dressed and his leather satchel, probably from Milan. Rita told the other girls, "You see that boy, the one with the leather satchel?" She pointed at him as they looked with doe eyes through the fence. "I'm going to marry him someday."

Nina wasn't home to feed her lunch so Lasia made her a meal of salami and cheese. But when Rita returned home after school, no one was there. She paced outside the door, kicking at the dirt. Why was her mother always gone? Why did she leave her with those miserable old hags at the convent or make her cater to Zia Evira? When she was older, married to that boy and living in America, she would attend marvellous parties with her papà and husband and dance every night.

Mamma and Lasia would be sorry! She sat on a rock next to her door. Where was Mamma? A knot tightened in her throat. The sky was turning a deep ochre as the sun set and she waited. Several times, the sound of footsteps shuffled outside the gate on the Via Calzen, but it only ended up being their neighbours. The wind blew, and as the sun lowered, she shivered but was adamant to wait and confront her mother. She picked at a scab on her knee and watched the tiny crimson stream oozing from it. She put a swipe of the blood on her finger and studied it, then wiped it on the bumpy stone of the house and went inside.

The next morning, Rita was in a better mood when her friend, Francesco, knocked on the door wanting to play in the pig shed. Her mother and sister were still upstairs, they wouldn't care and she saw no reason to tell them. Before long she convinced Francesco they should play a game of doctor. After explaining to him how she had seen the doctor give her uncle a shot in the *culo*, they went about finding sticks they could pretend were doctor's tools, placing them in a pail serving as the medical kit. Francesco was to be the doctor and Rita his patient, but she directed his actions. First, he had to take her temperature. Then he had to examine her throat. Just as they thought, she was sick and needed an injection. Rita pulled down her skirt in the back to reveal a white cheek and Francesco poked it with a stick. Just as he did, they heard Nina shouting as she burst through the pen door. "What are you doing? Pull up your skirt!" She grabbed Rita by the arm and swatted her *culo* with quick slaps, then set her free and did the same to Francesco. "Wait until your mother finds out about this!" she yelled while swatting him.

"But Mamma, the doctor does it!" Rita cried.

"Go to your room! Francesco, home, now!"

They both scurried off with tears stinging their eyes from the spankings and embarrassment.

Nina stood outside the pen, shaking her head in disbelief, then put her face in her hands and laughed until her sides ached. What a character her child was!

"Nina!" she heard Aurora's voice calling as she ran into the yard. She didn't ask what Nina was laughing about but stood, arms tight to her sides; the stance of someone about to deliver bad news. Nina stopped laughing. A thousand thoughts flashed through her head, was it something about Pietro?

"What's going on?" she finally asked.

Aurora met her eyes to deliver the news, "Italy's joined the war."

Nina froze. The mountains drew tight around her, closing her in and she couldn't catch her breath. The war. They'd joined the war. Leaving would be impossible. They would have to pray it was short. Pietro had abandoned them in Italy, and the war would separate them for longer. The thought of leaving for America or seeing Pietro melted into oblivion.

CHAPTER 25

The sun beat down, stifling Fonzaso and bringing sweat to every brow as the men who remained prepared to leave. Aurora's husband, Ippolito, and Vante who were both working in Africa were called up to fight against the British. Evira's husband was going. Toni would stay because of his rheumatism from the shrapnel injury in the Great War. Everyone else they knew was sending someone. But not Nina. She still hadn't heard from Pietro, and now the post was unreliable. It was more than a year since the last letter. She had waited and hoped for a long time, first not telling anyone but Aurora about the gap in communication. It reminded her too much of her uncle's abandonment of his family. She didn't want pity, she only needed to know he was safe. Aurora had secured the address of a *Fonzasino* Nina remembered him mentioning in Joliet, but she wasn't sure the address was right, or if anyone received it. There had been no response. Old news. She had two daughters to worry about and a war quaking around her. There wasn't time to pine for what could be. She prayed he was safe but cursed him at the same time. *Yet I have no regrets,* she thought. *I would do it all again.* What she regretted every day were the actions of another man – *il Duce,* who plunged Italy headfirst into a fight against Britain and France alongside Germany. What he hoped to gain was beyond her imagination. He said he wanted to return Italy to glory, but wasn't it more about his own? Hitler and Germany were the ones eating up Europe, yet Italians would die in the fight. She was glad her mother wasn't here to see this. She prayed Vante would be safe along with the others.

With many men away, Fonzaso was quiet. Rita was off playing and Lasia sat in the shade trying to remain cool. With a creaking of their gate, Nico appeared in her yard. Nina noticed Lasia perked up at the sight of him.

"*Ciao,* Nico, you look handsome! It's your name day, *sì?*" Nina said, noting he was wearing his dress shorts and a new shirt under his suspenders.

"*Grazie, santola.* I'm going to church. A gift, from my mother." Grinning, he handed her a bottle of wine. At twelve years old, it was already possible to see he would be a dashing man, with his golden hair and dark eyebrows.

"Come, give me a quick hug before you say hello to Lasia." She embraced the boy, then went inside to get him biscotti, wrapping them in a handkerchief. When she returned, she saw he had Lasia giggling about something.

"Here, Nico, eat this on your way to church. You don't want it turning to mush in your pocket."

"*Grazie, santola.* I'll pray for you at Mass."

She watched him go, remembering Lasia and him as babies. Time deceived her! She tried to imagine what the future would hold for them, but, with Italy at war and no letters from Pietro, it was hard to envision what was to come.

The war meant rationing, which put the family at the centre of the food chain with the Bianchis running the *alimentari* and Aurora managing their bakery. Aurora was awful at remembering to collect people's coupons, and Toni had to remind her repeatedly they could get in trouble if she wasn't careful. With food from the allotment, eggs from the chickens and milk from the goat, the family was lucky not to be hungry. Nina took it upon herself to use her better fortune to make meals for their neighbours for whom things were tighter, and she always took care of her in-laws' families. Pietro would have appreciated it.

While the bellies were not empty at her house, Nina knew something was missing. Despite the family around them, there was a loneliness to their home. She wanted to be a doting mother to her girls, but sometimes it was easier to find people who needed help outside the house. She could not give them a father. Theirs was far away, she rarely mentioned him anymore, and she wondered if the girls noticed. It added to her guilt. She wanted her girls to have good memories of their childhood, but she was usually too tired to make the effort.

That night, Nina remembered to tuck them in and to say prayers with them. She would try to do it more often. To give more of herself to them. Whatever was left to give. Nina stood on her balcony staring at San Micel as Fonzaso and her daughters slept. She had done well with the girls this week, sent them off to their cousins less; tried to focus less on the nonstop tucking in of chairs, picking up crumbs, closing open drawers, shutting cupboards and washing rags that drained her energy. The *Massaie Rurali* newsletter, a paper promoting fascism among the rural people, laid out housekeeping tips and child-rearing tips to bring up a good fascist Italian family but, with or without a husband, she failed to see how the expectation was realistic.

She rarely used the balcony off her bedroom for anything but hanging laundry, but tonight, she wrapped her mother's cardigan around her and sat outside on the wicker chair, letting the crisp air fill her lungs. Autumn was on its way. She loved hearing nothing but silence and the singing of cicadas under the full moon that illuminated San Micel. She made the sign of the cross, then prayed a Hail Mary, thinking about the Virgin. Mary, the mother of Jesus, one of the few women to have prominence in the Bible, who gave her body up for God's use, watched her only child tortured and killed. Not for the first time, she thought, *what women have to bear is shocking.*

A rustling movement in the yard got her attention. Nina swore she saw a figure squatting behind the shed. She thought twice about going to check, then padded downstairs, grabbed the handle of her heaviest pot and headed into the yard, leaving the girls asleep inside. In the darkness, she approached the back of the shed. A figure moved; it was something small – maybe a badger. But as she adjusted to the dark, she saw human eyes peering back at her.

"Get out!" Nina whispered loudly. She was about to scream, but the figure stood and spoke.

"Please, please," a voice whispered. Stepping into the moonlight appeared a young woman, her body swollen with child. "Please, no scream," she said, her Italian imperfect.

Nina assessed the refugee. She looked to be in her mid-twenties, likely from Austria based on her accent. The woman was dirty, wearing only one boot, her other foot wrapped in fabric. She wore a torn dress and jacket; there was a hole where she must have ripped off a Star of David patch.

"My husband dead, my baby all I have," she said, opening her jacket to reveal a clear bulge in front of her lithe frame.

"Be quiet. You wait here. I'll help you," Nina said.

"Please, no *polizia,* please," whispered the woman.

"No, no *polizia*. *Amica*." Nina pointed at herself. "I'm a mother too," she said. Leaving the woman in the shed's darkness, she paced back to the house. There could be repercussions for helping a Jew who fled German-annexed Austria, but, as a good Catholic woman, the daughter of Adelasia Argenta, she could not turn her back. She rushed around inside, grabbing a blanket and bread. The poor woman looked to be very far along, maybe seven or eight months pregnant. She couldn't imagine what this woman had gone through to end up in her shed. Without a sound, she went to the old trunk of Adelasia's clothes, pulling out a sweater her mother had worn. It would hang on this woman, but it would keep her warm. She paused a moment as she held the fabric, remembering it was the one the Captain had worn the day they sat together near *Sant'Anna*. *What else can I do?* she thought. Clothes her mother wore – hopefully they would help this woman. Nina paced catlike back behind the shed.

The silence of the night enveloped her; it was approaching two in the morning. They were the only ones not sleeping.

"What's your name?" Nina asked the woman, handing her the sweater and a piece of bread which she hurriedly bit into.

"Hannah," she said as she chewed.

"How far along are you?"

"Eight... I think." The woman slipped the garment on; it enveloped her, but she looked relieved having eaten and being wrapped in clean fabric.

"You can sleep in the shed tonight and stay there in the morning. We'll find somewhere else to hide you until you have the baby," Nina said. "I'm Nina." She gave her the reassuring smile she used with her pregnant patients. "I'll come tomorrow."

The next day, Nina watched the shed and her nerves sizzled on edge. While the war hadn't come to Fonzaso, there were several families with emphatically fascist beliefs who didn't like Jews and who could make trouble if they found out about Hannah. The race laws in Italy said Jews were outside Italian society. If Hannah was discovered, authorities would deport her. As always, most took the law as a suggestion. Many Italians had no issues with Jews, but she wouldn't risk it. Even Evira could make trouble if she found out. She hoped Tinetta, Federico and Giglio were safe. The last letter she received from them said they didn't get their paperwork on time. They hesitated too long to decide; the option to leave closed. Nina was unsure what was happening with them. The least she could do was to help this poor woman and her unborn baby. *How had she crossed the Dolomites on her own?* The strength of a woman with a child to protect was awe-inspiring. She must have kept going, step after step, incline after incline with death behind her and perhaps in front of her, but the life inside her was one she could save and she would have given every bit of her energy to make it to Nina's shed that night. She thought of Adelasia, how every time Nina's life seemed difficult, she added something onto it to help others instead of focusing on herself. This was no different. Maybe her mother had guided this woman to her.

Adelasia. The Captain.

Every day Nina lived as a woman and mother, she grew closer to her own. Funny how even death could not stop the relationship between mother and daughter evolving.

"Okay, Mamma," she whispered to herself aloud. "I'll do this. But you have to help me. I still need you."

Nina went around to her sisters and Corrado, asking them over for coffee. Her supply of real beans was depleting and everyone else except Onorina had run out so the invitation for a real cup was an easy way to ensure she had them at her house. She didn't invite Evira. They couldn't trust her in a situation like this.

When they were sitting with a hot cup in front of them, she explained about her visitor. They were astounded Hannah had crossed the mountains in her state and agreed helping her was a necessity. To start, they would move her somewhere safer. Nina remembered Pietro's childhood hideout behind the Madonna at *Sant'Anna.* Tangled overgrowth wove around the entrance, making it invisible, but she was certain they could reach it and create a safe hideaway for Hannah. From there, they could bring her food under the guise of praying to the Madonna. It would give them time to create a longer-term plan for what to do when the baby came.

In the late evening, they moved Hannah from the shed to the little hideout. Nina, Aurora and Hannah shrouded their hair in scarves and huddled together like three Argenta sisters going for a *passeggiata.* No one noticed that three women walked to *Sant'Anna,* but only two returned.

The next week began a dangerous routine. Each day the family conspired. Soon roasted chicory root substituted real coffee. They took turns bringing Hannah supplies: bread, blankets, a chamber pot, and Nina went every other day to see if the baby changed position. Hannah couldn't deliver where she was.

They would have to take her somewhere else to give birth. When Nina visited Hannah on the third night, she was agitated; it looked as though she had been pulling out her hair. Her scalp was red, and clumps of brown strands lay on the ground.

Hannah gripped her hands, eyes darting around the dim hut. In her shaking thinness, Nina thought she looked like a starving animal, scared to become the prey of a bloodthirsty predator.

"What's wrong?" Nina asked. Hannah rocked back and forth, attempting to calm herself enough to speak.

"No good to help me. I no deserve to live."

"What are you saying? Of course, you do," Nina spoke to her gently, touching her arm to calm her.

"What I did. How I got here. So awful!"

"You don't have to tell me. I'm going to help you no matter what. But if what happened is doing this to you, I'll listen." Something was eating at Hannah from inside. Nina knew the relief of confession, telling her sins to the priest, and the light feeling after absolution. She was no priest, and Hannah was not Catholic, but Nina could give her ear. She could try to understand this woman's pain.

"We live in Alps in Austria. My sister family in Vienna, when Jews a time no good. Must go away of Vienna. Sister had son, Adam, and my sister having baby. Things bad for us Jews. Very bad." Hannah squeezed her eyes closed, remembering, and continued.

"Sister husband, Rudolfo, jeweller and after shop broken four times, Jews no can have business. He close the shop and leave everything to live with us. In the country, not so much bad for Jews then. Neighbours far away and no hate us. We think we safe. I find out I with baby when Sonia and Rudolfo and Adam come. For months we live. We scared, but we hope things stop soon. Sonia have baby at my house. A beautiful girl name Edela for Austrian flower."

Nina could hear Hannah's voice tightening as she said the baby's name. She prepared herself for what was next, trying hard to listen to the woman's broken Italian and grim story. "Husbands go to town for food and come back say it not a good time. Come with *niente* because German in centre. We plan escape to the mountains but no good with baby and with me with baby. Then, we stay in house, eat from garden. Friend in the town bring us food and news. No friend. I think he tell Nazis about us." Hannah's eyes blazed as she continued.

"In morning two trucks with Germans come up hill to house. We run to yard to hide in trees behind house near mountains. I think my sister behind me, but she carry Edela and hold to little boy and husband. My husband, Nils, run upstairs for gun and hide to help us. I hide behind firewood. They grab Rudolfo and throw to wall in yard with boy and shoot them." Hannah scratched at her arms, rocking faster as she spoke.

"Sonia scream and hold Edela. So fast. Shots from the house. They kill my Nils." Tears ran down the thin woman's face, her voice becoming raspy. "Then. Then..." she stumbled. "Oh, God. Germans grab baby from my sister and tell to pull down dress. They animals. She reach for Edela and my sister did as they tell her then... oh God," she broke down again, crying and grabbing the hair around her temples with fists. "They take baby and swing her to wall, hit head over and over. My sister crazy scream... they hold her back. 'My baby'... she scream. When they done, they give baby to my sister... blood run on her breast. They leave baby on ground... make my sister go into the house. I don't know what they do to her. She scream and kitchen go on fire," she continued.

"Fire. Screams. My sister was there, she burn. I hide in

tree. I watch. I watch and I do *niente*. I watch they kill... I did *niente*. I should be dead. No here with you, tell you my story, confess my bad and coward. I no deserve to live. I need to go in fire and die. To burn, but now I burn with remorse. I deserve no to live and punishment is I do."

"Oh my God," cried Nina. "Please God, no."

"Yes. My God. Germans pure evil and I do *niente*. I hide and get sick and do nothing and my sister family I see die... my husband die."

"Hannah, there was nothing you could have done to change it." Nina grasped the woman's hands, wishing she could ease her pain. She was reminded looking at Hannah's swollen belly of Adelasia's words. *Women create, men destroy.*

"How I live? Only baby and I no know how I bring to this miserable world." She paused and continued.

"I wait for Nazis to leave and I climb into mountain. No sure if I live or die. I keep moving... remember paths my father show, eat what I find on way, not care if I die. I come over *Dolomiti* and your statue I see." She pointed into the air. "She no mine, but I know follow to your Mary, the mother of your saviour, hope. *Madre* of a Jew. And she bring me to you."

Rita fidgeted in her chair, the rough waist of her skirt scratching her ribs and making her itch. She made a face, turned her skirt and tried to settle herself once again. Ouch. There, now it was squeezing her side.

"I wish Mamma would let this out. It's too tight." She wriggled, trying to loosen the waist, twisting in her chair and biting her lower lip.

"Rita Pante, stop fidgeting," her nursery teacher, Sister Lina, called to her.

Madonna! she thought. *I'm always in trouble. I can't help it if my skirt is too tight – and so itchy.* She found the button and zipper and undid them.

Ah, that's better. Just as she released the pressure of her skirt, a gnat landed on her neck. She swatted it away. She was getting hot and let out a sigh.

The sound came out louder than she expected.

"Rita Pante, you are interrupting this class!"

"But I can't help it. It's hot, and I need to use the toilet," Rita protested.

"Let me finish the lesson, and I'll take the class." Sister Lina turned back towards the chalkboard.

"I can go. I know where the toilet is. I don't need you to take me."

"Fine," Sister Lina said, exasperated. "Come back right after." She pointed at the corridor.

I don't need anyone to walk me to the toilet. I'm not a baby, Rita thought as she left the classroom. Her skirt fell low on her hips, making the class giggle behind her.

The foyer was empty and dark. As she looked at the convent entrance, she had an idea. Could she escape? A column next to the door looked like the perfect hiding place. She ducked behind it. Mamma had been around little these past three days. Rita decided she would run home. Her mother would be there, maybe sitting at the table canning fruits. She'd smile at Rita when she came in, tell her to sit and help. Rita would bask in their time alone; maybe Mamma would spread raspberry jam on bread for her, she'd savour its sweetness then fall asleep for a nap by Mamma's side. It would be a glorious afternoon! The entry bell ringing interrupted her fantasy, indicating a visitor. She prepared herself, keeping hidden. Seeing a stick on the ground, she grabbed it, then jumped back to her spot as Mother Beatrice came to welcome the visitor. The nun led away the adult who entered as Rita's arm snuck around, poking the stick into the crack between the hinges. It stopped the door from clicking shut. Mother Beatrice closed the office door behind the visitor and Rita took her chance. She squeezed out the door, barrelling out onto the pavement, her little legs sprinting across town, up the road towards her house. She ran fast, sticking her palm out to swat the Giocomins' geraniums, leaving confetti of red petals behind her. Her shoe squished into the leftovers of a mule which slowed her down. She wiped her foot and kept running. *Mamma!* With every step, her excitement rose. A scruffy dog crossed her path then ran beside her for a few metres before the house came into view. She burst through the gate breathless and opened the door.

"Mamma!" she cried.

Her mother wasn't in the kitchen; maybe she was sweeping the sitting room.

"Mamma!"

No one was there.

She ran up the stairs. Perhaps she was napping after the late nights midwifing. Rita looked in her room.

No one.

Tears stung Rita's eyes, panic crept into her chest. The silence taunted her.

"Mamma?" she called, but no one answered. Rita's hope was deflating. What about the goat house? Maybe Mamma was tending to the animals; she could help. She closed the gate behind her. Tears rolled down her face.

"No one loves me; no one cares about me," she said aloud, making herself even more upset as the dramatic words left her mouth. Once inside the shed, she glanced around. There was no sign of her mother, but the goat stuck his tongue out at her and she reciprocated. A ladder leading to the hayloft above caught her attention.

What's up there? she wondered, curious and dismissing her sorrows in the wake of this new experience before her. She grabbed the rungs and climbed until she reached the loft.

"Oh! *Mamma mia!*" Hay stretched out in front of her. The unbundled, golden straw looked lush and squishy. She crawled into its warmth, inhaling the earthy smell, and sunk gently until she made her way to a shady corner with a view of the street. The excitement and tears had exhausted her; soon she was fast asleep.

"Rita. Rita are you up there?"

She awoke to someone calling her name. The sun, which had been shining brightly through the loft opening, was dim and cast a golden peach hue across the horizon outside. She crawled carefully to the opening to peek out. Below stood Nonno Corrado with Sister Lina.

"Rita, there you are! Please come down, or I'm going to be in trouble." The nun wrung her hands, pleading.

Sister Lina looked pitiful, younger than she did in the classroom. Rita felt a pang of guilt along with hunger in her belly, so she made her way down the ladder. Straw pricked out from her hair and her uniform was wrinkled. By the time she left the shed, Mamma had appeared. She grabbed Rita by the arm, swatting at her bottom, promising the wooden spoon when they got home. But it was okay with Rita, even if she was being spanked, at least her mother was paying attention to her.

CHAPTER 26

Nina tried to breathe, but breath escaped her. In the distance, Hitler stood in front of a crowd on a platform with Mussolini next to him. "*Heil*," the mob called. "*Heil Hitler,*" they repeated. She was holding onto Rita's hand, feeling the girl's small, sweaty palm. "Mamma, I want to watch the show," she said. Fear caught Nina's breath. They would catch her! They would take her children. Pietro would never forgive her. In an instant, Rita was gone. She scanned the crowd in a panic. She cried out, but no words came. The sun shone so brightly she had to squint. Coloured light in blues and oranges took over from the sunlight as if through stained glass, then turned to red. Rita's head appeared again in the crowd, Nina reached for her, but when the child turned around, it wasn't Rita but another girl of seven or eight in a lace Communion dress, with empty eyes and a Star of David on her chest. The sun shone brightly again and the girl disappeared. Nina gasped aloud, opening her eyes. Sweat drenched her nightdress as she realised it was a nightmare. She lay still, staring at the ceiling, heart racing until restless sleep came to her.

They devised a plan for Hannah. Her baby would stay with them until after the war while she attempted to get to Switzerland. She would stay in Aurora's cantina towards the last week of her pregnancy. They would seed a rumour, say the baby belonged to a cousin of Adelasia's in Rome. When Hannah was ready, and it was safe, she would come back for the baby. It was risky, but they knew the Captain was watching over them, and they could not turn back.

On a warm weekday before the planned move, Nina went to visit Hannah. Lizards scampered in and out of the rock walls. Pink oleander brightened the path. How serene and normal the world looked on the surface. When she arrived at the hideout and peered inside, it was obvious the time had come. The woman lay on the ground with a pinched look on her face, stifling her cries. She was in heavy labour and they needed to move her immediately. Nina ran back to alert the others. Corrado had his cart and donkey close by, their secret ambulance. They helped the woman in, covering her with blankets despite the heat of the day.

The cart jostled over bumps onto the street where Aurora lived. As soon as they arrived at the house, away from prying eyes, Aurora and Onorina pulled everything off Hannah as rapidly as they could.

"Are you okay?" asked Aurora.

Weakly, Hannah nodded. "Water, *per favore,*" she panted.

"Of course." They grabbed Hannah under her arms, rushing her down the stairs to the *cantina.*

A side room used for storing preserves became the birthing room and they laid an old mattress stuffed with corn husks on the ground. The temperature there was cool. "Here," Aurora said, handing her a cup of water as Nina helped her lie down. Hannah was unable to drink it before crying out in pain, "Aaahh!" She attempted to control the volume and whispered to Nina, "It starting."

"*Sì*, your baby is on the way. We'll take care of you. Here, drink a little," Nina said. This time she held Hannah's head, bringing the cup to her lips.

Aurora placed a damp rag on Hannah's forehead, cooling her down in between contractions.

The day dragged on. Nina worried about the baby. She'd struggled to hear the heartbeat through her Pinard horn but did not mention her concerns to Hannah. She needed her to be strong and focus on pushing the baby out. When it came time for Hannah to push, it was nearing ten o'clock. The families of Fonzaso were in for the night. Nina knew the cries of childbirth were hard to contain. The *cantina* would muffle the sound, but Hannah would have to hold in her pain. Aurora sat next to Hannah, squeezing her hand.

"She's ready," Nina said as she prepared the towels and the basin to clean the baby.

"Here," she bent to Hannah's side, handing her a towel. "Bite on this to get through the pain. It won't be long before you meet your baby."

Hannah did as she was told.

"Listen to me. I'll count, you push. Hold it until I tell you to let go. Do you understand?"

Hannah nodded yes.

Nina assumed her position between Hannah's legs. It was hard to stabilise herself on the floor-level mattress, but she had seen her mother do it many times.

Aurora and Onorina helped Hannah lean up to a near squatting position. She groaned, biting hard on the towel.

"Now push, 1-2-3-4-5." A small tuft of the baby's hair peeked out.

"Push," Nina said again. "Breathe, Hannah. You're doing well." Nina focused. For the moment, her mind did not worry about war, or children or anything but this woman in front of her and the life between her legs.

"Push, 1-2-3-4-5."

Again, Hannah bit down, crying as sweat beaded on her forehead.

"Push, 1-2-3..." Nina bent again. The baby's head was crowning. "The baby's coming," she told her. "Push, 1-2-3-4-5."

Hannah pushed. The head came out a few centimetres, then retreated into the wet folds of its mother.

"Hannah, one more push and the head will be delivered," Nina said, sounding calm, but excited as she always was at this point in a delivery. Hannah smiled through gritted teeth, gathering what energy she had left. Onorina and Aurora murmured words of encouragement, ready for the miracle of birth.

"My baby, my life," Hannah said.

"Here we go," Nina said. Aurora moved to the other side, preparing to take the baby to clean and wrap to limit the noise of the crying.

"Push, 1-2-3-4-5."

Hannah pushed with all her might, closing her eyes.

"Here it comes," Nina said, feeling the baby's shoulders twist free, pulling the baby smoothly from there.

Nina saw there would be no cry as she looked at the child, a little girl. Her flaccid body was dusky grey, a wilted flower. She was still.

No, God, she thought. *Please, no.* She looked up at Onorina and Aurora and shook her head.

"What's wrong?" Hannah gasped. "My baby? No cry?"

Nina's head was low; she handed the infant to Aurora, who

cleaned the baby, wrapped her little body in a blanket and sat next to Hannah on the ground.

"Hold her," Nina said. "For all this time, she felt your love, and she was with you through everything. Hold her. Say goodbye."

Trembling in agony, the broken woman reached out with love for her dead child. She kissed her little forehead and rocked her, whispering to the baby in a language foreign to Nina. When it was time, they put her in a small box and promised Hannah they would bury her safely so she could rest and then, eventually, move on.

A week later, Hannah, who spoke almost no words after the death of her daughter, left in the night, following their plans to get her to Switzerland.

After several weeks passed, they heard of a Jewish woman who drowned in Lake Como. Nina wondered if it was Hannah. She prayed she hadn't given up, with safety so close. Yet she imagined exactly what Hannah would have done. The same thing she wanted to do when Teo died – when it seemed there was no hope. Hannah would have walked in step by step, the blue ripples of the deep lake surrounding her, water entering her lungs, filling the emptiness her child left within her until she faded away forever.

CHAPTER 27

By 1941, Nina felt a shift within her. Over six years had passed without seeing Pietro, the longest since they were married. She hadn't received a letter in over two years. The men were gone. Pietro was long gone. He wasn't here to take up Mussolini's war. *Il Duce* had the world turning on Italy. He had followed his friend in Germany, declaring war on Britain and France. Canada, Australia, New Zealand and South Africa declared war against Italy. He brought his army into Greece, trying to replicate Hitler's advances. But, despite *il Duce's* attempts to cajole rural citizens, few of the women in town were nationalistic in the way he would have liked. They skimmed the *Massaie Rurali* newspaper for anything that might benefit them, soon realising the propaganda-filled paper was most useful for starting fires in their stoves.

One of the parish priests responsible for the church bulletin died, so *La Squilla di San Michele* stopped being published. It was sad. The end of an era. Nina used to fold it up and add it to her letters to Pietro. It made him so happy with its updates about life in Fonzaso. The last issue mentioned news of the Royal Army being sent into Russia, troops from Italy sent to the freezing Eastern Front to join Germany's invasion. Nina wondered how long it would continue.

This war, these times with the girls, it was all on her. There was fear, strangeness, but also freedom for women like her. She lay on the bed, revelling in it for a while. She controlled this small domain; she was powerful. She was her own captain.

Steam filled the windows in Aurora's house as the cold of the outside met the warm air and breath inside. They sat, huddled next to the fire with the radio on. Japan had bombed Pearl Harbor on Sunday. The next day, America had declared war on Japan, ally to Germany and Italy. They waited to find out what would happen next. Aurora adjusted the dials to manage the fuzzy sound around the foreign station. "Turn it up!" Corrado directed unhelpfully from the rocking chair.

"*Allora,* Papà, that's as loud as it goes." Aurora shook her hand towards their father.

Nina watched her daughter, sitting across from her on the sofa, knitting. Lasia winced at the squeak in airwaves. The girl hadn't spoken a word to Nina in three days, since she sent them to school with no coal. Mother Beatrice had slapped Lasia's hands hard with a ruler; hurting her in front of the class as punishment for not bringing a contribution. She had been humiliated; angry because they'd had coal, but Nina shared it with Pietro's family and Evira. Nina looked at her oldest daughter, soon to turn twelve, and noticed her nimble fingers, looping yarn around the needles. Piles of slippers in mismatched wools of yellow, grey, red and brown sat atop a basket filled with balls of tightly wound yarn of varying sizes, leftovers of Nonna Margherita. The slippers were Christmas gifts for the family, meant to keep their feet off cold floors. Nina studied her daughter. Despite the girl's thinness, breasts were budding in a dress long past needing to be replaced. Nina had taken for granted that Lasia would always be a child, but she realised a young woman, a capable *ragazza* sat before her.

Music played and Corrado, who had drifted off to sleep to the lull of the radio and the warmth of the fire, snored rhythmically. Aurora prepared polenta, waiting for her daughter, Milena, and Rita to return from playing in the snow. The fire kept their torsos warm, but their feet were perpetually cold, so Nina stretched her legs towards the flames to warm them.

"Mamma," Lasia said. Nina opened her eyes, waiting for the girl to speak. "I've decided." Whatever Lasia had to say, Nina was glad she was talking to her again. "I'm not going back to school after Christmas. I'd be done after this year, anyway. Silvia Moreno told me she'd take me as an apprentice seamstress. She'll even pay me. Then I can help you." Nina readied herself to argue, not prepared for the consideration Lasia might make choices of her own. She opened her mouth to object as the announcer came over the airwaves. Aurora raced into the room to be close to the radio and Corrado woke from his nap, straining to hear the broadcast.

It had happened.

America declared war on Japan so Germany and Italy had declared war on America. Nina put her head in her hands. The room spun. The flames which warmed her minutes before were now too hot, suffocating, and she couldn't get air into her lungs. Silence was heavy in the room. After a few endless minutes, Aurora turned the radio dial off with a click.

"Mamma, did you hear what I said before?" Lasia asked.

Nina lifted her head and with dead eyes, looked at her daughter. The realisation that her country was at war with Pietro's was already causing her temples to throb.

"Do what you want, Lasia. It doesn't matter now."

CHAPTER 28

Summer 1942 Nina's fair northern skin turned olive brown from days spent outside tending their plot, picking courgettes from under broad, prickly leaves and getting every tomato off its vine. The air was stifling. The sour odour of perspiration became permanent in clothes washed with soap made from animal fat. She divided her life between the land, the animals, cooking and midwifing occasionally. As for the girls, she felt she never saw them except in small bouts when Rita might chance by the house to grab her marbles, or Lasia brought her water. She stood at the doorway and watched them sleep each night, lying on their backs with their hands folded over their chests as she taught them and prayed to the Virgin Mary for their protection.

On the hottest day of the summer, Don Cavalli asked Nina to deliver Bettina Napoli's baby. It was an illegitimate birth; Bettina was a widow whose abusive husband died in Libya. She refused to remarry and had little family left. Nina remembered her as the beautiful girl, once the envy of so many, riding in the *Festa dell'Uva* parade. She had fallen from grace. Adelasia taught Nina not to judge – every woman deserved the same care, but this child's life would be a struggle. Bettina refused to name the father. Most people preferred not to know. While she was not a prostitute per se, men in the area knew that her door and her legs were always open provided a gift of lire or something equally valuable was exchanged.

It was the wrong time to be having a baby, in the summer heat when cool water was hard to come by, in the middle of a war making everything hard to come by. Nina wiped her forehead, walking back into the room. Her throat was dry, the thirst overwhelming. The air smelled stale with sweat and birth.

"Will you sit with me, Nina?" Bettina asked.

"*Sì,*" Nina said, sitting down in a rickety chair next to the bed, covered in papers she tossed to the ground, taking one to fan herself and her patient.

"I want to tell you something," Bettina said.

Nina hesitated. "You don't need to tell me what's not my business. It doesn't matter to me who the father of your child is, as long as the baby gets here safely."

What if Bettina named someone? Nina didn't want to know. She wouldn't judge, but she also was not a priest, and confessions of this nature were not her forte.

"I hope you know better than to judge me. I'm trying to survive like anyone else. If I want to eat, I have to get it from lying on my back. So what?" She winced as a contraction came. "No, I wanted you to know... this isn't my first baby."

"So, you know what to expect and what you'll need to do," Nina replied plainly, replacing the cloth on the woman's head with a fresh one.

Bettina continued, "I gave up my first baby. A little girl. She had thick black curls... so beautiful. The family who adopted her was rich. They longed for a child. She's in a good place." Nina could see tears on the rims of Bettina's eyes.

"I'm glad for it," Nina said, meaning it.

"Your mother helped me find the couple. She delivered the baby and took it to the family. She was a wonderful woman," said Bettina.

"Yes, she was," replied Nina. "She was."

Nina came home late; the girls were in bed but awake.

"Mamma, we were worried about you," Lasia said. "How did the birth go?"

She sat and told them. "An unmarried woman got pregnant. Her body nearly split in two giving birth. When I held the baby up, I saw his face was deformed with a nose like a pig's snout and missing parts behind his lip. I took him to the convent. The nuns will take care of him because his mother cannot. Pray for him."

"Mamma, will they go to hell? Since the mother wasn't married? Is that why the baby didn't come out right?" asked Rita.

"No, *bambina.* I blessed the baby myself; they'll baptise him and God isn't cruel. As for the mother, if she asks for forgiveness, he'll wash her of her sins and give her a place."

Lasia spent her days at Signora Morena's learning to be a seamstress. She'd traded the brutality of the nuns for a new cruelty. Nothing was good enough for Silvia Morena. Lasia stitched, Silvia ripped. The *signora* called everything uneven and tore apart perfectly acceptable work to be resewn until it was flawless. Lasia didn't complain. It was good of Silvia to give her the apprenticeship. Most of the time the work was in solitude, which suited Lasia. The *signora* was also one of the few people who had a radio which she played as they sewed. The enchanting voice of Alberto Rabagliati singing '*Sposi*' lulled in the background. If Lasia focused enough, she could forget where she was until the next time Signora Morena ripped the fabric from her hands. Content in the silence of her sewing, she could even dream of a time when things would return to normal. Sometimes, the news interrupted the music and Lasia would hear things she didn't understand about places she couldn't imagine like Singapore and Bataan. None of it was good; she worried about her uncles in Russia and Africa, wishing only music played from the radio.

Lasia tried to focus on her stitches, but her eyes were heavy. She struggled with the needle, poking it into her finger to awaken her senses. After four hours of sewing and having Silvia Morena sending terse looks her way, she had to use the toilet and it was time to go.

"May I take some scraps for my sister?" Lasia asked.

One of the neighbour's cats had ripped Rita's rag doll to shreds. Lasia was sure she had antagonised it. Their neighbour, Signora Curto, kept many cats outside in a miniature model house that was the ultimate curiosity for small children. She felt bad for her little sister. It was the only doll she had. Where was their father? What happened to the letters? The money he used to send? It seemed he had forgotten them.

"Take the scraps," Silvia croaked in reply, "but it comes out of your pay."

Lasia was excited to have a gift for Rita, grinning to herself as she walked through the piazza. When she passed the church, a group of boys appeared, kicking a *calcio* ball between them. A rogue kick sent the ball flying her way, landing with a plunk at her feet. A boy in shorts ran to collect it, from his light-blond hair she knew it was Nico.

"*Ciao,* Lasia! Do you want to play?" he asked, flipping the ball from one hand to the other in a smooth gesture.

"Oh no. I'm heading home for supper and to fix Rita's doll."

"You're lucky not to go to school anymore. All we do is talk about how great *il Duce* is... how we should long to fight for Italy. *Credere, Obbedire, Combattere!* Believe, Obey, Fight!" He shook his fist in the air as he repeated the mantra, then shrugged his shoulders, looking up at Mount Avena. "My papà's gone, did you know? I'd much rather have him home. I think he'd rather be home, too." Nico tossed the ball back to the other boys, then turned to Lasia, "I'll go with you."

They walked through the maze of streets while Nico updated Lasia about the kids at school. As usual, he bragged about his brother, Abramo, how he'd caught an enormous fish and was the third fastest boy in Fonzaso. She smiled, finding it endearing how he idolised his older sibling. When they said goodbye at the gate, Lasia swore she saw him linger until she was in the house, the sun setting behind his golden head.

She went upstairs and found Rita lying on their bed, asleep in her clothes. Lasia carefully repaired the doll then tucked it under Rita's arm for her to discover when she awoke.

At night, Nina lay awake staring at the ceiling. Was it possible for her to keep doing it all? Taking care of the animals, the children, midwifing, mending everything. She was falling behind, failing. She used to depend on the letters from Pietro and without them, hope of a life beyond

Fonzaso disappeared. The town that was her haven became her prison. She was trapped in Italy without knowing what was happening with her husband. Why did they choose these circumstances? How stupid they were. Maybe they shouldn't have married. Maybe she should have married someone who would have stayed in Fonzaso, who was off at war? Thinking it made her feel guilty. She gazed forlornly at her rosary. Was there any hope of her getting the life she'd dreamed about when she was young? It seemed hopeless. She let herself doze, giving in to the departure of her troubled thoughts.

While her mother slept, Rita had her own plan. A midnight adventure! She stood at her windowsill directing her friends who had tossed a stone into her bedroom to let her know they'd arrived. "Shhh, *silenzio!*" she whispered to Francesco, Carlo and Giovanni. "If you aren't quiet, my mamma will come. You won't have any fun without me!" They scolded and pushed each other, then referred to her for guidance.

"How will you get down? You'll break your arm if you jump. We can't promise to catch you," whispered Carlo.

"Make a staircase. You hold on to his shoulders. You get on his back. I'll climb down," she said. They looked at each other with quizzical faces, tried and failed. With further flurried directions from Rita, sharp whispers and frantic hand gestures, she got them in place. At seven, she was a slight girl; they barely felt her weight as she climbed over them to get down.

"Well?" They looked at their leader for the next move. "What should we do now? Where should we go?"

"The cemetery," she told them. "We'll play hide-and-go-seek then we can throw rocks at old man Spanini's window. *Il vecchio bacucco* will never catch us."

Carlo's eyes widened. "No way!" he said. "I'm not going to the cemetery at night! I'll throw rocks at Signor Spanini's again, but I'm not going to the cemetery."

"Yes, you are, you little baby, or else go home," Rita threatened him. She was nervous too, but had to maintain her tough reputation. They needed to recognise she wasn't their equal, but their leader, even if she was younger than them. The Fonzaso night was black, but the moon was low between the mountains. Its pearlescent glow lit their path.

"I can't believe we're doing this," said Giovanni. "It's crazy." They caught fireflies, watching them flash in their cupped hands, crinkling their noses at the acrid scent the frightened bugs gave off.

They reached the gate to the cemetery and lifted the latch. Finding it unlocked, they crept in, afraid of what or who might be there. Rita snuck behind a marble headstone as the boys proceeded forward. She wanted to scare them. Heart beating in her ears, she waited until Francesco whispered, "Where's Rita?" They looked around. She snuck closer, tiptoeing behind each headstone until she was within arm's reach of Francesco. The other boys moved ahead, and she reached out with her cold little hand and poked his neck. He jumped with a shout, growing close to tears until Rita revealed herself.

"You're a scaredy-cat," Rita said. "*Mio Dio,* are you three years old or eight?"

They picked up sticks and walked around, knocking rocks off headstones, then lay down on a grave, looking up at the stars.

"Wow, this is something," said Francesco. "Our parents would never guess we aren't in our beds sleeping!"

"Hmmph," Rita sneered in disagreement. "My mamma

could wake up tomorrow, go about making breakfast, kiss my sister goodbye and not even notice I wasn't there. She leaves me to myself. I don't care anyway. I like my freedom."

"She'd miss you," Carlo said. "And she'd have a wooden spoon to your *culo* if she knew you were out here! I know your mamma. You might not have a papà, but she's tough enough for two parents."

"I have a papà!" cried Rita, furious at his mention of her father. "He's a hero and a millionaire. He lives in America. He's getting everything ready so after the war ends I can go live there. I'll have a four-poster bed and lots of dolls and he's going to take me to every Shirley Temple movie. He'll make sure I have new dresses so I won't have to wear Lasia's cast-offs anymore. I'll go to an American school with *no* nuns!" She spurted out these details without hesitation. They were, after all, memorised dreams. She could even picture her mamma in a house in America and her future American friends.

The group got up and shuffled along, trading yawns. Sleep was becoming more enticing than strolling around the silent town, so they headed back towards their homes. As they passed the convent, a muted light glowed from the cellar of a nearby house. They crept closer to investigate. Three men and a woman sat around a candle wedged in a Chianti bottle. They spoke in low voices, but Rita thought she heard one of them call the other "Fumo". She swore the girl looked like her cousin, Mary, Zia Onorina's daughter. There was something clandestine about the meeting, and they looked at each other, acknowledging they should leave without being seen.

"I know them, but it's a secret," Francesco whispered to Rita while the others tiptoed backwards. "They're helping British soldiers hiding in the mountains. Your cousin's English comes in handy. She translates." Rita stared at Francesco jealous of his secret and not sure she believed him.

For a last bit of excitement, they headed to old Signor Spanini's and began their stone-tossing at his window, ready to run at any moment. When they were about to throw the third rock, the window opened and tepid liquid poured down on them, splashing on the cobbles. As they ran away, they heard Signor Spanini laughing behind them, calling out, "There you go, you little shits! You like teasing an old man? I saved my pee for a week. Come back when you want more!"

Disgusted, they jumped into the fountain in the piazza to rinse off. After, they ran home and struggled to get back into their houses, falling asleep with the smell of urine permeating their dreams.

The next week, Rita was in the care of her Zia Onorina while Nina saw about a birth. She joined her cousins playing on the mountainside while her aunt collected vegetables. Rita liked to show off to Onorina's kids, and today she educated them on how to light the end of long blades of straw and pretend they were smoking. Her box of matches was a secret treasure of which her mother was unaware.

When they were bored with their pretend cigarettes, they launched into a game of rolling down the hillside. Each of them ran up as high as they could, then lay down, rolling as grass tangled in their hair. On the fifth time up, Rita beat her cousins to the top and found herself alone, walking through a line of chestnut trees. She browsed mushrooms and watched ladybugs wrestle with each other on rocks. When she turned to go back down, she noticed two black boots sticking out of a pile of leaves. Her eyes widened as she inched towards them, then kicked one lightly with her toe. It didn't give. There was a leg attached.

Screaming, she ran down the hill to Zia Onorina with her cousins following behind her.

"Zia Onorina, there's a body!" she cried. "Right up there in the trees. I saw it."

Onorina hesitated. "Go get your Zio Toni. Show him what you've found."

Toni was at the *alimentari* and left Mary to watch the shop while he followed Rita.

"It's up there!" Rita explained to him, jumping from foot to foot with excitement. Toni followed Rita as she led him up the hill and into the chestnut trees. Sure enough, amid the leaves and branches, boots stuck up from the ground. Rita pointed but stood away, not wanting to see more. Toni shook his head.

"That's a soldier's body," he said. He leaned over to pull the boots off of the dead feet before they headed back to town to alert the *polizia*.

Rita followed her *zio* to the centre, wanting to see him tell the police about her find. She was ready for her congratulations. Maybe there was even a prize for finding dead soldiers. But the normal police officer wasn't at his station, so Toni placed the boots inside the doorway of his house on the Via Mezzaterra and continued towards the taverna to find another official. As they arrived, they could see something was amiss. Everyone was talking in the piazza. Something else had occurred in the mountains.

Rita loitered around the tables of old men playing cards to overhear the story of what happened from Signor Ceccon and Nonno Corrado. She heard the middle daughter of the Corsos married a man from Monfalcone. The couple was moving to her husband's family nearer to Trieste, with their toddler. They left two days before, and the family waited to hear they had settled.

"Those fascist idiots stopped them in the mountains...

asked for their papers and when Marco challenged, they became angry. Those Blackshirt fools only want to pick a fight. They can't read and have nothing of their own. They think because they are brutes of *il Duce* they can do what they please. One of them shot Marco and when Seraphina ran to him, they shot her. They went into the back seat where the baby was sleeping and..." Signor Ceccon was interrupted by Corrado. "Are you so sure it was the fascists who did it? This seems like something those partisan hooligans would have done, no? They're murderers and thieves, making life hell for everyone."

Corrado stopped as Rita peered from behind the table. No one had seen her. Signor Ceccon gave Corrado a grave look and pointed at Rita. Whoever had done it, the fascists or the bad partisans, she understood what had happened. They had killed the child, too.

The next day, when Rita went to the *Alimentari Bianchi* after school, she noticed her uncle's new boots. As she sat on a stool watching people come in, the bell rang. In walked a *fascista* soldier with his black shirt buttoned to his neck and a local girl on his arm. Rita had never seen him before, but the girl looked familiar, a young woman from Arten. The man stood at the counter, asking Zio Toni for tobacco. He handed the Blackshirt a pouch and took his lire with a smile.

In the winter of 1942, snow fell for six days straight, covering Fonzaso in white. Almost no one had coal left, so the family crowded into Nina's house to share the warmth. Corrado looked unwell, but he did his best not to complain even when Nina handed him a bowl of polenta with nothing to accompany it. He patted her arm and sat on the big chair as

Rita lounged on the floor next to him, taking advantage of her closeness to the fire to throw pieces of her hair in and watch them sizzle. They covered the lamps with black fabric, a new precaution. Lasia mended faded garments, having unwound a tablecloth for thread. The pile next to her was high, there was no such thing as replacing anymore.

Two weeks later, the cold was worse and rations more sparse. They celebrated Christmas with little flourish and Lasia's birthday along with it. Nina found herself, again, at the end of a year. She sat alone in her kitchen long after the girls had gone to bed. It felt silly to bother to wait until the year changed. What would the next year hold to look forward to? She poured herself a glass of Marsala wine, a gift from one of the latest deliveries, and watched thick flakes of snow fall outside on the Via Calzen. The sky was dark blue, stars shone through like pinpricks of the heavens between rooftops; the blackouts made them more pronounced. It was incredible. Even in times of great distress, even during war, there were moments like these. Moments of extreme peace and beauty that tricked you into remembering a time when there was no war, no *Führer*, no *Duce*. She touched the frosty glass and shivered. A voice from behind startled her.

"Mamma, I can't sleep." Lasia descended the last two steps. "Can I sit with you?"

"Of course, *mia bella ragazza*," Nina said. She smiled, watching Lasia pull out a chair. She felt sorry for this child. Their struggles were taking a toll on the sensitive girl. She should send her back to bed, but she appreciated the company.

Where Nina once found herself frustrated with Lasia as a coughing homebody, she now appreciated Lasia's dependability. She could see remarkable qualities in her oldest daughter. The concern and worry Lasia showed for

Nina's welfare was extraordinary; her patience with Rita was a godsend. Nina let Lasia grow up without making time to influence the outcome. Her baby was gone, there was no rewinding time.

"Here, try some, you're old enough." Nina poured a small glass of Marsala and slid it to Lasia. The girl sipped the red liquid and winced at the taste. The gesture caused memories to tumble into Nina's head. Corrado giving her a first drink of real wine, not watered down as they usually did for children, warm in the mouth, pungent but sweet. Then another memory, catching Pietro giving Lasia her first cup of coffee. She smiled. Her mind settled on a final memory, sitting across from Adelasia on a chilly night in the candlelight during the last war. She held back tears and thanked God for the child in front of her, eyes shining from the burn of the wine. On a snowy night sitting together during a war, they were happy.

"*Buon anno,* Lasietta," Nina said, holding her glass to the girl.

"*Buon anno.* Happy New Year, Mamma," Lasia replied, as they clinked glasses in the dim light.

CHAPTER 29

ugust 1943 Maria returned from Rome. Since the Allies landed in Sicily, it wasn't safe there any longer. Roman merchants were sandbagging their shops to prepare for bombings. King Vittorio Emanuele deposed Mussolini, had him arrested and held captive at *Gran Sasso.* The tides had turned for the great *il Duce.* Maria hoped to marry her sweetheart, Luigi Corso, when he returned. The tales she told from Rome were harrowing; stories of suspected partisans pulled in by the fascist Blackshirts and Nazis for questioning and then disappearing. People disappearing was normal, she said.

Murder was evil, and evil had become commonplace. The lives of men were a commodity. No one knew the whereabouts of the deported Jews. Nina heard of a train of cattle cars going through Padua filled with people begging for water as it moved north. *What if Federico and Giglio were on those trains?* The stories Maria told Nina made her sick. Each night in bed she pushed away images of toddlers being pulled from their parents, sent to camps where conditions were God knows what. She wanted to believe it was hearsay, but after Hannah's story, she knew the Nazis were capable of anything. The images tortured her, making her want to protect her daughters even more. The war was too close. The danger, too familiar. When joy and comfort are replaced with far off threats that haven't yet reached your gate, it was incredible how normal life could appear. Nina thought, *It appears people believe if their piece of life is intact, they can dispense of everything else.* Apathy comes when you have no control, when you are trying to provide; how little it takes for humans to turn into scavengers. Kindness is replaced with cynicism as people turn inward, shutting off the need to connect unless for their own gain or preservation.

On a grey day in the autumn of 1943, droplets of rain raced down the windowpanes outside Nina's kitchen where Aurora sipped chicory coffee. Nina sat across from her, observing her sister, noticing her sallow cheeks as she hummed and wrote a list of what she needed to do to prepare for winter. *How full and rosy her cheeks had been before the war!* Her eyes held the energy and optimism that was Aurora, but thin lines sprung from the corners. Nina thought fondly, she was still her good-humoured baby sister.

"So, I hear you're still having problems with rationing at the bakery," Nina teased.

Aurora shrugged. "Well, I'm not the brightest, you know, sometimes I lose a few things." She winked at Nina. The *Podestà* expected a strict inventory from Toni but Aurora always miscounted. Magically those with young children or a sweet *nonna* got an extra bit. Nico had helped at the bakery, too. Between them, much bread ended up where it was needed without coupons. "Be careful, Aurora. Don't bring any trouble to yourself."

"I have to do something. Things are getting worse. Besides, I was never good at maths. You know, I have a woman's brain," she said sarcastically and batted her eyelashes. Nina shook her head, remembering it was Aurora's strongest subject in school.

Aurora's expression turned serious and she leaned towards Nina. "We need a plan to protect the children. I don't mean to upset you, Ninetta, but have you heard the stories?"

"Yes, I hear things from Maria, and Corrado's careful but tells me sometimes what he finds out in the taverna. I think many more people are partisans than you realise, probably in the mountains too." Nina spoke only loud enough for Aurora to hear, not wanting to wake the girls upstairs.

"*Allora,* the partisans. You know they torment us too! They barged into the bakery and stole half what we had for Monday! And have you heard about the Russians fighting for the Germans?"

"The Russians are fighting with the rest of Europe, against Germany," Nina said.

"Not all of them. Since Mussolini's been captured, they're coming in to Italy and loads of Nazis as well. There's a group of these Cossack Russians out east. They're terrible. The stories I've heard, Nina! They're monsters: raiding towns, burning houses down if they think partisans live in them. And they take what they want." She glared at Nina with wide eyes. "*Anything* they want." The words settled between them. Silence held as they both imagined what 'anything' meant. Nina's mind flashed to Lasia.

"The world's ending; we're living in madness. It will come to Fonzaso any day," Aurora said, standing to grab a rag and wipe the table.

"Please be quiet." Nina kept her tone low. "I can't have the girls hear. Lasia's already nervous as it is."

"Do you think we could leave?" Aurora asked, as if she had just thought of the idea. "Take the children, go through Switzerland? I'm sure we could contact Pietro from there."

Nina shook her head. "Don't be crazy. We couldn't leave Papà and everyone else. Imagine what's in those mountains! Partisans and Germans. You dream." She paused, knowing even if she were willing, it would be impossible with little money, so many small children and no certainty of Pietro's whereabouts.

"*Allora,* I fear for us."

"Stop," Nina said, squeezing her sister's shoulder. "You're scared. So am I, but all we can do is pray. There's no leaving." She reached for her sister's hand, squeezed it and continued.

"We'll help each other, whatever comes. Don't forget Adelasia's blood runs through our veins."

In September 1943, Nina sat in Aurora's house, listening to the radio, waiting for the music to end to hear what was happening on the news. With Mussolini captured and the armistice between the King and the Allies, they hoped the end was in sight. She wanted it to be over. Closing her eyes, she let Alberto Rabagliati sing '*La Strada Nel Bosco*' to her. It played sweetly, filling the room with memories and regret. In her mind, Pietro appeared before her, with a warm smile.

The romantic notes filled her ears as he walked towards her. He wrapped his arm around her back, took her hand with his free one, pulling her close so she could feel the heat of his breath on her neck. He swayed her back and forth as the tune played. It spoke of a path, like the paths they had walked together long ago. The music continued; she could feel his arms around her, the solidness of him as if it were real. The sweet lyrics spoke of lovers following their hearts and love that would last forever.

He spun her around, flirting with her through his eyes. Their bodies met, and she arched into him, her mouth close to his as they swayed. She lay her head on his shoulder and whispered aloud, "Why did you ever leave me? My darling husband, why did you leave that day so long ago? Will I ever see you again?" The song ended. The image of Pietro faded, and the radio presenter came on, harsh and curt. He shared the news. In a dramatic turn, the Germans had rescued Mussolini from *Gran Sasso. Il Duce* was free.

The beginning of a terrible headache pulsed in her temples. The war was far from over; the nightmare would continue. Pietro had left on 16 April 1935. She hadn't seen him in over eight years, hadn't received a letter in over four. Maybe it was time to stop counting.

The clouds rolled into Fonzaso, and so did the Nazis. The air prickled with anxiety. No one went out in the piazza after eight o'clock, even before curfews were imposed. The stories were powerful enough to paralyse anyone from behaving normally. Fear permeated everything. Even children smiled less. Nina felt grimness around her: in her footsteps, in her shadow, in her reflection in the bakery window as she picked up their rations. At any time, for any reason, death might introduce itself to her, the girls, or her neighbours, and she would have to face it. Survival was chance; God hid, and destiny was whatever happened in the hour before the next nightmare. The town of Fonzaso was dense with fog and fear.

Nina awoke early with plans to go to the church and pray for Teo. She'd been thinking of him all the time lately. It seemed her thoughts were going backwards instead of forwards these days. She would do anything to survive with the girls, but it gave her solace to think if she died, she'd see her little boy again. Today, she wanted to talk to God and focus on Teo, to feel his presence and remind him of her unending love.

The wind bristled against her, tossing her hair in wild strands as soon as she stepped outside. She'd left the girls in bed. Lasia, a light sleeper, whispered to Nina before she left, "Say a prayer for him from me." Nina tugged her scarf around her head, tying it tightly under her chin. She hoped the wind would die down and the skies wouldn't open. The weather evoked an old memory. A windy day, a festival, a boy and a girl under a blanket, rain. Now, the boy was a man she barely knew, and the girl stood alone in the wind and cold.

Nina passed weathered propaganda posters as she headed straight for the church, focusing on her feet, making it to the *chiesa* in no time. She closed the large door behind her, shutting out the noise of the wind and enveloping herself in silence. She dipped her fingers in cold holy water, then made the sign of the cross. The pews were empty. Her footsteps echoed. No candles burned yet. Finding her way to the Virgin Mary by the dim light through the stained glass windows, Nina kneeled then lit two tapers, one for her mother, one for her son. She looked up at the Virgin, her eyes travelling to the base of the sculpture: the gentle bare foot smashing the attacking snake. Love overcoming evil. She thought of the Nazis. The snake. The candlelight illuminated Mary from below, and Nina studied her patient face; it held an expression of unconditional love of a mother for her child, the expression that could go from sheer elation to great despair, all dependent on the happiness and safety of her baby. Her calm face said, *Come to me. Tell me what's wrong. Let me make it better. Let my love surround you, shield you so you will feel no pain.* Nina bowed her head, remembering holding Teo. She prayed to Adelasia, telling her she knew she was holding him in Heaven. She told her mother how she missed her and prayed for strength to get through each dark day.

The church door creaked, telling Nina she was not alone. An old woman from one of the nearby villages walked in, making the sign of the cross. Nina could see, as she came into the light, she'd been crying. The pinkness of her face along with the redness in her eyes was proof something was terribly wrong. She approached the kneeler in front of the Madonna where Nina was praying. Nina gestured with her head to tell the woman she could join her.

The *signora* was petite; she reminded Nina of a baby bird. She looked to the Virgin Mary with a strained face, desperate, shaking.

"Is something wrong?" whispered Nina, wanting to offer her solace in the real world outside of her prayers. Silence filled the air without a response from the woman until she finally answered.

"I'm praying for my son. He... he's gone." The statement hung for a moment between them.

"Me, too." They both looked up at the Blessed Virgin, her glow stronger with the light of the additional candle. "What was he like?" Nina whispered, remembering the solace it gave her when someone asked about Teo, acknowledging his life.

"He was a hero. Small for his age, but he became a hero anyway – and yours?"

"He died at five months. He was chubby, such an eater, never happier than when he was sucking away. It showed in his cheeks."

"My son's nose. It was a little too big for his face."

"I remember Teo's toes, how he loved to eat them. I did, too," she said. Nina blinked back tears.

"His father's dead. I'm glad he didn't see this."

"His father's in America. I wish they would have met."

Silently, they looked at the Madonna and bowed their heads, two mothers praying for their dead sons.

The woman touched Nina's shoulder, then left, as if the Blessed Virgin had given her a mission she was off to complete. Nina finished her prayers and walked around the empty church. She stood in the pew where she prayed a lifetime ago. When Don Segala blessed a group of men emigrating to America. She could have never imagined their fate; that they would fall in love and years after she would remain here without him, in the middle of another war.

Nina stepped out of the church, into the chill and gasped when she looked across the piazza. On the high gate in front of the *Villa Vieceli,* a man hung from a rope, swaying from side to side. Besides the fact he was suspended in the air, it struck Nina that his clothing was perfectly in place. His striped shirt remained tucked into his trousers, belt buckle perfectly centred; his socks were bright white. Someone had kept them laundered for him, cared for him. Pinned to his shirt was a sign:

THIS IS THE END OF THE PARTISANS

The woman from the church had climbed onto the gate and was feverishly sawing at the rope with a kitchen knife. She hacked at the last strings before the body of the man released, collapsing to the ground. A group of men appeared with a wheelbarrow and gently helped her lay her son in it. Nina prayed and looked up to San Micel, but the fog was too thick, and the castle could not be seen.

CHAPTER 30

As the world fell apart around her, Nina lived a charade of ordinariness. She woke to stormy skies, lightning in the morning. It would be a day to stay inside and keep Rita entertained in the confines of the small house. She made herself chicory coffee then sat at the table in their *cucina,* closing her eyes to feel the thunder as pellets of rain shot at her windows with force.

It was all a mess.

Lasia came downstairs and joined her for a meagre breakfast. She ate one of the three dark pieces of bread, dipping it in her coffee. Only a dry wedge of dark bread remained and the few grapes they had salvaged were brown on the ends. Thank God they still had eggs and cornmeal.

"There's not much. I'll go out later to get our rations," Nina told Lasia, her stomach tensing to see her daughter with such a pitiful meal.

"I can't imagine how the larger families with boys who eat more than we do and get fewer extras survive," Lasia said.

"I think they're adding to what they have by hunting.

Anything they can get. I heard the barber's been butchering cats to eat," Nina said.

Lasia made a disgusted face and wiped sleep from her eyes. Nina observed her from across the table. She remembered being her age. Dancing with Pietro at the festival, thinking he loved her sister. Now, her sister and Toni were here, suffering through the war together. And where was Pietro? Where was he?

They climbed the stairs to get dressed as the rain fell in sheets, slapping at the windows. Three loud thumps beat at the front door and Nina jumped at the sound. She ran down the stairs, mind racing as she considered who it could be with such a demanding knock. A birth? She opened the door to six large men in uniform. Their huge thighs and thick bodies took her aback before she noticed fur hats and heard in their voices who they were – Russians, the Cossacks Aurora had told her about. On impulse, she tried to close the door but the soldier in front pushed it open. Her heart pumped in her ears as she tried to understand what they wanted.

"We're hungry. You will cook for us," he stated as he stomped into her kitchen with the others, surveying the place. His Italian was good but covered by a thick Russian accent. Her body gave away her fear as she trembled frantically.

"Mamma," called Rita from upstairs. "Who's here?"

"Go back to sleep, *bambina,* it's just the thunder," Nina called, her voice unsteady.

She returned to the soldiers standing in her kitchen.

"I have nothing, please, I have two children in bed with empty stomachs. There's nothing." The Cossack's face transformed like a wolf preparing to attack. He glared at her as if tearing into her, then stepped around the kitchen opening the cabinets. Realising she was telling the truth, he growled.

"We'll be back. Be ready for us," he said, then stomped out with his men.

Nina tried to control her trembling. Rita rushed to the window to see what she had missed. Lasia stood on the steps barefoot, holding the back of her nightdress out. A dark red spot was spreading through the fabric.

"*Mamma mia!* This is just what we need!" Nina cried.

"Mamma! I'm bleeding but nothing hurts," Lasia shrieked. "What's happening to me?" Nina crossed herself then looked out the window again. The men had disappeared from the Via Calzen. Her mind raced. She needed to get Lasia out of the house before they returned. She remembered Aurora's words, "They take anything they want."

She looked at Rita, scruffy and innocent. Should she send her too and be alone in the house with the men? No, if she kept the child with her maybe they would spare her as a mother. Maybe some decency would prevail. Thoughts flashed in seconds. She began ordering instructions.

"Lasia, go get dressed. You're not dying, it's normal. Run to Zia Aurora's. Stay there. Tell her you're bleeding, that it's your time and to explain. Tell her soldiers have decided to stay with us." She paused. "Tell her to stay away – Rita and the Captain are with me." Lasia did as she was told then raced down the road in the rain with Nina watching from the window.

She paced for an hour, second-guessing keeping Rita with her as she ran from room to room to see if there was anything to hide. What would they take? She launched into her Hail Marys as Rita peppered her with questions; she was too distracted to answer. The rain slowed and before long she heard rough voices coming up the Via Calzen. This time, she met them at the door, doing her best to look confident. Again, she noticed their appearance, like giants with black insignia hats, each carrying bags over their shoulders or with arms full of goods. Boots covered wide calves up to their knees, and they wore long brown tunics belted at the waist with leather holsters. The trembling returned as she noticed the pistols on their hips. Six men entered her house with muddy boots. Only the first man, the wolf-like leader, attempted to wipe them before entering. Nina stood out of the way, in the corner with Rita in front of her, hands on her shoulders, watching them pile item after item on her table then go upstairs to lay down their kits. They stacked the table high with eggs, cheese, flour, ham, bread, a dead chicken, real coffee, sugar, pasta and vegetables. She had never seen such abundance on her table, and she wondered where they had acquired everything; who would starve so they could feast? She directed Rita to pull out their pots then wiped her hands on her apron, looking at the soldier for direction as his men clamoured about dirtying her clean floors, their rough hands on her furniture. She winced as one soldier tossed a blanket her mother had knitted onto the floor. Why hadn't she moved that?

Her trembling continued despite her attempts to focus. *Think. Think, Nina.*

"Six men," he said. "Make enough food for six men."

She surveyed the ingredients. *Pasta. Primo piatto.* First things first. Just start. She looked up from the pot. They were opening drawers and cabinets as if they were in a shop and she had the urge to scream, *Stop!* but she knew she couldn't. *Keep your head about you, Nina. You'll get through this.*

"Cook!" he commanded her. Nina's entire body quivered as she tried to prepare the sauce, her shaking wrist made it impossible. Rita tightened to her side.

"Mamma," Rita whispered, "do you want me to stir it?"

Nina shook her head and glanced at the soldiers – one of them eyeing her. The Cossack captain crossed the room to Nina. His men continued in conversation while exploring her home. He walked up close to her until he was standing behind her at the stove and the others couldn't see, then reached into his jacket and she froze in fear. He pulled out a creased photograph. A stoic but attractive woman with golden hair held a baby in her arms and next to her stood a blonde curly-haired child who looked no more than five.

He kept his voice low. "Don't be scared of us," he said. "Don't shake. You think I want to be here? This is my family. This is where I want to be." He paused, staring out the window for a moment then straightened and said, "We won't hurt you."

He looked over at Rita then addressed Nina again.

"Don't serve all the food you make," he said. "Hold some back. When we leave, you keep the extra."

Nina nodded in shock. Fear and relief overwhelmed her. "*Grazie,*" she said. He dipped his head, returned his picture to his pocket and sat down for her to serve him.

Nina slept next to Rita with her hand on the girl's chest. They lay next to each other, looking at the ceiling, scared even to whisper. While the words of the soldier calmed her to an extent, she had no trust in his men. What if a soldier came for her at night or, God forbid, Rita? Each night she kept vigil for as long as she could keep her eyes open. *What would Pietro say?* He would be angry, maybe even jealous, but he wasn't there, was he? He wasn't caught up in the war like she was. She was in the centre of a nightmare with two young daughters. It would be a miracle if it ended and they were alive, much less unharmed and innocent. No one would leave this war unscathed. *I will make sure my daughters don't get hurt.*

Their minds might be poisoned with the evil they witness, but their bodies will remain innocent.

The Cossacks stomped around town during the day and her house at night. She kept out of their way, constantly cooking. Rita stayed in her sight at night but during the day, Nina sent her to Aurora's to get information. She reported back Cossacks were staying in two other houses in Fonzaso, one in the mountains and another near the boys' school.

After three nights passed, they left at sunrise, gone as quickly as they had arrived with only a nod from the soldier to Nina. They stole what jewellery she had forgotten to hide and left a mess: dirt encrusted on the floors, scratches and marks on the walls, a broken chair, along with a blessing: ten eggs, two skinned rabbits, a pouch of sugar, a large bag of flour, a canister of coffee and a collection of vegetables.

They joined up with the other Cossacks in Fonzaso. As the group marched across the bridge to Arsie, partisans waited for them – an ambush. The bridge exploded around them. There were no survivors.

The weather was overcast as the Pante women walked to Mass the Sunday after the partisans killed the Cossacks. As they strode down the aisle to take their seats, curious eyes surveyed them. Nina read the questions on their faces.

Had they attacked her? Had she shared any suspicions of who the partisans were?

Should they worry it would happen to them?

She knew no one would dare ask, and she had no desire to talk about it. For her, it was over. They were gone. They were dead. She prayed God would forgive them of their sins, thinking about the piles of food they left. Could that act of kindness be their salvation?

Lasia winced at the feeling of being observed. She was still too innocent to realise why her mother had sent her away but not Rita. Curious eyes searched for clues to what really happened in the way Nina carried herself and in Rita's face which, everyone knew, was easy to read.

The congregation took their places and the Mass began. Nico sang devoutly with his eyes closed. It made Lasia smile. He was the only boy she knew with the confidence to express himself and his faith without worrying about his pride. It made him stand out from the other boys his age. His closed-eyed singing and golden head gave him the look of an angel in the church against the dark-haired, drably dressed crowd. She wondered if she looked different now that her "time had come". She hoped no one would notice.

As for the adults, the congregation prayed harder than usual. More eyes closed tight for prayers; more voices sang with hope for God's mercy. Bad times were here. Terrible times. They prayed to be left safe with their families, for their men to return.

Don Cavalli stood for his homily, speaking about helping each other, not turning away those who were struggling more. He was so impassioned in his speech, he didn't hear the rumble of the trucks outside until they were right next to the church. A nun fumbled with her Bible, dropping it on the ground.

Old Signor Vieceli, who had skipped Mass, entered the church and walked at pace up the aisle as the congregation stared in disbelief. He delivered the message to Don Cavalli: Germans were outside, they wanted to speak to him. The priest asked everyone to remain in their seats and followed the man out through the great door. As he stepped into the daylight, the congregation saw a pack of German soldiers approaching him. Nina watched the pious man in his robes through the slit in the door. *Germans in Fonzaso,* she thought. The news spread over the faces of everyone in the pews. A child cried out, asking if they could leave and was hushed by three people. Fear kept them silent.

Don Cavalli walked solemnly back into the church. He stopped in the middle of the aisle. Standing closed-eyed in his robes, he gave the impression of praying, having a silent conversation with God before addressing them. When he spoke, his voice was grave. "My brothers and sisters, German soldiers are outside looking for partisans. I'm to tell you we must go into the piazza. Men on the right, women and children to the left." Nina imagined they must be looking for the partisans who had blown up the bridge.

Nina watched as he delivered the message, his body tense yet his voice assured. "May God be with us."

She pulled Rita and Lasia close to her and angled around the pew to stay near her sisters. She reached over to squeeze Corrado's hand as the congregation moved in a line in the opposite way they had just done to receive Communion.

In the piazza, the Germans stood, some planted with legs apart, while others paced with speed to the corners of the piazza. It was the first time she had seen German soldiers in a group; their biceps were wrapped with spidery swastika bands. She knew what it meant. Occupation. Death. The Germans would walk among them from now on.

An SS soldier with angry eyes and a chin which sloped directly to his neck climbed the stairs of the church then stood to face them. With his hands on his belt buckle, he saluted the *Führer,* and scanned across the eyes staring back at him, assessing their anticipation. Abruptly, he laughed, his expression changing to appear jovial. Something about the shift in his face made Nina's stomach turn.

"*Buongiorno.* I am High Commissioner Franz Hofer. I am in charge of this region. We now call it the Operational Zone of the Alpine Foothills." He spoke in perfect Italian with a strong German accent. "We are here to help secure your town. *Il Duce* and Hitler are friends. You will be safer with us here. You may have heard the enemy has invaded Italy. They are attacking in the south, on your soil. We will protect you. To do so, we need your help."

He introduced another man, SS Brigadier General Karl Brunner, who went through a list of regulations. Nina would have considered this man handsome if his demeanour wasn't so sinister. Nina listened intently as he called on the people to denounce any partisans. *These aren't friends,* Nina thought. *Friends who protect don't find it necessary to split families, hold the men apart. Protectors don't threaten.*

They stood for a long time listening to the new rules. An earlier curfew announced. Enemies defined – partisans, Americans, British, French and Jews. Hiding or helping the enemy would be punished by death. Italian speaking newspapers – banned. Radios – banned. Their houses were being ransacked as they stood in the piazza. The sounds of pots and furniture crashing played in the background. The soldier explained what behaviour was unacceptable, how the unacceptable behaviour would be punished with deportation to the transit camp in Bolzano, work camps in Germany, or death. Their reward for playing by the rules was being allowed to live.

Then, as suddenly as they had been summoned, the women were told to return home with their children. Frantic eyes sought husbands, fathers and sons. *They will be fine,* Nina told herself, trying to stay calm. Nothing would happen. *The Germans must have more to tell the men.* It would be fine.

Nina and the girls walked up the Via Calzen and back to a plundered home. Nina cried out. Everything the Cossacks left, they took. Every drawer was open, every cabinet emptied. She wept at the realisation of how close they'd been to having more days with full stomachs. The rug was flipped over. Upstairs, they'd overturned her jewellery box, everything stolen except her most humble rosaries; photos were strewn about haphazardly. She imagined them lobbing her beloved items into sacks that clinked while mixing with her neighbours' valuables. Wedding bands passed down for generations, diamond baby earrings and gifts from lovers lobbed into sacks as if they represented nothing.

For once, Rita was silent. They moved about the house closing drawers, putting things back in place, busying themselves while they waited for news.

After two hours, Nina couldn't take the waiting any longer. She was about to leave to investigate what was happening with the men when Aurora knocked on the door to tell them. Everyone had returned. According to Corrado, from what he heard afterwards, they found the partisans they were looking for in Arten. One boy hung from a tree there with a sign on his chest, and they hung and shot the others after interrogating them. Nina sat down, crying with relief that her family was safe.

"But those men. They hung them? Shot them?" Nina asked. "Do you know who they were? Mamma and I delivered every baby in Arten. Of the three of them, at least one would have been ours."

Aurora shrugged her shoulders. "I don't know who they were but, Nina, if they were partisans, and if they blew up that bridge, it's better they are gone. So many of them were bad in the first place. They'd only bring us trouble."

Nina leaned over and hugged her sister. They were both shaken from the day's events. She told her, "All we can do is pray we survive."

Aurora, holding her close, whispered in her ear, "They didn't find my radio. I hid it behind the outhouse."

CHAPTER 31

I n 1944, the Nazis based themselves at the new boys' school at the start of town near the *Albergo Sant'Antonio.* Each day a few patrolled the streets of Fonzaso while the others searched the mountains for enemies. It surprised the *Fonzasini* to find many of them friendly, particularly to the children. Nina knew it was a tactic to keep them under control but she pitied them and their young, smooth faces. Nina remembered the Cossack soldier who never returned to his family. *Would anyone be reunited when this was over? Did the Nazis go to bed dreaming of the wives who waited for them or babies they had never met?*

Two medic soldiers took up residence at the top of Onorina and Toni's house. One was Austrian, the other a German who had studied in England. The men heard about the large Bianchi house and Onorina had toured them around it as though they were her boarders in Canada. She showed them to the first floor, charmingly explaining to them this was the floor with the *kinder.* She knew sharing a floor with children would not interest them. Onorina brought them to the empty third floor. "We'll take it!" they said, as though they would pay rent. For days, they stayed in Fonzaso then went to treat German soldiers in the field, returning exhausted.

During the day, a permanent angst held Nina's stomach tight. Sometimes, it gave her a headache, especially when Rita peppered her with questions or bad news. The child roamed the town with her cousins when school finished and played on street corners with her few leftover marbles. Rita was the most well-known child in Fonzaso, but she was also the loneliest. Nina knew she needed her mother, desired her attention, but Nina couldn't help getting further away. In trying to survive, Nina built an island for herself. The retreat was palpable. Death became an accepted part of daily life. If something didn't happen in Fonzaso, then a story came from Arten, Agana or Feltre. The men tried to keep a low profile. More of them sided with the partisans, either in action or allegiance. Mussolini was somewhere in Lake Garda eating grapes, stuffing his face with food and making love to his mistress – while they worked to make sure there was enough food to last through winter.

Even when Germans bounced babies on their knees or handed sweets to children, Nina knew soldiers easily murdered as their duty. Insomnia invaded her nights as fear of what might happen refused to let her sleep. She developed scenarios and new worries until she was sick. Sleep only came if she willed her mind back in time. So, at night, Nina thought about Pietro. She imagined him in bed next to her and used her dingy pillow as if it were the crook of his arm, her head resting on his warm chest. It was hard to remember his face, his arms, his smell – what was that smell? Smoke and sun and earth and soap and him. She pictured him lifting her chin to kiss her and tell her they would be safe, he would take care of her and it would be over soon. In her fantasies, he chased her up the stairs and they were newlyweds again. She changed her reaction to him in her reveries, she was bolder. She reached for his hand and snuggled next to him under the blanket at the festival. She relived being in Padua and envisioned him there with her looking over the moonlit rooftops. She imagined him pulling her into the darkness of the *cantina,* kissing her against the wall, could almost feel his lips. She brought her fingertips to her own to make sure they were still there, could still feel a sensation where his once met hers. Her fantasies embarrassed her, yet she counted on them, depending on them to escape.

Why did we believe we had so much time? Young, stupid fools! He could have stayed. He could have worked with Toni. They would have had enough. They would have had each other. Or would he have hung in the piazza? Would he have been one of those pleading for his life and begging Nazis for pity? Would he be off freezing in a camp or dying in the Russian snow? Nine years. They hadn't seen each other in nine long years. What would she say if she saw him again? He was beyond a stranger to her. Full lives had been lived, and war had aged her. Grey speckled her hairline, and her cheekbones were cut with hunger.

The shelves of the *alimentari* were empty. Rations came and went. Days repeated themselves: wake up, work the fields, mind the children, clean the house, avoid trouble, check on the family, go to bed, repeat. Praise God nothing traumatic happened to your loved ones that day. But when she lay her head on her pillow, she was his Ninetta. From the bed, she could see the moon above San Micel, so she prayed her dreams may someday still be.

At one o'clock in the morning, when she was almost asleep, a pounding downstairs interrupted her reveries.

"Open the door!" Rough German accents ignored the fact that it was the middle of the night. Three SS soldiers stood outside the window. Rita and Lasia woke up, following behind their mother.

"Wait there," she said.

They stood frozen in the hall.

Nina opened the door, fear gripping her insides.

Two of the three Nazis bounded past her into the house and up the stairs. The third addressed Nina. "Who are you hiding? We know you have partisans coming through here, enemies you are hiding. Your cooperation ensures your life. Show us upstairs. Take us to the attic."

Nina nodded her head, but stood paralysed with fear.

"Upstairs!" he commanded.

She looked at the girls. "Stay here," she directed them, trying to calm herself.

In her bedroom, the two Germans were already rummaging through her things, pulling up the mattress. The other started tearing apart the girls' room.

She didn't care. If she was with them up here, the girls were safe downstairs. She had heard many horror stories about soldiers like these who had raped and beaten young girls. They could have whatever they wanted, but she prayed to God he would protect her daughters. She braced herself, trying to look cooperative, hoping they would leave.

"What are you hiding? Show us the attic," the commanding officer yelled. "We know you're hiding something."

"No, you've got everything. Even our rosaries. We're cooperating. I don't want any trouble," she said, clasping her hands and pleading with him.

She did her best to look him in the eyes so he didn't think she was lying. They would have no qualms about burning the house with her and the girls inside. They'd done it in many towns near Fonzaso – men, women and children burned to death in their homes or shot as they escaped the flames for nothing more than suspicion of acts against the Nazis.

"You lie."

"No, no...," she whispered. "Please, go up!" She pointed to the door to the attic, trying to focus as her heart thumped in her ears. If she could just get these Germans out of her home! She ran out of the room and down the stairs, pulling Lasia and Rita into her arms.

"Mamma!" they cried.

"It's okay, stay together. Pray in your head." Were these their last moments? Would they kill them all in a few minutes? She prayed an Our Father to ask for forgiveness before the impending end.

The men went through everything, when they found no partisans hiding, they took the small amount of chicory coffee and flour she had. *Bastards,* she thought.

"I will ask you one more time. Are you hiding anything?" The SS officer glared at her while she worked to hold his gaze, pleading with him through her eyes.

"No, you can see. I don't want any trouble."

He huffed. "We will be back," he said. "Let's go!" he called out, and they left as abruptly as they'd arrived, with Nina and the girls huddled in the chaotic mess of the kitchen.

The following week, Nina went to *Sant'Anna* to pray. The policing SS made it a nerve-wracking pilgrimage, and it had been too long since she made the walk. She felt a pull towards the sanctuary, a need to be on the land her mother held so dear, pray at the feet of the Madonna and reflect. Upon arriving, it saddened her to see the state of the place. The glass on the altar window was cracked so she could only see Saint Anne behind shards. The vineyards behind had been torn apart and fences hung forlorn and trampled. Dirt covered the statue of the Madonna. She could see that the Nazis had destroyed the hideout behind the grotto. Who had been hiding there last? What had become of them? Nina pulled out a handkerchief and wiped the Madonna's feet with care. It tore at her heart to know her mother's dream to build a pristine altar here was in such disarray. The men her mother had delivered were at war and the women were starving. Who would survive in the end?

Leaves whipped around the piazza as Rita scurried home from her cousins too close to curfew. A huge leaf caught her eye, distracting her up the church steps. As she chased it, she heard the sudden roar of engines, and three trucks with swastikas on the doors pulled into the empty piazza. Ducking behind a pillar, she peered out, watching the German soldiers push five men from the back of a truck. Their hands were tied in front of them and while four of them were silent, one begged desperately in a Belluno dialect, petitioning the soldiers.

"*Signor,*" the man pleaded, his high pitched voice filled the piazza. "Please, I have ten children. My family cannot survive without me. Have mercy."

Rita thought the soldiers couldn't have understood him as they spoke in German, laughing to each other. They directed him to kneel. He complied while continuing to beg, his hands folded together as though worshipping them. Maybe German was all they spoke except the word 'kneel'. Perhaps they didn't understand him explaining he had done nothing wrong; he was only a lonely old worker of the fields, he was a card carrying fascist. A blast put an end to his speech, and Rita's ears rang. The man fell to the ground, then a slow stream of red liquid pooled around his head.

More shots peppered the piazza, plaster flying. Rita stared, her eyes wide as she crouched behind the pillar. She dared not cry or call out to her mother as she wanted to. The men's bodies twisted, collapsing with the impact as the shots continued. They dropped to the ground, one here, one there. Blood streamed down the wall of the DeBonis' house facing the street.

Then, silence.

An SS officer walked up to each of the bodies, kicking them over to make sure their work was thorough. Fear pulsed through Rita's veins, heat spread to her face as her heart pounded in her ears. *Could the Germans hear the thumping?* She crouched lower, closer to the column. Out of the silence came another shot, swift and clean. They'd found a survivor and finished the work. "*Fortfahren!* Proceed," shouted the SS commander. The Germans mounted their truck, engine roaring. They drove off, leaving behind the corpses of strangers for the *Fonzasini* to attend to. An example. A warning.

Silence rolled over the piazza. Shock kept anyone from coming out. Time entered a purgatory. Rita stood, a curious dread pulling her towards the piazza. She walked methodically, approaching as the sulphury smell of gunpowder burned her nostrils. Blood spread around her worn shoes, pooling as she watched it fill the gaps between the cobblestones. As though stepping into a puddle of rain, she trod into it. Moving step by step among the bodies, her footsteps made crimson imprints. She paused, looking around. Here she stood, nine years old, a little girl among the remains: the twisted forms, bones and brain, flesh and death. This was her childhood. Tears pressed behind her eyes as she shook her head. She didn't want to understand this! She didn't want to learn to justify those men's actions! Rita looked around at the faces of someone else's fathers or brothers; she focused on one man, the one who had said he was a father of ten. His moustache looked soft; it curled at the corners. She had the desire to squeeze the ends of it, to pull it to see if it would detach. Maybe his children had sat on his lap and played with it this morning. His hair was matted around the hole in his head where blood streamed from it. She reached over, squeezing the corner of his moustache between two fingers. It *was* soft, she thought, then pulled her hand back as though he would awaken to reprimand her. She ran up the Via Calzen to tell the others what she had seen.

Nina vomited, unable to slow her heartbeat. Never had she witnessed something so violent. She had heard about atrocities like this, but today it was in front of her. Coming back from praying at *Sant'Anna*, she'd lost track of time, nearing the piazza at curfew when she heard the trucks pull up and ducked into a doorway. A father begged for his life before her eyes. She remembered the frozen face, his shattered head. How easily he changed from a man to a corpse. Hannah's words played in her head, "I watched and I did *niente*." She had done the same. She prayed, *Dear God, be with that man's family and all their families.* Her body was numb, moving an impossible feat. Even tears would not come.

They didn't deserve to die today. God, please keep us safe and end this war. She stood clutching a wall until she could calm her breathing. Wiping her mouth with a handkerchief, she thought about what she should tell the girls.

When she returned home, Lasia was waiting. "What happened? I heard shots coming from the piazza. I was worried. It's past curfew!" Nina walked past her and straight to the cabinet for a glass.

"I came down the hill after praying to the Madonna and there were Germans with prisoners in the piazza. There was a massacre." She filled the glass with water and rinsed the bile out of her mouth, then took another sip before continuing, "I didn't even know who the men were. I suppose they sentenced them to death in Bolzano. Brought here as an example to partisans." She paused as she saw the horrified look on Lasia's face, realising she'd said too much. "Where's Rita?" she asked, her anxiety creeping back.

"She's not here. I thought she was with you."

"No." Nina's head pounded, becoming fuzzy. "We need to find her."

As Nina opened the door, she let out a sigh of relief. Rita was there, swinging on the gate, gripping the rungs with her small hands. In her childish voice, she sang.

> *Giovinezza, giovinezza,*
> *primavera di bellezza,*
> *nel fascismo è la salvezza*
> *della nostra libertà.*

> Youth, youth,
> Spring of beauty,
> In fascism's the salvation
> Of our liberty.

Giovinezza, the anthem of the fascists. Her voice, usually loud, was low and unnerving. Nina shivered at the sound. It was as if her daughter was far away, out of reach.

"Rita, get in here, it's time for supper." She demanded her to come back to reality. The girl, still singing, came to the door, used one foot to coax off each shoe and left them in the entry as her mother told her. The still wet blood congealing on the soles went unseen. Nina was too grateful she was home to notice.

CHAPTER 32

The next morning, Onorina sat at Nina's table. "I need real coffee, real coffee!" Nina repeated, slamming drawers looking for a clean spoon. "I'm sick of this chicory sludge," she said. "It's bitter; it's no good." She sipped it and grimaced, wanting to throw the coffee cup across the room. "Disgusting."

It was the last of the chicory. Everything was diminishing: coffee substitutes, salt, soap, thread. Soon they would be stripped to nothing but bleakness and death. "How stupid is war?" Nina asked. "Men die, families are torn apart, everyone is poor and pathetic. Why do we ever go to war?"

"Because boys love to fight," Onorina said. "Listen, Nina, no one expects you to be strong all the time." She traced a chipped spot on Nina's table with her long finger, giving Nina a look as if she knew everything.

"*Senti,* last night I saw the executions in the piazza. I got sick behind your shop. But to make it worse, I came home and Rita wasn't here. She came in after curfew, not acting like herself. Singing *Giovinezza,* can you believe! This morning I found out why. Her shoes were filled with blood. She witnessed the whole thing too," Nina implored Onorina with her eyes. "I never wanted my children to experience what I did. Mamma shared too much with me. She told me awful stories during the Great War. So many disturbing details I didn't want to know. I've failed in this way too."

Onorina held her hand as she broke down. "We'll get through this war. It will be over soon." Onorina crooned, her voice was velvety smooth but did little to calm Nina.

"What's the point of all this pain?" she cried, her voice escalating as she stood up to pace the floor. "So men can gain more land? So Italy can be respected and great? I don't care! When my children watch their countrymen have their brains blown out onto the streets? When our cousins lose their husbands and sons because they're Jewish? I hate this war! I'm sick of being hungry and watching everyone around me suffer." Nina slapped her hand down on the table. "This is not the life I expected. My children shouldn't have to live like this. And to top it off, I'm one of the lucky ones!" She sat down, defeated by her own speech. "And you know what? I'll never know what Pietro is doing right now. And I hate him for leaving us. I hate him for leaving us behind."

That night, she looked in the mirror. War had done this to her. Her clothes, once vibrant and tailored, were colourless rags, with seams that had been sewn and resewn. She unbuttoned her blouse, wanting to shed the poverty from herself. Pulling it off, she observed her reflection. She stepped out of her slip, letting the tattered undergarment fall to the floor. There she was in the mirror. Grabbing her brush, she pulled her hair out of its chignon and let her uncut mane full of intermittent greys fall around her shoulders. She observed her arms, firm from picking in the fields; ran her hands down her hips, broad from giving birth to three children. Her hand moved to her collarbone, stroking her smooth chest. It was cool, and the touch of her warm hand consoled her. She was ageing. It couldn't be denied. She recalled herself ten years ago, before the war, when he had said goodbye; she had thought she was so old. What a joke God played on her! She was a woman loved, but she had been naïve. It had been an eternity since Pietro had loved her, so long since she touched his body and smelled his scent on hers. Her body had changed. But with the rags off, and her natural self standing before her, even at forty, something beautiful remained. Staring at her reflection, she felt a determination and a new certainty. Everything she needed to survive the war without her fantasies was in front of her. She didn't need a man to help her, she never had. This is what her mother had meant when she told her she was strong. Nina decided then, she would stop comforting herself with thoughts of Pietro. He wasn't her hero. She was her own. For the first time in months, she fell asleep without him.

The days came and went. More Nazis patrolled the streets of Fonzaso; they grew unpredictable – it was impossible to know if you would come upon an agreeable one or a monster. Partisans blew up Nazi vehicles and ammunition stockpiles, did anything they could do to make life difficult for the Germans until the Allies could advance. They helped prisoners of the transit camp in Bolzano escape and hid them in mountain shacks or recruited them into their ranks. Onorina whispered these things to Nina, and she didn't ask where the information came from. *Partigiani* actions agitated the Nazis against the *Fonzasini*. Resistance swarmed in the surrounding mountains. The Nazis knew it and suspected everyone.

The Germans announced Hitler's orders, *Rappresaglia Tedesca* – the command for German retaliation against the partisans. For any Nazi killed, they would take ten Italian lives. Word came that Nazis had raided Lamon hunting for enemies who accessed Italy through the mountains. Neighbours of Pietro's family had come back from church to find them ransacking their home. They were shot, blamed as partisans. In Arsie, Serena del Grappa and Agana stories flooded into the *alimentari* and taverna, more killed, shot in the streets, hung off trees, off gates, houses burned. Men, but also women and children. The desperate Nazis were not picky. Italians would pay as the partisans rose.

Christmas 1944 was brutally cold. There was little left to burn; everything was being used for firewood, and they had hacked down the trees leading up to Mount Avena. A tiny evergreen top stood next to the divan, their one decoration for Christmas. Rita and Quinto had trimmed it with gold foil sheets they collected when the Americans dropped them from planes to confuse German radio waves. Nina boiled water on the stove and made hot water bottles for them to keep at their feet. She filled a tin with hot ash from the fire to use as well.

"We'll sleep in my bed," she told the girls. The three of them squeezed together with Rita in the middle. Nina brought every blanket into her room. She placed the hot water bottles and ash box at the bottom of the bed, covered the girls and wrapped herself around Rita, kissing her hair. *At least we're together,* she thought.

Rita fell asleep, but Lasia stayed awake, and Nina could tell she wanted to talk. "Mamma, may I ask you something?" she started, whispering despite Rita's deep sleep.

"Tell me," Nina whispered back.

"You never say anything about Papà. Do you think we'll see him again?" Nina looked at the ceiling. She had wondered when this question would come. But she found herself without an answer.

"I don't know. I'm not sure anymore," her voice was flat as she spoke the words.

"I remember him. I remember his smile, his stories... the coffee." It pulled at Nina's heart to hear Lasia talk about Pietro. She hardly knew her father, yet she too comforted herself with thoughts of him.

"Good. Keep those memories. If we see him again or not, you'll always have those."

"We'll have to teach Rita," Lasia said, moving her sister's arm from where it had flopped across her belly.

"We have a lot to teach Rita." Nina laughed softly.

"She's a little wild," Lasia whispered.

"I don't know where she gets it!" They giggled together, and it felt good to laugh.

In the cold winter nights, their hearts were warmed by each other's stories. Nina remembered how she was Adelasia's gift. The chain continued as Lasietta became hers.

CHAPTER 33

A man in his Sunday best walked into a convenience store on Chicago Street in Joliet. His long fingers pushed the coins across the counter filled with offers for Wrigley's chewing gum and Miller beer. He took the paper from the cashier along with the bottle of Coca Cola, tucking the *Herald News* under his arm. "Have a good one," the fat cashier said from behind the register. He recognised this customer who bought the same thing each Sunday. A pop and a paper. Each week his customer's eyes faded, his shoulders sloped a little more. He might have been a good-looking man once, but with his hollow cheeks and deep purple arcs under his eyes, he looked perpetually weary.

The man walked down the busy boulevard as families shuffled by and couples rushed to cross the street to the Rialto for shows. The war brought industry to the city and the cool spring day had everyone out looking dapper. In his worn wool suit, he walked the mile to the house where he rented a room, then fumbled with the key, dropping the newspaper. Bending to pick it up, he winced at his aching bones. Once inside his room, he hung his jacket then took off his shirt, tossing it over the sofa. He pulled out a chair and sat in the undershirt he washed every night. After opening his pop, he laid the paper flat, then turned on the radio.

Advertisements for Dairy Queen and a new Western at the cinema caught his eye. Maybe he would go. He liked Westerns. It had been many months since he'd seen a flick because it was too hard to watch the beginning film reels of the European front. Guilt hung on him like a noose. At the show, people around him giggled and shuffled their popcorn as they watched the valour of the Allies, smiling pilots who dropped bombs from their planes on Europe to defeat the occupying Germans. They were on the ground now, in Italy, these Allies, making their way up the boot, fighting the Nazis. Italy was ablaze with war and he sat in a cinema watching it, a spectator. Voiceovers of Churchill and Roosevelt spoke of glory at all costs, battles to be won. Meanwhile, he was stuck in limbo. His family – he hadn't heard from them in six years. Once he'd recuperated from the accident, he'd written so many letters – even tried an expensive telegram service. He'd written not knowing when the post would stop. *Why hadn't he heard from her?* Logic told him time would have allowed for her to receive and respond to one of his letters. But there was nothing.

The cabinet with his radio looked more like an altar. It held photographs of them on their wedding day, baby Teo, her with the girls, and Lasia on her Communion day. Next to the pictures was the box that held his cheque book. There was plenty of money in the account these days. When the post stopped, his money stayed in the bank. He maintained his frugal ways, spending little on food and rent. He worked, saved, sometimes went to church or the occasional Western, chewed tobacco and drank two bottles of pop a week. Everything else, he saved.

His misery had turned to numbness. Did he really have a family? Was he married to the woman in the photographs? His marriage was never like couples around him. There used to be lots of others with long distance marriages, but not anymore. His miner friends had brought their families or started new ones. Only he was frozen like this. The men at the factory where he now worked teased him. "You're a good-lookin' guy. Come to one of these dances at St Joe's. You like Italian girls? What about a Polack? Those girls are fun. Come on. Come out." With so many young men at the Front, their pick of young women was abundant. Lovely girls with lipstick and pin curls. He wanted nothing to do with them; he was too old to start again.

A few times he'd joined them to see what it was about. But when slow dances played, he headed to the bathroom. With two hands on the sink, he observed the man in the mirror. Strong Italian genes. Ageing, but not as well as others. The sallow cheeks, tired eyes and the slight slump in the shoulders reduced the impact of his deep brown eyes, the still full tuft of hair and the lean muscles beneath his one Sunday suit.

Bing Crosby's 'I'll be Seeing You' started on the radio. It stopped him every time he heard it. The last line just got him, something about looking at the moon, seeing your lover. He smoothed out the open paper and sat back, remembering. There was a girl who had loved him. Who had looked at him as though he could give her salvation. Who had looked at the moon with him when he held her in his arms. Who let him take over her body, gave it to him freely. She had waited for him. Again, and again. He'd thought she always would. There was the little girl who looked up at him over a cup of milky coffee and a baby he'd held, whose cheek he had felt under his fingertips. Now there was nothing.

Page three. He reminded himself to focus on the paper. A

photograph of soldiers and Red Cross workers in Italy. He searched the picture for clues of where it was taken. It didn't say. He ran his hand through his hair and took a deep breath. After finishing his pop, he went to the drawer where he kept paper and pens, pulled out a sheet and wrote.

Cara Ninetta,

I don't know exactly what to write, but I'll try. It's been so long. Longer than I ever would have imagined we'd be apart. The silence all these years has been awful. I wish I'd moved faster to get you here. I walk around like a ghost of myself, not knowing if you and the girls are safe. I can't feel, I can't taste the food I eat, I can't smell or hear or see as I used to when I could at least write and know I'd get a letter in return. The last letters I received from you made it seem like you hadn't been getting mine. If you get this, please write. Let me know how you are. Do you still think of me when you look at the moon? I see it every night. I dream of you, and I remember lying next to you below San Micel and realising how lucky I was that you were my wife. You're so beautiful, Ninetta. So strong. When I see you again, I'll hold you and I'll do everything I can to take away the pain you have suffered. I pray you don't hate me. I'm working at a factory in Joliet. After the accident, I had to find a job outside the mines. I want to bring you here. It may sound ridiculous to you, but as soon as this war is over, if you're willing, you can come and we'll finish our lives together without one day apart, without one night not sleeping side by side. Promise me. Tell me you are safe. Tell me you still love me. Forgive me for not being able to bring you here and save you from whatever you are going through in Fonzaso. Tell me how I can help you. Tell me you'll come. Send my love to my girls. Lasia must be fifteen and how can it be the baby I held will be ten? And Maria, is she well? We will be together, Ninetta. If you still want me. We'll raise our girls here. They'll have

*their own families here one day. Your sacrifices will be rewarded.
You will be surrounded by more love than you can ever imagine. I
promise you. Be strong. Write.*

Ti amo, mia sposa,
Pietro

He folded the letter, then tucked it into an envelope,
scratching out the address in his neatest handwriting. This
time, he didn't bother with a stamp; the post was of no use.
The next day, he went to speak with people he thought might
get it to her, although he had no idea how. As he handed the
envelope to the Red Cross worker who listened to his story, he
had a renewed belief this letter would find its way to his wife.

CHAPTER 34

L asia woke up after another strange dream. She dreamt the war was over and Fonzaso was sparkling in the sunshine like it did when she was a child. The festivals started and she wore a red dress. Someone danced with her, holding her close, making her feel safe. Of all the girls in Fonzaso, the boy in her dreams found her the loveliest, despite her quietness. The light shining into her eyes brought her back to the reality she was living. She sat up, wishing the dream was real. All she desired was the Fonzaso of her childhood, quiet and colourful like when her *nonna* was alive, when Nico used to drop by with presents for her mother and tried to persuade her to play with him. He was the one good thing about her reality these days. Nico was different, gallant in his way. His confidence allowed him to sing happily at church long after the other boys became embarrassed to do so, and his easy manner made them want to be his friend. She smiled, thinking of him. Lasia loved the way he asked about what she was sewing when he visited. She watched him behind the counter at the bakery as he charmed every customer. Sometimes, he'd flash her a smile and signal to her he'd put something special in her bag. She would leave to find a little bread bird made from scrap dough. *Did he give those little birds to anyone else?* she wondered.

The sun rose in the sky, and her mother would be up soon so Lasia decided to start the coffee. They'd received a little from Zia Onorina, and Lasia knew her mother appreciated it. As Lasia stretched to grab the moka pot from the cabinet, she stopped. Outside the window was a tall man, ducking into the chicken coop across from their gate. His back was to her while he rummaged around, searching for something. He stood, then turned, looking her way. The swastika on his sleeve told her who he was. As soon as the revelation hit her, she pivoted sideways out of his view. Her mother began making her way down the stairs. Their eyes met. Both of them froze.

Nina sensed Lasia's panic. Halfway down the stairs, she bent to peek out the window as the soldier plodded around the yard. They waited, counting every long minute, fearing he would pound on the door. Lasia shrunk down below the window and ducked behind the stove, her eyes never leaving Nina's.

The chickens! Nina thought. He was looking for eggs. He wouldn't find any. Nina had caught Rita squeezing them to get their eggs the night before. She prayed he wouldn't take the birds. They counted on them for many meals. She heard another German voice shout a question towards to which he responded *"Nein"* then left to look elsewhere.

"*Ciao,* Corrado!" The barista greeted him as he walked into the empty taverna. He smiled and lifted his hand in response while pulling out a chair at his usual table in the centre of the room. He ordered a grappa and knocked it back, then ordered another to sip while he waited for the place to fill with men coming from the fields. These days, it was a never-ending hub of information and action. Rarely did good news make its way into conversations since the Germans had taken over northern Italy and the King aligned with the Allies. Any friendliness the Nazis showed before halted as their hold on the war slipped. They had orders which surpassed any level of underlying humanity. After Italy traded sides, word of executions was common from all over Belluno and the taverna was where the news broke first.

The bell on the door rang, and a group of labourers from Arten entered accompanied by the smell of stale sweat. Corrado nodded at them, recognising faces his late wife had delivered. They exchanged smiles and offered to buy him a drink.

A few months back, he was there when a travelling priest came in asking about the forest ranger, Perli. When someone pointed him out, the 'priest', an undercover partisan, shot him at close range. Perli, still a loyal fascist, had apparently told the Germans where English escapees from the Bolzano camp were hiding. The worst Italians were aligning with the Nazis, against their countrymen. There was a special place in hell for them in Corrado's mind and he conveniently forgot he had supported the fascists, worn his own black shirt years ago. The bell rang again, and the door swung open with force as a group of men from Frassenè piled in frantically.

"What's wrong?" Corrado asked. "What's happened?"

An older man in a worn plaid work shirt spoke first, catching his breath, "They're killing people in Frassenè. A partisan shot one of them..." The man was immediately cut off as the others started talking at the same time. Their voices growing loud with panic.

"A round-up! The women and the *bambini* too. All of them." Corrado heard from someone in the corner.

"Some Germans, looking for eggs. Damn partisans killed one... left the other to report it. Should've killed them both!" Two men surrounded him, adding more to the story.

"Don Cavalli came. That man's a saint. Told the SS to kill him instead!"

"If they didn't give up the partisans' names in five minutes, thirty would die." They pulled out chairs and sat with Corrado.

"Bastards!" They knocked back grappa. Glasses slammed on tables.

Then, a quieter voice stood out. "My wife's cousin was out there, with her little boys."

And another, "We came the back way, straight here, or we'd be dead."

"Nazi bastards," said everyone. Corrado nodded his head, agreeing.

"God help them."

"God help us all."

A pounding on the taverna window interrupted their chatter, and everyone looked up to see Abramo, Nico's brother, sprinting past. He ran up the Via Calzen. Immediately after, the urgent sound of boots on gravel followed as four SS soldiers chased behind him. Corrado stood on instinct as they ran up his street. Everyone he loved lived there. In one swift movement, he pulled a few lire out of his pocket and pushed the money onto the bar.

"I have to go," he said.

Rita sat on the street corner outside their house playing marbles with their neighbour, Maria Sofia. She had received a few for her birthday and sat whistling *Oy Marie,* a tune her new friend taught her. Maria Sofia had appeared six months before, another refugee from the bombed cities taking up with extended family in the country. The girl was intriguing to Rita; she knew lots of modern songs and spoke a little German, having a father of Austrian descent. Rita was about to explain more of the game when a figure flew past her, knocking her marbles across the cobblestones. He dashed down the street, then jumped through a lower window of the De Lazzer house. Abramo! He was always running. The fastest *ragazzo* in Fonzaso. As she reached to collect the mess, a group of SS officers appeared. They stopped and looked up the road, empty except for the girls. One of them pointed his bayonet at Rita, shouting in German. She stared at him, frozen. Maria Sofia spoke up in German explaining something Rita imagined had to do with her marbles. Her friend pointed to where Abramo dove into the house. They rushed to the ground floor window, bent down and shouted. One soldier stood guard as the others ran to the opposite entrance. "*Andiamo!*" Maria Sofia cried. "Go home and lock the door!" The girl urged Rita away before rushing off, but Rita insisted on collecting her marbles as she watched what was happening at the De Lazzer house. She heard screaming and cries of Signora De Lazzer. "Leave him! He's innocent! *Per favore!* Madonna save him!" In seconds the SS emerged from the house with their captive.

But it wasn't Abramo they held under the armpits; it was Nico.

His feet scrambled on the cobbles as they dragged him down the Via Calzen. She shouted, "Nico!" but he was already gone. Seconds later, Corrado came running around the corner. He grabbed Rita's hand, shouting, "*Dai, dai!* Come on!"

"Nonno, they took Nico, they took Nico!"

The pair burst into the house where Nina was preparing dinner with Lasia.

"They took Nico! Pulled him right out of his house!" Rita cried.

"What? What's happened?" Nina threw down her dish towel and immediately began untying her apron.

Corrado filled in the blanks and explained what he'd heard.

"Girls, stay here. I must go to Signora De Lazzer," Nina said, grabbing her sweater and reaching for the door.

"I'm going to Don Cavalli," Corrado said, "There must be something we can try. He's only a boy," He turned to Lasia and Rita and directed them with a face as serious as stone, "Stay here."

Lasia rushed upstairs to her mother's room and flung open the door to the balcony where she could see San Micel. She fell to her knees and prayed to the Madonna with everything in her heart for the sweetest boy she knew who now was in the clutches of the Nazis.

Signora De Lazzer wasn't at her house, so Nina headed to the piazza. She ducked into the *Alimentari Bianchi* where Onorina and Toni watched from the window. The SS were pushing men into the back of trucks, knocking them about and whipping them with the butts of their pistols. Signora Minella screamed, reaching for her boys only to get beaten herself with the end of a soldier's rifle; her head broke open like a pomegranate fruit, seeds of blood spilling over her face.

Inconsolable screams and cries filled the piazza. Engines revved. Abramo shouted as the trucks drove away, "It's me you want! Take me instead!" But it was too late. The trucks tore down the road kicking up dust behind them. In tears, the families dispersed, wondering if they would ever see their loved ones alive again.

No *Fonzasini* slept for fear the town would be burned and wondering what was happening to the captives. In the morning, they dashed between each other's houses, speculating about what would happen next – until a young girl pointed to something high on the cliff of *Cima Loreto*.

The men appeared at the edge of the precipice. They stood in a jagged row, facing the town. Nina insisted the girls go back to the house. But it was too late; two figures dropped down, followed by another. Shots rang out like firecrackers far away. One by one bodies floated off the edge, smooth, gliding until they disappeared behind the trees. Lasia watched, wondering which one was Nico. Her heart bounced to her throat, then plummeted as she glided down with him.

The skies opened; it rained with great fury. The next day a group attempted to recover the bodies but returned distraught. Nazis stood guard, shooting at them each time they approached. Two days later, when they finally reached them, animals had been there first. With a mixture of determination and tenderness, they collected the remains. They found the Minella brothers, Constantino and Antonio, a few feet apart from each other; the boys never could be separated, even in death. Nina found out later Nico's uncle had retrieved his body, having tenderly covered the boy's wounded head before delivering him to the arms of an inconsolable mother. As they were about to be executed, Nico had jumped, along with Silvio Marcon and Antonio Zucco. Brave boy. He had broken his leg and back when he hit the ground. People said they heard him calling out, "Mamma!" through the sounds of the storm. It was clear from his brutal injuries the Nazis had climbed down and finished him. The other two who jumped miraculously escaped.

There was silence as a wooden cart rolled down the mountainside with the four bodies inside. The *Fonzasini* lined up, wailing on either side of the road to watch their dead come home. No one met each other's eyes. The rain left a painfully dank smell in the air. Nina couldn't name the scent, but she was sure it was the smell of hopelessness. Rita shifted at her side, silent. Lasia stood next to her, holding Nina's arm for support. The cart creaked, moaning under the weight of the dead. It stopped at the top of the road where Nico's stoic mother and sister stood, still except for the tears rolling down their cheeks. Abramo leaned by his mother's side, hand over his eyes, curled over, knowing it should have been him.

They brought the bodies to the church where they joined six others who had been killed in Frassenè. Nina and her sisters volunteered to prepare them for burial. Corinna helped, but Lasia couldn't. She went to *Sant'Anna* and prayed for Nico's soul.

On the days before the funeral, while preparing the bodies for burial, the *Fonzasini* prayed the Germans wouldn't massacre them all. Families of the dead brought clothes to the church. Nina and her sisters washed the blood off each of them, trying to make them look the best they could. Nico's mother didn't want to leave his side. Nina cried with her. They had been together that night he was born. Nina had saved him at birth, but neither she nor his mother could protect him from the evil of men. Abramo, tormented with guilt, had run into the mountains to join the partisans and hunt down the Germans who'd killed his brother. He'd tried to apologise to his mother, but she acted as though he wasn't there. She couldn't register the actuality of her youngest being killed in such a way. How was it he was no longer of this Earth? Nico's smile wouldn't be waiting for her in the mornings, his sweet voice would never enter her ears again.

Word came through the resistance network. Mussolini was dead. Partisans had stopped him in Dongo, on the western shores of Lake Como, as he tried to escape to Switzerland. They found him; shot him and his actress lover near a gate overlooking the most beautiful part of Italy. They took his body to Milan, spat and pissed on it. The man who claimed he'd make Italy great hung like a pig in a petrol station; a fraud who traded his people to the wolves for power and pride.

With the end in sight, the Nazis in Belluno became ruthless, burning towns and killing indiscriminately. Rumour had it the partisans' actions had brought Fonzaso and Frassenè to their attention for more retaliation. The *Fonzasini* needed to be ready to run to the mountains at any moment if the town was set ablaze.

The night before the funerals, Nina lay awake, tormented by fear of what might come. It was three in the morning when an urgent knock pounded the door, and she rushed downstairs to find Aurora in her nightgown.

"It's over!" Aurora cried. "We've been liberated!"

"Shhh," Nina hushed her. "You'll wake up the girls." Nina looked over her sister's appearance. "Why aren't you wearing your clothes like we talked about?"

"Nina! It's over! We heard it on the radio!"

"Did you run over here in your nightgown? Come in." Nina urged her into the house, closing the door so it didn't slam.

"Listen to me!" Aurora tried again, ignoring her questions.

Nina interrupted, "You've lost your mind!"

"*Allora,* will you please let me speak!" Aurora said, exasperated. "It's been over for a week. The Germans are retreating!" Nina gaped at her sister in disbelief as she went on, "The school is empty of them! Do you realise what this means? We won't be hungry anymore. The children are safe!" Something in Aurora's face had been switched back on, and Nina suddenly remembered the little girl her sister had been long ago. "Come!" Aurora directed. "You should see how many Americans and British soldiers are in the piazza!"

Nina's head was cloudy. Her mind still contemplated how to survive. *After all these years, could this really be the end?*

"Americans, walking around in the piazza?" Nina asked.

"I'm telling you they're there now!" Aurora cried.

Euphoria washed through Nina as she considered it could be true. The fear, the hunger, the death. She had survived! The war was over. She rushed to the foot of the stairs, whispering loudly, "Lasia! Come down! Don't wake your sister. I'm not sure I believe it yet."

"Mamma?" Lasia hurried down the stairs.

Nina hugged her and looked at Lasia's young, worried face.

"Don't worry, *bella mia;* the war is over! Your Zia Aurora has run over in her nightgown to tell us," she laughed.

"Over?" said Lasia, her face brightening. "Over? The war is over!"

"Come!" Aurora urged. "Everyone is meeting at the piazza."

"Are you sure?" Lasia asked. "This isn't a trick?" Nina agreed, she couldn't believe it was true. She hurried to cover herself with a tattered shawl, then together the three women headed towards the piazza, leaving Rita in a deep sleep upstairs.

A fidgety Rita rolled back and forth in bed. She was dreaming of Nazis at the door, lifting bayonets at her, her sister and mother, the town burning outside her window. She sat up, gasping and sweating.

"Mamma?" she whispered. There was no response. Where was Mamma? Where was Lasia? They had both been there when she fell asleep, now they were gone. *Mio Dio!* Her heart dropped to her stomach. *They took them. The Nazis took them and left me here and they're going to burn the town!* she thought. A chill went through her. *Where are they?* Tears filled her eyes. It was her fault. She'd been bad, now they were gone, taken, maybe being tortured. She ran downstairs. There was no trace of them, but their shawls weren't on their hooks.

What do I do? I must run to Zia Aurora's and warn them or get help.

She threw on her cardigan, snuck out the door and looked around in case the soldiers were still nearby. A great commotion came from the piazza, buzzing dialect peppered with shrieks and cries. Her first instinct was to run to the mountains in case they were rounding up everyone to be shot. But she couldn't. *If my mamma and sorella are there, I have to help them.*

Her breath became measured as she headed towards the

noise, staying in the shadows. *This is it,* she thought as she inched towards the piazza.

A hand grabbed her shoulder and she turned in fear, coming face to face with her friend, Francesco.

"*Mio Dio!* Did you escape?" she whispered.

"What are you talking about?" he asked, smiling at her with imperfect teeth.

He was crazy or stupid.

Francesco began jumping up and down, holding on to Rita's arm. "Rita, the war is over! We're celebrating! Can you believe it?"

She looked at him, astonished.

"Over? Over? I thought Mamma and Lasia were..." She stopped as she spotted them near the church. Her aunts and cousins hugged and cried together. Instead of joy, pure jealousy coursed through her as she watched them. "They left me! They left me to believe they were dead and I was alone!" She ran until she reached them and pushed Lasia hard.

"Rita!" yelled Nina. "It's okay. The war is over! Everything is going to be better."

"You left me!" shouted Rita. "I came to save you from the Germans and here you are celebrating without me!"

"Oh, *bambina mia,*" Nina took the girl in her arms. "It's going to be good. I promise. Our lives can begin again and you will have some childhood left."

Lasia tugged her shawl tight across her shoulders, clasping it at her neck. She left her mother with Rita and went to talk to her cousins and old classmates. Candlelight in the hands of each *Fonzasini* lit the piazza, illuminating excited faces in a golden hue. Everyone's eyes sparkled knowing that when the sun rose, it would be a new day, without war. A new Italy! One yet to be defined, but free of Nazis and fascists. The end of the war! The piazza was packed like a festival. A few English and

American soldiers who had been hiding in the mountainside roamed freely, a sign of the end. Signora Marta came out covered in her jewellery, dancing and showing off every piece she had hidden. Everyone kissed each other's cheeks, embracing with relief. In the bustling of the crowd, Lasia found her back pressed against a young man. She recognised him as Bortolo Sebben, the boy who years ago had stolen her ribbon and teased her. He was tall and a smile filled his face. He didn't look like a bully anymore. The Nazis had killed three of his cousins in the Frassenè massacre. His family had lost much. But it was over; it was time to celebrate. He paused for the slightest moment and then kissed her on both cheeks, smiled and moved on.

Shadows danced on the walls where months earlier the men had been shot. Rita untangled herself from her mother's embrace and walked to the place on the cobbles where she had stood among the corpses. The blood on the ground had faded, but she'd always know it was there. She watched her mother moving from cluster to cluster and her sister talking to a tall boy. She saw Corrado helping the men from the taverna carry out dirt encrusted bottles of wine that had been buried, now dug up to celebrate. They wiped the necks, passing the bottles around for everyone to take a swig. Francesco snuck a bottle and sat next to her on the cool stone fountain steps to observe the crowd together. "Did you see what those bastard Nazis did to me? Stabbed me in the leg with their bayonets while I was hiding in the bushes." He lifted his shorts to reveal a long cut up his thigh, red and mid-healing, before continuing. "I helped, you know? I brought food to the Englishmen and the Americans hiding in the mountains. I've got the proof."

Not to be outdone, Rita commented, "I had one of those bayonets pointed right at my face!" A jovial American solider walked around handing out cigarettes to the most attractive women. Francesco and Rita exchanged glances and giggled.

"*Salute!*" Francesco said, raising the bottle to his lips for a long drink. "To the British and to the Americans!"

Rita grabbed the bottle, taking a deep swig. Who cared if Mamma caught her, for the moment, it didn't matter.

"To America!" she cheered.

CHAPTER 35

T he bells rang out the day of the funerals. Liberation. It was strange, a day mixed with goodbyes and hope twisted with a cruel joke of timing. Lasia prayed a Hail Mary standing next to each man's casket. The broken angles of their bodies couldn't be perfectly hidden; it unsettled her to be near the corpses of so many she knew. She walked to Nico's casket last. A bandage on the side of his serene face covered what they couldn't mend. There was no more ruddiness in his cheeks, but to Lasia he looked like a sculpture; she laid her hand against his cool cheek to say goodbye. A group of men carried the caskets to the cemetery followed by a parade of mourners. Lasia looked up to see Bortolo Sebben helping to carry of one of his three cousins. He bowed his head, acknowledging her.

They buried the men side by side. Don Cavalli gave a long blessing to a silent crowd. The families walked home, past the convent, up the road on a day that should have been one of the best of their lives, but they could not celebrate. Not everyone made it through. The bells of the church tolled again. Liberation was theirs.

The next days were strange for the *Fonzasini,* like emerging from a fevered illness. The Americans, British and partisans who had been hiding all over Fonzaso filled the piazza, passing chewing gum to the children. It was the Germans' turn to hide. There was a last shootout as they caught two Nazis behind Concetta Sebben's house. American soldiers killed them, but in the crossfire, they shot Concetta. The widow lay face up, eyes wide to Heaven; at peace.

Signora De Lazzer became part of her furniture. She lay in bed, day after day, looking at the *Cima Loreto* where her son had perished. She said nothing, ate nothing. He died and went to God; she died and kept living.

After church on Sunday, the older women of the town marched girls who the enemy had courted into the piazza. Bettina Napoli was the oldest among them, having opened her bed to the fascists and Nazis alike. Some of the young ones were Lasia's old classmates. The older women kicked and spat on them. "Nazi *puttane!*" They screamed. "Whores!" With razors in fists, they grabbed them by the hair and shaved them violently. Scalps nicked, bloody cuts appeared between patches of hair as the girls screamed for mercy. Some of the more savage partisans smeared the girls' bald heads with tar as their cries pierced the air and a crowd cheered. Nina couldn't watch. How could churchgoers pray to God then attack these poor women? Hadn't they seen enough violence? Bettina Napoli, the delicate girl on the float years ago, the victim of an abusive husband and dead family. What choice did life give her outside of marrying again? Nina tried to meet her eyes to comfort her, but the woman stared at the ground as they shaved and tarred her. When Rita asked why they were torturing them, Nina directed the girls to look the other way.

A few weeks later, fresh energy crept into Fonzaso. The *Fonzasini* became lively as more men returned, and families came to terms with those who wouldn't. It helped that summer was beginning, a time for optimism. On Sunday, they filled the piazza, and those who spoke English chatted to the Allies who remained.

Lasia stood in the piazza looking up at San Micel, and couldn't believe it all. She let her faith take away the sadness of loss and gave in to the sunny day surrounding her. The war was over. She could have a future. A voice interrupted her thoughts.

"*Ciao.*" Bortolo Sebben stood in front of her.

Lasia squinted, trying to see his face as a cloud moved and the sun shone in her eyes. She hadn't spoken to him since the night before the funerals.

"I saw you in church," he said. The mundane comment put her strangely at ease to talk to him.

"I'm very sorry about your cousins," she said, her voice sincere.

"*Sì.*" He was quiet. "I'm sorry about Nico. I know he was a good friend of your family. He was my friend too." She nodded, not meeting his eyes. A strange pause filled the space between them.

"Hey," Bortolo finally spoke, lifting his fist to crack his knuckles and twisting his torso. "The weather's nice. Do you want to go for a bike ride sometime in the hills with my friends from Frassenè?"

She bit her lip to hide the smile that crept onto her face, surprised she wanted to say yes to the Sebben boy. "I don't know. I... I guess so. Let me ask Mamma," she reasoned. "She's got an old bike in the shed. I think she'd let me use it. It was in such awful shape no one stole it. I'm not sure the tyres are any good. I don't know if I could keep up with you." How embarrassing that she couldn't stop talking. She had never noticed how attractive he was. How lean and tall he had become!

"So, you'll come?" he asked with a grin, encouraging her.

"*Sì,* if Mamma agrees," she said. He clapped his hands, surprising her as he nipped her chin with his thumb and forefinger, then gave her a wink. It was the second time in a few weeks his touch had surprised her.

"I'll come by on Wednesday. See you then, Lasia." He left her standing in the midday sun with a strange new feeling in her belly.

When they returned home with plans of making a Sunday dinner, they found a stranger on the Via Calzen. He wore an American flag pin on his lapel and a red cross on his green jacket. The man was studying each house with a letter in his hand. "Can we help you?" Nina asked.

"*Sì.* I'm looking for Nina Pante." The man spoke broken Italian with an American accent.

"I'm Nina Pante." Her heart leapt. *What was this?*

"I've a got letter for you from the States. I'm with the Red Cross in Bassano del Grappa." He handed the envelope to her, looking at the girls.

"I've had it a while." He watched Nina as she turned the letter over then asked her, "Do you have enough to eat?"

"We survive," she mumbled, too busy focusing on the letter. It felt strange between her fingers. He reached into his pocket and pulled out a chocolate bar, handing it to Rita.

"Share it with your sister, promise?" Rita's eyes grew large as she took the bar from him then immediately unwrapped it.

"*Grazie*," Nina said, staring at the handwriting on the envelope. Could it be? Could it really be?

Anticipation welled in her. The thought of her old dream being alive was ludicrous. But she tore open the envelope. Pietro was alive! She needed to read the letter thoroughly; it was hard to focus on the words. "Accident, what accident?" she whispered as she skimmed to the end. He wanted her to come to him. Nervous excitement had her dizzy. After over ten years apart from him and years of not hearing anything, not knowing if he was alive, if he still cared for his family – could it be? She wanted to shout aloud to San Micel but, instead, she cupped her hand over her mouth and walked into the house. She sat, rereading the letter as a thousand thoughts poured through her head. The girls spoke to her, but Nina couldn't hear and held a hand up to tell them to let her focus. Questions flew through her head. *Can he bring us to America soon? How soon?* Then again, she thought, *Thank God! Pietro is alive!*

Pietro. She closed her eyes and they were there together at San Micel.

Pietro. Standing in the church as she stood before him in her wedding dress. He had looked at her full of love and anticipation of their life together.

Pietro. He still loved her. She was his Ninetta. He wanted her. He had saved for years, built a life for them without knowing if he'd ever see her again.

Pietro. Appearing again and again after being gone so long, making love to her. Every time he was a stranger and every time there was something familiar.

The love of her life had returned to her in this letter. A war had kept them apart, but it was over. They could be a family again.

But she paused. How could she consider America now? Hadn't she been through the worst in Italy? How could she leave Papà? It would devastate him. When Pietro first left, she was young and America had been exciting, a welcome adventure. She didn't long for excitement. She needed peace. And Lasia and Rita, how would they feel? Lasia was almost sixteen, nearly as old as she had been when they married. Would she fight to stay behind? No, Lasia would listen to her mother and she would come, but it would break what was left of her spirit. In an instant, with one letter, the world that was righting itself turned upside down again.

CHAPTER 36

Summer 1946 Lasia walked into the water as far as her courage would take her, then relaxed her muscles, submerging her shoulders as her body, too, became liquid. She dared not go under. No father had taught her to swim. She stood, squinting as the August sun shone in her eyes. The mountains rose to the sky, roads winding around cliffs like amber ribbons. On the tiny pier, children sat, skipping stones. Sunbathers lay on rocks. If they were lovers, the men leaned on one elbow telling girls things that put smiles on their faces. Italian men were talented at charming women with little effort. She laughed, flipping onto her back to float; Bortolo had taught her to do that, at least. For the first time, happiness defined her life. From the day he took her on a bike ride they had become inseparable. Over the past year, they spent days visiting his friends in Agana and Arten, discovering fields of bluebells and returning with flour and olive oil for her mother. They rode as far as Feltre to visit the city as it was coming back to life. It was easy to ignore the way his eyes sometimes travelled over other women because he was her cicerone to life. He had taken her by the hand and introduced her to post-war freedom.

Bortolo made her feel attractive, even if it took teasing her to change her conservative ways. His taunting forced her to take chances. She had never been swimming with friends or revealed her body in a swimsuit. When he joked about her unwillingness to take off her day clothes and join everyone, she obliged awkwardly, then felt free. At sixteen, maybe life could be glorious. After years of knowing nothing but war, everything was taking on colour and texture. The world came into focus and he was the reason. She rose to her feet and looked back at the shoreline. A darkly tanned Bortolo stood, shirtless and lithe, with one hand on his hip and the other shielding his eyes from the sun. Finding her, he waved with gusto. She laughed despite herself, waved back and shouted, "I'm coming in," before treading her way back to shore.

"What will you do now the war's over? With your life?" she asked as they pedalled home.

"Is it over?" He laughed.

"What do you mean? Of course it's over!" she exclaimed, annoyed at his joking.

"Well," he said, "the war may have ended, but Italy will always be in conflict with herself. Your father, he has it right living abroad. Our country, it's beautiful. Our food, well, at least before the war, it's the best. Our artists – the greatest. Our women..." He winked at her and she blushed. "There are none like them, as I understand, but Italy can never be a truly great country."

She stopped her bike and glared at him. What was he saying?

"You're terrible!" she yelled. "How can you say that? How can you believe that? Look at what the Romans did. Their influence on cultures around the world." She didn't know much, but she knew the greatness of the Romans. He navigated his bike next to hers.

"Now you sound like *il Duce*. Look where it got him! If you want greatness, it's in America."

His words reminded her of the conversations going on at home. She decided it was time to tell him. "My father has been writing to us. He wants us to join him. Let's see if it happens," she said, glad it was finally out in the air, wondering how he would react to the thought of her leaving.

"I hope you do, Lasia. America is the place to go. There's nothing left here." He didn't act upset at the idea of her leaving; she could have announced what she was having for dinner.

"There's everything here! I don't want to leave. My family is here... and you." It was useless to try to control her emotions. They came out despite her attempts to hold back.

"Not for long," he said. "I'm going to figure out a way to leave. When I do, I'll come find you in America."

The more Nina watched Lasia live her life as a teenager, the more concerned she became. The girl was falling in love. Both the girls were growing up. Nina had to remind Rita not to join the boys when they gathered old bullets from the school where the Nazis had been stationed. Her friend, Giovanni, died when a leftover grenade exploded during a game. His mother cried because she could not save him from the war that would never end.

That summer had been the best of Lasia's life. Bortolo's family restarted their silk and textile trade, taking trips to Venice where their business recovered, slowly. Eventually, he could bring back fabric for her in bright colours, and she learnt to sew the newer fashions. Lasia was a meticulous seamstress who had inherited her father's frugal ways and his appreciation for make and quality. The war left her with a near-curveless five foot three, ninety-eight pound frame, but she could sew flattering styles that made the most of her figure. The more the letters moved back and forth between her parents, the more she dreaded leaving.

The *Fonzasini* decided the *Festa dell'Uva* would start up again. Lasia longed for the fun she and Bortolo would have, dancing and enjoying the wine. However, as the festival neared, Bortolo developed a habit of being late. A few afternoons, he failed to appear. On one of these occasions, when he was over an hour delayed, Lasia gave up and offered Rita her bicycle for the afternoon. The girl jumped on, pedalling fast down the Via Mezzaterra where she came upon a leisurely Bortolo talking to a buxom server at the taverna and ran into him with the bicycle. Accidental, she told Lasia, but he deserved it. If he had arrived on time, she wouldn't have taken the bicycle, and he wouldn't have been in her way.

On the day of the festival, Rita and Lasia both laughed as they stomped the harvest of grapes with their bare feet. Purple juice squirted from the fruit and the skins caught between their toes as the sweet smell permeated the air. Lasia thought she must look a funny sight, but her legs were pretty and well-shaped. She hoped Bortolo would admire them. As she searched among the crowds, she couldn't see him, and she continued her stomping disappointed. Her eyes trailed up to the *Cima Loreto,* and she flinched remembering Nico.

Bortolo didn't appear at the parade. He didn't see her in her crown of grapevines or come to the dance. When she heard he had left for Venice for an extended stay with his family there, she did all she could to hold in her devastation. The other girls twirled and tossed vines at their suitors, giggling. Lasia swayed in the crowd with her cousins and Rita, but slowly she made her way into the background where she was most comfortable, where her heart could not be broken.

In November, the final details of their move reached Nina. Pietro had planned everything. They would travel on the SS *Marine Perch.* Her extended Dalla Santa cousins, who had emigrated decades ago and lived in New Jersey, would pick them up. Nina felt like someone had spun her around, then told to walk straight. She went through their belongings, determining if there was anything left worth taking. Pietro promised if she didn't like America after five years, they could come back to Fonzaso. In her top drawer, she kept an eclectic mix of boxes filled with humble wooden rosaries the soldiers didn't bother taking. There was her mother's plainest rosary. Pulling it out, she dangled the object in her hand. She lay the crucifix in her palm, studying Jesus on the cross, thinking about gospels from church, the stories they had taught her to believe in. A book written by men in the interest of God. She thought of Hannah, the poor woman, and Federico and Giglio who, Tinetta wrote, were both missing, believed to have died in the camps. Her heart contracted thinking of them. How could one suffer so much for race and religion? How had the world gone so wrong they allowed an entire people to be annihilated? It was too much to comprehend.

But it was over, time to piece life back together, to move forward.

She'd never been so nervous as she was now. Toni and Onorina lent her a trunk, and she thought about what the girls should pack. She looked around the house at all the familiar things: furniture, baskets, copper pots. They would not live here anymore. She had to repeat it in her head to get it to sink in. Leaving Fonzaso had always been the plan, but as she began packing up, the trunk and bags weren't large enough to take her memories. *I never thought this would happen.* She squeezed the rosary beads in her palm, clasping them tightly between her hands. She fell to her knees next to the bed. "God, please be with us on this journey. Please give us the strength to take on this next test," she prayed. The fears were strong. War was horrible, sad, unnerving, but the unknown of this situation, leaving Fonzaso, moving to America, seeing Pietro after nearly twelve years apart, gave her a new kind of anxiety like the ground was being removed from under her feet. She cried out loud, confessing to Pietro and to God the way she would to a priest. "I've not kept my promises. I've failed you in every way. I'm not the girl you fell in love with, nor the young woman who was your wife all those years ago. I've been broken and put back together. I've scrounged and scavenged for food. I've lied. I've doubted your love, doubted my love for you. I have cast off God then come back to Him. I've questioned if I should be alive. I've thought about running away." She continued her confession, squeezing her elbows into the mattress. "I have hidden in our room while my children cried and ignored them because I had nothing left to give... looked at them with empty eyes, as though they weren't mine. I have envied my sisters and neighbours. I've been vain and full of regret and self-doubt. Convinced I don't deserve my dreams. I've not kept my promises to myself. It's all I can do to confess to you that what I am is an imperfect woman, yet I cannot be the only one."

Could she do this? At forty-two, wasn't she too late to follow old dreams? Aurora tiptoed into the room.

"*Allora,* who are you talking to? Are you going crazy?" she asked, sitting on the bed where Nina prayed.

"I can't believe this is happening. It doesn't feel real," Nina said. She pulled herself up and sat shoulder to shoulder with her sister.

"I know," Aurora said, smoothing her skirt. "I don't know what I'll do without you. What any of us will do without you."

"I promise we'll come back and visit," Nina said.

"Maybe I'll come to visit you, you never know," Aurora said, hesitating as if mustering courage then asked, "Do you still love him?"

Nina paused and studied her sister, looking at her honest eyes, the sturdy body. She could always trust Aurora. Nodding, she answered, "I think so."

"You're brave. You've been an inspiration. I wish you and the girls the best."

Nina pulled her younger sibling to her, hugging her with tears welling in her eyes.

"I'll miss you. Do you think it's right for me to go? I feel selfish."

"Mamma would have wanted you to do it," said Aurora.

"Yes, the Captain. She told me to go," Nina said.

"You've made her proud. You've followed in her footsteps, and you're doing something she never had the chance to do," Aurora said.

"All I've ever wanted was to be half the woman she was."

Aurora smiled. "Nina, you are much more than that. You've been the one to midwife, you've given everything you have and gone without to make sure our children had what they needed. This is your chance at happiness. You're the one who would have made her the most proud."

"She's always with us, isn't she? Her habits, her commanding, her love," Nina said.

"She gave us something special. Something we need to pass on to our girls," Aurora agreed.

"We will," Nina put the rosary in her pocket, above her heart, "and she'll continue to live on in them." Nina paused and reached for Aurora's hand. "Write to me. Have Papà write on the bottom. When I can, I'll send money back."

"I'll miss you, but I'm glad your time is here. It will be everything you've dreamed of."

"I hope so. If not, I'll be back."

A week later, a black Fiat drove up to the Via Calzen and Bortolo Sebben got out with a fedora in his hand. Lasia, watching from the kitchen window, wiped her hands on a dish towel before walking outside, feigning curiosity in the automobile. Her sadness quickly turned into anger. She'd never been more humiliated than she had been that night at the festival, convinced he didn't care about her. The other girls held onto their mementos from the night, but she had nothing. Who did he think he was? In her heart there was a fury mixed with hurt that made an explosive combination, out of character for her. She didn't want the street to hear her outburst, so told him to get into the car and sat in the passenger seat. As soon as the car door closed, she shouted at him.

"How could you? You didn't even say goodbye! You didn't even have the decency to tell me you were going away!" She surprised herself at the sharpness of her tongue, full of venom for him. He leaned back as her words hit him.

"Lasia, I went to visit family. It's not like we were going out. It's not like we ever did anything to make it seem like we were together," he said, reaching for her hand.

"Go to hell!" she yelled, grabbing at the handle to escape.

"Lasia, calm down," he pleaded with her.

Her body shook with anger.

"You think we can pick back up where we left off when you never even bothered writing? Were you too busy frequenting brothels under the canals?" She knew she was bordering on being ridiculous, but she was beyond caring. The anger was unfamiliar, like a release, unleashing months of pent up jealousy.

She turned from him to face forward. He did the same. They sat, staring silently out the dirty windshield at the mountains in front of them. He moved first, but did not speak. Instead, he opened his door, got out of the car, walked around the front of the Fiat and opened Lasia's door from the outside. She stepped out, hurrying towards her house without looking back at him.

"Lasia, please."

He caught up with her and grabbed her by the shoulder, twisting her towards him then put his lips to hers. With fervour, he kissed her. The second he relaxed his mouth, she pulled back and slapped him hard across the cheek with a power she didn't know she possessed. He winced, looking shocked. A giggle from a window above told her Rita had witnessed everything. The realisation infuriated her more.

She swung open the door to the house and slammed it behind her, closing him out forever.

As soon as she was alone in the kitchen, her heart sank and she burst into tears as she realised that might have been their last goodbye.

CHAPTER 37

O n Christmas Eve, 1946, their trunks sat ready to leave
as they huddled next to the stove, heat folding around
them. It was the last evening in their house. Nina looked at her
two daughters with awe. Lasia had turned seventeen the day
before. It was hard to believe she wasn't a little girl anymore. It
was their turn to have great loves and adventures, different
from hers. America was calling them. Pietro was waiting for
them. They would leave Fonzaso behind.

"Girls, I want you to know," she began, "I know I don't say
it often, but you both are my heart."

She stroked Lasia's hair and looked fondly at Rita from
across the room.

"Did you feel that way when you chased me down the
street with a broom?" Rita challenged her with raised
eyebrows. "Because it didn't seem like it."

"What do you expect? You were a little pain in the *culo* and
you reminded the taxman of everything we had!" Nina
laughed, remembering, then announced, "It's time to go to
bed. Say your prayers. Tomorrow is a big day."

When the fire died down, Nina climbed the stairs and sat on her bed. She looked up at San Micel and prayed. *Mary, please help us, watch over my family here in Fonzaso as I leave them, and watch over my children and me as we leave everything we know.* She held her rosary and said her prayers, ending her Hail Mary, "… now and at the hour of our death. Amen."

"Is everything packed?" Nina shouted as she paced the floor of the kitchen, now and then stopping to open a drawer or a cupboard as though it might hold something critical for their journey. It was early on Christmas morning but none of them could sleep the night before. It would be a Christmas like no other.

"*Sì*, Mamma!" they both exclaimed, answering the question she repeated to them.

Her nerves prickled with the anxiety of the unknown.

"First, we'll go to Genoa and stay the night. You must stay close the entire time. There'll be thieves and con artists everywhere. It's a port city; they know people are carrying their lives with them, and no one who's leaving would call the *Carabinieri* because they won't want to miss their ship."

Nina released every worry in her mind onto her daughters, as if saying them aloud might stop bad things from happening.

"Oh, Mamma," said Rita, rolling her eyes, "we won't be robbed. I'm excited to go to Genoa. There are street women there! Francesco told me ladies stand in the doorways and offer themselves to men."

"Margherita Pante, you shouldn't even know those things, much less say them! If I tell Francesco's mother you said that, she'll box his ears!" She was shocked, as usual, by Rita's knowledge and comfort in talking about such matters aloud, but at least it took Nina's mind off obsessing over the journey. A knock on the door interrupted their conversation. Lasia opened it to find Bortolo on the other side.

"Merry Christmas," he said. He rubbed his hands together as his breath met the cold air. "May I come in? It's freezing out here."

Lasia gestured inside towards the fire. She had already convinced herself she wouldn't see him again, but here he was shivering on her doorstep looking handsome and holding a beautifully wrapped box. Nina and Rita wished him a *Buon Natale,* then went upstairs for another round of packing checks.

They sat together in the fire-lit room. Lasia was stoic but after a brief silence, she asked him, "Why did you come back today? We're leaving in a few hours."

"I'm sorry," he offered. "I should have come sooner. But I'm here now."

"What did you think I would do? Stay here with you?" She pretended to watch the embers and secretly wished he was here to propose. To beg her to stay.

He looked at her, confused. "I don't know what to say. You have a whole other life waiting for you there. You won't want me writing to you, having you wait for me to come to you."

Her heart fell; she knew he was right. They weren't meant to be together, but she hated that he could be rational. Why wasn't he so caught up in love with her he couldn't think straight?

"Here. Happy birthday," he said, lifting the colourful box. "I want you to take this with you. Something you'll like, from Venice."

He put the box on her lap and she felt its weight. Whatever

it was would be difficult to take with her. She tore the wrapping, lifted the lid and looked inside. An elegant dish set was nestled in creamy satin fabric; white bone china with deep burgundy edges. Intricate hand painted gold script adorned them, Venetian-style. They were the most beautiful present she had ever received and, likely, the most expensive things she had ever owned. Her mouth dropped. "*Bellissima,*" she whispered as she dug through the large box, uncovering not only plates but bowls, cups and saucers.

"They're incredible. How can I accept these?"

"I knew you'd like them. They're like you, delicate and timeless. I wanted you to have them."

She ran her finger along the fine edges of the china. "How will I take this?" The practical side of her brain taking over.

"In a trunk; I'll pay for it to come with you. If things don't line up in America, sell them and come back."

"I *am* going to come back. As soon as I can. I want to be with my family, but I don't want to leave here." Tears sprang to the corners of her eyes. "I'm not asking you to wait for me. I'm not sure how long it will take. But please don't forget me." It was unfair. Why didn't he beg her to stay? Why not propose if he loved her? He stroked her hair and she closed her eyes, letting him, knowing it was too intimate. She should stay angry with him, but she didn't have the freedom to; she'd be gone by the end of the day. Her heart ached. It would have been easier if he hadn't come back at all.

"Okay," she agreed, "I'll take them with me. But I'll come back. Count on it."

The family surrounded them as they readied to go. Maria held her daughter on her hip, promising, with her husband Luigi, to take care of the house, with a plan to buy it if Nina stayed in America. Lasia convinced Nina to find space in their trunks to bring the china, the most impractical thing to carry overseas but the most important to her. Nina knew how hard it was for her daughter to leave Fonzaso and the girl never asked for anything, so when she begged to let her pack the beautiful china set, Nina agreed.

Rita played until the minute they had to go, sledding down from *Sant'Anna* on the icy slide she had made with Francesco. The boys stood around telling her they would hide her there. But she sledded down into a sea of her family members, and Nina said it was time to go. Everyone on the Via Calzen came out to say goodbye. Onorina hugged her and gave her a blue scarf she had knitted to keep her warm on the journey. Mary and Quinto promised to meet them in America someday. Francesco looked at Rita with weepy eyes, and his mother kissed Nina goodbye. Vante's wife, Antonietta, stood with Corinna, waving handkerchiefs at them. Nina held Aurora for the longest time, pressing her palms to her sister's back, trying to memorise the feel of her embrace. One of the few cars in town picked them up, everyone followed, crying and waving at them as they drove away.

When they turned the corner onto the piazza, Nina spotted Corrado leaning against the side of the taverna. He'd said goodbye and escaped earlier. Now he stood, his cap tipping sideways, wiping his tears with a handkerchief as he watched them go. Nina peered through the back window one last time. Corrado kissed his hand and waved. Her heart leapt into her throat and she made the sign of the cross, praying she would see him again.

They stood close together in the line for the ship, Rita pushing against her sister's side. Lasia looked annoyed, lost in her thoughts. Three women, heading to an unknown life. Nina wrapped her arms around Rita. She reached out to touch Lasia's face, but the girl turned away, pretending the line was moving, reaching to grab her bag.

We lived through a war. I've lived through two, Nina thought. *We will get through this.*

Rita pointed to the ship.

"Why is that man so dark? Did he drink a lot of coffee?" she asked. Nina looked up. Rita knew of black men and had seen pictures of the people in Africa in the newspapers, but in Fonzaso, she hadn't come across anyone with different skin to hers.

"Don't point, Rita. We aren't in Fonzaso anymore. Remember that."

As they boarded, the black man greeted them with a smile, ignoring Rita's stares. He guided them to their room, explaining through gestures where to go for dinner. They could understand something about Neapolitan ice cream in the dining hall. He promised Rita she could help him pass it out which made her happy. Never in her eleven years on Earth had she had Neapolitan ice cream, or had the chance to distribute it, or sailed on a ship. One thrill topped the next. Entering the room, their excitement diminished; it was dark and contained ten bunk beds squeezed into a small square space. Looking at each other but saying nothing, they dropped their bags and prepared to get used to their surroundings.

The boat shifted and groaned as Nina shivered in the room she and the girls shared with seven other passengers. Her cheek was flat to the thin mat serving as her bed, and the room swayed back and forth. She had eaten nothing in four days. Her stomach was concave; she was too weak to lift her head.

"Mamma, try to eat this." Rita sat on a stool next to the bed, holding out a small cup with two hard-boiled eggs in it. "Eat something, even if it comes back up."

Nina gaped at Rita and hoped she wasn't scaring her. She could feel her heart slowing. She was questioning if she could survive the rest of the voyage, if she would make it to America.

"Rita," she whispered, suddenly feeling like she needed to straighten things out with her youngest daughter. "That day, when you hid in the hay loft... do you know I went looking for you everywhere?" She coughed and shivered more but continued. "I was helping someone... hiding someone, and when I came home, you were nowhere to be found. Nothing else mattered when I thought you could be hurt. I prayed to *Sant'Antonio* and then you appeared."

She could see tears welling in the girl's eyes and the pursed lips that held back her feelings. Her strong-willed child. Rita cleared her throat and begged, "Please, Mamma. I got this for you," holding an egg out to Nina.

She grabbed the side of the bunk, took the egg from her daughter and braced herself to bite. It would take great effort to convince her stomach to ignore the swaying and keep it down.

Two days passed. Lasia watched over her mother while Rita helped distribute ice cream in the dining hall with her new friend. The girl had to regain his trust after the first time he asked her to help, when she had taken the ice cream, eaten as much as she could, then hid the huge box under her bed to save it for later. Despite the chilly room, the ice cream melted onto the floor and he'd had to clean it. It took her apologising repeatedly and promising not to do it again to convince him to give her another chance. Lasia was sure her sister found the whole escapade secretly hilarious.

She looked at her mother with concern, and Nina swallowed and opened her eyes.

"Have I let you down?" Nina whispered, as Lasia held her mother's bony hand and ran her thumb over the rivets across her knuckles. "I couldn't leave you behind. I know you could get along in Fonzaso, but I can't let you go yet. And your father..." Nina's eyes were pained as she looked at her eldest living child, "your father deserves to get to know you."

Lasia held back tears as she looked at her emaciated mother whose bright blue eyes sank deep in their sockets. Her mother's once full cheeks were sharp-angled and taut. Mamma had never spoken like this before, and Lasia didn't want to hear it now. Lasia's mind flashed to what could happen. She could not face her father without Mamma. She needed to get help.

The air was thick with fog, heavy and too warm. Nina shivered. Her hand reached out. A small white light came out of the periphery, drawing her to its glow. She reached for it but it floated forward. She stretched, calling out for it to come back. It was bright, peaceful. Too soon, it was out of reach. Other colours and shapes overtook it. Splotches of dark magenta and green, followed by dots of blue covering the light. This angered her and she cried out again. She floated backward, then turned. Drifting, she was leaving a room, and static spots surrounded her, guiding her floating body through the door. As she drifted, she could hear her breath as though a megaphone were amplifying it. *Huh, huh, huh,* scratchy, deep and slow, a seesaw of coarse exhales and inhales. Then she stopped floating. She stopped hearing the noise. She simply stopped.

CHAPTER 38

W hen Nina awoke, an older Italian woman was with Lasia and Rita. The *signora* checked her for a fever and pronounced it gone. "She's seasick, terribly seasick, but her fever has broken." The woman asked her to sit up.

"Drink this. It's ginger tea, it'll help with the nausea." She poured steaming liquid out of a flask and into a cup, then guided it to Nina's lips. "I brought it for my daughter, but she's fine. We're only a day and a half from port. You need to eat. If they think you're ill, they'll send you back."

Nina sipped the tea and thanked her. She inhaled deeply, realising she felt much improved. Her stomach rumbled from emptiness. With great effort, she dressed, then walked with the girls' help to the dining area. She chose two slices of toast with butter and coffee then afterwards poured herself more of the woman's tea. The girls watched her to see if the food would stay down. People from all over Europe dined in the modest hall: groups of young men in three-piece suits, raucous families, young women in belted coat dresses travelling alone to meet soldiers who had courted them in the war. Lasia had made friends with a few of these girls. Rita watched them strolling the ship.

After breakfast, they took a walk on deck. Nina breathed in the crisp, salty air, letting it fill her lungs, and exhaled, watching her breath appear in the frosty January air. Her nausea subdued, and a sense of a great adventure crept into her mind. Tomorrow she'd be in America.

America!

Icy air whipped at their cheeks. The sun made them squint. She felt alive! They laughed together, giddy with a sense of the future. When they had enough of the cold and sun, they went to pack their belongings for the next day's arrival. Before she knew it, she would see Pietro again.

Time sped. A crowd rushed on deck as the ship approached New York. There it was, right before their eyes. The sun streamed through the clouds, making the buildings glisten in the distance. *God loves America! The sun shines down on it from Heaven!* thought Nina. The splendour of the Statue of Liberty rose into the air and everyone cheered. Nina gazed at the tall statue and thought of the Madonna at *Sant'Anna* – two depictions of women, this one with her strong arm soaring to the sky, a determined look on her face. An assuredness in her stature with no sense of demureness or apology; she promised a future of life on her terms. Rita looked up at Nina and said, "It's like I'm a new person! I'm in America!" They were finally here!

The wind off the bay chilled their bones despite the excitement. Processing was nerve-wracking but went by quickly in their enlivened state. When they reached the front of the queue, the three of them tried to explain to the gentleman at the desk where they were from and why they were here. The spectacled clerk who checked their papers against the logbook seemed bored, at direct odds with their enthusiasm and nerves. Nina tried to explain when she saw everything spelled wrong and wasn't sure if it was because of her accent or the indifference of the scribes. Regardless, he let them through. Processed, they passed through and out to meet the Dalla Santa cousins who would take them on the next leg of their journey, as she and Pietro had planned.

Nina clung to her pocketbook filled with the precious $50 she had declared. Rita pointed out several of the girls Lasia had befriended on the ship, as they searched in vain for their lovers. Girls shouted, looking for men met during the war who were or were not waiting for them, "Mario, Mario," one girl cried out, unable to control her tears.

"How sad," Lasia said. "That girl paid her own way from Parma to meet a soldier she's been writing. I wonder what will happen if he doesn't come. What if she has to go back after that?"

Amid the crowd, Nina's Dalla Santa cousins held up a sign with NINA PANTE in bold letters. They found themselves hugged and kissed by these strangers that were family. First, their cousins took them to a restaurant in New York City. Walking in the streets among the gigantic buildings, they didn't know where to look next. Cars honked making them jump, people rushed past speaking languages they had never heard and the smell of unfamiliar spices and car exhaust overwhelmed them. Rita looked straight up between the buildings as they walked. "Mamma, I feel like a little pin! I've never seen buildings so tall!"

The ceiling at the restaurant was as high as the church steeple in Fonzaso, but the walls were pristine without a nick or scratch on them. Chandeliers brightened the room. Their cousins ordered as they glanced over menus that meant nothing to them. When the food came, it surprised Rita to see corn served on the cob. "What do they think we are, pigs?" she whispered to Lasia.

"Shhhhh," Lasia told her. "*Mangia, mangia*. This is a nice place. Just eat and smile."

A few days later, Nina shifted in her second-class seat on the overnight train from Newark to Chicago. After she and the girls had found their spots and settled in, two elegantly dressed women entered their cabin, complaining to the conductor in English, yelling at the man with grand gestures and flashing cherry-red polished fingertips. In the end they gave up, sat down and looked over Nina and the girls with raised eyebrows before dozing off. The girls slept, Rita next to Nina and Lasia in the seat across. An empty seat next to Lasia held their bags and allowed Nina to stretch out her legs.

She examined her own ankles and black-strapped shoes. They were newish, bought for the trip along with coats for her and Lasia. Rita was growing so fast it wasn't worth buying anything new for her. They gave her one of Mary's old coats, which she complained was patchy, and wore boys' shoes that the Corso cousins had sent from America in a charity box. Poor Rita. When they got settled, she'd encourage Lasia to make her something new. Nina peered across to where the two well-dressed women had fallen asleep, looking chic in crimson lipstick, silk stockings and well-cut wool coats with *Harper's Bazaar* issues across their laps. New or not, her shoes and hosiery looked dowdy compared to theirs. What would Pietro think when he saw her? His immigrant wife.

Beneath the angled brim of her hat, one of the ladies opened her eyes. Nina pretended she hadn't been staring at her.

"Can't sleep either?" the woman spoke in perfect Italian.

"*Parla italiano?* Your English seemed so strong! I couldn't even hear an accent." The thought of an American stranger speaking Italian to her made her feel somehow less foreign.

"*Sì.* My father moved us here when we were toddlers. My mother never learnt English. We're coming back from her funeral."

"I'm sorry."

"Ahhh," she dismissed the condolence with a flick of her hand. "She died happy. She lived a long life." The woman shifted, wincing as she pushed on her lower back. "We had a sleeper car, but they overbooked." She looked Nina over again. "And you? What brings you to Chicago?"

"I'm meeting my husband. It's been almost twelve years since we saw each other."

"I don't believe it! How romantic." The woman sat up and smoothed her hair, pinning loose strands under the hat.

Nina saw a flash of dangling gold and ruby earrings.

She responded, humbly, "I don't know about that. I was a different woman when he left." Why was she confiding in this woman? she wondered. Maybe because she'd shared that her mother just died.

"You've been in Italy all this time?"

"I have." It was surprisingly nice to be asked questions, to tell a stranger about herself.

"Through the war, then?" the woman asked, looking serious.

"*Sì.*" She whispered so as not to wake the girls.

"My God. You're a saint! How did you survive? They bombed our relatives in Rome to the gills!"

"*Sì*, I heard it was terrible there. I had a cousin whose child was born during the bombardment in Rome. He suffered from *paura della bomba* and was always a very upset baby. We're from Belluno, right next to the mountains. We were never bombed, but we heard them in Bassano Del Grappa and Vicenza."

"It couldn't have been easy. I admire you."

"*Grazie.* Thank God it's over."

The woman removed an ornate silver flask from a velvet pouch in her handbag then drank from it.

"Want some?" she asked, holding the flask across the aisle. "Here, brandy to help you sleep."

Nina hesitated before reaching for the flask and swigged back the potent liquid, letting the heat of it coat her throat and relax her nerves.

"I love your coat and lipstick. I'm afraid my style has suffered," Nina said, the alcohol loosening her tongue.

"Nonsense. Italians have style baked into our bones. Here, try some." She handed her a gold tube of lipstick and a jewelled oyster shell mirror from her pocketbook. Nina applied it carefully to her lips. By the low light of the cabin, she saw her face come alive with the colour.

"Look at you. It makes your eyes stand out. God, they're blue! Listen. You take that one. I bought a few tubes at Bloomingdale's. I can spare it. Consider it a good start in America from a fellow Italian. It'll give you a little extra confidence to meet that old husband of yours."

"Are you sure?" *I don't even know this woman and she's giving me lipstick,* Nina thought.

"I insist. It's nothing. Please." The woman flicked her hand up in a dramatic gesture and a powdery scent wafted from her wrist.

"*Grazie! Molte grazie!*" Nina said, reaching to squeeze the woman's delicate hand in her own, grateful for the small kindness that made her think how nice Americans were – at least the Italian ones. Maybe everything would be fine after all. The woman smiled, took another swig of brandy then fell asleep looking pleased with herself.

By the time the train pulled into Union Station in Chicago, Nina had recuperated fully. Her cheeks were still hollow but for the three of them, a combination of excitement and fear made their eyes shine and brought a flush to their cheeks. Everything was new! Everything was different and almost no one spoke Italian!

As the train neared the station, tall buildings rose outside their windows, Nina's heart raced in her chest. Eleven years and nine months had passed since she had last seen Pietro, holding Rita in his arms, and kissing her goodbye. Would she be able to step back into being a wife? Would he love her the way she was now? *I'm walking into the unknown.* She said a prayer in her head and crossed herself as they disembarked the train, stepping onto the crowded platform.

Rita ran in front, jostling through the crowds, stopping to pull her mother and Lasia along. She jumped, trying to see where they were headed, wondering if her father would be there with a sign. She wanted to see him first. Lasia held Nina's hand as they entered the Great Hall with directions to find him and a friend in the centre near the clock. "Mamma, Mamma, do you see him?" Rita called, her too-big shoes making a clapping noise on the marble station floors. A melange of people rushed by. Nina slowed the girls to get their bearings and looked around. Light filled the hall from a lattice window under a massive, blackened glass and steel roof. Soaring columns sparkled as they rose to the grand ceiling; atop them, golden statues of shrouded women holding birds looked down on the people below. Nina strained her eyes to search each face near the clock in the centre but her view was blocked again and again by passersby. People barked at her to buy something from a newsstand; everyone around them had their purpose. Who would help her if he wasn't there? If he'd decided not to meet her, like those girls looking for soldiers off the ship?

Rays of sunlight shone like spotlights on rushing businessmen and crying toddlers, but no Pietro. The crowd jostled behind her and she continued to search, her heart beating faster in her chest. The angle of the sun shifted and the rays to the right of the clock in the centre dimmed enough for her to see him before he spotted her. She froze, giving herself a moment to observe him for herself. This man she had waited for. Was it really him? He had aged; his jawline was slimmer, sharper, but it was him. So many years. There he was, next to two other men searching the thick crowd. Nina leaned over to Rita, pointed and said, "Over there. Which one do you think is your father?" The girl only knew him from the wedding photo in the hallway in Fonzaso – a picture from twenty-five years before. He held his hat in his hand, looking expectantly around the crowds until his eyes met Nina's, and his face broke into a spectacular smile. She couldn't help but do the same.

Rita broke the spell. "He's the man with the hat in his hand and the big smile, but the guy on the right's better looking," Rita giggled as she reasoned.

Nina rolled her eyes and laughed. There was no changing the girl.

The flurry of people moved them along as Pietro strode towards them, weaving through the crowd, eyes bright, arms out. When he reached them, he pulled Nina into an embrace, and with great urgency, kissed her. Then, after nearly twelve years apart, he reached for his girls, holding Nina and their daughters under the skylight of Chicago's Union Station.

The house he had rented on Adler Street in Joliet was only slightly larger than their home on the Via Calzen, and as she walked in, she observed the furniture, noting how it matched and looked fairly expensive.

"I hope you like everything," he said, still holding his cap, twisted in his hands. She could tell he was anxious too. He touched the walnut sideboard and explained, "I bought the furniture second hand from a teacher who took good care of it."

Nina smiled and nodded.

The girls walked uncertainly around this stranger's house step by step.

"Where can we put our things?" asked Lasia.

"You and Rita have a nice room back there, it overlooks the garden," he offered. The girls ran off to see it. Nina stepped into the kitchen, noticing the oven was yellow with buttons on top. *How am I supposed to use that?* she thought. She glanced at him as he watched for her approval. A man had decorated this house, but he had done it with love and with his family in mind. She would make it a home. They would make it a home.

"Should we make some coffee?" she asked.

When night came, she took a bath, revelling at the indoor bathroom, a luxury they hadn't had in Fonzaso. She had to ask Pietro to draw it for her, then closed the door and stepped in, one foot at a time, surprised at how hot the water was. The tub was enormous compared to the one they used in Fonzaso. She crisscrossed her legs so the water swooshed in waves around them. The soap was shop-bought, a brand called Ivory that smelled clean and sharp. When she dropped it in the water, it floated. *Allora, in America, soap floats!* She dried off with new towels that felt scratchy against her skin. Once in her nightdress, she headed to the room Lasia and Rita shared across from her and Pietro's, realising, with her bare feet on the cold wood floors, she had brought no house slippers.

"Mamma, aren't you going to sleep with us?" Rita asked, trying to arrange herself on the bed with a squishy mattress she wasn't used to.

"No, *amore,* I'll sleep in your papà's room." Nina looked at Lasia and asked her with her eyes to keep the girl in bed. Lasia nodded she understood.

"I don't know how you can sleep in there with a stranger, even if he is my papà," Rita scoffed to Nina then asked, "What will we do tomorrow?"

"Your papà's taking us shopping in the centre, there's a place called Woolworth's that sells everything – maybe like your *zia's* shop, we'll see. We can get some new things. Some American things." The girls were excited about the idea. They lay down and prayed the Hail Mary with Nina before going to sleep in their new room in America.

Nina crossed the hallway towards her and Pietro's bedroom, but first looked at the dark, silent house. She thought she'd like to rearrange some things. To move the sofa under the window and angle the armchair. Could she do that? *Is this mine? Is it ours? Is it his?* It didn't feel like hers. Would she have to ask him permission? The idea made her uneasy.

As she walked into the bedroom, the radio played a song in English she didn't recognise but liked. '*Mam'selle*' in Frank Sinatra's voice mingled in her ears. Pietro reached for her hand from his position on the corner of the bed and asked, "Did you ever think this moment would come?" Nina didn't reply. She gave him her hand while studying the room before bringing her eyes back to him. He spoke again to fill the silence.

"Here we are, needing to get to know each other again."

He stood, then pulled her close into his arms and swayed. She lay her head on his shoulder, feeling his bare arm on her cheek as they danced. The blue walls were sparse of decorations except for a crucifix. On the dresser, he had set the change from his pocket, sprawled on the wood. Silver coins in various sizes and bright, copper American pennies. She smiled, leaning back to look at her husband, *"Non ti preoccupare, ti conosco."* Don't worry, I know you, she whispered, and reached her hand to his chin, pulling his face to hers for a kiss.

CHAPTER 39

June 1947 Her eyes opened, and her body curved in the bed as light streamed in through the window. She was lusciously warm. The sheets were soft beneath her, the quilt cool and smooth on top of her as she lay with her arm tucked under a pillow. She wanted to arch and stretch, purring. A smile of satisfaction curled on her lips. She could hear Rita and Lasia's happy voices as they chatted with Pietro over breakfast in the kitchen. Six months had passed, and she was getting used to the comforts she never had in Italy.

The rich smell of fresh coffee wafted into the room. *Mmm, coffee.* It would be dark and strong, and she had shop-bought Stella D'Oro biscotti to dunk into it. She blinked at the bright sunshine bathing her face. She ran her hand over the sheets that had hung to dry in her new backyard where neighbours called over the fence to greet her. She hugged her fresh pillow, gazing at the room around her. There was a little desk in the corner with her stationery and a letter to Aurora in progress she would send to Italy later in the week. Hanging on the closet door was her blue and green housecoat, and on the ground beneath it were a pair of Daniel Green slippers to match. A little lamp with flowers painted on the base stood on the nightstand next to the bed. Her rosary lay on top of a crocheted lace doily Aurora had made for her in Fonzaso. She thought of the city, thousands of miles away from her little home in Joliet. She recalled the mountains and the winding streets. She remembered the *piazze* and the *chiesa*. The *Eremo di San Michele* looking down. She thought of her mother and the babies. Her father and his grappa. The red geraniums in the windows, the lush green grasses surrounding the Madonna at *Sant'Anna*. Her home on the Via Calzen. Fonzaso would always be part of her and, while the terror of the war had shaped her, thickened her resolve and tested her strength, that was not the Italy of her heart. A watercolour hung framed on the wall. It was the only artwork in the room – a painting of the Virgin Mary and baby Jesus. The Madonna looked down on the child with all-encompassing love, and her arms protected him eternally. It gave Nina a feeling of supreme peace.

The door cracked open. Pietro peeked in.

"*Buongiorno, bella mia,* Ninetta. Sleep well?"

"*Sì.* I'm getting up."

She glimpsed the scene at the kitchen table behind him. Lasia sipped coffee while refilling her father's mug. Rita had her head in a book given to her by a teacher who had taken the girl under her wing. They both wore pretty dresses Lasia had sewn for them. It was good. It was so good. She lay her hand on her belly. The future fluttered within her.

Life.

Gazing again at the sunlight, she inhaled the fresh summer air from the open window and sat up on the bed before walking out to greet her family.

AFTERWORD

The flutter in Nina's belly was Angela Pante, their fourth, and last child, born 17 December 1947, eleven months after Pietro and Nina were reunited.

Rita Pante started school in America and learnt English quickly. As she'd promised years earlier, she married Leonardo DeBoni, the boy with the fine leather satchel. They had eight children.

Lasia Pante worked as a seamstress at Hart Schaffner Marx to help the family and was briefly engaged to Bortolo Sebben. She eventually married a swarthy Italian-American bricklayer named Herman Manzi, whose family was from the shores of Lake Como. Lasia and Herman were my grandparents.

Aurora and Onorina continued to write to Nina, and Corrado wrote on the bottom of each letter until he died in 1958. They buried him in the cemetery next to his wife, the Captain.

In the early 1950s, Nina wrote to the priest in Fonzaso and sent him money she had collected from the immigrants in Joliet to raise funding for a proper altar and chapel at *Sant'Anna*. The *Fonzasini* christened the new building in 1957.

Afterword

On the wall of the altar at *Sant'Anna* are the names of important women who the monument pays honour to, and at the top of the list is Adelasia Dalla Santa Argenta under an inscription that simply states:

Ricordate le vostre mamme
Remember your mothers

Thank you for reading this story. It would mean so much to me if you would share your thoughts in a review on Amazon or Goodreads.

ACKNOWLEDGMENTS

Thank you to Margaret (Rita) Pante DeBoni and Angela (Angie) Pante Lopez, who helped me fill in the blanks when my grandmother died. Thanks to Corinna Argenta Pante, the late Maria Dalla Santa, Francesco Bof, Milena Sabbadin, Tinetta Sebben and Quinto Bianchi for sharing first-hand accounts of the events in this book.

Thanks to my editors throughout this process, including Angela Meyer and Sally Orson-Jones. I would have never finished this book without you both in my life!

Grazie to everyone in Italy, America and Canada who informed the content, provided translation for interviews and supported the process including, but not limited to: Ornella Bettega, Michela Corso, Marta Corso, Nikka Bisatti, Anita Mendoza, Valeria De Col, Anna Colesan, Don Alberto Vallotto, employees of the *municipio* of Fonzaso, Maria Giovanna Argenta, Jimmy Britt, Cristiano Vettori, Stephen Roberts, Manuela Speranza, Stella Thompson and Sylvia Bianchi. Thanks, Giovanni Battista Vieceli, for your lovely Fonzaso photos and videos.

I'm grateful to the writing community that supported me,

including my writing group in Chicago: Jian Ping, Susan Myrick, Timothy Gray, and Sharon Stangenes and my earliest editor, Emanuel Bergmann. Credit also goes to The Writers' Loft in Chicago under the late Jerry Cleaver, The UK Complete Creative Writing Workshop, The Writers' Workshop Getting Published Day and Jacq Burns of the London Writers' Club.

My dear beta readers who gave such incredible feedback and time have been instrumental including Kristie Price, Amanda Daniels, Jennifer Jarvis, Kristin Peterson Anton, Imogen Matthews and Mara Slongo. Thank you also to Alison Williams, Helen Baggott, Laurie Mucilli and Karen Loughrey for proofreading at various points.

Thanks to Professor Victoria de Grazia, Columbia University, for sharing her knowledge over wine, and Professor Richard Bosworth, Jesus College, Oxford, for sharing his over tea.

Thanks also go to Liesbeth Heenk at Amsterdam Publishers for seeing the potential in my novel and being committed to telling stories to keep history alive.

Thank you to my earliest teachers who encouraged my writing including Miss Wilson and the late Sister Mary of St. Mary Immaculate Catholic School in Plainfield, Illinois.

Special gratitude goes to my husband, Clint, for encouraging me every day and my daughter, Vivien, for being my critic and my inspiration.

Thanks to my parents: Gary Anton for teaching me to read and Nancy Manzi Anton for always being there for me and inspiring me to write this story.

Finally, love and gratitude to those who are no longer with us, especially my Grandma Lasia and Nonna Pante. I hope they see this book from heaven and know their legacy lives on.

GLOSSARY

autostrada – *highway in Italy*

albergo – *hotel*

alimentari – *grocery store*

allora – *filler word like 'so' or 'well'*

amico/a – *friend male/female*

amore mio – *my love*

andiamo – *let's go*

aperitivo – *snack and drink before dinner*

Babbo Natale – *Father Christmas*

bambini – *children*

basta – *enough*

bella – *beautiful*

bellissima – *very beautiful*

brava donna – *good woman*

buongiorno – *good morning*

buon anno – *happy new year*

Buon Natale – *Merry Christmas*

buon viaggio – *good travels*

caffettiera – *coffee pot*

caffè corretto – *coffee with a shot of alcohol*

Glossary

calcio – *football, European; soccer, U.S.*

cantina – *cellar*

Capitana – *Captain*

cara/o – *dear*

carabinieri – *military police*

cento baci – *one hundred kisses*

certo – *certainly/ of course*

che brutta/bella – *how ugly/beautiful*

chiesa – *church*

ciao – *hello/goodbye*

contadini – *peasants*

credere, obbedire, combattere – *believe, obey, fight*

crepi – *response to in bocca al lupo: may he die*

cucina – *kitchen*

culo – *buttocks*

dai dai – *come on, come on*

emigranti – *people leaving to go to a foreign land*

esatto – *exactly*

fagioli – *beans*

fascisti – *fascists*

festa/e – *festival/s*

Figli della Lupa – *children of the she-wolf/fascist organization for young children*

filó – *gathering where people shared gossip while working*

Fonzasini – *people of Fonzaso*

fratelli – *brothers*

ha sempre ragione – *he's always right*

il Duce – *the Leader, reference to Mussolini*

il vecchio bacucco – *term for decrepit old man*

in bocca al lupo – *literally: in the mouth of the wolf, saying for good luck*

La Befana – *witch that visits during the Epiphany*

la strada nel bosco – *the path in the woods*

lei è sono tua zia – *she is your aunt*

Glossary

leva obbligatoria – *mandatory military service*

luna – *moon*

macelleria – *butcher shop*

mammone – *adult man who lives with his mother*

mangia – *eat*

mio Dio – *my God*

moglie – *wife*

municipio – *municipal building/town hall*

niente – *nothing*

nonna/o – *grandma/grandpa*

Operazione Nationale Balilla – *fascist youth organisation*

oro alla Patria – *gold for the Fatherland*

ostetrica – *midwife*

panificio – *bakery*

parla italiano? – *you speak Italian?*

passeggiate – *walks*

paura della bomba – *affliction caused by fear of bombs*

per favore – *please*

perfetto – *perfect*

piacere – *pleased to meet you*

piazze – *town squares*

piccola italiana – *little Italian girl*

pizzelle – *flat Italian cookies with powdered sugar*

Podestà – *person put in charge of commune during fascist years*

polizia – *police*

primo piatto – *first dish*

procedi con cautela – *proceed with caution*

puttane – *prostitutes*

questura – *police station*

Risorgimento – *movement that brought the unification of Italy*

ragazza – *young woman*

salve – *casual greeting*

santola – *godmother (Belluno dialect)*

Glossary

sara la boca – *shut your mouth (Belluno dialect)*

senti – *listen*

sì - *yes*

signor/a – *Mr/Mrs*

signorotti – *upper class people*

silenzio – *silence*

soldi – *money*

sorellina – *affectionate term for younger sister*

mia sposa – *my bride*

squadristi – *fascist militia*

strega – *witch*

stronzo – *asshole*

tabacchi – *store selling tobacco and other items*

ti amo – *I love you (used for lovers/spouses)*

ti voglio bene – *I love you (used for children/family)*

topolino – *little mouse, Italian equivalent for tooth fairy*

tua – *your*

un altro bicchiere – *another glass*

uomini del mio cuore – *men of my heart*

vai subito per favore – *go now please*

viva il Duce – *long live the leader (reference to Mussolini)*

zanzare – *mosquitos*

zia/o – *aunt/uncle*

NOTES ON SOURCES

Apart from first-hand research interviewing *Fonzasini* who lived through this period and gaining access to files in the town hall and church, throughout the past fourteen years, I have sought out historical books, papers and films covering the time period to understand daily life for Italian women during and in between the Wars. Some of these included: *How Fascism Ruled Women* by Victoria de Grazia; *War in Italy, 1943-1945: A Brutal Story* by Richard Lamb; *Fonzaso Ieri* by Angelo Vigna; *Claretta: Mussolini's Last Lover* by R. J. B. Bosworth; *Women and the Great War: Femininity Under Fire* by Allison Scardino Belzer; along with *Peasant Women and Politics in Fascist Italy: The Massaie Rurali* by Perry Wilson. Caroline Brettell, Professor at Southern Methodist University, helped answer many of my questions over email based on her research for *Gender and Migration*. Jennifer Kosmin's PhD dissertation, *Embodied Knowledge: Midwives and the Medicalization of Childbirth in Early Modern Italy* confirmed the experiences of my midwife ancestors. *The Contrasting Image of Italian Women Under Fascism in the 1930s* by Jennifer Linda Monti was also informative.

The exhibition *Venire alla Luce,* curated by Giovanni Battista Nardelli and Maurizio Rippa Bonati, which I saw in Padua when I interviewed Gaetano Manfreda, Head of Didactic Services at the University of Padua, was incredibly helpful for understanding the lives of rural midwives. Sadly, Marina Cimino, whom I had seen quoted in many pieces of research, had helped curate the exhibition but died five months before I came to Padua hoping to meet her.

Atlante delle Stragi Naziste e Fasciste in Italia (www.straginazifasciste.it) is an incredible website that allows readers to pinpoint geographies in Italy and find the dates and details of atrocities documented in the local areas. At the request of *Associazione Bellunesi nel Mondo,* Enrico Bacchetti provided answers regarding Mussolini's visits to the area as well as photos. *The Statue of Liberty— Ellis Island Foundation Passenger Search* provided detail on dates of the voyages mentioned within the novel along with small details of the characters upon entry into the United States.

Under the Light of the Italian Moon is fiction based on real stories and events, so mindsets, dialogue and various situations had to be imagined and informed. In fiction, the book *Unspeakable Women: Selected Short Stories Written by Italian Women During Fascism,* edited by Robin Pickering-Iazzi, confirmed the everyday thinking of my characters beyond family stories. Giorgio Bassani's *The Garden of the Finzi-Continis* provided more into the changing mindsets of the day regarding Jews in Italy. *The Path to the Spider's Nests* by Italo Calvino and *Agostino* by Alberto Moravia gave insights into younger people's thinking. Ann Rubino's novel, *Peppino, Good as Bread* was a lovely fictional account of life under fascism and WWII in Italy told from the eyes of a child with a father abroad.

I am certain to be leaving out some sources because over

the past fourteen years, there has not been a video, article, essay, film, website, or history book covering this time period that I did not gravitate to. The above were the most memorable and useful. I have specifically documented them for this reason.

BOOK GROUP QUESTIONS

1. "War is to man what maternity is to a woman." – *Benito Mussolini*. From the beginning of the book, we see Adelasia and Nina bringing life and caring for life while, we see Mussolini aiming for power and ultimately bringing more and more death. Eventually, Mussolini's quest undoes so much of their work, as men who Adelasia helped deliver as babies die by the hands of the Nazis because of Mussolini's actions. Are men more likely to want power and willing to kill than women? Does this make women unfit to be leaders and do you think, deep down, it is something Mussolini said but that most societies still at their core believe?

2. Why do you think Nina chooses a long-distance marriage? Do you think her mother wanted that for her or helped orchestrate it? Do you think Nina could have been happy with a man who was always around?

3. Adelasia is the stronger personality in the relationship with Corrado. Do you think he was her first love? Why do you think she married him?

4. Is Nina's reaction to the birth of Lasia normal? Do you think Nina could have suffered from postpartum depression? How did their relationship change over time, and why?

5. Adelasia has many lines that make her a strong, opinionated woman, yet she has very traditional values about family and the church. Would you consider her a feminist? She goes against Mussolini's policies knowingly. Is she a rebel? A criminal?

6. How does the Virgin Mary play as a key symbol in this book? Why do you think most major religions are all based around males? Have women not tried or have they been actively repressed?

7. What assumptions about *La Donna Brava*, good women, still exist today? Do you think there is any hope in reprogramming these deeply embedded values?

8. Do you think Pietro tried hard enough to bring them together? Why do you think it took so long for them to finally reunite?

9. Who is your favourite character in the book? Who do you relate to the most? Why?

10. At the beginning of the book, Nina is ten years old, then we flip to her being fifteen. At the end, Lasia is seventeen and Rita eleven. What similarities do you see in her daughters at the end to her in those years? If you are a mother, can you relate to remembering your own milestones as your children reach teen years?

11. When Adelasia dies, Nina looks through her mother's jewellery box and finds mementos, some of which cannot be explained. Can you relate to the line, "we forget our mothers were once girls?"

12. Do you think women lose a piece of their identity when they become mothers, or does their identity develop and deepen?

ABOUT THE AUTHOR

Jennifer Anton is an American/Italian dual citizen born in Joliet, Illinois and now lives between London and Lake Como, Italy. A proud advocate for women's rights and equality, she hopes to rescue women's stories from history, starting with her Italian family.

In 2006, after the birth of her daughter, Jennifer suffered a life-threatening post-partum cardiomyopathy, and soon after, her Italian grandmother died. This tumultuous year strengthened her desire to capture the stories of her female Italian ancestors.

In 2012, she moved with her family to Milan, Italy and *Chicago Parent Magazine* published her article, *It's In the Journey,* chronicling the benefits of travelling the world with children. Later, she moved to London where she has held leadership positions in brand marketing with companies including ABInbev, Revlon, Shiseido and Tory Burch.

Jennifer is a graduate of Illinois State University where she was a Chi Omega and holds a master's degree from DePaul University in Chicago.

Under the Light of the Italian Moon is her first novel, based on the lives of her Italian grandmother and great grandmothers during the rise of fascism and World War II.

Review the book on Amazon, Goodreads and Bookbub

Join her mailing list at www.boldwomanwriting.com

Made in the USA
Middletown, DE
07 March 2021

34994378R00234